In the background on the cover of this book is the image of Jaroslav Hašek's letter of resignation from the Czechoslovak Corps in Russia:

To the Branch of the Czechoslovak National Council

I hereby let it be known, that I do not agree with the policy of the Branch of the Czechoslovak National Council and with the departure of our Corps to France.

Therefore I declare, that I am leaving the Czechoslovak Corps until such time, that both within it and the whole leadership of the National Council, a new direction prevails.

I request, that this decision of mine be noted. I will even now continue to work for a revolution in Austria and the liberation of our nation.

Jaroslav Hašek, in own hand

---

*This edition was not prepared
for prevailing habits of reading.*

*It was prepared for readers
willing to meet the conditions it already inhabits.*

The Fateful Adventures of
**THE GOOD SOLDIER
ŠVEJK** [sh-vake]
During the World War

Book One

presents
still as a samizdat

The Centennial Edition
of The "Chicago Version" English rendition of

Jaroslav Hašek's

The Fateful Adventures of The Good Soldier

Švejk

During the World War

Book One

Visit our websites
zenny.com
SvejkCentral.com
for additional information and enjoyment of the
Good Soldier Švejk

Copyright© 2026
Zdeněk "Zenny" K. Sadloň
All rights reserved.
ISBN: 979-8-9943084-1-7

v. 12/25/2025

Dedication

To **Antonín Bukovjan**, *1890 - †1964
  Farmhand
  Infantry man, 25th Reserve Regiment, Austro-Hungarian Army
    Wounded
    Captured: September 17, 1915, Rovno, Volhynian Governorate, Russian Empire (currently Rivne, Ukraine), imprisoned in a POW camp
  Private, 8. Rifle Regiment, Czechoslovak Legions in Russia,
    Enlisted: September 1, 1917
    End of service: March 30, 1918

This translation is based on ***Osudy dobrého vojáka Švejka za světové války***, edited by Jaroslava Myslivečková (**Praha: Odeon, 1968**). For certain readings, I consulted the Book One and Book Two manuscript transcripts (Book(s) Three & Four not yet transcribed) by Jaroslav Šerák (svejkmuseum.cz), which contain at least two lines inadvertently omitted and several typographical errors. Where variant readings or uncertainties arose, I confirmed the correct text by reference to high-resolution manuscript scans provided by Jomar Hønsi. The translation does not rely on the manuscript transcript alone for any passage where significant textual doubt or error is possible.

Table of Contents

Dedication..v
Step Into the World of Švejk..ix
Preface...xi
Acknowledgments..xiii
Editorial Notes..xvii
Comparative Notes on Methodology.......................................xxxi
František Josef and the Grammar of Czech Subjecthood
   in Hašek's Opening Line..xli
Introduction to The Centennial English Edition............................1

Book One
IN THE REAR[1]

INTRODUCTION...5
1 THE GOOD SOLDIER ŠVEJK ACTS TO
   INTERVENE IN THE WORLD WAR 9
2 THE GOOD SOLDIER ŠVEJK AT POLICE
   HEADQUARTERS..18
3 ŠVEJK BEFORE THE COURT PHYSICIANS..........................26
4 THEY THREW ŠVEJK OUT OF THE MADHOUSE...............32
5 ŠVEJK AT THE DISTRICT POLICE STATION
   IN SALMOVA STREET..36
6 ŠVEJK AT HOME AGAIN, HAVING BROKEN
   THROUGH THE VICIOUS CIRCLE.......................................43
7 ŠVEJK GOES IN THE MILITARY SERVICE..........................53
8 ŠVEJK AS A MALINGERER...59
9 ŠVEJK IN THE GARRISON PRISON.....................................74
10 ŠVEJK AS A MILITARY SERVANT
   TO THE FIELD CHAPLAIN...94
11 ŠVEJK RIDES WITH THE FIELD CHAPLAIN
   TO SERVE A FIELD MASS..115
12 A RELIGIOUS DEBATE...124
13 ŠVEJK GOES TO PROVIDE THE LAST RITES..................131
14 ŠVEJK AS A MILITARY SERVANT UNDER
   SENIOR LIEUTENANT[2] LUKÁŠ..144
15 THE CATASTROPHE..182
AFTERWORD to the First Volume: "In the Rear".....................194

Endnotes 197
About the Author...314
Bibliography of Editorial Notes...322

Step Into the World of Švejk

Step into the world of *The Good Soldier Švejk* as never before.

This three-volume Centennial English Edition presents Jaroslav Hašek's masterpiece in a **faithful English translation that preserves Czech syntax, phrasing rhythms, idiomatic structures, and the internal contradictions, imagery, and voices of the original**, rendering the text with rigor, clarity, and scholarly fidelity.

In addition, virtually all of Jomar Hønsi's entries in his unmatched collection of curated historical, military, and cultural realia from the novel appear as endnotes, alongside extensive prefatory essays, comparative notes on translation methodology, and critical analysis.

Across these volumes, **you** follow Švejk through pubs, the madhouse, police headquarters and district stations, prisons, towns and villages, transport trains, and military interrogations, encountering the world Hašek so meticulously constructed, a world that can, in part, be read as a **historical record**.

Whereas the only other complete unabridged English translation, by Cecil Parrott, provides the narrative core, the Centennial English Edition **adds comprehensive context and interpretation**.

By integrating a fully annotated apparatus, critical commentary, and historical framework with the translation, this edition presents Hašek's work in its full historical, cultural, and linguistic richness — offering a reading experience that is both **entertaining and enlightening**.

Preface

If you haven't read the first edition of the "Chicago version" translation of this title or come across my explanation elsewhere of why I decided to produce it and would like to know, here it is.

Born and raised in Czechoslovakia, I couldn't escape the knowledge of who Švejk was and is. But I managed to escape the envy of the decadent West, the Czechoslovak Socialist Republic, in which the Communist Party had a "leading role" that was embedded in the country's Constitution. Eventually I ended up in the United States. Having left the factory floor and studying at a university, I had to read the then just published first unabridged translation of the work. Having found it odd, a thought flashed through my mind: "Maybe I should translate it one day."

Nearly a quarter of a century later, as an International Radio Broadcaster of Voice of America, I was goaded by a colleague to do it, after he read the Parrott's translation I had lent him. I told him I needed such project like a hole in my head. In the end, I gave in, provided he would collaborate on it with me. In three months Book One was completed. A couple of years later I started translating the remaining volumes alone, with proofreading help from a volunteer. I managed to publish them twelve years after the first volume was being sold initially as a digital file.

Only much later I came across the following quote, which made my weary heart flutter with joy and hope. Joy, because I wasn't alone, and hope that others might see the light:

"Our translations, even the best ones, proceed from a wrong premise. They want to turn Hindi, Greek, English, into German instead of turning German into Hindi, Greek, English. Our translators have a far greater reverence for the usage of their own language than for the spirit of the foreign works… The basic error of the translator is that he preserves the state in which his own language happens to be instead of allowing his language to be powerfully affected by the foreign tongue. Particularly when translating from a language very remote from his own he must go back to the primal elements of language itself and penetrate to the point where work, image, and tone converge. He must expand and deepen his language by means of the foreign language. It is not generally realized to what extent this is possible, to what extent any language can be transformed, how language differs from language almost the way dialect differs from dialect; however, this last is true only if one takes language seriously enough, not if one takes it lightly."- Rudolf Pannwitz in *Die Krisis der europaischen Kultur* (quoted by W. Benjamin in *The Task of the Translator*[1])

Only a few weeks ago I read another just published encouraging text. It is a take on one of the important aspects of literary texts, touching even on the challenge of translating a very complex text, which Hašek's *Good Soldier Švejk* is:

"One thing some of the better books teach is that good writing is very often unexpected and surprises the reader with novel takes on familiar and well-worn scenes or tired tropes, whether it's from the thematic and storyline standpoint, to even the grammatical sentence level one." – Simplicius in Subvert [Artifice] = Retain [Self][2].

As the Czech linguist František Daneš wrote in *The Language and Style of Hašek's Novel The Good Soldier Švejk from the Viewpoint of Translation*[3]: "Firstly, in 'The Good Soldier Švejk', more than in a great majority of other literary works, the difference between particular languages, their (social) stratifications, along with cultural, historical and ethnic specificities are highly involved, so that to find or contrive truthful translational equivalents is in many instances extremely difficult and in part simply impossible."

That is the gauntlet I picked up, against all advice and odds. The history of my first attempt and its languishing result is 27 years long. As an uninvited and non-commissioned outsider, I have learned quite a bit about the industry of creating and publishing translations of foreign works over that time. But I have also gained an even greater appreciation of Hašek's text and confidence that I was on the right track. This time, I've stuck to my guns.

---

[1] Benjamin, Walter. "The Task of the Translator." In Walter Benjamin: Selected Writings, Volume 1: 1913–1926, edited by Marcus Bullock and Michael W. Jennings, 253–263. Cambridge, MA: Harvard University Press, 1996.

[2] Simplicius. "Subvert[Artifice]=Retain[Self];". Substack, 18 Apr. 2024, https://darkfutura.substack.com/p/subvertartificeretainself.

[3] František Daneš, "The Language and Style of Hašek's Novel 'The Good Soldier Švejk' from the Viewpoint of Translation," in Studies in Functional Stylistics, ed. Jan Chloupek and Jiří Nekvapil (Amsterdam: John Benjamins Publishing Company, 1993), 223–247.

Acknowledgments

Having decided to pick up the challenge of producing a better English translation of Jaroslav Hašek's unfinished novel has had many repercussions. The most immediate was the impact on my family. Adding this task to the full-time job and a part-time business deprived my wife and daughter of the time, which could and should had been spent with them and for them during the almost fifteen years so far. (But they got to know very well the back of my head, I'm told.) I've been fortunate, that not only behind great men there are great women, but even I have been blessed with a great wife, Mary Keenan-Sadlon, without whose loyal support, prayers, advice, unwavering directness and honesty, and above all love and understanding, my labor would have never been rewarded with the existence of the new translation, *The Fateful Adventures of the Good Soldier Švejk*. Thank you, dear Mary. And, Lucille, even though I can't make up for the lost time, its fruit is for you. No longer just snippets of the text you read on the scrap paper supplied for your childhood needs, but the whole published volume.

This volume wouldn't exist, if the first edition of it didn't. Therefore, the first thanks go to Emmett Michael Joyce, whose persistence prevailed over my resistance to the audacious attempt to produce a better English translation of Švejk. Having read the first unabridged version by Cecil Parrott, Mike told me: "Well, I don't want to run your life, but you've got to retranslate this thing." He resisted just as vehemently, when I made his collaboration a condition for me to do it. So we both ended up submitting to the other's demand. Immediately the work on Book One of *The Fateful Adventures of the Good Soldier Švejk* began.

This time around I have worked alone. One of the challenges of translating the multilevel, multifaceted text written by Jaroslav Hašek is the vast amount of realia. *The Good Soldier Švejk* is replete with historical, literary and geographical references. In this regard, two resources have been most useful and enlightening, and their compilers most helpful.

Jomar Hønsi is an active Norwegian amateur historian/researcher. He specializes in the life and writing of the Czech author Jaroslav Hašek, with a focus on his famous satirical novel *The Good Soldier Švejk*. When he first contacted me in 2004, he was already fluent not only in his mother tongue and English, but had a good command of both spoken and written German and Spanish. His intensifying passion for the subject, and his "geo-nerdish fundamentalist inclinations", led him to spend six months retracing the footsteps of both Švejk and Jaroslav Hašek on his anabasis from Prague across the Eurasian continent to beyond Lake Baikal in Siberia. In 2015 he became President of the *World Society of Jaroslav Hašek*. In the process of becoming one of the world's leading authorities on the subject, he has added Czech to the languages he can communicate in. An accomplished software engineer driven by pursuit of verifiable empirical facts, Jomar still manages to unearth new facts in various European archives after 100 years since the publication of the novel and passing of the author. His website, honsi.org/svejk, devoted to the subjects of his research, is an unequaled treasure trove for all interested in the subjects. But above all for a translator, who doesn't merely read and absorb the text, but has to understand each word, phrase, sentence and paragraph beyond any doubt, in order to do his work. Jomar has graciously allowed me to cite his encyclopedic entries in the Endnotes of this volume and proofread the text. (Any remaining errors are of my own doing.) Thank you, Jomar.

The second, a Czech language resource for the effort to improve the text for this edition, was the *Virtual museum of Jaroslav Hašek and Josef Švejk*, at svejkmuseum.cz, owned and operated by Jaroslav Šerák in Prague. Jarda is also a wikipedian: *"I was most pleased that I managed to create a page for Margarette Reiner, murdered by the Nazis in Auschwitz, who was completely forgotten by the Czech public, although she contributed to its promotion among the German population with her translations of Czech literature before the Second World War. She was the first to translate Jaroslav Hašek's novel The Fateful Adventures of the Good Soldier Švejk during the World War into another language. My resolution is to find as many similar people as possible, mainly Czechs, who have contributed something to humanity and especially the Czech nation, but somehow have been forgotten. And memorialize these personalities in Wikipedia."* He also graciously allowed me to cite his entries. Díky, Jardo.

Russian prose writer, trained as mining engineer, Sergey Soloukh in Siberia, provided the momentum, which breached the walls of the pressurized brain inertia, that stalled the first attempt to produce The Centennial Edition of *The Fateful Adventures*. Just as Jomar Hønsi,

Sergey did what untold numbers of researchers and writers studying, analyzing and writing about Jaroslav Hašek and his Švejk failed to do for one hundred years: "...to understand [the book] fully...[o]ne must understand Jaroslav Hašek himself. And what struck me, when I started to read the numerous biographies of him and memories related to him, [was] that most of them if not totally ignored, then mentioned as something completely insignificant, his life-long love to Jarmila Mayerová. ... And most of Jamila's letters that survived haven't been even transcribed, let alone published. Hundred years old, they still lay buried in the PNP files. ... And they gave me the key."

I hope that you can read the original Russian or the great Czech translation of Sergey Soloukh's resulting book *Nothing Will Happen to Anyone: The Romance/Novel of Jaroslav Hašek and Jarmila Mayerová*. An English translation must be produced. Thank you, Sergey.

Editorial Notes

As this work is a translation[1] of the original Czech, it will inevitably be compared to it. The "Chicago version" now exists in two editions: the first edition (1998–2009) and The Centennial Edition (2024–2026). There are a number of levels on which such comparisons can be made.

The reviewers might be subscribers to one of the current translation theories: sociological, communicational, hermeneutic, linguistic, literary and semiotic, or perhaps another. While such theories provide great analytical tools, I have not felt the need somehow to make a choice among them and pick my approach to the empirical enterprise of producing this translation accordingly.

The Preface has already pointed to the most fundamental choice I've made regarding the interplay of the language pair involved in the translation: The source language has supremacy over the target language, in order to retain the meaning, style and form of the original work. "This is extremely challenging because it involves understanding and transmitting all the nuances and double meanings in the original text, while also making the translation read naturally in the target language."[2]

In The Report[3] on the experimental project of the first edition of the "Chicago version" Book One, I addressed the fact, that extraordinary amount of *"The realia of 'The Fateful Adventures' cause no small problems for their translators"*[4]:

"How should the differences in linguistic, cultural and historical context be solved? One option is footnotes. With the exception of several mostly inevitable cases, such as the footnote about using the pronoun 'oni', we had decided not to use footnotes as they are distracting. Instead, we strove to integrate pieces of information into the text, because such pieces of information were and to a great extent

---

[1] *Text in italics* indicates it is a translation of the original
[2] Literary Translation, Acantho I&C, Professional Translators and Translations
[3] https://svejkcentral.com/The%20Report
[4] Několik editologických poznámek k románu Jaroslava Haška Osudy dobrého vojáka Švejka za světové války (*A few editological notes to Jaroslav Hašek's novel The Fateful Adventures Of The Good Soldier Švejk During The World War*), by Jiří Fiala, in Acta Universitatis Palackianae Olomucensis Facultas Philosophica Philologica 84 – 2004, Studia Bohemica IX

even today are a part of the frame of reference of the Czech reader, for whom they are then practically included in the perception of the original text and he does not have to look for them outside of it. As with most things in life, even here the situation is not ideal and there's no single possible solution. We rejected the third possibility, i.e. neither footnotes nor information integrated into the text, as depriving the reader of information and therefore unacceptable."

After reading it, Jiří Fiala, in his editological[1] notes concluded: *"...but the concept of the English translation of the realia of 'The Fateful Adventures' presented by Zenny K. Sadlon curiously disturbs the author's text."* Although unrelated to his characterization of our attempt to solve the problem of mounting endnotes, earlier in the text he allowed that *"The decision whether or not to provide an explanatory note to the text in question is not always easy..."*[2] The authors were first charged in connection with integrating parts of the native Czech readers' frame of reference into the text two years earlier already: They "feel that they need to guide the reader through the text...falsely in the guise of Hašek's language,..."[3]

The first edition of the "Chicago version" of Book One was indeed experimental. We tried to avoid the disruptive nature and clutter of footnotes or endnotes, while at the same time preserving the meaning and impact of the original text by occasionally inserting the information into the text. It was produced quickly and without strict guardrails.

A year after the new translation was finished, the authors of the Czech language *Encyclopedia for Those Who Love Švejk* cataloged the ever growing number of expressions, the meanings of which are inevitably moving into the category of misunderstood or unknown. Thus the need for footnotes or endnotes keeps increasing. *"In this context, it is worth mentioning the opinion of publisher Emil Šolc and attorney A. Červinka, who on August 20, 1923 appraised the copyright of Jaroslav Hašek regarding the Fateful Adventures with a prognosis: 'After 10 years, the contents of the book will be unclear to the new*

---

[1] Editology is an area of translation research that is focused on the theoretical and critical reflection on the editorial and publishing practice of translated literature

[2] *A few editological notes to Jaroslav Hašek's novel The Fateful Adventures Of The Good Soldier Švejk During The World War*

[3] Michelle Woods reviews *The Good Soldier Švejk (Book One)*, Jacket 18 — August 2002

generation and there will hardly be readers for this work.' (see Jaroslav Hašek in the photo, Prague 1959, p. 138)."[1]

That prognosis was uttered one hundred and one year ago. With time slipping into the future, it is apparently futile to think, that simply translating the text will preserve it for passing it onto the future generations. What is to be done? Unfortunately, and, as it appears, inevitably, the answer is more explanatory notes.

The second charge made against the authors of the first edition of the "Chicago version" was "dismantling the layout of the text. They literally signpost Švejk's meanderings by cutting them up into short three or four sentence paragraphs and suggest a logical rhetoric being put forth by Švejk."[2]

"It is true that punctuation and hard returns break up the format that forces the reader to read 'as Švejk speaks — without a breath.' We decided to do that in Book One so that modern readers wouldn't asphyxiate before the end of the book, as the goal was to convey the whole novel. There are two factors mitigating our structural crime: [the first of two factors is that] larger portion of Švejk's spirit lives in the other aspects of the text: point of view, syntax and semantics."[3] As for the question of convergence of the points of view of the author and the translator, see The Contextual Point Of View, in The Report.[4]

To address the remaining mentioned issues of syntax and semantics, which the translator has to solve, one must examine how "all of the domains of linguistic knowledge (morphology, lexicon, semantics, and syntax)"[5] manifest themselves in the text being translated.

I have already addressed the ignored lexical improvements the "Chicago version" translation contains in comparison to the currently "authoritative translation".[6]

The Czech language has a very rich morphology, "a very high

---

[1] *A few editological notes to Jaroslav Hašek's novel The Fateful Adventures Of The Good Soldier Švejk During The World War*

[2] Michelle Woods reviews *The Good Soldier Švejk (Book One)*

[3] Summary, in A response to Michelle Woods' review of «The Good Soldier Švejk (Book One)», Jacket 40 — Late 2010

[4] The Contextual Point Of View, in The Report on the experimental project of the first edition of the "Chicago version" Book One

[5] Trends in Language Acquisition Research

[6] Lexical Accuracy Issues, in A response to Michelle Woods' review of «The Good Soldier Švejk (Book One)», Jacket 40 — Late 2010

degree of inflection. For example, a noun can have up to 14 different forms depending on the case and number (singular or plural). The situation is even worse with pronouns and numbers whose morphological form is controlled by the gender and other attributes of the adjacent noun. Three possible grades (standard, comparative and superlative) result in further tripled amount of forms that can be derived from a single adjective. In case of verbs the variability is the largest one due to the dependency on person, gender, number, tense, mood, etc."[1]

There is interaction between morphology (structure and formation of words) and syntax (rules governing sentence structure) in a language. In this combination, called morphosyntax, grammatical structures and word forms interact to convey meaning in sentences. Due to rich morphology, the Czech morphosyntax has a very important byproduct: "**The free word order in Czech sentences allows for situations where, for example, the sentence subject controlling the verb phrase may appear in various and sometimes very distant positions.**"[2] This [bolded by me] aspect of the Czech, as the source language for the text you're about to read, is one of the means, with which the translator is urged to "expand and deepen his [target] language".[3] Concurring with that dictum, I decided to keep the original syntax to the utmost degree.

"A comparison of English with Czech shows that some syntactic functions performed by the developed Czech inflection are beyond the purview of the relatively poor English inflection, which creates the need to use other means of expressing syntactic relations, primarily auxiliary (functional) words and word order."[4]

"Languages with a 'rich' morphology (i.e. with expansive case systems, agreement of nouns with adjectives, rich verbal systems with person marking for all main participants, etc.) will tend to have a freer word order than languages that lack such markings. In the languages that lack such markings, word order will often take over the role of

---

[1] Combining Lexical And Morphological Knowledge in Language Model For Inflectional (Czech) Language, by Jan Nouza, Jindra Drabkova
[2] Combining Lexical And Morphological Knowledge in Language Model For Inflectional (Czech) Language
[3] Die Krisis der europaischen Kultur (p.242), by Rudolf Pannwitz
[4] Mluvnice současné angličtiny na pozadí češtiny (Grammar of Contemporary English against the background of Czech), Electronic edition, Dušková, Libuše et al.

indicating grammatical roles in the sentence, and for this reason will tend to become fixed, as **changing the word order in such languages would likely cause misunderstandings**."[1] I have endeavored to replicate the Czech language sentence structures, which are unfamiliar to the English reader, but make them understandable, even though requiring some effort at times to overcome the expectations formed by long-standing habit of anticipating the standard flow of how thoughts are expressed, before actually reading their record in the translated written sentence.

If "long, involved sentences and paragraphs are...as much constitutive of the meaning in the novel as the choice of words or ideas"[2] and are "integral to the meaning and tone of the novel,"[3] a maxim we purposefully violated in the first edition of Book One, what of **translating of meanings resulting from differing morphosyntax of the source language into the target language**? The iconic opening phrase of the book is an excellent example of this phenomenon.[4] To our surprise, it hasn't been commented on by any of the academicians, who had anything to say about the first edition. Only a lone reader remarked: "I tried a sample of the new translation and was so **stunned even by the difference in the meaning of the dialogue of the opening scene**, I embarked on the story again from page 1."[5] [See the essay "František Josef and the Grammar of Czech Subjecthood in Hašek's Opening Line".]

The decision to replicate the syntax of the original may impact two aspects of the text: the goal of "making the translation read naturally in the target language"[6] and "aesthetic functions"[7] of the literary work. "[E]ach art form has its own system for the judgment of aesthetics."[8] The syntax of the language is certainly a component of the aesthetics of a literary text. In order to appreciate the syntax aesthetics of the original text, the reader of the translation has to be

---

[1] Languages with stricter and less strict word order?, Linguistics Stack Exchange
[2] Michelle Woods reviews *The Good Soldier Švejk (Book One)*
[3] ditto
[4] The Plunge, in The Report on the experimental project of the first edition of the "Chicago version" Book One
[5] Corto 's Reviews > The Fateful Adventures of the Good Soldier Svejk During the World War, Book(s) Three & Four
[6] Literary Translation, Acantho I&C
[7] Literary translations, POLYGLOT
[8] Aesthetic Elements in Prose Translation, by Jin Li

first exposed to it: "**the aesthetic perspective of a translator determines in which aspects he will bring out the aesthetic beauty of the original** and his aesthetic competence determines to what extent he can blend the artistic properties on different levels into a well-organized unity;"[1]

The next issue was touched upon by another retail customer's review: "A note on **the translation**: it is very colloquial, very funny but I believe it **overuses the past progressive tense**, which must be a lot more common in Czech than in English."[2]

I will tag this issue by the label:
ON THE USE OF THE PROGRESSIVE AND CONTINUOUS TENSES, AND PERFECTIVE AND IMPERFECTIVE *VID*/VERBAL ASPECT.

"*The* **'vid'** *of a verb is a category that is in the greatest degree represented in Slavic languages. In other language groups (for example, in the Romance or Germanic languages* [such as English]*), this category is reflected only on a limited scale and **is usually referred to as* **'aspect'***.*[3] "*The issue of verbal aspect has been for many decades the subject of research in general linguistics and the linguistics of individual languages, however,* **in connection with the theory of translation, this issue remains to a large extent** *terra incognita.*"[4]

"Although **English** largely separates tense and aspect formally, its **aspects** (neutral, progressive, perfect, progressive perfect, and [in the past tense] habitual) **do not correspond very closely to the distinction of perfective vs. imperfective** that is found in most languages with aspect. Furthermore, the separation of tense and aspect in English is not maintained rigidly."[5] "The Slavic languages make a clear distinction between perfective and imperfective aspects; it was in relation to these languages that the modern concept of aspect originally developed."[6] "With a few exceptions, each Slavic verb is either perfective or imperfective. Most verbs form canonical pairs of one perfective and one imperfective verb with generally the same meaning. However, each Slavic language contains a number of bi-

---

[1] Aesthetic Elements in Prose Translation
[2] Amazon Customer Review, by Edmund Pickett
[3] On the Rendition of Verbal Aspect in English and Spanish Translations of Zdeněk Jirotka's Saturnin, by Nikola Janotová
[4] ditto
[5] Grammatical aspect in Slavic languages, Wikipedia
[6] Grammatical aspect, Wikipedia

aspectual verbs, which may be used as both imperfective and perfective. ... **Aspect in Slavic languages is a superior category in relation to tense or mood.** Particularly, some verbal forms (like infinitive) cannot distinguish tense but they still distinguish aspect."[1]

If this sounds confusing to the average reader of novels, it is natural. These passages from academic theoretical papers express concepts, which are discoveries *ex post facto*. They've existed in the language before anybody started studying them. Not knowing about them doesn't preclude a native speaker from using them and doing so "correctly", i.e. according to the theories defining the concepts and prescribing how they are to be implemented in one's speech or writing.

*"A Czech is growing up already [immersed] in the category of verbal aspect, from a very young age he hears the use of differences of verbal aspect in thousands and tens of thousands of sentences, he already **thinks and formulates his thoughts in this category.**"*[2]

This is not just metaphor — it is phenomenological fact. The preconscious structuring of reality through aspectual boundaries is so deep that, the Czech child instinctively distinguishes šel = "he went" (once; a single completed motion) vs. chodil = "he used to go" or "he would go" (repeated or habitual motion), udělal = "he did" or "he made" (once, and finished) vs. dělal = "he was doing" or "he used to do" (ongoing, incomplete, or habitual action), not just semantically but ontologically. The English child, meanwhile, parses time more through tense and lexical choice, rarely encoding completion as part of the verb's essence.

*"The category of vid, as a purely Czech (Slavic) phenomenon, permeates all layers of our national language, and even if one may not be aware of it, **from the point of view of translation, it is one of the most frequent problems that a translator encounters during his work.**"*[3] *"The question of the adequate translation of this category in an aesthetically demanding [literary] work into a language with considerably different grammatical system could therefore become a kind of touchstone for evaluating the quality of a translation. If **in Slavic languages verbal aspect is an integral part of the expression***

---

[1] Grammatical aspect in Slavic languages
[2] Sloveso v překladu, (*Verb in Translation*), Slavica Pragensia, by Josef Václav Bečka
[3] On the Rendition of Verbal Aspect in English and Spanish Translations of Zdeněk Jirotka's Saturnin

and formulation of ideas, its traces can be found at all levels of the text: not only purely grammatical, but also, for example, at the level of expressing the speaker's attitude towards a certain event or rendering the atmosphere of the situation, thereby potentially moving the analysis from a purely linguistic level to the level of narratology."[1]

As a result, a Czech speaker cannot speak about events without positioning them within the continuum of done / in progress / habitual / attempted — it is as essential as subject or object. English, in contrast, can remain aspectually vague, or defer it to adverbials (already, still, again), tense shifts, or periphrastic forms.

This issue cuts to the very core of the translational abyss between Czech and English: **verbal aspect/vid isn't just a grammatical feature in Czech — it's a mental orientation**. The native Czech speaker breathes it; the native English speaker does not live it.

In response to the kind Amazon reviewer, who triggered this discussion, we can now say: *"[For] what the Czech expresses by verbal aspect, the French uses the system of verb tenses, which characterize time relatedness.* **The Englishman leaves these distinctions categorically unstated.***"*[2]

I hope the above discussion will help any reader to understand the complexity of the translator's job. Jaroslav Hašek added a wonderful burden to it by the complexity of his text and stretching the limits of the language, in addition to breaching the boundaries of tradition and expectations.

Following are several additional editorial notes.

ON THE USE OF *ITALICIZATION:*

Starting with the later versions of the first edition of Book Two, changes were made to the solution of the complicated problem of rendering the many non-Czech words, phrases, proper names, titles and even a few blue-streaks into English. To give the reader the flavor of the real-world multi-culturalism of Austria-Hungary, in Book One and the first versions of the remaining volumes, the original German, Polish and Hungarian and other foreign language phrases were left in,

---

[1] On the Rendition of Verbal Aspect in English and Spanish Translations of Zdeněk Jirotka's Saturnin
[2] Sloveso v překladu, (*Verb in Translation*)

italicized, and followed by a comma and the English translation.

During reader testing of Book Two this original solution hampered readability and diminished reading enjoyment. Švejk is now on his way to the front with the military, in which German is the official language, he travels through Hungary and Poland, meeting local residents and soldiers from all corners of the Empire, and eventually even soldiers fighting for the other side. The number of utterances in foreign languages increases accordingly. To overcome the reported readability problem, the most reasonable option appeared to be to omit the foreign language text wherever we can assume, that the average Czech likely to read the book in the 1920s would have understood it. Instead, only the translations are included, written in *italics*, to indicate that *the words were spoken or written in a foreign language*. After applying this solution, however, the identity of the foreign language is not immediately apparent. Yet, which foreign language the words originated in can usually be discerned from the context or by direct reference.

The italicized *"They"* or *"they"* and their morphological variants are an important exception to this *italicization* rule. Why? The word isn't foreign, but its use is, in a very significant way: *"They"* is the English word for the Czech "oni" pronounced "'oh-nyi", which is used in place of "vy", i.e. second personal plural "you".

During the 300 years of Austrian imperial regime, the German language virtually replaced Czech among the successful and ambitious Czechs. The process of Germanization didn't stop with them. When in the 18th century the Czech National Revival started, programmatically driven by the intellectuals, much of the writing, including treatises on the Czech language, was done in German. European languages, with the exception of English, retain the device of **showing respect** by addressing another person using a form of the personal pronoun other than the second person singular. Most, with the exception of at least German and Finnish, do it **by using the second person plural** of the personal pronoun and the corresponding form of the verb.

To complicate things further, in modern English there is no way to indicate whether the speaker is addressing one person or many people when saying "you". Unless, of course, he's from the American South and makes himself clear by saying "y'all". The means of the familiar address, the second person singular pronoun in English used to be "thou". 'You' was reserved for the second person plural. "You" eventually replaced "thou". Therefore, using the pronoun "you" among the masses of secular mortals nowadays, when addressing a single person, it is as if actually showing mutual respect and maintaining distance. At the same time, in a linguistically and socially bizarre twist we refer to even casual acquaintances and strangers we merely conduct business with by their first name. (The capitalized "Thou" is retained only among some Christians to address God, with whom we're supposed to be on first name basis and on really good terms and show respect to at the same time.)

Now, consider this: the **Germans use** "Sie", the capitalized form of "sie", i.e. the **third person plural** pronoun "they", when addressing a stranger or showing respect to age, position, or maintaining distance. It was probably the Czech "petty bourgeoisie" under the German speaking Austrian rule, who introduced, spread and maintained the habit of using this German rule of grammar, when speaking Czech: using the third person plural pronoun 'oni' in place of the second person plural "Vy", i.e. "You" (capitalized in writing in conformance with the German grammar and to distinguish it from the standard form of the second person plural "vy"). Germanisms, most often simply German words with Czech endings and spelling, persist in the Czech language and are still used today. Fortunately, **using "they" instead of "you"**, a particularly onerous Germanism, has disappeared at last. However, among the snobbish "petty bourgeoisie", a cultural equivalent of the latter day U.S. "upper middle class", it was in use **even after the demise of the Habsburg rule of 1918**.

Can you image living in a society where foreigners and their language rule? Can you imagine the successful and the turncoats among your own people twisting your own language to conform to the unique rule of the oppressors' language? Perhaps you can now begin to ponder how many levels of communication there are when, as you'll read later on, a police station chief addresses an old hag gofer of his in the manner signifying respect or distance that he borrowed from the language of the foreign oppressors. Is the hag being given respect, is it just a habit to address her in such a way because she is older, or is she being mocked? Some would argue, that the police station chief is mocking her, his mocking is habitual and the manner of speech is mocking-habit-forming. Imagine hearing this speech phenomenon for another twenty years after your country had been liberated and become free and independent. And that is just a single point of language.

On the use of "missis" for "paní":
In English, "a man always goes by 'Mr.' or 'Mister' regardless of his marital status, whereas how you refer to a woman depends on her marital status …"[1]

There are two main female characters in the novel: Mrs. Müller and Mrs. Palivec. The latter is the wife of pubkeeper Palivec, so her marital status is known. As for the former, a cleaning lady, we don't know whether she is or ever was married. In Czech, one word is sufficient. In English there's for adult females no single counterpart to the label "mister", reserved for adult males.

Czech: "Támhle ta **paní** uklouzla na ledě."
"Nevíš, kdo ta **paní** je?"
"Jo, já jí znám. To je **paní** Palivcová."
"Počkej, ne, není. To je **paní** Müllerová."
English: "That **woman/lady** over there slipped on ice."
"Would you know who that **woman/lady** is?"
"Yeah, I know her. That is **Mrs./missis** Palivec."
"Wait, no, it isn't. That's **Mrs./ missis** Müller.

Is the reader going to deduce from the abbreviation "Mrs." that both of the women are married? To avoid a potential error, what word corresponding to the marital-status-neutral "mister" designation for females should we choose? I've settled on "missis", when referring to a known woman of uncertain or irrelevant marital status. While I would refer to an unknown female as a "woman" or "lady", I can't refer to a known female as "woman" or "lady" followed by her last name. If I use "Mrs.", the implication seems to be she's married. Let's see what the dictionaries tell us about the terms:

missis - per Collins dictionary online
    in American English
      1. one's **wife** *also used with the*
      2. the **mistress of a household** *used with the*
    Word origin: <u>altered < mistress</u>, Mrs.[2]
      Mrs. - is used before the name of **a married woman**

---

[1] Mr and Mrs, Ms, and Miss: Meanings, Abbreviations, and Correct Usage, Hannah Yang
[2] missis, Collins online dictionary

when you are speaking or referring to her.[1]

missis – per Merriam-Webster online
variant of missus
1. informal + old-fashioned: **WIFE**
2. British, informal —used to address **a woman whose name is not known** [Note: What about a woman whose name is known?]
3. dialect: MISTRESS sense 1a— the **female head of a household**

mistress
5a—used archaically as a title prefixed to the name of **a married** or **unmarried** woman
5b—chiefly Southern US and Midland US[2] —used as a **conventional title of courtesy** except when usage requires the substitution of a title of rank or an honorific or professional title before a married woman's surname: MRS. sense 1a

Mrs.
1a—used as a conventional title of courtesy except when usage requires the substitution of a title of rank or an honorific or professional title before a married woman's surname
b—used before the name of a place (such as a country or city) or of a profession or activity (such as a sport) or before some epithet (such as clever) to form a title applied to a married woman viewed or recognized as representative of the thing indicated
2: WIFE

---

[1] Mrs., Collins online dictionary
[2] "According to author Colin Woodard, this is the region that 'extends from Quaker territory in Pennsylvania and Delaware through populated Midwestern areas in Ohio, Indiana, and Illinois, down through the Plains states of Iowa, Nebraska, and Kansas, and stretching out to include parts of Oklahoma, the Texas Panhandle, and New Mexico. It includes some of what we consider the American Heartland and Middle America. Midlands society is 'pluralistic and organized around the middle class'." - This map shows the US really has 11 separate 'nations' with entirely different cultures, by Mark Abadi in Business Insider

Since "missis" originated as an alteration of "mistress", which in turn is used as a conventional title of courtesy in much of the U.S. area "organized around the middle class", I think it appropriate to use it for the translation of the Czech marital-status-neutral term "paní".

ON THE CHOICE TO USE TIMES NEW ROMAN TYPE:
While having tested several types of print that were readable and appealing and could have served Jaroslav Hašek's text well, I've finally settled on the Times New Roman type. It was designed for a newspaper and is perhaps the most popular of all fonts. But "thanks to its ubiquity, it can come off as lacking character."[1] A type, which conveys the news of the day from around the world and virtually any other information to the reader of newspapers, while lacking character of its own, and lets the character of the stories come across unpolluted by the character of the print type? That is actually the perfect combination for *The Fateful Adventures of The Good Soldier Švejk*:

The News that Matters!
The news you need to know!
Now!

---

[1] 10 Popular Newspaper Fonts, Issuu digital publishing platform

Comparative Notes on Methodology

In my work on *The Fateful Adventures of the Good Soldier Švejk*, I have made clear my fidelity to the principle, that the source language must shape the target, not the reverse — a notion most forcefully articulated by Rudolf Pannwitz, who wrote that a true translation "does not turn the German into the target language, but lets the target language be powerfully affected by the foreign tongue."

But does this make mine an isolated case, or is it part of a broader tradition of radical fidelity in literary translation? A search for an answer turned out five prominent cases, where translators of complex, often linguistically experimental authors have been lauded for going as far as their originals demand:

1. **Gregory Rabassa** (Jorge Luis Borges, Gabriel García Márquez) His method involved deeply inhabiting **the original language** and **allowing its rhythm and structures to reshape the English**. He emphasized that a good translator must "betray the reader to be faithful to the author."[A]

2. **Richard Pevear and Larissa Volokhonsky** (Dostoevsky, Tolstoy, Chekhov): Their translations **prioritize syntactic fidelity over fluency**, often echoing Russian sentence structures in English. They have been both praised and criticized for this uncompromising approach, which they defend as essential to preserving the author's voice[B]. As Pevear himself explains, the translator's task is not to create an easy or "lovely" surface but to reproduce the seams, awkwardness, and premeditated resistance that mark the original. "Terms like 'gorgeous,' 'sonorous,' and 'lovely' simply have no relevance to Tolstoy's work," he notes, adding that Tolstoy "was not only unconcerned with such artistic qualities, but quite openly despised them."[C]

3. **John E. Woods** (Arno Schmidt): Woods' translation of *Zettel's Traum*, a notoriously untranslatable modernist text, required radical innovation in English. He **echoed** Schmidt's playful **multilingualism and syntactic fragmentation** with painstaking care, and was celebrated for doing so.[D]

4. **Barbara Wright** (Raymond Queneau): Her rendering of *Exercises in Style* captured not just content but form, **mirroring** Queneau's **structural experiments in a target language** where

xxxi

such devices had no precedent. Her approach to form-as-content translation has been lauded as a model of creative fidelity.[E]

5. **J. A. Underwood** (Karl Kraus): Underwood tackled Kraus's **compressed syntax, linguistic satire**, and cultural density with a strategy that **preserved** the difficulty rather than smoothed it. He received critical recognition for refusing to compromise Kraus's aggression and intricacy.[F]

The common ground among these translators lies in their methodological **refusal to naturalize the foreign**. They do not treat their target language as a dominant or self-contained norm, but as a medium malleable enough to absorb the alien structures of the source. Their English is shaped by the source, not the other way around.

This is the central tenet of my own practice, and aligns with what I have articulated in both my *Editorial Notes* and in The Report (*Challenges of Translating Švejk into English – A Report on the Experimental Project of its "Chicago Version."*) Such choices have long carried a personal cost for me, since fidelity often meant standing apart from colleagues who preferred the ease of naturalization[1].

METHODOLOGICAL COMMITMENTS:
INSIGHTS FROM THE REPORT

The original 15-page Report, composed six years prior to my formal 29-page response to Michelle Woods in Jacket Magazine, outlined in unambiguous terms the guiding methodological principles behind the experimental Book One of the "Chicago version" English translation of Švejk: My collaborator and I "agreed on the method of literary rendition of, as I had named it, the 'raw translation'.

---

[1] I had already practiced this approach years before I encountered Pannwitz. While working at the Voice of America from 1986, I was once chided for "not even sounding Czech" in my reportages — for translating "word for word." The same Pannwitzian instinct was already at work, misunderstood and mislabeled by a colleague: allowing English meanings to reshape Czech rather than smoothing them into the expected idiom. I encountered the same problem in reverse — translating from English into Czech — for example with the term 'credit card.' Here I resisted the easy adoption of an anglicism and insisted on the direct rendering "úvěrová karta," not knowing what, if any, terminology existed in Czech banking at the time. This form was later adopted officially, though in colloquial usage "kredit karta," and eventually "kreditka," prevailed. To my disappointment, my colleagues adopted the colloquial anglicism in their official broadcasting work.

The raw translation I was producing for our purposes was something between a literal translation and a proper translation. A raw translation contains, e.g., original idioms translated in such a way as to communicate the Czech idiom by English words, not by an English idiom, so that it is possible to discuss its content in English without any knowledge of Czech. Similarly, the raw translation often keeps the original sentence structure if it is needed to preserve logical inferences that would disappear by adjusting it. That way there is always enough to discuss or to fight for in the course of producing the final translation."

Twenty eight years later, The Centennial Edition has taken the maximalist approach "to keep the original syntax to the utmost degree." I've kept the, by critics yet unassailed, iconic opening sentence of the novel in its expanded form. "We sacrificed the structure of the original sentence in our translation in order to preserve the information contained in it." I didn't do it "to integrate cultural context into the text itself rather than using footnotes," but to bridge a structural gap between Czech and English: the Czech sentence contains an ethical dative (nám), a grammatical function that English cannot express syntactically.

"Call me Ishmael."

"Mother died today."

"As Gregor Samsa awoke one morning from uneasy dreams he found himself transformed in his bed into a gigantic insect."

"Tak nám zabili Ferdinanda."

Placed beside these canonical openings, the first sentence of Švejk is equally fixed in cultural memory.

Czech original:
"Tak **nám** zabili Ferdinanda," řekla posluhovačka panu Švejkovi...

Parrott's literary translation and industry-sanctioned English version:
*"So they've killed **our** Ferdinand," said the charwoman to Mr. Švejk...*

That my expanded English form of it drew no comment from critics is a fact that requires acknowledgment before any discussion of method can proceed. It is the point that should unsettle any serious reader of translation.

The Chicago non-commissioned version's expanded form:
So *they've done it **to us**, they've killed **our** Ferdinand," said the cleaning woman to Mr. Švejk...*

The choice to divide Hašek's single sentence into two English clauses was not a loss of Czech structure, but an adjustment of English surface form to preserve the Czech emotional stance encoded in that ethical dative. The Czech ethical dative (nám) cannot be reproduced in English without violating the native syntax; the translator must bend English to carry it. I bent it — publicly, in the first line of the book. That is the methodological signature.

Indeed, the disparity in critical focus was striking. The same critics who seized on matters as trivial as my use of the word "mutants" — which Michelle Woods dismissed as a "modish slang term" or who, like Oxford's James Partridge, urged respect for Parrott's "devotion to Hašek" while noting the awkwardness and flatness of Parrott's diction, remained silent about the one decision that announced my method most unmistakably: the expanded form of the novel's first sentence.

That silence is telling. They nitpicked smaller matters while leaving unremarked a transformation at the very gateway of the book, a transformation that openly declared my refusal to naturalize Hašek's Czech into a smoother English idiom.

The category of verbal aspect, discussed in the preceding Editorial Notes, is not the only grammatical system a Czech grows up already immersed in, one that shapes his perception of events and agency. Another grammatical feature in Czech that determines his mental orientation is the reflexivity of verbs. It is not the reflexivity in itself that distinguishes the Czech from the English in their perception of the world, but the way it is expressed.

In English, these verbs use reflexive pronouns (such as myself, yourself, himself, herself, itself, ourselves, yourselves, themselves) to indicate that the action is reflected back onto the subject. Reflexive verbs often describe actions someone does to himself, but in Czech, the subject is not limited to people. Reflexivity is a built-in, routine part of Czech verb morphology and syntax, with both semantic and aspectual consequences.

In Czech, the reflexive marker "se" can be attached to transitive verbs to make them intransitive (otevřít – otevřít se, *to open – to open itself*), to create a middle voice¹ (rozpadá se, *it falls apart*), or to mark impersonal constructions (žije se tu dobře, *it is lived well here / life is good here*), or to denote habitual, reciprocal, or passive-like meaning. This system works across both animate and inanimate subjects and does not rely on pronominal identity between subject and object. As such, it introduces a broader, more abstract **form of reflexivity — one that need not point to psychological or volitional selfhood, and one that can function as a marker of voice, aspect, or event framing**.

In English, by contrast, reflexivity depends on agency and personhood. "He washed himself" is grammatical; "The door opened itself" is awkward or poetic at best. English resists reflexivity with inanimate subjects and often requires passive or circumlocutory rephrasing. "The door opened" in English is not reflexive, even though the Czech "Dveře se otevřely" formally is. This mismatch puts pressure on the translator to disambiguate, to choose voice, and to either suppress or render explicit the agentless neutrality that Czech reflexivity often preserves.

This is not just a grammatical divergence — it's a mental one. **The Czech reflexive system allows a speaker to remain ambiguous about agency, to center the unfolding of events without forcing them into active/passive binary categories. English**, on the other hand, **demands clarity: Who did what to whom? Was it done or did it happen?** These demands shape not only the translator's syntax but the entire rhythm and tone of the resulting sentence. In Hašek's prose, where irony, deflection, and structural vagueness often carry narrative weight, such pressures can be deforming.

The Czech reflexive clitic "se" does not merely alter syntax; in combination with verbal aspect, it reshapes how events are framed, how agency is assigned, and how time is perceived. From a translator's perspective, **the cumulative effect of aspect and reflexivity defines the deep divide between Czech** (and other Slavic

---

[1] English lacks a true middle voice and rarely uses reflexive syntax to express impersonal or intransitive events. Czech reflexivity, by contrast, routinely carries both syntactic and semantic weight: it can shift agency, remove it altogether, or reframe the subject-object relation. These constructions are not idiomatic but grammaticalized — that is, built into the structure of the language as a systematic Czech way of encoding perspective.

languages) **and English, making the work not only harder but equally more important.**[1]

And it is precisely these puzzles, if not attended to with the same determination as semantic challenges, that may frustrate the reader's quest to find what it is like to be the foreign author's compatriot and soulmate.

"The purpose" of my project to translate the novel, 75 years old at the time, "was to create the most faithful translation possible which would unmask Švejk for readers of English."

METHODOLOGICAL COMMITMENTS REAFFIRMED:
MY RESPONSE TO THE REVIEW

If fidelity to the author's world is the translator's primary duty, then the case of *The Good Soldier Švejk* places that duty under exceptional strain. The linguistic, political, and tonal textures of Jaroslav Hašek's novel do not merely resist domestication — they actively subvert it. Any attempt to smooth these surfaces in the name of reader comfort or fluency risks obscuring the very mechanisms through which the novel achieves its critique. It is precisely in this domain that the methodological choices made in my translation, particularly in relation to the early criticism levied by Michelle Woods in her Jacket 18 review, can be understood, not as eccentric deviations from best practice, but as principled attempts to align the English text with the Czech reader's experience of Hašek's original.

At the time Woods conducted her review, only the online version of Book One had been completed, a version that bore the traces of experimentation, some of which I later revised or abandoned

---

[1] As a former interpreter for a President of the United States, I can't help but reflect on how profoundly worldview is shaped and expressed by language. The structural differences between English and Slavic languages, including Russian, are not merely grammatical: they frame perception, agency, and responsibility. Such divergences, I believe, do not remain confined to private cognition. They shape diplomacy, war, and the interpretation of truth itself.
Just yesterday (8/26/2005), President Donald J. Trump responded to the Russian foreign minister Lavrov's statement that Russia could not sign a peace deal with Ukrainian President Volodymyr Zelensky: "We recognize him as the de facto head of the regime…But when it comes to signing legal documents…we would need very clear understanding by everybody that the person who is signing is legitimate." President Trump: "Doesn't matter what they say. Everybody's posturing. It's all bullshit, OK? Everybody's posturing".

entirely.^G But even in that early form, the translation was anchored in a commitment I had not yet formalized but practiced: the conviction that the target language must not remain intact, but be reshaped under the pressure of the source, as Rudolf Pannwitz demanded when he warned translators against preserving "the state in which [their] own language happens to be." Woods, opposed to domestication, read certain experimental features of Book One — paragraph divisions, slang choices, and added glosses — not as methodological fidelity but as errors of simplification.

Woods charged the translation with simplification of style, Americanized slang, and appropriative additions that she saw as domesticating and explanatory. What she identified as flaws — loss of Hašek's looping structure and register subtlety — we regard as conscious decisions to make Hašek's tone audible in English. As I wrote in my response to the review, the work was "characterized by Partridge as marked by clumsy diction"[1] and by Woods as a simplification of syntax and domestication, but those surface qualities were essential to the strategy of radical fidelity.

This was especially evident in her charge that our version simply transplanted Parrott's formulations while adding "modish" or "American-influenced slang." In her analysis, words like "mongrel mutants" or idiomatic constructions such as "how they got into this mess" were held up as examples of a deliberate Americanization, as if the point of departure from Parrott were merely one of cultural flavor or national idiom. But these were not instances of lexical frivolity. They were rooted in a semantic investigation that privileged context over substitution. The term "mutants," far from being plucked from pop culture, was selected through etymological triangulation, drawing on the Czech term "obluda" and its relation to "netvor", "zrůda", and the semantic field of monstrosity, deformity, and mutation. Likewise, "mess" was not slang inserted for local color, but the idiomatic rendering of a Czech situational phrase (jak se do toho dostali) whose referent was not a physical location, but a bureaucratic and moral quagmire. Woods' reading failed to account for the cultural embeddedness of the Czech original, and therefore mischaracterized

---

[1] Partridge's description of the translation as "clumsy" is not a neutral stylistic observation but a normative judgment, measuring the English against expectations of idiomatic fluency rather than against the structural and tonal demands of Hašek's Czech.

the effort to replicate that embeddedness in English as a distortion, rather than a methodological fidelity.

Her critique of our early structural decisions — particularly the breaking up of Hašek's famously long paragraphs — deserves more careful parsing. It is true that in Book One we experimented with paragraph breaks to avoid overwhelming readers unaccustomed to the breathless cascades of indirect speech and nested digression that characterize Hašek's style. That decision was later reversed in the remaining three books, which I translated independently. But even in Book One, the aim was not to impose rhetorical clarity where none existed. Rather, it was to prevent premature reader abandonment. As I stated elsewhere: "We decided to do that in Book One so that modern readers wouldn't asphyxiate before the end of the book." It was not a concession to fluency, but a triage measure, and one I ultimately judged unnecessary. What matters more, and what remains consistent across all volumes, is the preservation of Hašek's syntactic tempo, idiomatic layering, and the sociolinguistic register of his speakers. In other words, even when the paragraph was shortened, the sentence was not domesticated.

Equally revealing is Woods' treatment of our strategy toward cultural specificity. She objected, for example, to our elaboration of the word borovička as "that liquor that tastes like pine wood," claiming that such insertions were misleading acts of appropriation. But this objection assumes that Czech readers encounter the term borovička with no interpretive effort, as if its connotations were obvious and transparent. In truth, the Czech word is already a diminutive derived from borovice (*pine*), even though the liquor is made from jalovec (*juniper*). Hašek's readers might have tasted pine not in the chemistry of the drink, but in the metaphor embedded in the word's morphology. To replicate that synesthetic ambiguity in English not with a footnote, but with a phrase inside the line, was a decision born of respect for readerly experience, not an indulgence in explanatory gloss.

It is important, too, to address the evolution of the translation's method over time. Woods was reviewing a project in motion. Book One, the only volume she assessed, was shaped by early compromises and reader-response experimentation. After my colleague's departure, I completed the remaining volumes alone, with full methodological clarity. I abandoned explanatory insertions. I reinstated paragraph lengths. I removed the last traces of domesticating compromise. The voice of Švejk, and of the novel's surrounding bureaucratic chorus, was allowed to speak in English with the same syntactic strangeness and rhythmic density as in Czech. The result is not a smoother text, but a more faithful one. As Don DeGrazia wrote, Švejk is not a "dainty classic" but a "bellowing barroom brawl of a book" — and the translation had to carry that volume and vehemence into English without distortion.

In this light, what appeared to Woods as inconsistencies or stylistic intrusions were in fact signs of a translator grappling, publicly and imperfectly, with the ethics of representation. The decision to preserve Czech morphosyntax, to maintain aspectual distinctions, to embed the authority of German into English while still translating it, and to replicate the layering of literary and vernacular registers: none of these were aesthetic embellishments. They were methodological commitments. And while the first edition of Book One contains the record of early compromises, The Centennial Edition, and especially Books Three & Four, stand as the mature result of those same commitments brought to completion.

Ultimately, what Woods called for — greater transparency about the technical decisions of the translation process — is precisely what I have aimed to provide, both in direct response to her critique and in the broader methodological reflections that shape this edition. If the translation remains controversial, it is not because its method is obscure. It is because its method refuses to do what most English-language readers, critics, and publishers have been trained to expect: a text that reads like English first and like Švejk second. Mine does not. It reads like Švejk, in English.

As one reviewer, reading the translation alongside its predecessor, put it: "The Parrott seems like how Hašek would have written if English were his primary language, while the Sadlon seems like how Hašek would tell us the story in his second language."

[A] Gregory Rabassa, "No Two Snowflakes Are Alike: Translation as Metaphor," *Translation Review* 64 (2002): 8.

[B] Richard Pevear, "Translating Tolstoy's 'War and Peace'," *The New York Times*, October 21, 2007; see also *Translation Review* 64 (2002) for extended discussion of Pevear & Volokhonsky's methodology.

[C] Richard Pevear, comment posted to The New York Times online Reading Room discussion, October 29, 2007, https://archive.nytimes.com/readingroom.blogs.nytimes.com/2007/10/29/the-art-of-translation/#comment-199

^D John Tebbel, interview with John E. Woods, "Professor Horrdendo Discovers on Page 23 That He's a Translator," *San Diego Reader*, August 14, 1997.

^E *Asymptote Journal*, "Raymond Queneau's Exercises in Style (Barbara Wright, trans.)," review essay, 2013.

^F J. A. Underwood, introduction to *The Castle*, by Franz Kafka, translated by J. A. Underwood, 7–8 (London: Penguin Classics, 2000).

^G The digital version of Book One was available on my website (zenny.com) as early as 1998, initially in downloadable EVY format and later as a PDF. While the earliest capture of the site by the Wayback Machine is dated March 2, 2001, this postdates both the initial online publication and Michelle Woods' personal request for a review copy. She contacted me to request the digital text prior to the paperback's release on June 12, 2000, but did not indicate at the time that she intended to publish a review of it, nor inform me of its existence when she did so. Her critique appeared without forewarning in *Jacket Magazine* 18 (2002), which I discovered only incidentally several years later. While academic reviewers are not formally obligated to notify authors, it is generally considered good scholarly practice, particularly when one has proactively requested a free review copy. Based on later online research, I surmised that Michelle Woods may have been a postgraduate student at Charles University in Prague at the time, possibly of Czech heritage through her mother Yvonna Woods. It is conceivable that my translation of *Švejk* served a university-related purpose, given the timing and subject matter.

[Editorial Note]
The next essay is positioned between the Comparative Notes on Methodology and the Introduction to The Centennial English Edition because it bridges the translator's methodological commitments with the reader's historical and cultural orientation. It articulates the linguistic and emotional grammar underlying Hašek's opening sentence and imperial nomenclature, establishing the conceptual ground on which the Introduction's broader historical and contemporary reflections proceed.

František Josef and the Grammar of Czech Subjecthood in Hašek's Opening Line

Jaroslav Hašek begins *The Good Soldier Švejk* with a sentence so familiar to Czech readers that its strangeness can go unnoticed: "Tak nám zabili Ferdinanda." Much could be said about its humor, its offhand tone, its folk peculiarity. Yet the true force of the sentence resides in a single word: "nám", i.e. *"to us," "for us," "upon us"*.

This small dative pronoun encodes an entire social order: the emotional grammar of a subject population living under a ruler whose fate is theirs, whether they like it or not. When Mrs. Müller announces the Archduke's death, she does not simply report it; she experiences it as something done to her, as an event that happens upon the Czech people, as if imperial blood were somehow mixed into their own lives.

This is why, in The Report, explaining the decision to expand the form of the single-phrase iconic opening of the novel, I rendered the logic of "nám" as:

"They've done it to us, they've killed our Ferdinand…"

This expanded rendering is not a literal reproduction of Hašek's Czech syntax; it is the only faithful English translation if the meaning carried by "nám" is to be preserved.

This rendering is not meant as an English paraphrase but as a way to expose the emotional entanglement encoded in the grammar: ownership without affection, implication without consent, the peculiar intimacy of those who are ruled by people they neither chose nor necessarily even care about.

It is within this same emotional logic that Hašek makes a linguistic choice that can be easily overlooked: he refers to the Emperor exclusively as "František Josef." Not once in narration or dialogue does Hašek use the German imperial form "Franz Josef," even though bilingual Prague was saturated with it. Contemporary Czech historians gloss the Emperor as "císař František Josef I., lidově Franz Josef, (*Emperor František Josef I, popularly 'Franz Josef'*)" indicating that the German form "Franz Josef" was widely used as a popular form of the Emperor's name among Czechs, alongside official Czech "František Josef" in print.¹ My own 1960s recollections match this: in everyday Czech speech "Franz Josef" was used, seemingly always carrying a shade of ironic, Švejkian respect. Hašek's consistent use of the fully Czech "František Josef" in the novel, by contrast, seems deliberate — folding the Emperor into Czech domestic phonetics, within the same emotional grammar as "Tak nám zabili Ferdinanda."

Hašek's refusal to use the German name is therefore intentional and nontrivial.

To understand why this matters, one must hear what the Czech ear hears.

"František" is not a diminutive, but it sits right on the edge of the diminutive sound-family. Its phonetics — the soft -tišek cluster, the DUM-da-da rhythm characteristic of many Czech diminutive-adjacent words — place it near names like "little Vilouš" from the first Chapter of Book Four, "Viloušek", or "Ježíšek" (*little Jesus*, saturating broadcasts, print and personal speech in the third most atheistic society in the world every Christmas season), the diminutive of the most popular Czech male name "Josef" "Pepíček", then words like "koloušek", "kožíšek", and even the trochaic-meter-title of a children's 1955 animated film about a little ball "Míček Flíček" (*Balley the Speckle*). These affectionate or domestic diminutive patterns impart a tonal softness to the Emperor's name. Meanwhile, the familiar form "Franta" has the same hard, clipped profile as "Franz", revealing a nearly one-to-one acoustic correspondence between the familiar Czech male name and its German counterpart.

In this soundscape, "František Josef" does not feel imperial; it feels domestic, local — almost as if the Emperor were a figure in the Czech village.

This is not affection. It is Czech deflation of imperial grandeur through linguistic domestication. Hašek thus pulls the Habsburg monarch into the Czech speech-world. The Emperor becomes "ours"

---

¹ For example: Český rozhlas Plus: "Císař František Josef I., lidově Franz Josef…" (2020); https://plus.rozhlas.cz/nenavideny-nebo-milovany-franz-josef-7445774; "Dobrá historie" website links to that article using the same formula: *Emperor František Josef I, popularly 'Franz Josef'*; https://dobrahistorie.cz/dokument/3316-2-12-1848-den-kdy-nastoupil-na-trun-cisar-frantisek-josef

not because he is beloved, but because his authority saturates the lives of those who neither chose him nor can escape him. The Czech linguistic form insinuates him into the everyday: a presence that governs, interferes, and accompanies, whether welcome or not.

This mirrors the same psychological structure encoded in the opening "nám". The rulers' fates happen "to us"; and in the same way, the Emperor is named not with a distant imperial title but with the Czech version of his German name that folds him into the domestic, communal universe of the subjects. Hašek's satire works by showing how imperial authority is experienced from below: not as majesty, but as a familiar, nearly neighborly intrusion in daily life.

The grammatical domestication of authority did not disappear with the collapse of the Habsburg monarchy. It re-emerged, in altered ideological form, in the interwar cult of "tatíček Masaryk" ("*Daddy Masaryk*" or "*Papa Masaryk*"). The affectionate diminutive did not merely express admiration for Tomáš Garrigue Masaryk; it performed the same linguistic operation as Hašek's "František Josef": the conversion of political authority into a familiar, quasi-familial presence. As with the Emperor, power was not held at a rhetorical distance, but drawn inward, made grammatically intimate and unavoidable. The Czech subject does not stand opposite authority; he is placed in relation to it—as someone for whom the ruler is "ours," whether as imposed sovereign or as moral father.[1]

This familialization of authority was not merely rhetorical. It was formally codified in 1930, when the National Assembly adopted Law No. 22/1930 Sb., commonly known as Lex Masaryk. The law consists of a single declarative sentence: T. G. Masaryk zasloužil se o stát—a formula crediting Masaryk with the establishment of the Czechoslovak state—followed by an injunction that this statement be carved in stone in both chambers of parliament for eternal memory.

---

[1] Early documented uses of *tatíček Masaryk* ("Daddy Masaryk" or "Papa Masaryk") include Karel Teige's 1918 formulation "tatíček Masaryk, dědic Chelčického," Gustav Jaroš-Gamma's *Náš tatíček Masaryk* (1918–1925), and Arnošt Caha's *Tatíček Masaryk—Osvoboditel* (1921). The nickname arose organically around the founding of the Czechoslovak Republic and became central to Masaryk's interwar leader cult, framing him as a paternal moral authority and "father of the nation" (*otec národa*). He was also widely styled *Prezident Osvoboditel* ("President Liberator"). While these epithets were common in public discourse, literature, and visual culture, Law No. 22/1930 Sb. itself employs a deliberately spare grammatical formulation rather than any of these titles.

Authority here is neither narrated nor argued; it is grammatically asserted and monumentalized. As with Hašek's "František Josef," power is rendered linguistically intimate and unavoidable—embedded not only in speech and sentiment, but in law itself.[1]

Thus, the use of "František Josef" and the force of "nám" belong to the same thematic architecture. Both expose the ambivalent intimacy between subjects and sovereigns, between the powerless and those who preside over them. The Czech people in Hašek's world neither wholly love nor wholly hate their rulers; they live with them — as facts, as burdens, as unavoidable neighbors in the shared house of empire.

Hašek captures this condition not through manifesto or polemic, but through the grammar of a pronoun and the sound of a name.

Taken together, the emotional grammar of "nám," the Czech domestication of imperial authority in "František Josef," and the lived logic of subjection that Hašek records do not belong only to the world of the "war to end all wars". They anticipate the masked and intricate forms of subjugation that have since been technologically created, fortified and secured in the 21st century. The Introduction that follows places this continuity in context, showing how Švejk's world illuminates the contemporary structures in which events still happen "to us," often without our consent or participation.

---

[1] Law No. 22/1930 Sb. ("On the Merits of T. G. Masaryk"), adopted on February 26th 1930 on the occasion of Masaryk's 80th birthday, mandated that the sentence T. G. Masaryk "zasloužil se o stát" be carved in stone in both chambers of the National Assembly, where it was duly inscribed.

Introduction to
The Centennial English Edition

The original edition of this volume was published as an electronic EVY format file on the Internet in 1998. As professor Charles Sabatos noted twenty years later, "…despite the translator's active attempt to replace Parrott as the authoritative translation, this version reached only a limited readership." It is still true in 2024, a quarter of a century since it was published.

In the Introduction to the first edition of Book One of the "Chicago version", Mike Joyce wrote for both of us: "This new translation and rendition of *The Good Soldier Švejk* is our attempt to make this Central European masterwork accessible to the modern reader of English." He's more literary and well-read than I, and argued well for that approach. That's why I slightly compromised my personal goal of presenting the most faithful translation of the work. Yet, even so, our translation was much closer to the original than the reigning "authoritative translation". I argued that case in the online magazine Jacket 40 — Late 2010.

The long-brewing idea of producing The Centennial Edition of the "Chicago version" of the English translation of Švejk was to start being realized in early 2020. Just then came The Ultimate Unraveling…

最終的解開

As the unraveling has been exposing previously hidden or unperceived realities throughout the institutions of the society and personal lives alike, it has produced a positive value. Even its personally agonizing effect of delaying The Centennial Edition project now appears to have been a catalyst for a major, positive breakthrough. It is my hope, that the resulting crystallization and sharpening of the ideas driving this project, have produced a public good.

"Over the past few decades Americans have been subjected to some of the same social, political, economic, and moral phenomena that Europeans have endured for ages and which are the backdrop to this iconoclastic and soul probing epic. Now more than ever before, Americans will be able to relate to the story and its main character. And they will enjoy doing it."

That statement appeared on the website devoted to the "Chicago version" in 2012, and migrated from the bottom of the landing page to become the website's virtual masthead in 2018. Since then, the quintessentially un-American experiences, that my fellow Americans have been living through, have only increased in scope and intensity, reaching unprecedented and destructive levels since the beginning of The Ultimate Unraveling. That is why I still believe, with yet greater conviction, that even "Americans will be able to relate to the story and its main character." Whether they will enjoy it or not, is to be found by each reader alone.

The much diverse Czechoslovak First Republic, a patch carved out of the multiethnic, multilingual — and in this respect modern — cloth of the Austro-Hungarian Empire, full of long-standing grievances and tensions in 1918, was only four years and two months old when war veteran Jaroslav Hašek passed away, 116 days short of celebrating his 40th birthday.

The environment into which Jaroslav Hašek was born, in which he lived and created as well, was engendered by the effects of the industrial revolution and is the background of the novel set in the times of World War I in Austria-Hungary.

The rise of a large working class at the end of the 19th and beginning of the 20th century spawned a cultural revolution. The Austro-Hungarian Empire ignored the accompanying changes and became more and more decrepit and anachronistic. As the system decayed, it became absurd and irrelevant to ordinary people. When forced to respond to dissent, the imperial powers did so, more often than not, with hollow propaganda and repression.

"In a world where the greedy and ambitious slam the public from crisis to crisis," wrote on Christmas Eve of 2000 Bob Hicks in the Portland Oregonian, "gratuitously wrecking daily life as they destroy states and pull down civilizations, Švejk represents the underground — a passive-aggressive resister who beats the rules of the game by applying his own crazy logic to them. ... Unlike K., fellow Czech Franz Kafka's stunted stand-in for modern intellectual man, the rascal Švejk belongs to the men and women of the workaday world — the bartenders, cleaning women, gamekeepers, petty larcenists, lathe operators, janitors, drunkards, office workers, shopkeepers, undertakers, adulterers, nightclub bouncers, butchers, farmers, cab drivers and others who populate Hašek's imagination as they stumble through the lunacies of the first World War."

All those people, and many like them, still populate our world today. They've been labeled "deplorables" and have proudly taken that insult as their *nom de guerre*.[1] The increasing number and burden of absurdities they deal with is putting them in a position to relate to and viscerally understand Švejk, i.e. the book, the character, and the method. Untold hundreds of thousands [as originally stated in 2001] and perhaps even millions [certainly millions now, in 2024] of Americans experience and operate in "**švejkárna** [sh-vake-car-na] (*svejkardom* [sh-vake-car-dom])". This is a younger derivation of the original term "švejking". "Švejking" is the method for surviving "švejkárna (*svejkardom*)", which is a situation or institution of systemic absurdity requiring the employment of "švejking" for one to survive and remain untouched by it.

In Book One, Jaroslav Hašek paints a picture of a society transitioning from the "normal" state on the way to the catastrophe. He does it by weaving stories and fragments of stories of familiar archetypes of people and their institutions without any apparent rhyme or reason. The book has been hailed as an antiwar book, perhaps even only the second one of the genre after Red Badge of Courage. It's no accident. Hašek started writing it when the war was much on everybody's mind, a little over two years after the end of the WWI. He poured his soul into *The Good Soldier Švejk* between 1921 and 1922. He breathed his last on January 3rd 1923, fifteen years and nine months before the infamous Munich Agreement.[2] The official start of WWII, the German invasion of Poland, happened the same month a year after Messrs. Chamberlain, Daladier, Hitler, and Mussolini decided the fate of "people of whom we know little". When Jaroslav Hašek had his hero Švejk report in 1914 that he had read in the newspaper "the dear motherland has been has been swaddled in very dark clouds", could he have envisaged that those clouds would be back so quickly, in 1938, and then again in 1948, and once more in 1968?

But the book is much more than an antiwar novel:

"*The Good Soldier Švejk*, in fact, is a truly great satire (perhaps the greatest of them all) on the most central feature of social life in the

---

[1] Assumed name, under which a person engages in combat or some other activity or enterprise.

[2] Settlement reached on September 30, 1938 by Germany, Great Britain, France, and Italy that permitted German annexation of the Sudetenland, in western Czechoslovakia – hence the Czech saying "about us, without us", the equivalent of the American "not in the room, not in the deal"

past century and a half (at least) in most modern industrialized countries—the ubiquitous presence of huge, labyrinthine bureaucratic structures ostensibly set in place to make modern society more efficient, equal, and fair, but, in fact, reducing life for those who have to deal with them to what often amounts to an incomprehensible and out-of-control game whose major players never tire of announcing in noble-sounding prose and stirring poetry the importance of the structure and its alleged purpose but who, in their daily practice, show no signs of any significant humanity in dealing with subordinates or those whom the bureaucracy is supposed to serve. That target is something we all understand (because we have to deal with it, no matter where we live), and thus the impact of this satire extends well beyond the particular social and political realities of the world it depicts." - Ian Johnston

Jaroslav Hašek drew on his unusual life experiences, powers of observation, and extraordinary memory to expose and ridicule not only war, but anything that wasn't genuine, righteous, natural, or kind. Now it's time for you to take the plunge and enter the world of Švejk.

What Hašek did in his monumental text has been talked and written about, and studied for full one hundred years. To read some of the material to clue yourself into the world of Švejk and Hašek, you can start at https:/svejkcentral.com/Analyses.

INTRODUCTION

Great times demand great people. There are unrecognized heroes, unassuming, without the fame and history of Napoleon[3]. The results of an analysis of their character would overshadow even the glory of Alexander the Great of Macedon[4]. Nowadays you can run into a shabby man in the streets of Prague[5], who himself doesn't even know what significance he actually has in the history of the new great era. He walks modestly on his way, not bothering anybody, and he too isn't bothered by journalists, who would be begging him for an interview. If you were to ask him what his name was, he would answer you very simply and modestly: "I'm Švejk..."

And this quiet, unassuming, shabby man is indeed the old good soldier Švejk, heroic, valiant, whose name was once upon a time, during the Austrian rule, on the lips of all the citizens of the Czech Kingdom[6], and whose fame will not fade even in the Republic[7].

I very much like the good soldier Švejk, and presenting his fateful adventures during the World War, I am convinced that all of you will sympathize with this modest, unrecognized hero. He did not torch the temple of the goddess in Ephesus[8], as did that moron Herostratus, to get himself into the newspapers and classroom readers.

And that is enough.

THE AUTHOR

Book One

IN THE REAR

1

THE GOOD SOLDIER ŠVEJK ACTS TO INTERVENE IN THE WORLD WAR

"So they've done it to us, they've killed our Ferdinand[9]," said the cleaning woman to Mr. Švejk who, having left military service years ago when a military medical commission had pronounced him definitely to be an imbecile, made a living selling dogs, ugly mongrel mutants, for which he forged their pedigrees.

In addition to this occupation he was plagued by rheumatism and was just now rubbing his knees with camphor ice.

"Which Ferdinand, missis Müller?" asked Švejk, continuing to massage his knees, "I know two Ferdinands. One is the pharmacist Průša's[10] servant and he once drank up a bottle of some hair potion there by mistake, and then I also know the one Ferdinand Kokoška, who collects those dog turds. Neither one would be of any loss."

"But merciful Sir, the lord Archduke Ferdinand, the one from Konopiště[11], the fat one, the pious one."

"Jesusmaria," yelled Švejk, "that's good. And where did it befall him, the lord Archduke?"

"They whacked him in Sarajevo, merciful Sir, with a revolver, you know. He was riding there with that Archduchess[12] of his in an automobile."

"There you have it, missis Müller, in an automobile. Yeah, a lord like that can afford it, and it doesn't even cross his mind how such a ride in an automobile can have an unfortunate ending. And in Sarajevo on top of it, that's in Bosnia, missis Müller. The Turks probably did it. In short, we shouldn't have taken that Bosnia and Hercegovina[13] from them. So see, missis Müller. He is then, the lord Archduke, resting in the truth of the Lord[14] already. Did he suffer long?"

"The lord Archduke was done for right away, merciful Sir. *They*[15] know that with a revolver it's no child's play. Not long ago, a man in our Nusle neighborhood[16] was also playing with a revolver and blasted away the whole family, even the custodian, who went to take a look to see who's shooting there on the third floor."

"Some revolvers, missis Müller, won't go bang, even if you were to lose your mind trying to make them. There are many such systems. But for the lord Archduke they surely bought something better, and I would also like to bet, missis Müller, that the man who did it to him, dressed nicely for it. You know, taking a shot at the lord Archduke is a very tough job. It's not like a poacher taking a shot at the game warden. Here the problem is how to get to him, you can't go hunting a lord like that in some rags. You have to go with a top hat on so a cop wouldn't pinch you beforehand."

"There were more of them, they say, merciful Sir."

"That goes without saying, missis Müller," said Švejk, as he finished massaging his knees, "if you wanted to kill the lord Archduke or the lord Emperor[17], then you would surely consult somebody. More people means more brains. This one will advise this, that one that, and then the job will succeed, as it says in our anthem[18]. The main thing is to lie in wait for that moment, at which such lord is riding by. Like, if *they* recall that mister Lucheni[9], who ran that file through our late Elizabeth[20]. He was strolling with her. Then go trust somebody; since that time no empress goes out for a stroll. And this awaits many others. You'll see, missis Müller, that they'll even get to that Czar and Czarina[21], and could be, God forbid, even lord Emperor, since they have already started it with his nephew. He has, the old man, a lot of enemies. Even more than that Ferdinand. Just like the other day a man at the pub was saying, that the time will come, that those emperors will be dropping dead, one after the other, and that even all the state prosecutors won't be able to help. Then he didn't have enough to cover his tab, so the pubkeeper had to get him pinched. And he slapped him across the face once and the patrolman twice. Then they drove him away in a košatinka[22], so he'd come to. Yeah, missis Müller, the things that happen nowadays. It's again a big loss for Austria. When I was in the military service, an infantryman there shot a captain dead. He loaded a rifle and went to the office. There they told him that he had no business there, but he kept insisting that he needed to talk to mister captain. That captain came out and right away slapped him with confinement to the barracks. He raised the rifle and plugged him right in the heart. The bullet flew out of the captain's back and still managed to do damage in the office. It broke a bottle of ink, which spilled onto official documents."

"And what happened to that soldier?" asked after a while missis Müller, as Švejk was dressing.

"He hanged himself on suspenders," said Švejk, cleaning his bowler. "And the suspenders weren't even his. He borrowed them from the prison guard, that his pants were falling down. Was he to wait until they shoot him dead? *They* know missis Müller that in a situation like that everyone's head spins. The prison guard was demoted for it and they gave him six months. But he didn't do all of his time. He ran off to Switzerland[23] and today he is a preacher of some church denomination there. Nowadays there are few honest people, missis Müller. I imagine that the lord Archduke Ferdinand over there in Sarajevo misjudged the man, who shot him[24]. He saw some man and thought: There's an upright man, since he's chanting glory to me. And instead that mister plugged him. Did he give him one or several?"

"The newspaper writes, merciful Sir, that the lord Archduke was like a sieve. He emptied the gun and hit him with all the bullets."

"It goes extremely fast, missis Müller, terribly fast. For something like that, I'd buy a Browning[25]. It looks like a toy, but in two minutes you can mow down twenty archdukes, thin or fat ones. Although between you and me, missis Müller, you'll hit a fat lord archduke more likely than a thin one. If *they* recall how that time in Portugal they mowed down their own king[26]. He too was such a fat one. You know that a king is not going to be skinny, after all. I'm now going to The Chalice pub then, and should somebody come for that little ratter, which I took a down payment for, *they* tell him it's in my kennel in the country, that I recently clipped its ears and that it can't be transported until the ears heal, so they wouldn't catch cold. The key you leave with the custodian woman."

At The Chalice pub there was sitting only one guest. He was the plainclothes patrolman Bretschneider, standing in service for the State Police[27]. The pubkeeper Palivec was washing porcelain coasters and Bretschneider was in vain trying to engage him in a serious conversation.

Palivec was a well-known foul mouth, every other word of his was butt or shit. Still, he was well-read and urged everyone to read what wrote about the last item Victor Hugo[28] when describing the last answer Napoleon's Old Guard gave the English in the battle at Waterloo[29].

"That's a nice summer we're having," initiated his serious conversation Bretschneider.

"It's all worth shit," replied Palivec, putting his coasters away among the glassware.

"They sure did it to us nicely over there in Sarajevo," piped up with a weak hope Bretschneider.

"In what Sarajevo?" asked Palivec, "that wine bar in Nusle? There they fight every day, you know, Nusle."

"In the Bosnian Sarajevo, mister pubkeeper. They shot there the lord Archduke Ferdinand dead. What do you say to that?"

"I don't get myself mixed up in such things; regarding that everybody can kiss my ass," answered politely mister Palivec, lighting up his pipe, "nowadays getting mixed up in it could break anybody's neck. I'm a small businessman, when somebody comes in and orders a beer, then I draw it for him. But some Sarajevo, politics or the late Archduke, that's nothing for us, it holds no promise, but Pankrác[30]."

Bretschneider turned silent and was in disappointment looking around the deserted pub.

"There used to hang a picture of our lord Emperor here," he let himself be heard again after a while, "right where the mirror hangs now."

Yeah, you're right," answered mister Palivec, "it used to hang there and the flies kept shitting on it, so I put it in the attic. You know well, somebody could dare to make some remark and it could result in unpleasant difficulties. Do you think I need that?"

"Over there in that Sarajevo it must had been probably ugly, mister pubkeeper."

To this sneakily direct question mister Palivec replied with unusual caution:

"Around this time in Bosnia and Hercegovina it is usually terribly hot. When I served there, they used to have to put ice on our senior lieutenant's head."

"Which regiment did you serve with, mister pubkeeper?"

"I don't recall such trifle, I was never interested in such bullshit and couldn't be less curious about it," replied mister Palivec, "too much curiosity is detrimental."

The plainclothes patrolman became definitely silent and his gloomy expression improved only upon the arrival of Švejk, who, having entered the pub, ordered himself a dark beer with this remark:

"In Vienna today they are also in mourning," said Švejk. Bretschneider's eyes lit up with full hope; he said succinctly:

"At Konopiště there are ten black pennants."

"There should be twelve of them," said Švejk, when he took a swig.

"Why do you think twelve?" asked Bretschneider.

"To make it fit the count, the dozen, it's easier to count and by dozens one always gets it more cheaply," answered Švejk.

Silence reigned, which Švejk himself broke with a sigh:

"So he is there already, in the truth of the Lord, give him eternal glory Lord God. He didn't even live to be Emperor. When I was serving in the military, then one of our generals fell off his horse and got himself killed quite calmly. They wanted to help him back into the saddle, give him a boost, and were surprised that he was totally dead. And he was also to be promoted to Field Marshal. It happened during a parade review of the troops. These reviews never lead to any good. In Sarajevo there was also some kind of parade review. I remember that at one time, I was missing during such a parade review twenty buttons on my uniform and that they locked me up because of it in solitary for two weeks, and for two days I was lying still like lazar[31], hogtied. But there has to be discipline in the military, otherwise nobody would take anything seriously or fear anything. Our Senior Lieutenant, Makovec, he would always tell us: 'Discipline, you stupid boys, must be enforced, otherwise you would be climbing trees like monkeys, but military service will turn you into humans, you stupid idiots.' And isn't that the truth? Imagine a park, let's say Charlie's[32], and in every tree one soldier without discipline. That's what I always feared most."

"Over there in that Sarajevo," returned to the thread Bretschneider, "it was the Serbs, who did it."

"You are mistaken," retorted Švejk, "the Turks did it, on account of Bosnia and Hercegovina."

And Švejk expounded his opinion of Austria's international policy in the Balkans. The Turks lost in 1912 to Serbia, Bulgaria and Greece. They had wanted Austria to help them, and when that didn't happen, they shot Ferdinand.

"Do you like Turks?" Švejk asked, turning to Palivec, "do you like those pagan dogs? You don't, right?"

"A guest is a guest," said Palivec, "even a Turk. For us, who are in business for ourselves, politics has no currency. Pay for your beer and sit in the pub, and babble all you want. That is my principle. Whether it was a Serb or a Turk, who did it to our Ferdinand, or a Catholic, Mohammedan, anarchist, or Young Czech[33], it's all the same to me."

"Alright, mister pubkeeper," let himself be heard Bretschneider, who was again losing hope that either of the two could be caught, "but you will admit, that it is a great loss for Austria."

Instead of the pubkeeper answered Švejk:

"A loss it is, that cannot be denied. A terrible loss. Ferdinand can't be replaced by some dimwit. Only he should had been still fatter."

"How do you mean that?" said the revived Bretschneider.

"How do I mean that?" answered contentedly Švejk. "Altogether only like this. Had he been fatter, then he would surely had been hit with a stroke before this, when he was chasing after those broads at Konopiště, when they were collecting twigs and mushroom in his forest district there, and he didn't have to die such a shameful death. When I think about it, a nephew of the lord Emperor, and they shoot him dead. Now that's scandalous, the newspapers are full of it. Years ago, in our Budějovice, they stabbed during one of those petty arguments in the marketplace a livestock dealer, some Břetislav Ludvík. He had a son Bohuslav, and wherever he came to sell pigs, nobody bought anything from him and everyone would say: 'That's the son of the one, who was stabbed, he too is probably quite a scoundrel.' He had to jump from that bridge in Krumlov[34] into the Vltava[35] and they had to pull him out, they had to try reviving him, had to be pumping water out of him and he had to die in the doctor's arms, when he gave him some injection."

"You sure come up with odd comparisons," said Bretschneider meaningfully, "you speak first about Ferdinand and then about a livestock dealer."

"But I don't," was Švejk defending himself, "God spare me from wanting to compare anybody to somebody else. Mister pubkeeper knows me. Say that I have never compared anybody to somebody else, right? I just wouldn't want to be in the skin of the widow left by the Archduke. What now is she going to do? The children are orphans, the lord's estate at Konopiště without its master. And to be marrying again some new archduke? What's in it for her? She'll go with him to Sarajevo again, and she'll be widowed the second time. There was in Zliv[36] by Hluboká years ago a gamekeeper, he had such an ugly name, Littlepecker. Poachers shot him dead and he left a widow with two little children and a year later she again married a gamekeeper, the Šavels' Pepík from Mydlovary[37]. And they shot him dead for her too. Then she married for the third time and again took a gamekeeper for husband and said: 'Third time lucky. If it doesn't work out this time, I don't know any more what I'll do.' It figures that they shot him dead for her again, and by now she had had six children altogether with those gamekeepers. She went all the way to the office of the Prince of Hluboká[38] and complained that she had had torment with those gamekeepers. So they recommended fishpond warden Jareš from the

Ražice[39] pond ward cottage. And what would you say, they drowned him for her while fishing out the pond, and she'd had two children with him. Then she married a gelder from Vodňany, and he whacked her with an ax one night and went to turn himself in voluntarily. When they were then hanging him at the district courthouse in Písek[40], he bit off the priest's nose and said that he had no remorse for anything, and he also said something very ugly about the lord Emperor."

"And would you know what he said about him?" asked Bretschneider in a voice full of hope.

"That I cannot tell you, because no one dared to repeat it. But it was, it is said, something so terrible and dreadful that a councilor of the court, who was there, lost his mind over it and until this day they keep him in isolation so that it won't come out. It was not just a common insult to the lord Emperor, the kind made while drunk."

"And what kind of insults to the lord Emperor are made while drunk?" asked Bretschneider.

"I beg you, gentlemen, turn the page," sounded up the pubkeeper Palivec, "you know, I don't like it. This or that is blabbered out and then man regrets it."

"What kind of insults to the lord Emperor are made while drunk?" repeated Švejk. "All kinds. Get drunk, have them play the Austrian anthem and you'll see what you start saying. You will make up so much about the lord Emperor, that if only half of it were true, it would be enough for him to live in shame for the rest of his life. But the old man really doesn't deserve it. Let's take this. He lost his son Rudolf[41] at a very young age, full of manly vitality. His wife Elizabeth they ran through with a file, then he lost Johann Orth[42], and the brother, Mexican Emperor[43], they shot dead in some fortress by some wall. Now again, in his old age, they blew away his nephew. Given all that, a man better have nerves of steel. And then out of the blue some drunk decides to start calling him names. If something were to break out today, I would volunteer and serve the lord Emperor until my body was torn to pieces."

Švejk took a thorough swig and continued:

"You think that the lord Emperor will let this go? Then you know him very little. There must be a war with the Turks. You've killed my nephew, so here comes your kickass beatdown. A war is guaranteed. Serbia and Russia will help us in that war. It will be a rumble."

Švejk appeared beautiful in that prophetic moment. His simple-minded face, smiley like a full moon, shone with enthusiasm. To him everything was clear.

"May be," he continued his exposition of Austria's future, "that in case of a war with Turkey, the Germans will attack us, because Germans and Turks stick together. They're such bitches, that they don't have an equal in the world. However, we can join with France, which has it in for Germany since 1871. And that'll get it going already. There will be war, I'll say no more to you."

Bretschneider stood up and said ceremonially:

"You don't have to say any more, come with me to the hallway, I'll tell you something there."

Švejk followed the plainclothes patrolman into the hallway, where a small surprise awaited him, as the beer drinking companion showed him the little eagle badge and proclaimed that he was arresting him and would immediately take him to the police headquarters. Švejk tried to explain that the gentleman was probably mistaken, that he was totally innocent, that he had not uttered even one word, which could have offended anyone.

Bretschneider however told him, that he had really committed several criminal offenses, among which was numbered even the crime of high treason.

Then they returned to the pub and Švejk said in the direction of mister Palivec:

"I've had five beers and one roll with a sausage. Now give me a shot of slivovitz to boot and I have to go already, because I'm under arrest."

Bretschneider showed mister Palivec the little eagle, for a moment was looking at mister Palivec and then asked:

"Are you married?"

"I am."

"And can your wife run the business in your place during your absence?"

"She can."

"So it's all right mister pubkeeper," cheerfully said Bretschneider, "call your wife here, turn it over to her and we'll drive by tonight to pick you up."

"Don't let it make you feel bad," Švejk was consoling him, "I'm being taken in only for high treason."

"But what for I?" lamented mister Palivec. "I was so careful, after all."

Bretschneider flashed a smile and triumphantly said:

"For having said that the flies kept shitting on the lord Emperor. They will, no doubt, knock that lord Emperor out of your head."

And Švejk left The Chalice pub under the escort of the plainclothes patrolman, whom, having followed his face with his good-hearted smile, he asked, once they walked out into the street:

"Should I get off the sidewalk?"

"Why so?"

"I'm thinking that, since I'm under arrest, I don't have the right to walk on the sidewalk."

As they were entering the gate of the police headquarters, Švejk said:

"The time went by quite nicely for us. Do you come often to The Chalice?"

And while they were taking Švejk to the arraignment office, at The Chalice mister Palivec was handing over the pub to his weeping wife, soothing her in his own peculiar way:

"Don't cry, don't bawl, what can they do to me on account of a shitty picture of the lord Emperor?"

And so the good soldier Švejk intervened in the World War in his lovable, charming manner. Historians will be interested to know that he saw far into the future. If the situation later developed differently from how he was expounding it at The Chalice, we have to keep in mind that he hadn't had preparatory education in diplomacy.

2

THE GOOD SOLDIER ŠVEJK AT POLICE HEADQUARTERS

The Sarajevo assassination filled police headquarters[44] with numerous victims. They kept bringing in one after another and an old inspector in the arraignment office would say in his good-natured voice:
"That Ferdinand will cost you!"
When they locked Švejk up in one of the numerous holding rooms on the second floor, Švejk found a company of six people there. Five were sitting around a table, and in a corner on a bunk was sitting, as if he were shunning them, a middle-aged man.

Švejk began to inquire of one after the other, why they were locked up.

From the five sitting at the table, he received virtually the exact same answer:

"Because of Sarajevo!" — "Because of Ferdinand!" — "Because of the murder of the lord Archduke!" — "For Ferdinand!" — "Since they bumped off the lord Archduke in Sarajevo!"

The sixth one, who was avoiding the other five, said, that he wanted nothing to do with them, lest he fall under any suspicion, as he was sitting there merely for the attempted robbery and murder of a goodman from Holice.

Švejk sat down, joining the company of conspirators at the table, who were for the tenth time already telling each other, how they had gotten into this.

All of them, except one, were caught up with either in a pub, a wine bar or a coffeehouse. The exception was an unusually fat gentleman with glasses, his eyes cried out, who was arrested at home in his apartment, because two days before the assassination in Sarajevo he had paid the tab for two Serbian engineering students at Brejška's[45], and was spotted by detective Brixi in their company, drunk, at The Montmartre[46] on Řetězová street where, as he already confirmed by his signature on a statement to the police, he had paid for them as well.

In response to all the questions during the preliminary interrogation at the police district station he kept stereotypically wailing:

"I have a stationery store!"

Whereupon he was getting also a stereotypical answer:
"That doesn't excuse you."

A small gentleman, to whom it happened at a wine bar, was a history professor and he had been explaining to the wine bar keeper the history of various assassinations. He was arrested just at the moment he finished the psychological analysis of all assassinations with the words:

"The idea of an assassination is as simple as the egg of Columbus[47]."

"Just like the fact that Pankrác awaits you," added to his pronouncement during the interrogation the police inspector.

The third conspirator was the chairman of the charitable club Dobromil in Hodkovičky. The day the assassination was carried out, Dobromil was hosting a garden party with a concert. The State police sergeant came to ask the participants to disperse as Austria was in mourning, whereupon the chairman of Dobromil replied good-naturedly:

"*They,* wait a moment until they finish playing Hey, Slavs![48]"

Now he was sitting here with his head down and moaning:

"In August we're having new board elections, if I'm not home by that time it could happen that they won't elect me. I'm the chairman for the tenth time already. I won't live down the shame."

The late Ferdinand had strange fun with the fourth arrestee, a man of sterling character and a spotless escutcheon. He had avoided any conversation about Ferdinand for two days, until the evening at a coffeehouse, when during a hand of mariáš[49], while trumping the king of acorns with a seven of rounds, he said:

"Seven rounds, like in Sarajevo."

The fifth man, who, as he himself said, was sitting in jail "because of that murder of the lord Archduke in Sarajevo", had still today the hair on his head and in his beard standing on end from fright, so that his head was reminiscent of a stable pinscher[50].

This one hadn't uttered even one word at the restaurant where he was arrested, and what's more, he hadn't even read the newspaper accounts of the killing of Ferdinand and had been sitting at a table absolutely alone, when some man came up to him, sat down across from him and quickly said to him:

"Have you read it?"

"I haven't."

"Do you know about it?"

"I don't."
"And do you know what it's about?"
"I don't, and I don't care about it."
"And yet, it should be of interest to you."
"I don't know, what is it that should be of interest to me? I'll smoke my cigar, drink my few glasses, have dinner and I don't read the papers. Newspapers lie. What should I get upset for?"
"So even the murder in Sarajevo is of no interest to you?"
"To me no murder at all is of any interest, regardless of whether it's in Prague, in Vienna, in Sarajevo or in London. That's what you have authorities for, the courts and the police. If sometime somewhere they kill somebody, it serves him right, why is the dimwit so careless, that he lets himself get killed."

Those were his last words in this conversation. Since that time he's only repeated loudly in five-minute intervals:

"I'm innocent, I'm innocent!"

He screamed those words even in the gate of the police headquarters, he'll repeat those words even during his transfer to the criminal court in Prague, and with those words he'll even enter his prison dungeon.

Once Švejk had listened through all the dreadful conspiratorial stories, he judged it fitting to explain to them the utter hopelessness of their situation.

"It's very bad for us all," he began his words of consolation, "it is not true, as you have been saying that to you, to us all nothing bad can happen. What do we have the police for if not to punish us for our bad mouths. Since the times are so dangerous that they shoot archdukes, then nobody should be surprised that they're taking him to the headquarters. All of this is done for polish, so that Ferdinand will have publicity before his funeral. The more of us are here, the better it'll be for us, because we can cheer each other up. When I was serving in the military, sometimes half of us in the company gang were locked up. And the number of innocent people that used to be found guilty. And not only in the military, but by the courts too. Once, I remember, some woman was found guilty of having strangled her newborn twins. Even though she swore that she couldn't have strangled twins, since she had given birth to only one little girl, whom she had managed to strangle quite painlessly, she was still found guilty of double murder. Or the innocent gypsy in Záběhlice, who broke into that grocery store on Christmas night. He swore that he went there to warm up, but that didn't help him at all. Once a court takes something in hand, it's trouble. But that trouble is necessary. Perhaps not all people are such rascals, as can be presumed about them; but how can you tell nowadays the good one from the hoodlum, especially today, during such serious times, when they blew away that Ferdinand. Where I was, when serving in the military in Budějovice, they shot the captain's dog in a forest on the other side of the training ground. When he found out about it, he called us all together, had us stand and said that every tenth man should step forward. It goes without saying that I also was a tenth, so we stood at attention and didn't as much as blink. The captain is walking around us and says: 'You hoodlums, villains, scum, spotted hyenas, I would so love to slam you into solitary for that dog, chop you into noodles, blast and mow you down and turn you into carp au bleu[51]. So that you know I won't be going soft on you, I'm giving you all two weeks of confinement to the barracks.' So you see, back then it was the matter of a doggie, and now it's the matter of even no less than the lord Archduke. And that's why there has to be dread, so that the mourning will be worth something."

"I'm innocent! I'm innocent!" repeated the bristled-up man.

"Christ the Lord was also innocent," said Švejk, "and they crucified him too. Nowhere, at no time, did an innocent man matter to anybody. Keep your mouth shut and keep on serving! — as they used to tell us in the military. That is the best and most beautiful."

Švejk lay down on a bunk and contentedly fell asleep.

In the meantime they brought in two new ones. One of them was a Bosnian. He kept pacing around the holding room, gritting his teeth and every other word of his was: "*I fuck your soul.*" He was tortured by the thought that his peddler's basket would get lost at the police headquarters.

The second new guest was the pubkeeper Palivec who, having noticed his acquaintance Švejk, woke him and in a voice full of tragedy exclaimed:

"I'm here too already!"

Švejk cordially shook his hand and said:

"I'm really glad. I knew that the gentleman would keep his word when he told you, that they would come to pick you up. Being on time like that is a good thing."

Mister Palivec remarked however, that being on time like that is worth shit, and asked Švejk softly, whether the other men weren't thieves, because that to him, as a small businessman, could be detrimental.

Švejk explained to him that all of them, save one, who was there for the attempted robbery with murder of a goodman from Holice, were part of their company on account of the Archduke.

Palivec took offense and said that he wasn't there on account of some stupid archduke, but on account of the lord Emperor. And because the others started taking interest, he recounted to them how the flies had soiled his lord Emperor.

"They mucked him up for me, the bitches", he ended telling his story, "and in the end, they got me thrown in the slammer. I will not forgive those flies for that," he added threateningly.

Švejk went to sleep again, but didn't sleep long, because they came for him, to take him to interrogation.

And so, ascending the staircase to Section III to be interrogated, Švejk carried his cross to the top of Golgotha[52], not noticing himself anything about his own martyrdom.

Having beheld the sign that spitting in the corridor was forbidden, he asked the patrolman to allow him to spit into a spittoon, and radiant with his simplicity, he entered the office with the words:

"I wish you Gentlemen, one and all, a good evening."

Instead of a reply somebody poked him under the ribs and pushed him in front of a desk, behind which sat a man with a cold official face with features of animal cruelty, as if he had just fallen out of Lombroso's[53] book On Criminal Types.

He looked bloodthirstily at Švejk and said:

"Don't look so stupid."

"I can't help it," answered Švejk seriously, "I was released from military service for stupidity after an examination by the superior commission and officially proclaimed to be an imbecile. I'm an official imbecile."

The man with the criminal countenance chattered his teeth:

"That, which you are accused of and which you have committed, bears witness that you haven't lost any of your marbles."

And now he enumerated for Švejk a whole list of various crimes, beginning with high treason and ending with offending His Majesty and members of the imperial house. At the center of the constellation shone the crime of approving of the murder of Archduke Ferdinand, from which sprung another branch of new crimes, among which glared the crime of sedition, because it all had happened in a public space.

"What do you say to that?" asked victoriously the gentleman with the features of animal cruelness.

"There's a lot there," answered Švejk innocently, "too much of anything is detrimental."

"There you go, you admit it."

"I admit everything, there must be strictness, without strictness nobody would get anywhere. Like when I served in the military…"

"Shut your trap!" screamed at Švejk the police councilor, "and speak only when I ask you something! Understand?"

"How could I not understand," said Švejk, "I dutifully report, Sir, that I understand and that in everything *they* desire to say I am able to get my bearings and find my way around."

"Whomever do you have contacts with?"

"With my cleaning woman, yergrace."

"And don't you have any acquaintance in the local political circles?"

"That I do, yergrace, I buy for myself the small afternoon edition of *National Politics*, the little bitch[54]."

"Out!" screamed at Švejk the man with animal visage.

When they were taking him out of the office, Švejk said:

"Good night, yergrace."

Having returned to his holding room, Švejk informed all the arrestees that such interrogation is fun. "They scream at you there a bit and in the end they chase you out. — In the old days," continued Švejk, "it used to be worse. I read in a book long ago, that suspects used to have to walk on red hot iron and drink molten lead, to discover whether one was innocent. Or they put his feet in the Spanish boots and jacked him up on the rack, when he didn't want to confess, or they burned his sides with a fireman's torch, like they did to John of Nepomuk[55]. He, they say, screamed as if they were lifting him up on tips of knives, and didn't stop, until they threw him off the Elisabeth Bridge in a water-proof bag. There were more of such cases and afterward they would still quarter the man or impale him on a stake somewhere by the Museum[56]. When they only threw him into the hunger pit, then such a man felt as if reborn. — Nowadays it is easy fun to be locked up," continued Švejk with delight, "no quartering, no Spanish boots, we have bunks, we have a table, we have a bench, we're not crammed cheek to jowl, we get soup, they give us bread, bring a jug of water, we have the toilet right under our yap. In everything one can see progress. True, it's a little bit too far to interrogation, all the way across three corridors and one floor up, but on the other hand, the corridors are clean and full of life. They're taking one hither, another one tither, a young one, an old one, male and female. You're glad that at least you're not here alone. Everybody goes contentedly on his way and doesn't have to fear that in the office they will tell him: 'So we consulted one another and tomorrow you'll be quartered or burned at the stake, according to your own wish.' That would certainly be a tough decision to think about and I think, gentlemen, that many of you could be totally stumped in a moment like that. Yeah, nowadays circumstances have already improved to our benefit."

He had just finished his defense of the modern incarceration of citizens, when a guard opened the door and yelled out:

"Švejk, *they* get dressed, *they're* going to interrogation."

"I'll get dressed," replied Švejk, "I have nothing against that, but I'm afraid that there's been some mistake, I was already kicked out of an interrogation once. And then I'm afraid that the rest of the gentlemen, who are here with me, might be angry with me since I'm going to interrogation second time in a row, and they haven't been there as of this evening even once yet. They could become jealous of me."

"*They* crawl out and stop blathering," was the answer to Švejk's gentlemanly concern.

Švejk found himself again in front of the gentleman of criminal type who, without any further introductions, asked him toughly and inescapably:

"Do you confess everything?"

Švejk gazed intently with his good blue eyes at the merciless man and said softly:

"If *they* wish, yergrace, for me to confess, then I'll confess, that can't hurt me. But if *they* say: 'Švejk, don't confess anything,' I'll fib and wiggle until my body is torn to pieces."

The stern gentleman wrote something in a document and, handing Švejk a pen, he challenged him to sign it.

And Švejk signed Bretschneider's denunciation and this addendum:

All of the above shown accusations against me are based on truth.
Josef Švejk

After he signed, he turned to the stern gentleman:

"Am I to sign anything else? Or should I come back in the morning?"

"In the morning, they'll drive you to the criminal court," was the answer he received.

"At what time, yergrace? So I don't — forchristhelord — oversleep."

"Out!" was the scream hurled at Švejk for the second time today from the other side of the desk, in front of which he stood.

Returning to his new home behind bars, Švejk told the patrolman, who was accompanying him:

"Everything here goes just like it's been greased".

As soon as they closed the door behind him, his fellow prisoners showered him with various questions, to which Švejk replied clearly:

"I just confessed that I probably killed Archduke Ferdinand."

Six men curled up in fright under their flea-infested blankets, only the Bosnian said:

"*Welcome.*"

Laying himself down on the bunk, Švejk said:

"It's too bad they don't sound reveille for us here."

In the morning though they woke him up even without a reveille and exactly at six o'clock they were driving Švejk in a Green Anton[57] to the regional criminal court.

"A morning bird gets to hop farther," said Švejk toward his fellow passengers, as the Green Anton was rolling out of the gate of the police headquarters.

3

ŠVEJK BEFORE THE COURT PHYSICIANS

The clean, cozy little rooms of the regional "as criminal" court[58] impressed Švejk most favorably. Whitewashed walls, window bars painted black, even the fat Mr. Demartini, the head prison guard of the pretrial detention, with purple shoulder boards and border on his government-issue cap. Purple is the prescribed color not only here, but also during religious ceremonies on Ash Wednesday and Good Friday.

The famed history of the Roman[59] rule over Jerusalem[60] was returning. They were bringing out the prisoners down to the ground floor and standing them before the Pilates[61] of the year 1914. And the examining magistrates, Pilates of the new times, instead of honorably washing off their hands, would sent for a pepper[62] and Pilsner[63] beer from Teissig's[64] and were passing a stream of new charges over to the State Prosecutor's Office[65].

Here all logic mostly disappeared and winning was the article of law, the article of law strangled, the article of law goofed, the article of law fretted and fumed, the article of law laughed, the article of law threatened, the article of law killed, and the article of law would not forgive. They were jugglers of statutes, eaters of the letters in the legal code, devourers of the accused, tigers of the Austrian jungle, measuring the distance for their jump onto the accused according to the numbers of the articles of law.

An exception was constituted by several gentlemen (just like at police headquarters), who didn't take the law quite so seriously, because everywhere wheat can be found among the corn cockle.

To one such gentleman they brought Švejk for interrogation. An older man of good-hearted appearance who, when interrogating a notorious killer Valeš once, had never failed to tell him: "Please, sit down Mr. Valeš, it just so happens that there is one empty chair here."

When they brought Švejk in, he asked him with his inborn adorability to sit down, and said:

"So you are then this Mr. Švejk?"

"I think," answered Švejk, "that I must be him, since even my daddy was a Švejk and mommy missis Švejk. I can't bring such shame to them, as to deny my own name."

A kind smile fluttered across the face of the interrogating court councilor:

"But you have messed up pretty good. You have quite a lot on your conscience."

"I always have quite a lot on my conscience," said Švejk, smiling even more kindly than the court councilor; "I have, it might be, even more on my conscience than pleases you to have on yours, yergrace."

"That's evident from the statement you signed," replied in no less kind tone the court councilor, "didn't they pressure you in any way at the police station?"

"Oh no, yergrace. I myself asked them whether I should sign it, and when they told me to sign it, then I obeyed them. It goes without saying I wasn't going to get into a brawl with them on account of my own signature. I definitely wouldn't help myself by that. Order must be maintained."

"Do you feel, mister Švejk, completely healthy?"

"Completely healthy, that just isn't the case, yergrace mister councilor. I have rheumatism, I rub myself down with camphor ice."

The old man smiled kindly again: "What would you say if we were to have you examined by court physicians?"

"I don't think that I'm so bad off, for those gentlemen to be wasting unnecessarily time on me. Some doctor at the police headquarters already examined me to see if I have gonorrhea."

"You know, mister Švejk, we will try it after all with those gentlemen court physicians. We'll assemble a nice commission, have you put in pretrial custody, and in the meantime you'll rest nicely. For now, one more question: You're said to have been, according to the statement, declaring and disseminating that a war will now break out sooner rather than later?"

"That, if you please yergrace councilor, will break out as soon as possible."

"And don't you have some seizures once in a while?"

"That, if you please, I don't, only once I was almost seized by some automobile at Charles' square[66], but that's already a number of years ago."

Thereby was the interrogation finished, Švejk offered his hand to the court councilor, and having returned to his little room, he addressed his neighbors:

"So on account of the murder of the lord Archduke Ferdinand, the court physicians will be now examining me."

"I also was examined by court physicians," said a young man, "it happened back when on account of carpets I ended up in front of a jury. They found me to be feebleminded. Now I absconded with a steam thresher, and they can't do anything to me. My lawyer was telling me yesterday that since I was pronounced feebleminded once already, then I have to benefit from it for the rest of my life."

"I don't trust those court physicians at all," remarked a man of intelligent appearance. "When I was forging checks at one time, I attended lectures of doctor Heveroch, to prepare, just in case, and when they caught me, I feigned to be paralytic, just the way doctor Heveroch used to describe it. I bit one of the court physician's leg during the commission's proceedings, drank up all the ink from an inkwell, and I relieved myself, if you will excuse me, in front of the whole commission in the corner of the room. But because I bit through the calf of one of them, they found me to be absolutely healthy and I was done for."

"I don't fear an examination by those gentlemen at all," declared Švejk; "when I was serving in the military, I was examined by a veterinarian and it turned out quite well."

"Court physicians are sons-of-bitches," piped up a small, crouching human, "not long ago by some chance they dug a skeleton out of my meadow and the court physicians said that the skeleton had been murdered by blows of some blunt object to the head forty years ago. I am thirty-eight and I'm locked up, even though I have my birth certificate, a copy of the entry in the birth registry, and my domicile certificate[67]."

"I think," said Švejk, "we should try to be fair. Anybody can make a mistake, and he's bound to make a mistake the more he's thinking about something. Court physicians are people, and people have their flaws. Just like once in Nusle, right by the bridge across Botič, a gentleman came up to me at night, while I was returning from Banzets'[68], and he whacked me with a blackjack across my head, and when I was lying on the ground, he shined light on me and said: 'There's been a mistake, it's not him.' And he got so mad at the fact he had made a mistake, that he whacked me once more across the back. It's just like that in the human nature, that a man will make mistakes until his death. Just like the gentleman, who found a half-frozen rabid dog at night and took him home with him and he shoved it in his wife's bed. As soon as the dog warmed up and got comfortable, he bit the whole family and the youngest one in the crib he tore up and devoured. Or I'll tell you an example of how a lathe operator in our building once made a mistake. With a key he opened a little church in Podolí[69], thinking he was at home, took off his shoes in the sacristy, because he thought it was the kitchen of their home, and he laid down on the altar, because he thought he was at home in his bed, and he covered himself with some of those doilies with holy inscriptions and under his head the gospel and some other sanctified books, to keep his head up high. In the morning the church custodian found him and the lathe operator quite good-naturedly tells him, when he came to, that it was a mistake. 'A nice mistake,' says the church custodian, 'when on account of such mistake we'll have to have the church sanctified again.' After that the lathe operator faced the court physicians and they proved to him that he was absolutely sane and sober, because had he been drunk, they said, he would not had been able to hit the mark and insert the key in the lock of the church door. After that the lathe operator died at Pankrác. I'll also give you an example of how in Kladno[70] a police dog made a mistake, a German Shepherd belonging to that well-known police Captain Rotter[71]. Captain Rotter bred those dogs and conducted experiments on itinerant bums, until all itinerant bums started avoiding the Kladno region. So he gave an order for the state policemen to bring in someone suspicious, one way or another. So one time they brought to him a quite properly clothed man, whom they found in the Lány forests, sitting on some tree stump. Right away he had them cut off a piece of the man's coattail, gave it to his police dogs to sniff and then they took the man to some brick yard outside of the town and set on his foot trail the trained dogs, who found him and brought him back again. Then the man had to climb up some ladder into an attic, jump over a wall, jump into a pond and the dogs after him. In the end it turned out, that the man was a Czech radical[72] deputy, who took a ride into the Lány forests for an outing, when he'd had grown tired of the Parliament[73]. That's why I say that people are prone to errors, that they make mistakes, whether one is learned, or a stupid, uneducated idiot. Even government ministers make mistakes."

*

The commission of court physicians, that was to decide whether Švejk's mental horizons were or weren't consistent with all those crimes, with which he was being charged, was composed of three unusually serious gentlemen with opinions, among which the opinion of each individual differed markedly from the opinions of whichever of the other two.

Here were represented three various scientific schools and

opinions of psychiatrists.

If in Švejk's case an absolute agreement arose among these diametrically opposed scientific camps, it can be explained clearly only by the stunning impression, which Švejk made on the whole commission when, having entered the hall, wherein his mental state was to be examined, he yelled out, having noticed a picture of the Austrian monarch hanging on the wall: "Long live, gentlemen, the Emperor František Josef I!"

The case was completely clear. Švejk's spontaneous utterance had made a whole number of questions disappear, and only some most important remained, so that from the answers could be confirmed the first impression about Švejk on the basis of the system set up by doctor of psychiatry Kallerson, doctor Heveroch[74], and the Englishman Weiking.

"Is radium heavier than lead?"

"I have, if you please, not weighed it," answered with his charming smile Švejk.

"Do you believe in the end of the world?"

"First I would have to see the end of the world," answered in a carefree manner Švejk, "but definitely I will not get to see it tomorrow."

"Would you be able to calculate the Earth's diameter?"

"That, if you please, I wouldn't be able to do," answered Švejk, "but I myself, gentlemen, would also like to pose to you a riddle: There is a three-story building, in that building on each floor eight windows. On the roof there are two dormers and two chimneys. On each floor there are two tenants. And now tell me, gentlemen, in what year passed away the resident custodian's grandmother?"

The court physicians gave one another meaningful looks, nevertheless one of them posed yet this question:

"Would you know the greatest depth in the Pacific ocean?"

"That, if you please, I don't know," was the answer, "but I think that it'll be definitely greater than below the Vyšehrad rock in the Vltava.

The chairman of the commission tersely asked "Enough?", but one of the members still insisted on this question:

"How much is 12,897 times 13,863?"

"729," answered Švejk without batting an eye."

"I think that will be absolutely sufficient," said the chairman of the commission, "you may take the accused back to his old spot."

"Thank you, gentlemen," piped up Švejk deferentially, "for me it's also absolutely sufficient."

After his departure the collegium of three agreed, that Švejk was a notorious imbecile and an idiot according to all the natural laws invented by psychiatric scientists.

In the report turned over to the interrogating judge appeared, among other things: "The undersigned court physicians insist on the finding of total mental dullness and congenital cretinism of, to the aforementioned commission presented, Josef Švejk, expressing himself with words such as 'Long live the emperor František Josef I.', which utterance is totally sufficient to shed light on the mental state of Josef Švejk as a notorious imbecile. The undersigned commission therefore recommends that: 1. the investigation of Josef Švejk be stopped. 2. Josef Švejk be sent for observation to the psychiatric clinic in order to determine to what extent his mental state is dangerous to others around him."

While this report was being drafted, Švejk was telling his fellow prisoners: "They paid no mind to Ferdinand and conversed with me about even stupider things. In the end, we told one another that we had enough of what we conversed about, and we parted company."

"I don't trust anybody," remarked the crouching little human in whose meadow they had by chance dug up a skeleton. "It is all thievery."

"Even that thievery must exist," said Švejk, laying himself down on a straw mattress, "if all people had good intentions toward others, then they would mutually smash themselves out of existence at the earliest."

4

THEY THREW ŠVEJK OUT OF THE MADHOUSE

When later Švejk was describing life in the madhouse[75], he did it in the manner of unusual eulogy: "I really don't know why the nuts are angry when they're being held there. One can crawl there naked on the floor, howl like a jackal, rage and bite. If one were to do that on a promenade, people would be surprised, but in there it is counted among things as common as dust. There's in there such freedom, about which even the socialists haven't dreamt! One can even be passing himself off as the Lord God or the Virgin Mary[76] in there, or the Pope[77], or the English King[78], or the lord Emperor, or St. Wenceslaus[79], although the last was always bound up and naked and lying in isolation. There was also one, who kept screaming, that he was an archbishop, but he didn't do anything other than stuffing his face 'til fit, and then he'd do another thing, which, if you'll excuse me, you know, can rhyme with it, but in there nobody feels any shame for it. One was even impersonating the saints Cyril and Methodius[80], in order to get two portions. And one gentleman there was pregnant and kept inviting everybody to the christening. A lot of chess players, politicians, fishermen, Scouts, stamp collectors and amateur photographers were locked up there. One was there on account of some old pots that he called the ash cans. One was kept constantly in a straitjacket to prevent him from calculating when the end of the world will come. I also met several professors in there. One of them kept coming to me and was telling me, that the cradle of the Gypsies was in the *Giant Mountains*[81], and the second one would explain to me that inside this Earth's globe there is yet another, much larger one than the upper.

Everybody there could say what he wanted, and whatever just happens to come to his tongue with the saliva, as if he were in the Parliament. Sometimes they would tell one another fairy tales and get into a brawl, when some princess came to a very bad end. The one raging the most was one gentleman, who presented himself as the 16th volume of Otto's[82] Educational Dictionary and kept begging everybody to open him, and find the entry 'Cartonage stapler', that otherwise he'd be done for. He calmed down only when they put him in a straitjacket. He took great pleasure in it, thinking he had been put into a printing press, and was begging they give him a modern bookbinder's trim. All-in-all, living there was like being in paradise. You can holler, scream, sing, weep, bleat, shriek, jump, pray, do somersaults, walk on all four, skip on one foot, run in a circle, dance, hop around, squat all day and climb the walls. Nobody will come up to you and say: 'You can't do this, it is, Sir, not proper, you should be ashamed, you call yourself an educated man?' Yet it's also true that there are totally quiet lunatics there. Like there was an educated inventor, who kept digging in his nose and only once a day he'd say: 'I've just discovered electricity.' I'm telling you, very nice it was there and the few days, which I've spent in the madhouse, belong among the most beautiful moments of my life."

And truly, the welcome alone already, that awaited Švejk in the madhouse, after they drove him there for observation from the regional criminal court, surpassed his expectations. First they stripped him naked, then gave him some sort of khalat[83] and led him to have a bath, having taken him intimately under his arms, while one of the attendants amused him by telling him some jokes about Jews. In the bathroom they submerged him in a bathtub filled with warm water and then they pulled him out and stood him under a cold shower. This they repeated with him three times and then asked him how he liked it. Švejk said that this was better than that spa[84] near the Charles' Bridge[85] and that he loved to take baths. "If you also cut my nails and hair, there will be nothing missing to complete my total happiness," he added, smiling pleasantly.

Even this wish was accommodated, and when they also rubbed him down thoroughly with a sponge, they wrapped him in a bedsheet and carried him to a bed in the first ward, wherein they deposited him, covered with a blanket and asked him to please fall asleep.

Švejk to this day relates the story with fondness: "Imagine, they were carrying me, carried me all the way, and I was at that moment in total bliss."

And on that bed he also blissfully fell asleep. Then they woke him up to present him with a cup of milk and a braided bun. The bun was already cut into little pieces, and while one of the attendants held Švejk's both hands, the other was dunking the pieces of bun in the milk and fed him, just as a goose is fed with fattening balls. After they had fed him, they took him under his arms and brought him to the bathroom, where they asked him to please satisfy both number one and number two bodily needs.

Even of this nice moment Švejk speaks with fondness and I surely

33

don't have to reproduce his words of what they did with him next. I'll mention only that Švejk says:

"One of them was holding me all along in his arms."

When they brought him back, they deposited him again in the bed and again asked him to please fall asleep. After he fell asleep, they woke him up and led him to an examination room where Švejk, standing totally naked in front of two doctors, was reminded of that glorious time he was drafted. Unwittingly, across his lips slipped:

"*Fit for duty.*"

"What did you say?" asked one of the doctors. "Take five steps forward and five back."

Švejk took ten of them.

"I told you, didn't I," said the doctor, "to take five of them."

"I'm not a stickler about a couple of steps," said Švejk.

After that the doctors asked him to sit in a chair and one was knocking on his knee. He then told the other that the reflexes were completely correct, whereupon the other shook his head and himself started knocking on Švejk's knee, while the first one was forcing Švejk's eyelids open and examining his pupil. Following that they both walked to the desk and exchanged several Latin expressions.

"Listen, can you sing?" asked one of them of Švejk. "Couldn't you sing some song for us?"

"No problem, gentlemen," answered Švejk. "Although I don't have a voice, or a musical ear, but I'll try to satisfy your wish, since you want to be entertained."

And Švejk let them have it:

> "Why's the young monk in that armchair,
> His forehead into his right hand bowing,
> Two bitter, burning tears
> Down his pale cheeks are rolling…

"I don't know the rest of it," continued Švejk. "If you want, I'll sing for you:

> What loneliness round my heart,
> That heavily, painfully lifts up my breast,
> When silently I'm sitting, into distance gazing
> There, there into distance my desire…

"And I don't know the rest of it either," sighed Švejk. "I know the first stanza of 'Where Is My Home,'[86] and then 'General

Windishgrätz[87] and the military lords started a war at sunrise,' and still a couple of such national folk songs like 'Preserve for us, Lord God,'[88] and 'When we marched to Jaromeř,'[89] and 'A thousand times we hail Thee...'[90]

Both physicians exchanged looks and one of them put a question to Švejk: "Has your mental state ever been examined already?"

"In the military service," answered Švejk ceremonially and proudly, "the military's gentlemen physicians officially found me to be a notorious imbecile."

"It seems to me that you are a malingerer," yelled out the second physician at Švejk.

"I, gentlemen," defended himself Švejk, "am no malingerer, I am a real imbecile, you can check with the office of the 91st Regiment in České Budějovice or with the Replenishment Command in Karlín[91]."

The older of the physicians waved his hand hopelessly and, pointing at Švejk, told the attendants: "Return this man's clothes and lock him up in the third-class[92] in the first corridor, then one will return and take all the files about him to the office. And tell them there to process him quickly, so that we won't be stuck with him here for too long."

The physicians cast one more time a crushing look at Švejk, who deferentially shuffled backwards to the door, bowing politely. To the question of one of the attendants, what were the silly things he was doing, he answered:

"Because I'm not dressed, I'm naked and I don't want to be making the gentlemen to look at anything, so they wouldn't think that I'm impolite or vulgar."

From the moment when the attendants received the order to return Švejk's clothes, they stopped showing any signs of care for him, whatsoever. They ordered him to get dressed, and one took him to the third class ward, where during the several days the office took to process a written order to boot him out, he had the opportunity to carry out his fine observations. The disappointed physicians diagnosed him as a "malingerer with a feeble mind," and because they were releasing him before lunch, a minor incident arose.

Švejk declared that when they kick someone out of a madhouse, they cannot throw him out without lunch.

The disturbance was brought to an end when the doorman called for a police patrolman, who then brought Švejk to the district police station in Salmova[93] street.

5

ŠVEJK AT THE DISTRICT POLICE STATION IN SALMOVA STREET

After the beautiful sunny days in the madhouse, Švejk was now visited upon by hours full of persecution. Police Inspector Braun set the stage for his meeting with Švejk with the cruelty of Roman henchmen from the time of that charming emperor Nero[94]. Harshly, as in those days when they used to say: "Throw that hoodlum Christian to the lions," inspector Braun now said: "Put him behind the iron gate!"

Neither one word more, nor less. Only the eyes of police inspector Braun flashed at that moment with peculiar, perverse pleasure.

Švejk bowed and said proudly:

"I am ready, gentlemen. I think that 'the iron gate' must mean the same as segregation, and that's not exactly that bad."

"Don't *they* be sprawling out in here," replied the police patrolman, whereupon Švejk let himself be heard: "My needs are modest and I'm grateful for everything that you'll do for me."

In the segregation cell-block there sat a gentleman on a plank bunk, lost in thought. As he was sitting there apathetically, one could see in his countenance that when the key screeched to open the door, he didn't believe that the gate to freedom was opening for him.

"I bend my knee, honorable Sir," said Švejk, while taking a seat next to him on the plank bunk, "About what time might it be?"

"Time is not my master," responded the man lost in thought.

"It's not bad in here," Švejk continued his attempt at a conversation, "This plank bunk was made of sanded lumber."

The serious man didn't answer, stood up and started walking quickly in the small space between the locked door and the plank bunk, as if he were in a hurry to save something.

In the meantime Švejk was observing with interest the graffiti scribbled on the walls. There was an inscription, in which an unknown prisoner promised heaven a life-or-death struggle with the police. The text read: "You'll get yours." Another prisoner wrote: "Dry up and blow away, pigs." Yet another simply stated a fact: "I was sitting here doing time on June 5th, 1913, and I was treated decently. Josef Mareček, trader from Vršovice[95]." There was also an inscription that was jolting in its profundity: "Mercy, great God…" and underneath it: "Kiss my a." The letter "a" was crossed out, however, and beside it was written, in capital letters, COAT TAIL. Next to that, some poetic soul wrote in verse:

"By the brook mournful I'm sitting, behind the mountains the sun his cover is taking, I'm gazing onto the illuminated hills, there, where my dear lover dwells."

The man, who kept running between the door and the plank bunk, as if he wanted to win a marathon[96], stopped, and out of breath he sat down in his old spot, lowered his head in his hands and suddenly screamed: "Let me out!"

"No, they won't let me out," he was telling to himself, "they won't and they won't. I've already been here since six o'clock this morning."

In a fit of talkativeness he stood up straight and asked Švejk:

"You don't by chance have a belt on you, so that I could end it all?"

"Glad that I can be of service in that regard," answered Švejk, unbuckling his belt, "I've never yet seen people hanging themselves in segregation with a belt. — Only, it's a pity," he continued while looking all around, "that there's no hook here. The window handle won't hold you. The only way you can hang yourself is kneeling by the plank bunk, the way that monk did in the Emmaus monastery[97], who hanged himself by his crucifix pendant, on account of some young Jewess. I like people, who commit suicide, very much, so just go ahead with gusto."

The gloomy man, into whose hand Švejk inserted the belt, took a look at the strap, threw it into a corner and started to weep, smudging the tears on his face with his black hands, while emitting shrieks:

"I have kiddies, I'm here because of drunkenness and immoral life, jesusmaria, my poor wife, and what will they tell me at the office? I have kiddies, I'm here because of drunkenness and immoral life" and so on without end.

In the end he did calm down a little, went to the door and began kicking it and banging on it with his fist. Behind the door could be heard steps and a voice: "What do you want?"

"Let me out!" he said with such a voice, as if he were left with nothing to live for. "Where to?" was the question coming from the other side. "To the office," replied the unfortunate father, husband, office worker, drunkard and immoral man.

Laughter, horrible laughter broke the silence in the corridor, and the steps moved to a distance again.

"It seems to me that gentleman hates you, since he's laughing at you so," said Švejk, as the hopeless man sat down next to him again. "A policeman like that, when he's angry, can do a lot, and when he gets even angrier, he's capable of anything. Just keep sitting here calmly, since you don't want to hang yourself, and wait to see how things will unfold. If you're an office worker, are married and have little children, it is, I admit, horrible. You're probably convinced they'll fire you from the job at the office, if I'm not mistaken."

"I can't say for sure," he sighed, "because I myself don't remember all the silly things I did, I only know that they threw me out of some place, and that I wanted to go back in there to light up my cigar. But first it began quite nicely. The chief of our department was celebrating his name's day[98] and invited us to a wine bar, then we all went to a second, a third, a fourth, a fifth, a sixth, a seventh, an eighth, a ninth…"

"Don't you want me to help you count?" asked Švejk. "I'm quite familiar with this, one night I visited twenty eight different tap-rooms. But to my credit, nowhere did I have any more than three beers."

"In short," continued the unhappy subordinate of the chief, who had celebrated his name's day in such a grand manner, "after we went through about a dozen of those little dives, we noticed that we had lost the chief, even though we had tied a string to him and walked him along like a little dog. So we went looking for him again everywhere and in the end, we all lost each other, until finally I found myself in one of those all-night coffeehouses in Vinohrady[99], it was a very decent establishment where I kept drinking some liqueur straight from the bottle. What I did after that, I don't remember, I only know that here at the district police station already, once they brought me here, both of the policemen reported that I got drunk, behaved immorally, beat up a lady, with a pocket knife cut somebody else's hat, which I took off a coatrack, dispersed a female band, accused the head-waiter in front of everybody of stealing a twenty crown bill, broke in two the marble top of the table I was sitting at, and spat intentionally into the black coffee of a man sitting at the next table. I didn't do anything else, at least I can't recall that I would have had done something else. But believe me, I'm such a proper, intelligent man, who doesn't think of anything else but his family. What do you say to it all? I'm no hoodlum breaking the peace after all!"

"Did it take a lot of work before you broke the marble top in two," asked Švejk with interest instead of answering, "or did you break it all at once?"

"At once," responded the intelligent man.

"Then, you're done for," Švejk said thoughtfully. "They'll prove that you'd been getting ready for that through diligent exercise. And the stranger's coffee that you spat into, was it with rum or without rum?"

And not waiting for an answer, Švejk clarified:

"If it was with rum, then it'll be worse because it's more expensive. At the court everything gets counted and put together, so that it would climb to at least a felony."

"At the court...," whispered dejectedly the conscientious father of a family, and having bowed his head, fell into an unpleasant state, in which a man's conscience devours* him.

"And do they know at home," asked Švejk, "that you're locked up, or will you wait until it's in the papers?"

"You think it will be in the papers?" asked naively the victim of his superior's name's day.

"That's more than a sure thing," was Švejk's straightforward answer because it had never been his habit to hide something from another. "This story about you will give all the readers of the newspapers enormous pleasure. I too like to read the section about those drunks and their breeches of the peace. Not long ago at The Chalice, one customer did nothing else except break his own head with a stein. He threw it up in the air and stepped under it. They drove him away, and in the morning we were already reading about it. Or like when in Bendlovka[100] I slapped an undertaker and he slapped me one back. In order for us to reconcile, they had to arrest both of us, and right away it was in the small afternoon edition. Or when in the coffeehouse At the Corpse[101] that office administrator broke two coasters, do you think that they spared him? He too was in the newspaper right away the next day. The only thing you can do from the prison is to send a correction to the newspaper, saying that the news item published about you has nothing to do with you and that you're neither related to the gentleman named in the paper, nor associated, and write home to have them cut out the correction and save it, so that you can read it when you will have sat through your

---

* Some writers use the expression "conscience gnaws." I do not view this expression to be exactly fitting. Even a tiger devours a man, rather than gnaws on him.

sentence. – Aren't you cold?" asked Švejk sympathetically, having noticed that the intelligent gentleman was shivering. "We're having a rather cold end of summer this year."

"I'm impossible," moaned Švejk's companion, "there goes my promotion."

"You're right about that," Švejk willingly concurred. "After you will have sat through your sentence, if they don't take you back at the office, I don't know whether you'll find another job any time soon, because even if you want to be a carrion collector's assistant, everybody demands you produce a certificate of moral intactness. Aye, such a moment of indulgent pleasure, like the one that you've allowed yourself, isn't worth it. And does your missis with your children have anything to live on during the time you'll be sitting in jail? Or will she have to go out begging and teach the kiddies various vices?

The sound of sobbing rang out:

"My poor babes, my poor wife!"

The careless penitent stood up and started talking about his children: He had five, the oldest was twelve and was one of those Boy Scouts. He drank only water and should have been an example to his father, who had done this for the first time in his life.

"One of the Scouts?" exclaimed Švejk. "I love to hear about those Scouts. Once in Mydlovary, near Zliv, *judicial district* Hluboká[102], *administrative district* České Budějovice, just when we, the ninety-first-regimenters were having exercises there, the farmers from the area had themselves a hunt for the Scouts in the village forest, who had multiplied in there like jack-rabbits. They caught three. When they were tying him up, the smallest one wailed, squealed and moaned so, that even we, hardened soldiers, couldn't watch it and chose to step aside. As they were being tied up, those three Scouts bit eight farmers. After the torment at the mayor's, under a cane, they confessed that there wasn't one meadow in the area that they hadn't flattened while catching some sun, further, that the field of standing rye, just before harvest, near Ražice, burned by pure chance, when in the rye they were roasting for themselves on a spit a doe, which they stalked with knives in the village forest. In their den in the forest they found more than one hundred pounds of poultry and game bones picked clean, a stunning volume of cherry stones, a lot of cores from unripe apples and other good things."

The poor father of the Scout was however disconsolate.

"What have I done?" he wailed, "my reputation is ruined!"

"It sure is," Švejk said with his native sincerity; "after what has happened, your reputation must certainly be ruined for life, because when they're reading about this in the newspaper, people you know will add more to it. That's the way it's always done, but don't let it bother you. The number of people, who have ruined or damaged reputations in this world, is at least ten times the number of those with spotless reputations. That's just a mere and hardly noticeable minuscule detail."

The sound of resolute steps was heard in the corridor, then the key rattled in the lock, the door opened, and a police patrolman called out Švejk's name.

"Excuse me," Švejk said in a courtly manner, "I've been here since only twelve o'clock noon, but this gentleman's already been here since six o'clock in the morning. I'm not in such a hurry."

Instead of an answer the strong hand of the police patrolman pulled Švejk into the corridor and in silence led him up the stairs to the second floor.

In the second room sat behind the desk the police inspector, a fat gentleman of jovial appearance, who said toward Švejk:

"So then you are that Švejk? So how did you end up here?"

"In a manner as common as dust," answered Švejk; "I came here escorted by one mister patrolman, because I wouldn't put up with being thrown out of the madhouse without lunch. That's as if they considered me like some streetwalker kicked to the curb."

"You know what, Švejk," said kindly the inspector, "why should we here at Salmovka station be bothering ourselves with you? Won't it be better if we just send you to police headquarters?"

"Sir, you are, as the saying goes," Švejk replied contentedly, "the master of the situation; a walk down to police headquarters now, toward evening, would be a quite pleasant little stroll."

"I'm so glad that we are agreed," the police inspector said merrily, "isn't it better when we reach an understanding? Isn't it true, Švejk?"

"I also love very much to consult with others," Švejk answered; "believe me, mister inspector, I'll never forget your goodness."

Having bowed deferentially, he was walking away with the police patrolman down to the guard house and a quarter of an hour later, Švejk could be seen already at the corner of Ječná street[103] and Charles' square, being escorted by yet another police patrolman, who was carrying under his arm a voluminous book with the German title

Arrestees Book.

At the corner of Spálená street[104], Švejk and his escort met a band of people pressing around a poster.

"That's the proclamation of the lord Emperor declaring war," the police patrolman told Švejk.

"I predicted it," said Švejk, "but in the madhouse they still don't know anything about it, although they should have got it first-hand."

"How do you mean that?" the police patrolman asked Švejk.

"Because in there are locked up a lot of officer gentlemen," Švejk explained, and when they reached another crowd pressing in front of the proclamation, Švejk yelled out:

"Hail to the Emperor František Josef! This war we will win."

Someone from the enthusiastic crowd pulled Švejk's hat down over his ears and so as people were quickly gathering, he stepped out and walked once again through the gate of the police headquarters.

"This war we will win quite certainly, I repeat it one more time, gentlemen"; with these words Švejk bid good-bye to the crowd that had seen him off.

And somewhere in the far removed distant parts of history, descending upon Europe[105] was the truth that tomorrow would wreck the plans of the present, as well.

6

ŠVEJK AT HOME AGAIN, HAVING BROKEN THROUGH THE VICIOUS CIRCLE

Through the building of the police headquarters wafted the spirit of foreign authority, which was charged with finding out to what extent was the population enthusiastic for war. Except for a few exceptions, the people who didn't deny that they were the sons of a nation that was doomed to bleed itself empty for interests totally alien to them, the police headquarters was home to the most beautiful gathering of bureaucratic birds of prey, who had use only for the dungeon and the gallows as a means of defending the existence of convoluted articles of law.

At the same time they were handling their victims with caustic kindness, weighing each word beforehand.

"I'm very sorry," said one of the black-and-yellow[106] birds of prey when they brought Švejk to him, "that you fell into our hands again. We thought that you'd straighten out, but we've been disappointed."

Švejk silently nodded in agreement and had such an innocent look on his face that the black-and-yellow predator looked at him quizzically and snapped:

"Stop making stupid faces."

He immediately switched to a kind tone however and continued:

"For us it's certainly very unpleasant to keep you in custody, and I can assure you that in my view, your guilt isn't so great, because given your little intelligence, there's no doubt that you've been put up to it. Tell me, mister Švejk, who is it really, who entices you to commit such silly acts?"

Švejk coughed and spoke up:

"Please forgive me, but I don't know of any silly acts."

"Is it not silliness, mister Švejk," said the artificially fatherly tone, "when you, according to the report of the police patrolman, who brought you here, caused people quickly gathering in front of a proclamation concerning the war that was posted on a corner and when you incited these people by exclaiming 'Hail to the Emperor František Josef! This war is won!'?

"I couldn't stay idle," declared Švejk, straining his good eyes, fixing them onto the eyes of the inquisitor, "I got upset when I saw that they all were reading the proclamation about the war and not showing any signs of being glad. No chanting of glory, no hoorays, absolutely nothing, mister Magistrate. It was as if it had absolutely nothing to do with them. And at that moment, I, an old soldier from the 91st Regiment, couldn't stand watching it, so I shouted out those sentences, and I think that if you were in my place, you would have done exactly as I did. When there is a war, it must be won and 'Glory to the lord Emperor!' must be shouted, and nobody can talk me out of that."

Outdone and crushed, the black-and-yellow predator couldn't withstand the gaze of the innocent lamb, lowered his own onto the official files and said:

"I agree fully with your enthusiasm, but if it were only manifested under different circumstances. But you yourself well know you were being escorted by a police patrolman, so such a patriotic outburst could and had to strike the audience ironically, rather than seriously."

"When somebody is being escorted by a police patrolman," Švejk replied, "it is a tough moment in his human life. And if, at even such a tough moment, a man doesn't forget what the proper thing to do is, when there is a war, then, I think, such a man is not all that bad."

The black-and-yellow predator growled and once more looked directly into Švejk's eyes.

Švejk answered with innocent, soft, unassuming and tender warmth of his gaze.

For a moment the two were just looking at each other.

"The demons take you, Švejk!" the official chin finally said, if you end up here one more time, then I won't bother asking you anything and you'll be on your way to the military court[107] at Hradčany[108]. Do you understand?"

Before he knew what was happening, Švejk stepped up to him, kissed his hand and said:

"May God repay you for everything, should you ever need a pure-blooded little dog, please condescend to turn to me. I have a dog business."

And so Švejk found himself free again and on his way toward home.

His musing about whether he should stop first at The Chalice pub ended by his opening the very door, out of which he left some time ago, in the custody of detective Bretschneider.

In the taproom reined grave-like silence. Several guests were sitting there, among whom was the church custodian from Saint Apollinaire[109]. All of them wore gloomy faces. Behind the tap-counter sat the pubkeeper's wife, Mrs. Palivec, and was gazing at the beer taps with a dull expression.

"So I'm back already," Švejk said cheerfully, "give me a stein of beer. Now where is our mister Palivec, is he too home already?"

Instead of giving an answer, Mrs. Palivec started to weep, and concentrating her misfortune into a peculiar stress on each word, she moaned:

"They — gave — him — ten — years — a week — ago."

"Well, there you go," said Švejk, "then he's already got seven days behind him."

"He was so careful," wept Mrs. Palivec, "he always said so about himself."

The guests in the tap room were stubbornly reticent, as if Palivec's spirit was wandering there and exhorting them to even greater caution.

"Caution is the mother of wisdom," said Švejk, taking a seat at a table behind a stein of beer topped with foamy head, in which there were little openings, resulting from tears of missis Palivec dripping into the foam as she carried the beer to Švejk and sat it before him on the table, "times are such that they force a man to be careful."

"Yesterday we had two funerals," said the custodian from Saint Apollinaire, switching the conversation to another subject.

"Then apparently somebody died," said a second guest whereupon the third added:

"Did the funerals make use of the catafalque?"

"I'd like to know," said Švejk, "what the military funerals are going to be like now, during the war."

The guests got up, paid and left in silence. Only Švejk now remained alone with missis Palivec.

"It didn't cross my mind," he said, "that they would sentence an innocent man to ten years. I've already heard that they sentenced one innocent man to five years, but ten years, that's a little too much."

"But my old man confessed," said the weeping Mrs. Palivec, "the things he said in here about those flies and about the picture, he repeated them both at the police headquarters and in court. I was at the trial proceedings as a witness, but what could I have testified to since they told me that I was in a familial relationship with my husband, and that I could withhold my testimony. I got so spooked by that familial relationship notion, lest something be made of it, so I withheld my testimony and he, the poor old soul, gave me such a look, until I die I won't forget those eyes of his. And then, after sentencing, when they were escorting him out, he yelled out for them in the corridor, as he'd been stupefied from it all: 'Long live Free Thought![110]"

"And Mister Bretschneider doesn't come in here anymore?" asked Švejk.

"He's been here several times," the pubkeeper's wife answered, "had a beer or two, asked me who comes here, and listened to the guests talk about soccer. When they see him, they always talk only about soccer. And he was all fidgety, as if at any moment he could go berserk and writhe. During all that time he only got one upholsterer from Příčná street to swallow his bait."

"It's a matter of training," Švejk remarked, "was the upholsterer a dim-witted man?"

"Just about like my husband," she answered, as she wept. "He asked him whether he would shoot at the Serbs, and he told him that he didn't know how to shoot, that he was once at a shooting gallery, and shot up a crown[111]. Then we all heard mister Bretschneider say, as he pulled out his notebook: 'Look here, again we have a new nice high treason!', and he left with that upholsterer from Příčná street, who has never returned."

"There will be more of those, who won't return," remarked Švejk, "give me rum."

Švejk was just having a second shot of rum poured for him, when into the tap-room came undercover patrolman Bretschneider. Having cast a quick look around the tap room and into the empty pub, he sat down next to Švejk, and having ordered a beer waited for what Švejk would say.

Švejk lifted some newspaper off the rack and scanning through the classifieds on the back page he spoke up:

"Look here, this Čimpera fellow in Straškov, number 5, serviced by the Račiněves post office, will sell a farm with its own thirteen acres of fields, a school and a railway at the location."

Bretschneider nervously drummed his fingers and turning to Švejk said:

"I'm surprised that a farm should interest you, mister Švejk."

"Ah, it's you," said Švejk, extending a hand to him, "I couldn't recognize you right away, my memory is weak. The last time we parted, if I'm not mistaken, was in the arraignment office of police headquarters. What is it you have been doing since then, do you come here often?"

"I came today on your account," said Bretschneider, "I was told at police headquarters that you sell dogs. I need a nice little ratter, or a Spitz, or something similar."

"I can provide you all that," responded Švejk. "Do you wish a pure-blooded animal or something from the street?"

"I think," replied Bretschneider, "I'll end up going with a pure-blooded animal."

"And what about a police dog, wouldn't that be your wish?" asked Švejk, "the kind that snoops everything out right away and leads to the trail of the crime. A butcher in Vršovice has one and it pulls his little wagon, and that dog, as the saying goes, has missed out on his true vocation."

"I'd like a Spitz," Bretschneider said with calm restraint, "a Spitz that won't bite."

"Do you then desire a toothless Spitz?" asked Švejk, "I know of one. A pubkeeper in Dejvice[112] has it."

"Then rather a little ratter," tentatively said Bretschneider whose knowledge of canines was only in its infancy, if it hadn't been for the direct order from police headquarters, he would never have found out anything about dogs.

But the order's tone was specific, clear, and tough. Get to know Švejk on more familiar terms through his dog-selling business, for which purpose he was given the right to choose assistants and have funds at his disposal for purchases of dogs.

"The little ratters come both bigger and smaller," said Švejk, "I know of two smaller ones and three bigger ones. All five can be cradled in your lap. I can recommend them to you with the utmost enthusiasm."

"That would suite me," proclaimed Bretschneider, "and how much would one cost?"

"Now you're talking size," answered Švejk. "It depends on size. A little ratter is not a calf, with little ratters it's just the other way around, the smaller, the more expensive."

"I'm inclined to get bigger ones that could be guard dogs," replied Bretschneider, afraid to strain the secret fund of the State Police.

"All right," said Švejk, "the bigger ones I can sell for fifty crowns apiece and the yet bigger ones for forty five, but we've forgotten one thing. Are they supposed to be puppies or older dogs, male doggies or bitches?"

"It's all the same to me," answered Bretschneider, who was dealing with problems here he knew nothing about, "get them for me and tomorrow at seven in the evening I'll come by your place to pick them up. Will they be to be had?"

"Do come, they will be," Švejk responded dryly, "but in this case I'm forced to ask you for a deposit of thirty crowns."

"No problem," said Bretschneider, paying out the money, "and now let's each have a quarter-liter of wine on my account."

When they drank it up, Švejk bought them a quarter-liter on his account, then Bretschneider, urging Švejk not to be afraid of him, pointing out that he was off duty and today one could talk to him about politics.

Švejk declared that he never talked about politics in a pub, that the whole of politics was for little children.

Bretschneider in contrast expressed even more revolutionary opinions and said that every weak State was foreordained to extinction, and asked Švejk what was his opinion of this matter.

Švejk declared that he had nothing to do with the State, but that he had once cared for a weak St. Bernard[113] puppy, which he fed military biscuits, and that it also croaked.

After they each had a fifth quarter-liter, Bretschneider proclaimed himself to be an anarchist and asked Švejk, which organization he should sign up with.

Švejk said that an anarchist had once bought a Leonberger[114] from him for one hundred crowns and that he still owed him the last payment.

During the sixth quarter-liter Bretschneider spoke of revolution and against mobilization, whereupon Švejk leaned toward him and whispered in his ear:

"A customer walked just now into the pub, so be careful that he doesn't hear you, or you might have some unpleasant difficulties from it... You can see, the pubkeeper's wife is already weeping."

Missis Palivec was indeed sobbing in her chair behind the tap counter.

"Why are you crying, missis pubkeeper?" asked Bretschneider, "in three months we'll win the war, there will be an amnesty, your husband will return and then we'll really wet our whistles in this place of yours. — Or don't you think that we'll win it?" he turned to Švejk.

"Why keep kicking a dead horse," Švejk said, "it must be won, and that's it, but now I have to go home already."

Švejk paid his tab and returned to his cleaning woman missis Müller, who was greatly startled when she saw that the man using a key to open the door of the apartment for himself, was Švejk.

"I thought, merciful Sir, that *they* wouldn't be back until years from now," she said with her customary sincerity, "in the meantime I rented your apartment out of pity to a doorman from an all-night coffeehouse, because they had already conducted a house search in here three times, and when they couldn't find anything, they said then that you were done for, because you're cunning."

Švejk was immediately able to verify for himself that an unknown foreigner had settled in absolutely comfortably. He was sleeping in Švejk's bed and was even so magnanimous that he was satisfied with half of it and on the other half he had placed some long-haired creature, which was sleeping out of gratitude, having had her arms wrapped around his neck, while various articles of both male and female clothing lay intermingled around the bed. From the chaos it was apparent that the doorman had returned from the all-night coffeehouse with his lady in a merry mood.

"Mister," said Švejk shaking the intruder, "don't let yourself be late for lunch. I would feel terrible if you were telling everyone that I threw you out when you couldn't anymore get anything for lunch anywhere."

The doorman from the all-night coffeehouse was very drowsy with interrupted sleep, and it took a long time before he got to understand that the owner of the bed had returned home and was laying a claim to it.

As is the custom of all doormen from all-night coffeehouses, even this man expressed himself saying that he would beat up anybody, who tried to wake him up, and he attempted to keep on sleeping.

In the meantime, Švejk picked up articles of the man's wardrobe and brought them near the bed for him, and having shaken him vigorously, he said:

"If you don't get dressed, then I'll try to throw you, just as you are, out into the street. It would be of great advantage to you if you fly out of here dressed."

"I wanted to sleep until eight in the evening," muttered the dumbfounded doorman, pulling on his pants, "I pay daily two crowns for the bed to that woman and I can bring young ladies here from the coffeehouse. Tough Mary, get up!"

By the time he was putting on his collar and knotting his tie, he'd come to his senses enough to be able to assure Švejk that the all-night coffeehouse Mimosa[115] was really one of the city's most respectable night rooms, accessible only to ladies whose police registration booklets were in absolute order, and he was inviting Švejk cordially to come for a visit.

In contrast to that, his female companion was in no way satisfied with Švejk and used several very decent expressions, the most decent of which was "You high-priest punk!"

After the departure of the intruders, Švejk went to straighten things out with missis Müller, but he found no trace of her, except for a bit of paper, on which there was scribbled in pencil the disorderly handwriting of missis Müller's, who with uncommon ease expressed her thoughts regarding the unfortunate incident of subletting Švejk's bed to the doorman from the all-night coffeehouse:

"Do forgive me, merciful Sir, that I won't be seeing *them* anymore, because I'm going to jump from a window."

"She's lying," said Švejk and waited.

A half-hour later the unhappy missis Müller crept into the kitchen, and from the crushed expression on her face it was apparent that she was expecting from Švejk words of comfort.

"If you want to jump out of a window," Švejk said, "go into the bedroom, I've opened the window there. I would not recommend to you that you jump from the kitchen window, because you would fall onto the roses in the garden and you would crumple the bushes and have to pay for it. From the bedroom's window you'll fly down beautifully onto the sidewalk, and if you get to be lucky, you'll break your neck. If you have bad luck, you will only break all your ribs, arms and legs, and you'll have to pay the hospital."

Missis Müller started to weep, departed silently for the bedroom, closed the window, and when she returned she said: "There's a draft and it would not be good for your merciful Sir's rheumatism."

Then she went to make the bed, was unusually diligently putting everything in order and having returned to Švejk in the kitchen, with tears in her eyes she remarked: "Those two puppies, merciful Sir, that we had in the yard, are dead. And the St. Bernard, he ran away when they were conducting a house search here."

"Oh forchristhelord", exclaimed Švejk, "that dog could get himself into a pretty mess, the police will surely be looking for him now."

"He bit a mister police inspector when he was pulling him out from under the bed," continued missis Müller, "because before that one of those policemen said that there was somebody under the bed, so they commanded the St. Bernard in the name of the law to crawl out, and when he didn't want to, they then dragged him out. And he wanted to swallow them, then he charged out of the door and has never returned. They also interrogated me, asking who visits us, whether or not we receive any money from abroad, and then they were insinuating that I was stupid, when I had told them that money from abroad came only seldom, the last time from that manager in Brno[116], the deposit of sixty crowns for an Angora[117] cat you had advertised in the *National Politics*, instead of which you sent him that blind fox-terrier puppy in the empty box of dates. After that they spoke with me very kindly and referred to me that doorman from the all-night coffeehouse, so that I wouldn't be afraid in the apartment, the same one you threw out..."

"I just have such bad luck with the authorities already, missis Müller, now you'll see how many of them will be coming here to buy dogs," sighed Švejk.

I don't know whether those gentlemen, who examined the police archives after the regime changed, ever deciphered the items listed in the secret fund of the State Police that read:

B...40K, F...50K, L...80K, etc., but they were definitely mistaken if they thought that B, F and L were the initials of some gentlemen, who for 40, 50, 80 or more crowns used to sell the Czech nation to the black-and-yellow eagle.

B indicates a St. Bernard, F fox-terrier and L denotes Leonberger. Bretschneider brought all of these dogs from Švejk to police headquarters. They were hideous mutants and didn't have the slightest trait in common with a pure-blooded breed, which Švejk was passing them off as such to Bretschneider.

The St. Bernard was a mix of a mongrel poodle and some stray street pooch, the fox-terrier had the ears of a basset and was the size of a butcher's dog with twisted legs, as if he had suffered from rickets. The Leonberger's hairy head was reminiscent of a stable pinscher's snout, had his tail chopped off, the height of a basset and butt bare, like those famous naked American dogs.

Next was sent to buy a dog from Švejk detective named Kalous[118], and he returned with a dazed freak, reminiscent of spotted hyena with the mane of a Scottish sheep dog, and a new item was added to the secret fund: D...90 K.

That mutant beast was now officially playing the part of a Great

Dane...

But Kalous did not manage to spy out anything out of Švejk either. He did only as well as Bretschneider. Švejk managed to switch even the most nimble political conversations to treatments of puppies' distemper, and the cleverest of sneaky snares ended with Bretschneider taking away with him from Švejk another new, inconceivable crossbred mutant.

And that was the end of the famous detective Bretschneider. By the time he already had in his apartment seven such abominations, he shut himself in the back room with them and wouldn't give them anything to eat for so long, until they devoured him.

He had been so conscientious, that he saved the state the funeral expense.

In his personnel file at police headquarters, entered in the section "Career progression," were these words replete with tragedy:

"Devoured by own dogs."

When Švejk later found out about this tragic event, he said:

"I only keep wondering, how will they at the Last Judgment put him back together?"

7

ŠVEJK GOES IN THE MILITARY SERVICE

At the time when the forests along the river Raba[119] in Galicia[120] saw Austrian troops fleeing across the Raba, and down in Serbia one Austrian division after another was getting a long-deserved kick in the seat of the pants, the Austrian Ministry of MilitaryAffairs[121] remembered even Švejk, to help the monarchy out of the mess.

When they brought him the notice that he was to appear in one week at Střelecký Island for a medical exam, Švejk just happened to be lying in bed, stricken again with rheumatism.

Missis Müller was making coffee for him in the kitchen.

"Missis Müller," Švejk's soft voice was heard coming from the bedroom, "missis Müller, come here for a moment."

Once the cleaning woman stood by the bed, Švejk said again in such a soft voice: "Sit down, missis Müller."

There was something mysteriously festive in his voice.

When missis Müller did sit down, Švejk declared, suddenly rising up in his bed: "I'm going in the military service!"

"Virgin Mary," exclaimed missis Müller, "what will *they* do there?"

"Fight," answered Švejk with a grave voice, "Austria is in big trouble. Topside the enemy is already creeping up on Krakow[122], and down under into Hungary[123]. We're getting threshed like rye wherever we look, and that's why they're calling me up into military service. Remember after all how yesterday I was reading to you from the newspaper that the dear motherland has been has been swaddled in very dark clouds?"

"But *they* can't even move."

"That doesn't matter, missis Müller, I will ride to military service in a wheelchair. You know the confectioner around the corner, he has such a wheelchair. Years ago he used to push his paralyzed nasty grandpa in it out into the fresh air. You, missis Müller, will push me into military service in that wheelchair."

Missis Müller started crying:

"Shouldn't I, merciful Sir, run to fetch a doctor?"

"You will go nowhere, missis Müller, I am, except for my legs, absolutely healthy cannon fodder and at a time when it is so grim for Austria, every cripple must be at his post. Be calm and keep brewing the coffee."

While missis Müller, tearful and trembling, was straining the coffee, the good soldier Švejk was singing on his bed:

> General Windischgrätz[124] and the military lords
> Started a war at the rising of the sun;
> hop, hop, hop!
> A war they started, and cried like this:
> Help us Christ the Lord and Virgin Mary;
> hop, hop, hop!

Frightened by the dreadful battle song, missis Müller forgot about the coffee and her whole body trembling, she listened full of fright, as the good soldier Švejk continued singing on the bed:

> With the Virgin Mary and those four bridges,
> Build for yourself, Piedmont[125], stronger advanced posts;
> hop, hop, hop!
> 'Twas a battle, there 'twas, near Solferino[126].
> Much blood flowed there, blood up to your knees.
> hop, hop, hop!
> Blood up to your knees and meat by the wagonload,
> After all, 'twas the eighteenth gang[127] brawling there;
> hop, hop, hop!
> Eighteenth gang, don't you be afraid of want,
> After all, behind you they're bringing you money on a cart;
> hop, hop, hop!

"Merciful Sir, for-God's-sake I beseech *them*," came the pitiful request from the kitchen, but Švejk was already finishing his war song:

> The money on a cart and the mess rations in a carriage,
> Now, which regiment can this manage?
> Jumpity, jumpity, jump!

Missis Müller charged out the door and ran to fetch the doctor. She came back an hour later, while Švejk had a nap.

And so he was awakened by a pudgy man, who held his hand on his forehead for a moment and said:

"Don't be afraid, I am doctor Pávek from Vinohrady — show me your hand — put this thermometer under your arm... That's it — show me your tongue — farther — hold your tongue — what did your father and mother die of?"

And so at the time, when Vienna wished that all the nations of Austria-Hungary[128] would be offering to the empire its most exquisite specimens of loyalty and dedication, doctor Pávek prescribed bromide for Švejk as an antidote to his patriotic enthusiasm and he also recommended that this brave and nice private not even think about the military:

"Keep lying down straight and remain calm, tomorrow I'll come again."

When he did come the next day, he asked missis Müller in the kitchen how the patient was doing.

"He's worse, doctor, Sir," she answered with true grief, "in the night he sang, forgive me please, when his rheumatism flared up, the Austrian anthem."

Doctor Pávek found himself forced to react to his patient's new expression of loyalty by an increased dosage of bromide.

On the third day missis Müller reported to him that Švejk was even worse.

"At midday, doctor, Sir, he sent for a map of the battlefield, and in the night he was struck by the fantasy that Austria will win it."

"And he's taking the powder pills exactly according to the prescription?

"He hasn't, doctor, Sir, even sent for them yet."

Doctor Pávek left, having brought down on Švejk a storm of recriminations, with the assurance that he would never again come to treat a man, who refuses his medical help with bromide.

Only two days were left before Švejk was to appear in front of the draft commission[129].

In that time Švejk carried out the appropriate preparations. First of all he sent missis Müller to buy a military cap and second he sent her to borrow the wheelchair from the confectioner around the corner, the one, which once upon a time long ago the confectioner had used to cart his nasty paralyzed grandpa out into the fresh air. Then he remembered that he needed crutches. Fortunately, the confectioner held even onto the pair of crutches, as a familial memento of his grandpa.

He still lacked recruit's flowers for his button-hole. Even those were chased down for him by missis Müller, who over the course of those days noticeably lost weight, and wherever she went she wept.

And so on that memorable day appeared in the streets of Prague a moving case of loyalty:

An old woman, pushing in front of her a wheelchair, in which was sitting a man wearing a military cap with a freshly polished brass frankie[130], waving his crutches. And on his coat there stood out the eye-catching brightly colored recruit's flowers.

And this man, waving his crutches again and again, was yelling into the street of Prague:

"On against Belgrade! On against Belgrade[131]!"

Following him was a crowd of people, which kept growing from the barely noticeable huddle that had gathered in front of the building from where Švejk began to ride into military service.

Švejk was able to state that police patrolmen, standing at some intersections, had saluted him.

In Wenceslas square the crowd around the wheelchair with Švejk in it grew to a headcount of several hundred, and at the corner of Krakovská street it beat up a German fraternity student, who yelled toward Švejk:

"*Hail! Down with the Serbs!*"

At the corner of Vodičkova street, the mounted police rode into it and dispersed the crowd.

When Švejk showed the district police inspector that he had it in black and white, that today he had to appear in front of the draft board, the district inspector was a bit disappointed and in order to prevent any breech of the peace, he had the wheelchair with Švejk in it escorted by two mounted patrolmen to Střelecký Island.

An article about this whole event appeared in the *Prague Official Newspaper*[132]:

> Patriotism of a cripple: Yesterday forenoon pedestrians at main Prague thoroughfares witnessed a scene, which speaks beautifully of how in these great and serious times, even the sons of our nation can give the most brilliant examples of loyalty and devotion to the throne of the dear old monarch. It seems to us that the times of ancient Greeks and Romans have returned, during which Mucius Scaevola[133] had them take him into battle, disregarding his burned-off hand. These most sacred emotions and interests were beautifully demonstrated yesterday by a cripple on crutches,

whom his dear old mother pushed in a wheelchair for the sick. This son of the Czech nation voluntarily, disregarding his infirmity, let himself be led into military service, so that he could give his life and possessions for his Emperor. And if his cry of "On against Belgrade!" had such a vigorous reception in the streets of Prague, it's all only a convincing testimony that the inhabitants of Prague provide model examples of love for one's homeland and the ruling sovereign's house."

In the same sense wrote even the Prager Tagblatt[134], which concluded its article with the words that the cripple volunteer was seen off by a crowd of Germans, who wanted to protect him with their bodies from lynching[135] by Czech agents of the well-known Entente[136]

Bohemie[137] published this news item demanding that the crippled patriot be rewarded, and announced that it was accepting for the unknown man gifts from German citizens at the newspaper's administration office.

If according to these three magazines the Czech Lands could not deliver a nobler citizen, the gentlemen of the draft board did not share that view.

Especially not the chief military physician, doctor Bautze. He was an obstinate man, who saw in everything a fraudulent attempt to dodge the military, the front, the bullets and the shrapnel.

Well known is his statement:

"The whole Czech nation is a pack of malingerers."

Over the ten weeks of his activity he had weeded out 10,999 malingerers from 11,000 civilians and he would have gotten the eleven-thousandth, if that lucky soul, just as the doctor suddenly screamed at him *"About face!"* wasn't hit with a fatal stroke.

"Carry that malingerer away!" said Bautze after he had realized the man was dead.

And in front of him stood on that memorable day Švejk, like the others, fully naked, covering up chastely his nakedness with the crutches he was leaning on.

"That is really a peculiar fig leaf," said Bautze, "there were no such fig leaves in paradise."

"Declared unfit for stupidity," remarked a master sergeant looking at the official documents.

"And what else is wrong with you?" asked Bautze.

"I dutifully report that I'm a rheumatic, but I will serve the lord

Emperor until my body is torn to pieces," Švejk replied modestly, "my knees are swollen."

Bautze gave Švejk a horrifying look and screamed: "*You are a malingerer!*", and turning to the master sergeant with icy calmness he said: "*Lock this guy up immediately!*"

Two soldiers with bayonets were taking Švejk to the garrison prison[138].

Švejk walked on his crutches, and with horror was noticing that his rheumatism was beginning to disappear.

Missis Müller, who had been waiting for Švejk on the bridge above with the wheelchair, when she saw him, being led away under bayonets, started crying and walked away from the wheelchair, never to return to it again.

And the good soldier Švejk continued to walk modestly under the escort of the armed defenders of the state.

The bayonets glistened in the glow of the sun and in front of Radetzky's[139] memorial statue in the Small Side[140] Švejk turned to the crowd, which was seeing him off:

"On against Belgrade! On against Belgrade!"

And from atop his memorial Marshall Radetzky was dreamily watching the good soldier Švejk, with the recruit's flowers on his coat, hobbling along on the old crutches, increasing the distance between them, while some serious gentleman was telling the people around him that they were escorting a deserter[141].

8

ŠVEJK AS A MALINGERER

In these momentous times, military physicians took unusual care to exorcise the demon of sabotage out of malingerers and return them to the womb of the army.

Several degrees of torment were instituted for malingerers and people suspected of malingering, which were: consumptives, rheumatics, or people with a hernia, kidney disease, typhus, diabetes, inflammation of the lungs and other illnesses.

The torment the malingerers were subjected to was systematized and the degrees of torment were these:

1. An absolute diet, a cup of tea in the morning and evening for three days, while to all, without regard to what the patients complained about, aspirin was given to induce sweating.

2. Being served in copious portions, so that the malingerers would not think military service was a bowl of honey, was quinine in powder form, that is, the so-called "quinine licking".

3. Flushing out the stomach twice a day with a liter of warm water.

4. Enemas, using soapy water and glycerin.

5. Wrapping in a bed sheet soaked in cold water.

There were courageous people, who suffered through all five degrees of torment and let themselves be taken away in a simple coffin to the military cemetery. There were however other people of little heart, who, when having progressed to the enema, proclaimed they were well already, and that they wished for nothing else but to leave with the earliest march-battalion[141] for the trenches.

In the garrison prison they stashed Švejk in the hospital building among just such a group of dejected malingerers.

"I won't hold up anymore," said his neighbor on the bed, whom they just brought back from the procedure room, where they had flushed his stomach out for the second time.

That man was feigning shortsightedness.

"Tomorrow I'll ride to the regiment," decided a malingerer to the left of Švejk, who had just received an enema, feigning to be as deaf as a tree stump.

On the bed by the door was dying a consumptive, wrapped in a bed sheet soaked in cold water.

"He's the third one already this week," remarked a neighbor on the right, "and what's wrong with you?"

"I've got rheumatism," answered Švejk, whereupon followed hearty laughter of all around. Laughing was even the dying consumptive feigning tuberculosis.

"Don't barge in here with rheumatism to be one of us," a fat man notified Švejk seriously, "rheumatism has about as much currency around here as corns; I'm anemic, half of my stomach is gone and five ribs are gone, and nobody believes me. There was even a deaf mute here, for two weeks they would every half hour wrap him in a bed sheet soaked in cold water, every day they'd give him an enema and pump his stomach. All the ambulance corpsmen already thought he'd won his freedom and that he'd be going home, until the doctor prescribed something to make him gag. It could have torn him up, and here's where he lost his heart. 'I can't', says he, "pretend to be a deaf mute anymore, my speech and hearing have returned.' All the guys in the sickbay kept telling him not to doom himself, but he stood his ground, insisting he could now hear and speak just like others. And that's also the way he reported it the next morning during the doctor's rounds."

"He kept it up for quite a while," remarked a man feigning that one of his legs was shorter than the other by whole four inches, "not like the one feigning that he had a stroke. Three quinine lickings, one enema and a one-day fast were enough. He confessed, and before the time came to pump his stomach, not even a memento of the stroke remained. The longest held out the one, who was bitten by a rabid dog. He would bite, howl, it's true, and he did know how to do that remarkably well, but he just couldn't whip up foam at his mouth. We tried to help him any way we could. We tickled him many times for the whole hour before the doctor's rounds, until he got cramps and turned blue on us, but the foam wouldn't come to his mouth and it just never did. It was something horrible. As he was giving himself up one morning during the doctor's rounds, we felt pity for him. He stood himself up by his bed straight as a candle, saluted and said: 'I dutifully report Chief Medical Officer, Sir, that perhaps the dog that bit me wasn't rabid.' The chief medical officer gave him such a weird look that the bitten man's body started shaking all over and he continued: 'I dutifully report, Chief Medical Officer, Sir, that no dog bit me at all, it was just I myself, who bit my own hand.' After this confession they investigated him for self-mutilation, said that he wanted to bite off his own hand, so that he wouldn't have to go into the field."

"All such illnesses, where you need foam at your mouth," said a fat malingerer, "are hard to feign. Like for example the falling sickness[142]. There was once also a guy here with the falling sickness, he was always telling us that he didn't care about one seizure, so he would stage maybe ten of them in one day. He was writhing in those convulsions, clenching his fists, bugging his eyes far out, looking as if he had them hanging out on stems, he would slam his body around, stick his tongue out, in short, I'll tell you, an exquisite, first-class falling sickness, kind of sincere. All of a sudden, he got furuncles, two on his neck, two on his back, and that ended his writhing and slamming himself to the floor, since he could neither move his head, nor sit, nor lie down. He got fever and in the fever during the doctor's visit he told everything on himself. He really did it to us with those furuncles, because having them he had to lie among us for three more days and was getting another diet, in the morning coffee and a braided bun, for lunch soup, gravy and dumplings, in the evening soup or porridge, and we, having hungry pumped-out stomachs on a complete diet, had to watch that guy feeding his face, smacking his lips, and snorting and burping fully satiated. Thereby he tripped three guys, they also confessed. Those had been laid up on account of a heart defect."

"The best", opined one of the malingerers, "which one can feign, is lunacy. In the next room, there are two from our teachers faculty, one keeps constantly screaming, day and night: 'The pyre of Giordano Bruno[143] is still smoldering, reopen the trial of Galileo[144]!' and the other one barks, first three times slowly: woof — woof — woof, then five times in quick succession: woof woof woof woof woof, and again slowly, and so it goes without stopping. They've already managed to keep it up for three weeks. I originally also wanted to pretend to be a lunatic, a religious nut, and preach about the infallibility of the Pope, but in the end I got myself a case of cancer of the stomach from a barber in the Small Side for fifteen crowns."

"I know a chimney sweep in Břevnov[145]," remarked another patient, "for ten crowns he will give you such a fever that you'll jump out of the window."

"That's nothing," said another, "in Vršovice there is a midwife, who, for twenty crowns, will dislocate your foot so bad that you'll be a cripple for the rest of your life."

"I got a dislocated foot for a tenner," piped up a voice from the row of beds by the window, "a tenner and three beers."

"My illness has cost me over two hundred already," complained his neighbor, a dried-out little bean-pole, "name me any poison and you won't come up with one that I haven't used. I am a living warehouse of poisons. I drank sublimate, inhaled mercury vapor, munched on arsenic, smoked opium, drank opium tincture, sprinkled morphine on bread, swallowed strychnine, drank a solution of phosphorus in carbon disulfide, even picric acid. I've ruined my liver, lungs, kidneys, gall bladder, brain, heart, guts. Nobody knows what illnesses I have."

"The best thing is," somebody from somewhere near the door was explaining, "to inject kerosene under the skin of your hand. My cousin was so happy when they had to cut his arm off up to the elbow, and today he's done with the whole military service and left in peace."

"So you see," Švejk said, "all of this everyone must suffer for the lord Emperor. Even stomach pumping, even that enema. When I was serving with my regiment years ago, it was worse yet. They'd hog-tie such a sick man and throw him in the slammer, so that he would get better. There were no bunk beds like here or spittoons. Bare plank beds, and on them were lying sick men. At one time one really had a true case of typhus and another next to him had small pox. Both were hog-tied and the regiment's doctor would kick them in the stomach, saying that they were supposedly malingerers. Then when both those soldiers died, it got into the Parliament and it was even in the newspapers. They immediately forbade us to read newspapers and conducted a search through our suitcases, to find who had a newspaper. And as I always have bad luck, among the whole regiment they didn't find anyone with a newspaper, but me. So they escorted me to regimental report and that colonel of ours, such an ox, Lord God let him in heaven, he started screaming at me, ordering me to stand straight and tell him who wrote it to the newspapers, or else he he'd rip my mouth from ear to ear and have me locked up until I turned black. Next came the regiment's doctor, swinging his fist under my nose and screaming: '*You runaway dog! You shabby beast! You hapless hunk of barnyard crap!* — You socialist punk!' I'm looking them all sincerely in the eyes, not blinking even once, keeping quiet, the right hand on my cap and the left one on the crease of my pants. They were running around me like dogs, barking at me, still getting nothing from me. I'm quiet, rendering military honors and the left hand on the crease of my pants. After they had been going crazy like that for about half an hour, the colonel ran toward me screaming: 'Are you an idiot, or are you not an idiot?' — 'I dutifully report Colonel, Sir, that I am an idiot.' — 'Twenty one days of strict regimen imprisonment for idiocy, two days of fasting a week, a month of confinement to the barracks, manacles for forty-eight hours, lock him up immediately, nothing to feed, bind him up, to show him that the military doesn't need idiots. We will, you churl, knock that newspaper nonsense out of your head', decided the Colonel after a long time of running around. — While I sat there doing my time, wonders were happening in the garrison. Our Colonel forbade the soldiers to read anything, even if it were the *Prague Official Newspaper*, in the mess they couldn't even wrap hot dogs or syrečky[146] in newspapers. From that time on the soldiers started to read and our regiment became the most educated. We read all the newspapers and at each company gang, they composed little verses and songs targeting the Colonel. And when something would happen in the regiment, there was always found some good soul among the men, who would put it in the newspaper under the title 'Cruel Maltreatment of Soldiers.' And that wasn't enough for them. They'd write to the Parliamentary deputies in Vienna, asking that they take up their cause, and those deputies started making one motion after another, declaring that our Colonel was an animal, and similar things in that vein. Some minister of the government sent a commission our way, to investigate it, and some Franta Henčl from Hluboká got afterwards two years in prison, because it was he, who turned to the deputies in Vienna on account of the slap in the face the Colonel had given him on the training ground. After the commission left, the Colonel had us all fall in, the whole regiment, and said that a soldier is a soldier, that he must shut his trap and keep on serving; that if there was something the Colonel really didn't like, it was insubordination. 'So you hoodlums thought that the commission would help you,' says the Colonel, 'like shit it did. And now each company gang will march in formation before me and loudly repeat everything I have said.' – So we did, one company gang after another, right-faced to where the Colonel stood, one hand on the slings of our rifles, and we hollered at him: 'So we hoodlums thought that the commission would help us, like shit it did!' — Our Colonel laughed so hard that he kept grabbing his belly, until the eleventh company gang marched by in formation. They came along, stomping hard, and when they reached the Colonel, nothing, silence, not even a tiny sound. The Colonel turned red like a rooster and sent the eleventh company gang back to do it again. They marched back again in formation, silent, only rank after rank stared insolently into the Colonel's eyes. '*At ease!*' the Colonel said, pacing up and down the yard, lashing at his boots with a riding whip and spitting, then all of a sudden, he stops and screams '*Fall out!*', mounts his old nag and is already outside of the gate. We were waiting to see what would happen to the eleventh company gang, and lo and behold, nothing. We waited a day, the second day, the whole week, and lo and behold still nothing. The Colonel didn't show up at the garrison at all, which the rank and file, the noncoms[147], and all the officers rejoiced over very much. Afterward we got a new colonel and it was rumored that the old one was in some kind of sanitarium because he wrote a letter, in his own hand, to the lord Emperor, that the eleventh company gang mutinied."

Soon the time for the afternoon doctors' rounds approached. Army[148] doctor Grünstein went from bed to bed, followed by an ambulance corpsman non-commissioned officer[149] with a records book.

"Macuna?!"

"Here!"

"Enema and aspirin! - Pokorný?!"

"Here!"

"Flush out the stomach, and quinine! - Kovařík?!"

"Here!"

"Enema and aspirin! - Koťátko?!"

"Here!"

"Flush out the stomach, and quinine!"

And so it went, one after the other, without mercy, mechanically, briskly.

"Švejk?!"

"Here!"

Dr. Grünstein looked at the new addition.

"What's wrong with you?'

"I dutifully report that I have rheumatism!"

During the course of his medical career, Dr. Grünstein had become accustomed to being subtly ironic, which manner produced a more solid effect than shouting.

"Ah, rheumatism," he said toward Švejk, "then you have a tremendously serious illness. It really must be by chance getting rheumatism at a time when there is a World War and a man is to go in the military service. I think that this must make you feel terribly sorry."

"I dutifully report, Chief Medical Officer, Sir, that I do feel terribly sorry."

"There you have it, he feels sorry about it. That is tremendously nice of you, that you've remembered us with that rheumatism of yours just now. In peace time, such a poor guy undoubtedly runs around like a yeanling, but when a war breaks out, right away he's got rheumatism and right away his knees won't serve him. Don't your knees ache?"

"I dutifully report that they do ache."

"And you can't sleep for whole nights at a time, isn't that true? Rheumatism is a very dangerous, painful and serious illness. We've already had good experience here with rheumatics. Our absolute diet and our different manner of healing have proven to work very well. You will get healthier here much faster than in Piešťany[150] and you'll soon be marching off to a front-line position so well, that only the kicked-up dust will be left behind you to watch you go."

Turning to the ambulance NCO, the doctor said: "Write this down: Švejk, complete diet, flush out the stomach twice a day, once a day an enema and we'll see how it goes from there. For the time being, take him to the procedure room, flush out his stomach and give him, when he comes to, an enema, but give it to him really good, until he calls on all the saints, so that the rheumatism of his gets spooked and runs out of him."

Turning toward all the beds in the room, he then gave a little speech filled with nice and sensible sentences:

"Do not think that you're facing some ox that allows himself to be fooled every time. Your behavior will not throw me off balance in any way. I know that you all are malingerers, that you want to deserteer from the military service. And I am dealing with you accordingly. I've survived and outlived hundreds and hundreds of soldiers such as you. On these beds have lain a whole lot of men, who lacked nothing but military spirit. While their buddies were fighting in the field, they thought that they might roll around in a comfortable bed, getting hospital food, and wait until the war has blown over. But they made a damn colossal mistake, and all of you also will have made a damn colossal mistake. Twenty years from now, you'll still be screaming in your sleep when you dream of how you were malingering while here with me."

"I dutifully report, Chief Medical Officer, Sir," a faint voice squeaked from a bed by the window, "I am already healthy, I noticed last night already that my asthma has disappeared."

"Your name is?"

"Kovařík, I dutifully report Sir that I'm to get an enema."

"All right, you'll still get the enema for the road," decided Dr. Grünstein, "so that you don't complain that you were not getting treatment from us.

"So, and now all the sick men whose names I've called follow the ambulance NCO, so that each will get what he's got coming."

And so it was that each did get an honest portion, as it had been prescribed for him. And if some of them tried to influence those executing the doctor's orders by pleas or threats, that they would join the ambulance corps, and could be, that one day they too would in turn fall into their hands, Švejk held his own with courage.

"Don't spare me," he prodded the henchman, who was giving him an enema, "remember your oath. Even if your father or your own brother were lying here, give them an enema, not even batting an eye. Just think to yourself that Austria stands on such enemas, and victory is ours."

The next day during his rounds Dr. Grünstein asked Švejk how he liked being in the military hospital[152].

Švejk answered that it was an establishment both correct and noble. As a reward, he received the same as the day before, except for the aspirin and three powder capsules of quinine, which they emptied into water and told him to drink them up immediately.

Even Socrates[153] wasn't drinking his goblet of hemlock with such composure as Švejk, on whom Dr. Grünstein tried all his stages of torment, his quinine.

As they were wrapping Švejk in a wet bed sheet in the presence of the physician, Švejk answered his question, how did he like it now:

"I dutifully report Chief Medical Officer, Sir, that it is like being at the municipal swimming pavilion or at a spa by the sea."

"Do you still have rheumatism?"

"I dutifully report, Sir, that it refuses to get any better."

Švejk was then subjected to more torment.

At that time, the widow of an infantry general, Baroness von Botzenheim, had gone through a lot of trouble to search out the soldier, who was the subject of a news item published recently in the Bohemie, how he had them drive him in a wheelchair, he, an invalid, as he shouted "On against Belgrade!", which patriotic expression prompted the Bohemie's editors to call on its readers to take up collections for the benefit of this loyal hero invalid.

The Fateful Adventures of the Good Soldier Švejk

Through an inquiry at the police headquarters it was found at last, that it was Švejk, and after that locating him was easy. Baroness von Botzenheim brought along her lady companion, and a footman carrying a basket, and they rode to Hradčany.

The poor thing Baroness had no idea, what it meant, when somebody was laid up in the military hospital of a garrison prison. Her calling card opened the door of the prison and in the office they treated her with immense kindness, and in five minutes she already knew that "the good and courageous soldier Švejk," about whom she inquired, was lying in the third barrack, bed number 17. Dr. Grünstein himself, who was silly from it all, went with her.

Švejk was just then sitting on the bed following the usual daily therapy prescribed by Dr. Grünstein, surrounded by a group of emaciated and starved malingerers, who had yet not given up and were tenaciously wrestling with Dr. Grünstein in the arena of complete diet.

Anyone listening to them would have had the impression he found himself in the company of culinary experts, in an advanced chef's school, or attending a course for gourmets.

"Even the lowly suet cracklings are edible", narrated just then one lying here with 'a neglected inflammation of the stomach', "if they're warm. When the suet is rendered down, the cracklings should be squeezed until dry, salted, peppered, and I'm telling you that goose cracklings can't equal them."

"Leave goose cracklings out of it," said a man with 'stomach cancer', "nothing tops goose cracklings. Ones made from pork lard just can't touch them. It goes without saying that they must be rendered until goldish, like the Jews do it. They'll take a fat goose and strip the fat with the skin and render it down."

"Do you know that you are mistaken when it comes to pork cracklings?" remarked Švejk's neighbor, "then again, I'm talking about cracklings from home-made lard, as they're called home-made cracklings. Not of a brown color, but also not yellow. They must be something between those two hues. Such a crackling can't be either too soft, or too hard. It can't be crunchy, or then it's overdone and burnt. It must dissolve on the tongue and as it's happening you must not have the impression, that you have lard running down on your chin."

"Who among you has eaten cracklings from horse lard?" somebody's voice was heard, but nobody gave an answer because an ambulance NCO ran in: "Everybody in bed, some archduchess is coming here, and nobody better show his dirty feet from under the blanket!"

Not even an archduchess could have entered as solemnly as did Baroness von Botzenheim. Behind her was rolling in a whole procession, which wouldn't be complete without the hospital's accounting master sergeant, who saw in all of it the mysterious hand of an inspection, which would take him from his fat trough in the rear and deliver him as a desert to the shrapnel and barbed wire of the front-line positions.

He was pale, but even paler was Dr. Grünstein. Dancing in front of his eyes was the small calling card of the old Baroness, with the title "a general's widow", and all that, which could be associated with that title, like connections, access, complaints, transfer to the front or other horrible things.

"Here we have Švejk," he said, maintaining an artificial calm, leading Baroness von Botzenheim to Švejk's bed, "he behaves very patiently."

Baroness von Botzenheim sat down on a chair placed next to Švejk's bed for her and said:

"Chekie zauldjer, gooht zauldjer. Kreepl zauldjer, be kahreyjes zauldjer. I luf veree moch zee Chekie Austrian."

All along she was caressing Švejk's unshaven cheek and continued:

"I reed ohl in zee paypehr. I breeng you munchie, bitie, smokie, suckie, Czekie zauldjer, gooht zauldjer. *Johann, come here!*"

The footman, by his bristly side-burns evoking the image of Babinský[154], dragged a voluminous basket to the bed, while the old Baroness' lady companion, a tall dame with her eyes cried out, sat on Švejk's bed and straightened out the straw pillow under his back, being fixated on the idea that this was the proper thing to do for sick heroes.

The Baroness was in the meantime pulling her gifts out of the basket. A dozen roasted chickens wrapped in pink silken paper and bound by a black-and-yellow silk ribbon, two bottles of some war-time liqueur with the label *"God punish England*[155]*!"*. On the other side the label bore a picture of Franz Josef and Kaiser Wilhelm[156], holding hands, as if they wanted to play "Bunny is sitting in his little hollow all alone; what's ailing you, poor little one, that you can't be jumping up and down."[157]

Next she pulled out three bottles of wine for the convalescents, and two boxes of cigarettes. She spread everything elegantly on the empty bed next to Švejk, whereto was also added a nicely bound book entitled Stories from the Life of Our Monarch, which was written by the current and esteemed editor-in-chief[158] of our official newspaper Czechoslovak Republic[159], who doted on the old Frankie, of whom he saw much in himself. Then packets of chocolate appeared on the bed, with the identical inscription *"God punish England!"* and again with the likenesses of the Austrian and German emperors. On the chocolate they were not holding hands anymore and each kept to himself, showing each other their backs. Nice was the double-row toothbrush with the inscription "Viribus unitis,"[160] so that everybody, who is brushing his teeth, would think on Austria. An elegant and very fitting little gift for the front and the trenches was the set for cleaning finger and toe nails. On the box was a picture of a shell bursting and a man in a coner[161] rushing forward with a bayonet. Underneath it: *"For God, the Emperor, and the Fatherland!"*

No picture was on the package of cookies, but there was a verse:

Österreich, du edles Haus,
Österreich steck deine Fahne aus,
lass sie im Winde weh'n,
Österreich muss ewig stehn!

with the Czech translation placed on the reverse side:

Austria, you noble house,
Austria, hang out your flag,
Let it wave in the wind
Austria must stand forever!

The last gift was a hyacinth in a flowerpot.

When all of it lay unwrapped on the bed, Baroness von Botzenheim was so moved she could not hold back tears. Several starved malingerers had saliva drooling from their mouths. The lady companion of the Baroness was propping up the seated Švejk and was also shedding tears. There was church-like silence, which Švejk suddenly interrupted, having clasped his hands:

"Our Father, who art in heaven, hallowed be Thy name, Thy kingdom come...pardon me, gracious lady, that's not it, I wanted to say: Lord God, heavenly Father, bless for us these gifts, which from

Thy generous bounty we're about to consume. Amen!"

After these words he took off the bed a chicken and tore into it, being watched by the horrified glare of Dr. Grünstein.

"Ah, the soldier boy is so enjoying it," whispered the old Baroness with enthusiasm to Dr. Grünstein, "he is certainly healthy already and can go into the field. I am really very glad how this came just in time for him."

Then she went from bed to bed handing out cigarettes and chocolate pralines, and returned from her stroll to Švejk again, stroked his hair with the words *"God protect you all,"* and led her whole procession out of the door.

Before Dr. Grünstein returned from downstairs, where he went accompanying the Baroness, Švejk passed out the chickens, which were devoured by the patients with such speed, that instead of chickens Dr. Grünstein found a pile of bones, gnawed so clean, that it looked as if the chickens had fallen alive into a nest of vultures, and on their gnawed-clean bones the roasting sun beat down for several months.

What had also disappeared were the war-time liqueur, and the three bottles of wine. In the stomachs of the patients had also disappeared the packets of chocolate, and the package of cookies. Somebody even drank up a vial of nail polish, found in the manicure set, and took a bite out of the toothpaste enclosed with the toothbrush.

When Dr. Grünstein returned he again assumed fighting stance and made a long speech. It was as if a rock of burden fell off his heart when the visitor had left. The pile of bones gnawed clean hardened his view that they were all incorrigible.

"Soldiers," he launched, "if you had half a brain, you would have left it all alone and thought to yourselves: if we devour it, the chief medical officer won't believe that we are seriously sick. You yourselves have hereby given testimony that you don't appreciate my goodness. I pump your stomachs, I give you enemas, I'm trying to make you stick to a complete diet, and you overstuff your stomachs on me. Do you want to get a stomach catarrh[162]? You are mistaken, before your stomach even tries to digest it, I'll clean it out for you so thoroughly, that you'll be recalling the memories of it as long as you live and you'll be the last one to die, and you'll still be telling your children how you once devoured chicken and gorged yourselves on other various goodies, but how it didn't stay in your stomach for even a quarter of an hour, because we pumped your stomach out while it was still warm. And now file behind me one after the other, so you won't think that I'm some kind of an ox like you, but in the end a little bit smarter than all of you put together. Besides that I'm letting you know, that tomorrow I'll send the commission here to sic them on you, because you've been lying around here too long and none of you has anything wrong with him, since you can in a few of those minutes mess up your stomachs and turn them into swine-filth so nicely, as you have just managed. So forward, march!"

When Švejk's turn came, Dr. Grünstein looked at him and some sort of reminiscence of the day's mysterious visit forced him to ask: "Do you know her ladyship, the Baroness?"

"She's my stepmother," answered Švejk calmly, "when I was of tender age, she ditched me and now she's found me again…"

Dr. Grünstein said tersely: "Afterward give Švejk again an enema."

In the evening sadness reigned on the bunks. Several hours earlier, they all had in their stomachs various good and tasty things, and now, all they had in there were weak tea and a slice of bread.

From near the window, number 21 let himself be heard:

"Would you guys believe that I prefer fried over roasted chicken?"

Somebody growled: "Give him the blanket treatment," but they were all so weak after the ill-fated banquet, that nobody made a move.

Dr. Grünstein kept his word. In the forenoon came several military physicians from the renowned commission.

They solemnly went through the rows of beds and nothing else could be heard but "Show your tongue!"

Švejk stuck his tongue out so far that his face contorted into a weird grimace and his eyes squinted shut:

"I dutifully report Command Medical Officer, Sir, that I can't make my tongue any longer than that."

An interesting discourse commenced between Švejk and the commission. Švejk claimed that he made the remark fearing they would think he was hiding his tongue from them.

As for the members of the commission, they differed superbly among themselves in their judgments of Švejk.

Half of them insisted that Švejk was *"an idiotic guy,"* while the other half claimed he was a rogue, who wanted to make fun of the military service.

"There'd have to be the devil's thunder in this," screamed at Švejk the chairman of the commission, "if we were not to get the best of you!"

Švejk watched the whole commission with the divine calm of an innocent child.

The Command Chief Physician stepped within an inch of Švejk: "I'd like to know, you sea pig, just what you're thinking now."

"I dutifully report that I'm not thinking at all."

"*Heaven's thunderstorm!*" hollered one of the members of the commission, clanking his saber, "so he doesn't think at all. Why is it, you Siamese[163] elephant you, that you don't think?"

"I dutifully report that the reason I don't, Sir, is, that it is forbidden for soldiers in the military service to think. When years ago I was with the 91st Regiment, our mister Captain would always say: 'A soldier must not think on his own. His superiors think for him. As soon as a soldier starts thinking, he's not a soldier anymore, but some kind of mangy civilian. Thinking doesn't lead…'"

"Shut your trap!" the chairman of the commission interrupted Švejk furiously, "we've already got the word about you. This guy thinks: they'll believe that I'm a real idiot… You're no idiot, Švejk, you're smart, you're cunning, you're a scoundrel, a street punk, a louse, you understand…"

"I dutifully report that I understand."

"I've already told you to keep your trap shut, didn't you hear me?"

"I dutifully report, that I've heard to keep my trap shut."

"*Heavenly-lord-God*, then keep the trap shut, since I ordered you, you know well, that you're not to talk back."

"I dutifully report, that I know, that I must not talk back."

The military overlords looked at one another and called in the Master Sergeant. "You will escort this man", said the Command Chief Physician of the commission pointing at Švejk, "down to the office and wait there for our message and report. At the garrison prison they'll knock that talking back out of his head already. The guy's as healthy as can be, he's malingering and talks back on top of it and makes fun of his superiors. He thinks that they are here just for his amusement and that the whole military is fun, a thing of merriment. Švejk, they will show you at the garrison prison, that military service is no shitty joke."

Švejk was on the way with the Master Sergeant going to the office, and on the path across the yard to the office he hummed for himself:

I've always thought to myself,

that military service was fun,
that I'd be there for a week or two,
then home again I'd run...

And while in the office the duty officer was screaming at Švejk, that such guys like Švejk should be shot, the commission upstairs in the hospital rooms was slaying the malingerers. Of seventy patients, only two saved themselves. One, whose leg had been blown off by a grenade, and another with a real bone-eating disease.

Only these two didn't hear the little phrase *"fit for duty"*, all the rest, not excepting even the three dying of consumption, were acknowledged as being capable of service in the field, while the Command Chief Physician didn't miss this great opportunity for a rhetorical exercise.

His speech was interspersed with quite a variety of epithets and as for content it was brief. All of them are cattle beasts and dung, and only if they will fight courageously for the lord Emperor can they return to the human society, and only after the war will they be forgiven for wanting to get out of military service and malingering. He himself however doesn't believe it and thinks that rope awaits them all.

Some young military physician, a pure of soul and yet unspoiled, asked the Command Chief for permission to speak too. His speech differed from his superior's by optimism and naiveté. He spoke in German.

He spoke at length about how each of those leaving the hospital to be with their regiments in the field must become victors and knights. That he is convinced they will be skilled at arms, on the battlefield, and honest in all matters of war and private lives as well. That they will be invincible warriors, mindful of the glory of Radetzky and prince Eugen of Savoy[164]. That they will make fertile, with their blood, the monarchy's wide fields of glory and victoriously fulfill the role, which history had foreordained for them. With daring courage, disdaining their lives they will rush forward under their regiments' banners shot full of holes, toward new glory, toward new victories.

Afterward, in the corridor, the Command Chief Physician told this naive, young man: "My dear colleague, I can assure you that it is all in vain. Not even Radetzky or your prince Eugen of Savoy could turn those hoodlums into soldiers. Speaking to them in an angelic or demonic manner, it's all the same. They're a bunch of gangsters."

9

ŠVEJK IN THE GARRISON PRISON

The last refuge of people, who didn't want to go to war, was the garrison prison. I knew a substitute teacher who, as a mathematician, didn't want to shoot at others with the artillery and that was why he stole a watch from a senior lieutenant just to get into the garrison prison. He did so with deliberate forethought. The war neither impressed nor enchanted him. Shooting at the enemy and killing equally unlucky substitute teachers and mathematicians on the other side by shrapnel and grenades, he viewed as idiocy.

"I don't want to be hated for my violence," he said to himself and calmly stole the watch. First they probed into his mental state, and when he declared, that he wanted to enrich himself, they transported him to the garrison prison.

There were a few more such people, who were doing time in garrison prison for theft or fraud. Idealists and non-idealists. People, who viewed the war as a source of income, the various accountant NCOs both in the rear and at the front, who committed all possible manner of fraud with supplies and with the soldiers' pay, and then the simple petty thieves, a thousand times more honest than the guys, who sent them in here. Next, also sitting in garrison prison were soldiers doing time for various other infractions of purely military nature, breeches of discipline, attempts at mutiny, and desertion. Then a peculiar type were the politicals, of whom eighty percent were completely innocent, and of whom again ninety-nine percent were found guilty and sentenced.

The apparatus of the auditors was grandiose. Such judicial machinery is in the possession of every government of any country before a comprehensive political, economic and moral crash. The radiance of bygone might and glory bolsters these courts, as well as the local police, the State Police, and all the whoring informer scum.

In every part of the military Austria had its snoops, ratting on the comrades, who slept on the same bunks with them and shared bread with them on the march.

The State Police supplied material also to the garrison prison — Messrs. Klíma, Slavíček & Co.[165] The military censor incarcerated the authors of correspondence between the front and those they left behind in desperation at home. This is where the state policemen would bring in even old retired farmers, who sent letters to the front, and the military courts hung the noose of twelve years in prison around each of their necks for their words of solace and describing their domestic misery.

One path from the Hradčany prison led also through Břevnov to the military training grounds in Motol[166]. In the lead of a procession of bayonets would walk a man with chains on his wrists and behind him a cart with a coffin. And at the Motol training ground, a brusque order: "*Ready-aim! Fire!*" And at all the regiments and battalions they read the regimental orders of the day, that a soldier was shot for mutiny when he was drafted, and a mister captain used his saber to cut down his wife, who had a hard time letting go of him.

At the garrison prison, the trio of Garrison Staff Warden Slavík, Captain Linhart, and Master Sergeant Řepa, also known as "The Executioner," was fulfilling its role. How many had they beaten to death in the solitary! Could be, that today Linhart is still, even in this new Republic, a captain. I wish that he would get credit for his years of service at the garrison prison. Slavíček and Klíma, of the State Police, have had them credited. Řepa has returned to civilian life and continues to perform his job as a masons' foreman. Could be, he got it because he's a member of patriotic associations in the Republic.

Garrison Staff Warden Slavík became a thief in the Republic and today he's incarcerated. The poor soul has not cast his anchor as well in the Republic as many other military bosses have.

*

It is quite natural that Garrison Staff Warden Slavík, when accepting Švejk into his custody, shot at him a look full of mute reproach:

"Your reputation is so wrecked that you made it all the way here into our midst? Well, little boy, we will sweeten your stay here like we do for all, who have fallen into our hands, and those hands of ours are not some ladies' little hands."

To add weight to the look he cast, he then put his muscular fist under Švejk's nose and said:

"Take a whiff, you hoodlum!"

Švejk took a whiff and remarked:

"I wouldn't like to get it in the nose with this one, it has the fragrance of a cemetery."

His calm, deliberate speech struck a chord with the Garrison Staff Warden.

"Ha," he said, poking Švejk in the belly with his fist, "stand straight, what do you have in your pockets? If you have a cigarette, then you can keep it, money you'll turn over, so nobody would steal it from you. You don't have more? Really, you don't? Don't lie, a lie gets you punished."

"Where are we going to put him?" asked Master Sergeant Řepa.

"We'll put him in the sixteen," decided the Garrison Staff Warden, "among the ones in long johns, can't you see that Captain Linhart wrote on his file *Watch! Closely guard!*? — "Oh yeah," he proclaimed festively to Švejk, "dealing with scum, you've got to use a scum bag. If somebody resists, then we drag him into solitary and break all his ribs there for him, until he croaks. We've got the right to do that. Like we did with that butcher, remember, Řepa?"

"Well, he sure made us work, Garrison Staff Warden, Sir," answered dreamily Master Sergeant Řepa, "what a body! I stomped all over him for five minutes before his ribs started cracking and blood pouring out of his snout. And he still lived another ten days. Almost a perfect diehard."

"So you see, you hoodlum, how it goes here when somebody resists," Garrison Staff Warden Slavík was winding down his pedagogic exposition, "or when he wants to escape. It is then actually a suicide, which here at our place, is also punished. Or God forbid, you little shithead, you get an idea, when the inspection detail shows up, to complain about something. When the inspectors show up and ask: 'Do you have any complaints?' then you must, you stench, stand at attention, give a salute and answer: 'I dutifully report that I don't and that I'm totally satisfied.' — How will you say it, you vile filth, repeat it!"

"I dutifully report that I don't and that I'm totally satisfied," Švejk repeated it with such a lovable expression on his face, that the Garrison Staff Warden mistook it to be a sincere effort and honesty.

"So strip down to your long johns and you're going to number sixteen," he said amiably, without adding hoodlum, vile filth or a stench, as he was accustomed to doing.

In the number sixteen Švejk met nineteen other men with no pants. These were all those, on whose files there was the written note *"Watch! Closely guard!"* and who were now looked after caringly, so they wouldn't run away.

If their underwear had been clean, and if there were no bars on the windows, at first glance you might get the impression that you were in the locker room of some spa.

Švejk was handed over from Master Sergeant Řepa to the room unit commander, an unshaven man in an open shirt. He wrote down his name on a piece of paper hanging on the wall and told him:

"Tomorrow we've got a great theater going on here. They will escort us to the chapel[167] for a sermon. All of us in long johns must stand right under the pulpit. Wait until you see what fun it will be!"

As in all jails and penitentiaries, so in this garrison prison the in-house chapel enjoyed great popularity. It was not that the mandatory visit to the prison chapel would bring the visitors closer to God, or that the prisoners would learn more about morality. There can't even be any talk of such silliness.

The divine services and the sermons were a nice break from the boredom of the garrison prison. It wasn't about being closer to God, but that on the way there was the hope of finding in the corridors and crossing the yard a piece of a tossed away cigarette or cigar. God was completely shoved off to the wayside by a little butt lying hopelessly in a spittoon, or somewhere on the ground in the dust. That little stinking object conquered God and the salvation of the soul.

And then yet the sermon the entertainment and the fun. The Field Chaplain Otto Katz was after all, a delightful man. His sermons were unusually riveting, funny, and refreshing in the boredom of the garrison prison. He was so good at babbling about the endless mercy of God, strengthening the debauched prisoners and dishonored men. He was so good at delivering a beautiful tongue-lashing from both the pulpit and the altar. He was so good at wonderfully screaming out his *"Go, the mass is ended,"* performing the whole divine service in an original manner and mixing up the whole sequence of the Holy Mass, inventing, when he was really drunk, completely new prayers, his own rite, something that the world had never seen before.

And then the fun when sometimes he slipped and fell with the chalice, or with the exalted sacrament or with the missal, and loudly accusing the penal company's altar boy of purposefully tripping him, and immediately, in front of the very exalted sacrament, he would slam him with the solitary and manacles.

And the afflicted man is joyful, because he is part of the fun in the convicts' chapel. He plays a great role in the schtik and acquitted himself with dignity.

Field Chaplain Otto Katz, the most perfect of military chaplains, was a Jew. That, by the way, is not at all odd. Archbishop Kohn[168] was also a Jew, and a friend of Machar[169], to boot.

Field Chaplain Otto Katz had an even more checkered past than the famous Archbishop Kohn.

He studied at a business academy[170] and served in the army as a one-year volunteer. He was so well versed in the laws of bills-of-exchange and in using these money drafts, that in one year he was able to force the firm of Katz & Co. into bankruptcy so famous and accomplished, that the old mister Katz left for North America[171], having finagled some settlement with his creditors without the knowledge of the latter or of his associate, who left for Argentina[172].

So when the young Otto Katz had unselfishly bestowed the gift of the firm of Katz & Co. upon America, both North and South[173], he found himself in the situation of a man, who had absolutely nothing to inherit, who didn't know where he might lay his head, and who must get himself on active duty in the military service.

Prior to that, however, One-Year Volunteer Otto Katz had thought up an immensely famous thing. He had himself baptized. He turned to Christ, so that He would help him land a successful career. He turned to Him with absolute trust, that it was a business matter between himself and the Son of God.

They baptized him ceremoniously at the Emmaus Monastery. Father Alban[174] himself dunked Katz in the baptismal font. It was a gorgeous show, also present were a religious major from the regiment where Otto Katz served, an old maid from the institute of noblewomen in Hradčany, and some bulldog-faced representative of the consistory[175], who stood up as his godfather.

The officer exam turned out well and the new Christian, Otto Katz, stayed in the military. At first it seemed to him it would go well, he even wanted to pursue studying Command Staff Courses.

But one day he got drunk and went to a monastery, turned in his saber, and put on the frock. He visited the archbishop at Hradčany and got into a seminary[176]. He got smashed before his ordination at a very solid house[177] with ladies' service staff in the alley behind the Vejvodas'[178], and straight from the vortex of sensual pleasure and entertainment he went to get himself ordained. After he was ordained, he sought refuge in the protection of his regiment, and when he was appointed as field chaplain, he bought a horse and would crisscross through Prague and partake merrily in all the drinking bouts with the officers of his regiment.

In the hallway of the building, where he had his apartment, the sound of curses of unsatisfied creditors could often be heard. He would also keep bringing girls into the apartment from the street or send his military servant to fetch them. He very much liked to play ferbl[179], and some made suppositions and assumptions that he cheated, but no one ever proved that he had hidden an ace in the wide sleeve of his military cassock. In the officers' circles, they called him holy father.

He never prepared for his sermons, in which regard he differed greatly from his predecessor, who also used to visit the garrison prison. That one was a man, who suffered from a fixation, that troops locked in a garrison prison could be reformed from the pulpit. That honorable chaplain would roll his eyes piously and tell the locked up men, that reform of harlots, reform of the care for unwed mothers were a necessity, and speak of bringing up children born out of wedlock. His sermons were of an abstract nature and had no connection at all to the current situation, were boring.

In contrast, Field Chaplain Otto Katz preached sermons that everyone looked forward to.

It was a festive moment when they escorted the room sixteen in long johns into the chapel, because dressing them posed a risk, that one of them would get lost. They stood the twenty white long johns and angels under the pulpit. Some of them, to whom lady luck had given a fleeting smile, were chewing the cigar butts they had found on the way, because they didn't have — naturally — pockets and there was nowhere to hide the things.

Around them stood the rest of the garrison prison's inmates and amused themselves by gawking at the twenty long johns under the pulpit, up into which climbed the Field Chaplain, clanking his spurs.

"*Attention!*" he yelled, "let us pray, everyone repeat after me what I'm saying! And you in the back, you hoodlum, don't blow your nose into your hand, you are in the temple of the Lord, I can have you locked up for that. Could it be, you rascals, that you have also forgotten your Our Father? Then, let's try it — — — Well, I knew you couldn't do it. No way the Our Father, maybe two portions of meat and bean salad, gorge yourselves, lie belly down on your bunks, pick your noses and not think of the Lord God, am I not right?"

He looked down from the pulpit at the twenty white angels in long johns, who were tremendously entertained, as was everyone else. In the back they were playing meat[180]!

"It is very good," whispered Švejk to his neighbor on whom stuck the suspicion, that for three crowns he had cut all the fingers off his friend's hand with an axe, so that he could get out of the military service.

"The best is yet to come," was the response, "today he is again properly blasted, so he'll be talking about the thorny path of sin."

The Field Chaplain was today indeed in an excellent disposition. Even he didn't know why he was doing it, but he kept leaning over from the pulpit and could have easily lost his balance and fallen off.

"Sing something boys," he yelled down, "or do you want me to teach you a new song? Then sing along with me:

> Of all, the most beloved
> is the love I have,
> I don't go after her alone,
> many more also pursue her,
> of lovers she has thousands,
> and my most beloved
> is the Virgin Mary — — —

"You churls, you'll never learn it," the Field Chaplain continued, "I'm for having you all mowed down by guns; do you understand me well?! I declare it from this divine spot, you scoundrels, because God is something that is not afraid of you and will tear into you so, that you will become dimwits from it all, because you hesitate to turn to Christ and you choose to walk down the thorny path of sin."

"It's here already, he's properly tanked," whispered joyfully to Švejk the man next to him.

"The thorny path of sin, you stupid boys, is the path of battle against vices. You are prodigal sons, who would rather lie around the solitary than return to the Father. Only farther and higher train your sight into the lofty heavens and you'll be victorious and peace will make a home in your soul, you street punks. Now I must insist that whoever it is in the back that's snoring and neighing must stop. He is not a horse, and he is not in a stable, he is in the temple of the Lord. I bring that to your attention, you little darlings of mine. So wherever did I stop. *Yes, about the peace in the soul, very good.* Remember, you depraved animals, that you are human and that you have to look even through the dark cloud and into distant space and know, that everything here lasts only for a time, but that God is forever. *Very good, is it not, my gentlemen?* I should be praying day and night for you, so that the merciful God, you stupid boys, would pour His Soul into your cold hearts and with his Holy Grace wash away your sins, so that you would be His forever and so He would love you rascals, always. But you are mistaken. I will not be ushering you into that paradise —" The Field Chaplain burped. "And I won't," he repeated stubbornly, "I won't do anything for you, it won't even occur to me, because you are all incorrigible scoundrels. You won't be guided on your paths by the goodness of the Lord, the breath of God's love won't waft through you, because it won't even occur to the beloved Lord God to deal with such rogues. Do you hear that, you down here in those long johns?"

Twenty long johns looked up and said as in one voice:

"We dutifully report, that we hear."

"It's not enough just to hear," continued his sermon the Field Chaplain, "the dark cloud of life, in which a divine smile won't take away your sorrow, you numbskulls, because the goodness of God has also its limits, and you, the mule in the back, don't look like you're choking with laughter, or I'll have you locked up until you turn black. And you all down there, don't think that you're in a pub. God is merciful to the utmost, but only for proper people, and not for some outcasts of a society, which does not administer itself by His laws or even by the service regulations. That's what I wanted to tell you. You don't know how to pray and you think coming to the chapel is part of some kind of fun, that this is some theatrical production or moving picture show. And I'll chase these thoughts right out of your head, so that you don't think that I'm here to entertain you or to add some joy to your life. I'll assign you all to seats in solitary, that's what I'll do with you, you hoodlums! I waste my time with you and see, that it's all in vain. That even if the Field Marshall or the Archbishop himself was here, you wouldn't repent, wouldn't turn to God. And yet one day you will remember me and know that I intended to do well by you."

In the midst of the twenty long johns, loud sobbing was heard. It was Švejk, who had burst into tears.

The Field Chaplain looked down. There stood Švejk, wiping his eyes with his fist. All around him could be seen signs of joyous approval.

Pointing to Švejk, the Field Chaplain continued:

"Let everyone have this man for an example. What is he doing? He's weeping. Don't weep, I'm telling you, don't weep. You want to change for the better? You won't accomplish that so easily, boy. Now you're weeping, and when you return to your room, you'll be just the same kind of hoodlum as you were before. You must still dwell on the ceaseless grace and mercy of God, take great care, in order to enable your sinning soul to find the right path, on which it is to tread. Today we see that one man of ours here has broken into tears and wants to repent, and what are the rest of you doing? Nothing at all. That one over there is chewing something, as if his parents were ruminants, and over there they're searching in the temple of God for lice in their shirts. Can't you at all scratch yourselves at home and do you have to leave it to do right now, during divine services? Mister Garrison Staff Warden, you too don't pay attention and notice anything. After all, you're all supposed to be soldiers, and not some numbskull civilians. You are supposed to behave as becomes soldiers, even if you are in a church. Get going, goddamit, searching for God, and for lice search at home. With that, I'm done you street punks, and I'm asking you to behave properly during the mass, so it won't happen like the last time, when in the back they were trading government issue linen for bread and feeding on it during the Elevation of the Host."

The Field Chaplain descended from the pulpit and went into the sacristy whereto he was followed by the Garrison Staff Warden. A short time later the Garrison Staff Warden reemerged, turned directly to Švejk, pulled him out of the group of twenty long johns and escorted him into the sacristy.

The Field Chaplain was sitting very comfortably on a desk, and was rolling a cigarette for himself.

When Švejk entered, the Field Chaplain said:

"So here you are. I have already thought everything over and I think I have seen right through you good and proper, do you understand me, man? This is the first case of anybody to have ever broken into tears here in church for me."

He jumped off the desk and jerking Švejk by the shoulder he was screaming from under a big, gloomy painting of Francis de Sales[181]:

"Confess, hoodlum, were you bawling like that just for fun?!"

And Francis de Sales gazed quizzically from the painting at Švejk. From the other side, from another picture, stared at Švejk dumbfoundingly some martyr, who just then had in his butt the teeth of a saw, with which some unknown Roman mercenaries were sawing him. In the face of the martyr at the same time wasn't discernible any suffering, or joy or martyr's glow. He only looked dumbfounded, as if wanting to ask: How have I gotten myself into this, what is this, gentlemen, that you are doing to me?

"I dutifully report, Field Chaplain, Sir," Švejk said measuredly, betting everything on one card, "that I am confessing to God Almighty and to you, Reverend Father, you, who stands in God's place, that I bawled really just for fun. I saw that your sermon lacked only a reformed sinner, whom you searched for in vain during your sermon. So I wanted really to make you happy, so you wouldn't think that there were not to be found any righteous people anymore, and for myself I wanted to make some fun, to lighten my misery."

The Field Chaplain cast a probing look at the simpleminded face of Švejk's. A ray of sun frolicked on the gloomy picture of Francis de Sales and gently warmed up the dumbfounded martyr on the opposite wall.

"I'm beginning to like you," the Field Chaplain said, taking a seat again on the desk. "Which regiment do you belong to?" He began to hiccup.

"I dutifully report, Field Chaplain, Sir, that I both belong and don't belong to the 91st Regiment, that I don't know at all, what my situation actually is."

"Why is it actually you are sitting here doing time?" asked the Field Chaplain, unable to stop his hiccups.

From the chapel carried the sounds of a harmonium, substituting for an organ. The musician, a teacher locked up for desertion, was wailing on the harmonium with the most nostalgic of church melodies. Those sounds were fusing with the field chaplain's hiccups into an entirely new Doric scale.

"I dutifully report Field Chaplain, Sir, that I really don't know why I'm sitting here, and that I'm not complaining that I'm sitting here. I just only have bad luck. I always mean to do everything right and in the end it all turns on me for the worse, like on the martyr in that painting."

The Field Chaplain looked at the picture, smiled, and said:

"I really like you, I'll have to ask the judge advocate about you and now I'm done talking to you. I can't wait to be done with this Holy Mass! *About face! Fall out!*"

When Švejk returned to his native group of long johns under the pulpit, he answered the questions of what it was the Field Chaplain wanted to see him about in the sacristy, very dryly and succinctly:

"He's blasted."

The latest performance of Field Chaplain's, the Holy Mass, was being observed by all with great attention and open sympathy. One under the pulpit even bet another that the Field Chaplain would drop the monstrance from his hand. He bet his whole portion of bread against two slaps in the face and he won.

That, which filled the souls of all those watching the rituals of the Field Chaplain, was not the mysticism of the faithful or the piety of genuine Catholics. It was a feeling such as being in a theater, when we don't know the content of the play, the plot is becoming entangled and we are eagerly waiting to see how, it will evolve. They immersed themselves in the scene, which was being provided for them with great selflessness by the Field Chaplain at the altar.

They devoted themselves to feasting esthetically on the chasuble[182], which the Field Chaplain had put on inside out, and with fervent attention and a high level of excitement watched everything that was taking place at the altar.

The red-haired altar boy, a deserter from the orbit of the Church, a specialist of petty thefts at the 28th Regiment[183], struggled honestly to recall from memory the whole process, technique and text of the Holy Mass. He was serving concurrently as both the altar boy and the prompter for the Field Chaplain, who with total carelessness was transposing whole sentences and instead of ordinary mass, he got in the missal all the way to the Advent morning service songs, which he started singing to the universal delight of his audience.

He had neither the voice, nor musical ear and under the vaulting of the chapel resounded such squealing and shrieking, as in a pig sty.

"He sure is drunk today," said with full satisfaction and joy those in front of the altar, "he's tied one on. It seized him big time again! For sure he got smashed around the broads somewhere."

And for perhaps the third time already came from the altar the sound of the Field Chaplain's singing *"Go, the Mass is ended!"* like the war cry of the Red Indians, until the windows were rattling.

After that the Field Chaplain looked one more time into the chalice, in case there might be after all a drop of wine left, gestured as if annoyed and turned to his listeners:

"All right already, you hoodlums, you can go home now, it's over. I observed that you were not showing the genuine piety, which you are to have, when you're in church, in the presence of the face of the holiest sacrament of the altar, you street punks. Though you are face-to-face with the Highest God, you're not ashamed to laugh out loud, cough, clear your throats, or shuffle your feet, even in front of me, who represents the Virgin Mary, Christ the Lord, and God the Father, you jerks. If this happens again next time, I'll nail you all proper and so that you'll know, that there isn't only one hell, the one I preached to you about the last time, but that there is also a hell on Earth, and even if you might be able to save yourselves from that first one, from the second one you won't save yourself to avoid me. *Fall out!*"

The Field Chaplain, who so beautifully and in practice explained that damned old thing about visiting prisoners, left for the sacristy, changed his clothes and had them pour the church wine from a demijohn into a jug, drank it up and with the help of the red-haired altar boy, he mounted his cavalry horse tied up in the yard, but then he remembered Švejk, dismounted and went into the office to see the military Judge Advocate Bernis.

The Investigating Judge Advocate Bernis was a social man, charming dancer and moral degenerate that was awfully bored, wrote German verses for girls' memorial albums, just to have a ready supply on hand at all times. He was the most important component in the whole machinery of the military court, because he had such a horrible quantity of unfinished cases and confused files, that he commanded the respect of the entire Chief Military Court in Hradčany. He would constantly lose the prosecution's material and was forced to invent new one. He would switch names, lose the threads leading to indictments and spin new ones, as they might occur to him. He judged deserters for theft and thieves for desertion. He could jumble up even political trials, which he could pull from thin air. He conducted a wide assortment of hocus-pocus sessions to convict men accused of crimes they would never even dream of. He invented insults against His Majesty and would always attribute the made-up, incriminating statements to someone, whose indictment or denunciation of him had been lost in the continuous chaos of his official files and memoranda.

"Greetings," said the Field Chaplain, extending his hand, "How is it going?"

"Not too well," answered the Investigating Judge Advocate Bernis, "they have mixed up my material so much, that even a demon couldn't find his way through it. Yesterday I sent material upstairs, that had already been processed, regarding a man accused of mutiny, and they returned it, that the case against him was not mutiny, but a theft of a can of food. And I had even put a different number on it, but how they ever got their hands on it, only God knows." The Judge Advocate spat.

"Do you still go out and play cards?" asked the Field Chaplain.

"I've lost everything playing cards; the last time we played Macau[184] with that bald colonel and I ended up stuffing all my money down his gullet. But I know of a girl. And what have you been doing, holy father?"

"I need an orderly," said the Field Chaplain, "the last one I had was a really old accountant without academic education, but a first-class dumb beast. He only whined constantly and prayed for God to protect him, so I sent him to a march-battalion headed for the front. The word is, that battie[185] was completely shredded. Then they sent me some guy, who wouldn't do anything, but sit in a pub all day and drink on my account. He was still bearable, but his feet sweat. So I sent him with a march-battalion as well. Today during the sermon I found a man, who broke out in tears on me, just for fun. I need a man like that. His name is Švejk and he's sitting in the sixteen. I would like to know why they locked him up and whether it could somehow be arranged, so I could take him out of here."

The Judge Advocate looked through his drawers for a file on Švejk, but as usual he couldn't find anything.

"Captain Linhart will have it," he said after a long search, "only demons know, where all the files here with me disappear to. Apparently I sent them to Linhart. I'll phone over there immediately — — — Hello, this is Senior Lieutenant Judge Advocate Bernis, Captain, Sir. I beg to ask, whether you might not have files there regarding someone Švejk... That Švejk has to be here with me? I'm surprised... That I accepted the transfer from you? I'm really surprised... He's sitting in the sixteen. I know, Captain, Sir, that I have the sixteen. But I thought, that the files on Švejk were lying around over there by you somewhere... That you object to my speaking to you like that? That there's nothing lying around over there? Hello, hello..."

Judge Advocate Bernis sat down at the desk and angrily decried the disorder in how investigations were being conducted. Between him and Captain Linhart had long reigned animosity, in which they were both very thorough. Should a file belonging to Linhart get into the hands of Bernis, Bernis would file it in such a way, that nobody could make any sense of it. Linhart would do the same with the files belonging to Bernis. They kept losing each other's addenda.*

---

* Thirty percent of the people, who were sitting and doing time in the garrison prison, sat there throughout the whole war without going to interrogation once.

(Švejk's records were eventually found in the archives of the Military Court, but only after the regime had changed, with this note attached: "He intended to throw off his hypocritical mask and come out publicly against the person of our monarch and against our State." The records were tucked inside the files having to do with one Josef Koudela. On the jacket was a little cross and under it "Resolved" and the date.)

"So Švejk has disappeared on me," said Judge Advocate Bernis, "I'll have him called in, and if he doesn't confess to anything, I'll let him out and have him escorted to you and you can then talk it over and make a deal at the regiment."

After the Field Chaplain left, the Judge Advocate sent for Švejk and left him standing in the doorway, because he just received a telegram from police headquarters, that the requested material pertaining to prosecution file number 7267, regarding an infantryman named Maixner, had already been received at the office number 1, and signed for by Captain Linhart.

In the meantime Švejk looked over the Judge Advocate's office.

That it made a very favorable impression, especially the photographs on the walls, one couldn't say. They were photographs of various actions, taken by the army in Galicia and Serbia. Art photographs of burned-out cottages and of trees, the branches of which were straining from the weight of the human bodies hanging from them. Especially pretty was a photograph from Serbia of a hanged family. A small boy, the father and the mother. Two soldiers with bayonets are guarding the tree with the executed on it and some officer is standing like a victor in the foreground and is smoking a cigarette. On the other side, in the background, can be seen a field kitchen hard at work.

"So how is it with you, Švejk?" asked the Judge Advocate, as he inserted the telegram into the records, "what is it that you have done? Would you like to confess, or wait until an indictment against you is composed? It can't go on like this any longer. Don't think you're in some court, where you're being questioned by some stupid civilians. Here with us, there are only military courts, Imperial and Royal Military Courts. Your only hope of deliverance from a stiff and just punishment can be if you confess."

Judge Advocate Bernis had a special method, when he lost the prosecution material to be used against the accused. As you see, there wasn't really anything special about it and therefore we must not be amazed, that the results of such an investigation and interrogation in each case equaled zero.

And here Judge Advocate Bernis felt himself to be so foresighted, that having no material against the accused, not knowing what he was charging him with, or why he was sitting doing time in the garrison prison, by observing the behavior and the physiognomy of the man brought in for interrogation, he tried to piece together, for what reason they had locked this human in the garrison prison.

His foresight and his knowledge of people were so great, that he once charged a gypsy, who got to the garrison prison from his regiment for the theft of several dozen articles of clothing (he was on hand for the storekeeper in the warehouse), with political crimes, for supposedly in a pub somewhere he had discussed the establishment of a new nation-state in the lands of the Czech Crown and Slovakia[186], with a Slavic king at the helm.

"We have documents," he told the unfortunate gypsy, "there is nothing left for you but to confess, in which pub you were saying it and from which regiment were the soldiers, who were listening to you, and when was it."

The hapless gypsy made up a date, named a pub, and even from which regiment was his alleged audience, and when he was leaving after the interrogation, he ran away from the garrison prison altogether.

"You don't want to admit to anything," said the Judge Advocate Bernis, when Švejk kept silent like a grave, "you don't want to say why you are here, why they have locked you up? You could at least tell me, before I tell you myself. I'm putting you on notice one more time to confess. It would be better for you, because it would make the investigation easier and mitigate the punishment. In that way, it is the same here as it is with the civilians."

"I dutifully report," Švejk's good-natured voice proclaimed, "that I'm here in the garrison prison as a foundling."

"How do you mean that?"

"I dutifully report, that I can explain it in a tremendously simple manner. In our street there is a coal peddler and he had an absolutely innocent little two-year-old boy and one day he got on foot from Vinohrady all the way to Libeň[187], where a patrolman found him sitting on a sidewalk. So he brought the little boy to the district police station[188], and they locked him up in there, a two-year-old child. He was, as you can see, the little boy, absolutely innocent, and yet he was locked up. If he could talk and someone were to ask him, why he is sitting doing time there, then he wouldn't know either. With me it is something similar. I too am a foundling."

The wary gaze of the Judge Advocate scanned Švejk's figure and face and shattered itself against them. Such indifference and innocence radiated from the entire being standing in front of the Judge Advocate, that Bernis began pacing angrily around his office, and had he not promised to the Field Chaplain, that he'd send him Švejk, only demons know how Švejk would have ended up.

Finally however he stopped again at his desk.

Švejk nonchalantly gazed off into the distance.

"Listen," he said to Švejk, who was looking indifferently straight ahead, "if you cross my path one more time, you'll never forget it. — Take him away!"

While they were escorting Švejk back to the sixteen, Judge Advocate Bernis had them call in Garrison Staff Warden Slavík.

"Until further notice," he said briefly, "Švejk is being sent to be at the disposal of mister Field Chaplain Katz. Draw up release papers and have Švejk escorted by two men to mister Field Chaplain."

"Should we put him in handcuffs for the trip, Senior Lieutenant, Sir?"

The Judge Advocate hit the desk with his fist:

"You're such a dumb ox, mister! I told you clearly to draw up release papers, didn't I?"

And all that, which had accumulated throughout this day in the soul of the Judge Advocate, including Captain Linhart and Švejk, gushed forth like a wild river at the Garrison Staff Warden and finished with these words:

"And do you understand now, why you are the crowned dumb ox?"

Obviously, one should title thusly only kings and emperors, but even the simple Garrison Staff Warden, with his head never crowned, wasn't satisfied by it. Having left the Judge Advocate's office, he kicked a swabber prisoner cleaning the corridor until he curled up into a ball.

As regards Švejk, the Garrison Staff Warden then made up his mind, that Švejk had to spend at least one more night in the garrison prison, so he could savor still some more.

─ ─ ─ ─ ─

A night spent at a garrison prison always belongs among the

pleasant memories.

Next to "the sixteen" was "ajnclík", a gloomy hole — solitary, from which resounded even that night the howl of some locked-up soldier, as Master Sergeant Řepa, ordered by Garrison Staff Warden Slavík, was breaking his ribs for some breech of discipline.

When the howling stopped, what could be heard in the sixteen was the cracking of the lice, that ended up between the fingers of the soldiers during an inspection.

In an opening on the wall above the door, a kerosene lamp equipped with a protective grille released both a dim light and sooty smoke. The stench of the kerosene blended with the natural vapors of unwashed human bodies and the odor of a bucket, which after each use pushed apart its crusty surface only to hurl another wave of foul odors into the sixteen.

Bad nutrition made the digesting process difficult and the majority suffered winds, which they released into the nocturnal silence, answering each other with those signal to the accompaniment of various jokes.

In the corridor could be heard the measured pace of patrols, once in a while a portal in the door would swing open and a guard would peer through the peep hole.

From the middle bunk came the sound of discreet narration:

"Before I wanted to escape and before they put me in here with you afterward, I used to be in the number twelve. There they put, like, the lighter cases. Let me tell you, once they brought this man in from somewhere in the country. This charming man got two weeks for letting some soldiers sleep over at his place. First they thought it was part of a conspiracy, but then the explanation came down, that he had been doing it for money. He was supposed to be locked up with the lightest cases, but because it was filled to capacity there, he ended up among us. You wouldn't believe all the stuff he brought in with him and all that they would send him from home, because somehow he was allowed to take meals on his own and get hold of extras. He was even allowed to smoke. He had two hams, these giant loaves of bread, eggs, butter, cigarettes, tobacco, well, in short, whatever man could think of, that he had on him in two backpacks. And the guy thought, that he must devour it by himself. We started begging him to share, since he didn't figure out on his own, that he must share with us, as others always did, when they got something, but he, the stingy guy, kept saying no, that he was going to be locked up for two weeks and would ruin his stomach with the cabbage and rotten potatoes they give us as rations. He said he would give us his whole ration and his commissary bread, that he didn't care about them and it would be up to us to divide it among ourselves or take turns.

    Let me tell you, he was such a refined man that he didn't even want to sit on the bucket and waited until the next day for the stroll, to do it in the latrine in the yard. He was so spoiled that he had even brought in with him toilet paper. We told him we would piss on that portion of his, and we suffered one day, the second, and the third. The man was gobbling down ham, spreading butter on bread, peeling eggs for himself, in short, he was living it up. He smoked cigarettes and wouldn't even give a drag to anyone. We must not smoke, he said, because if the guard saw him giving us a drag, they'd lock him up. As I said, we had suffered for three days. In the night of the fourth day we acted. The man woke up in the morning, but I forgot to tell you that every day in the morning, at noon, and in the evening, before he would start stuffing himself, he prayed, for a long time he prayed. So after he prayed, he starts looking for his backpacks under the plank bunk. Well, the backpacks were there, but they were shriveled up like dried prunes. He started screaming that he had been robbed, that they left for him there only the toilet paper. Then he thought of it for about five minutes, that we pranked him, that we just hid his stuff here and there. He still says sort of joyfully: 'I know that you're little cheats, I know that you'll give it back to me, but boys, you really got me good.' There was among us one guy from Libeň and he says: '*They* know what, just cover *themselves* with the blanket and count to ten. And then *they* look into those backpacks of *theirs*.' He covered himself like an obedient boy and began counting: 'One, two, three...' And that guy from Libeň says: '*They* must not count so fast, *they* must go very slowly.' And so he, under the blanket, counts slowly, with pauses: 'One — two — three...' When he finished counting to ten, he crawled out of the bunk and inspected his backpacks. 'Jesusmaria, people," he started screaming, 'but they're as empty as they were before.' And all the while this stupid grimace on his face, we all could have ripped ourselves open laughing. And the guy from Libeň says: '*They* try it one more time.' And would you believe that he was so stupid from it all, that he tried it one more time and when he saw, that again there was nothing in there, except his toilet paper, he started beating on the door and screaming: 'They've robbed me, they've robbed me, help, open up, forchristhelord, open up.' So the guards flew in there right away, called the Garrison Staff Warden and Master Sergeant Řepa. To a man we all said the guy had just gone nuts, that yesterday, even long into the night, he had been gorging and must have devoured it all. And he wept and kept saying: 'But there have to be little crumbs somewhere.' So they searched for little crumbs and didn't find any, because we were smart enough for that too. What we couldn't wolf down ourselves we sent on a string up to the second floor. They couldn't prove anything against us, even though that idiot kept his whining: 'But the little crumbs must be somewhere.' All that day he didn't eat anything and was on the lookout to see whether anybody was eating anything or smoking. The next day at lunchtime he still didn't touch the ration, but by the evening the rotten potatoes and cabbage were doing him good, except he wouldn't pray anymore like he used to before he'd launch into that ham and eggs. Then one of us somehow got cheap smokes from the outside and that's when he first started to talk to us, asking us to give him a drag. We gave him nothing."

"I was afraid that you did give him a drag," remarked Švejk, "you would have spoiled the whole tale. Such magnanimity is to be found only in novels, but in a garrison prison, under such circumstances, that would have been stupid."

"You didn't give him a beating under the blanket?" somebody's voice piped up.

"We forgot that."

A quiet debate began about whether the man should have gotten the blanket in addition to all the rest, or not. The majority was for it.

The talk slowly gave way to silence. They were falling asleep, scratching their armpits, chests and bellies, where in their underwear the lice liked to hang on the most. They were falling asleep, pulling their lice-infested blankets over their heads, so that the light from the kerosene lamp wouldn't disturb them…

At eight in the morning they called on Švejk to go to the office.

"On the left side by the office door there is a spittoon, they throw butts in there," one was instructing him. "Then on the second floor you go past another one. They don't sweep the corridors until nine, so there should be something there."

But Švejk dashed their hopes. He returned no more to the sixteen. The nineteen remaining long johns were left to speculate and guess all sorts of things.

Some freckled soldier from the Land Defense[189], with the wildest imagination, spread the story that Švejk had taken a shot at his captain and that today they took him to the Motol training ground to be executed.

10

ŠVEJK AS A MILITARY SERVANT TO THE FIELD CHAPLAIN

1

Once again his odyssey begins under the honorable escort of two soldiers with bayonets, who were to transport him to the Field Chaplain.

His escorts were men, who complemented one another. If one was a tall beanstalk, the other was short, fat. The beanstalk had gimpy right leg, the fat one limped with his left. Both were serving in the rear, because long before the war they were both fully exempt from military service.

They walked earnestly alongside the sidewalk, occasionally stealing sidelong glances at Švejk, who marched smartly between them and saluted just about everyone. His civilian clothes had been lost in the garrison prison store room, along with the military cap, that he wore on the way to military service. Before they released him, they gave him an old military uniform, that had previously belonged to someone with a huge belly and was a head taller than Švejk.

Into the pants, that he wore, could have fit still three more Švejks. The endless folds of cloth, from the feet all the way up over his chest, were causing him to be spontaneously admired by many onlookers. A huge military blouse with patches on the elbows, greasy and dirty, dangled from Švejk like a coat on a scare crow. The pants hung on him like the costume on a clown from a circus. The military cap, that they had also given him in exchange in the garrison prison, slid down over his ears.

The smiles of onlookers Švejk answered with his own soft smile, the warmth and tenderness of his good-natured eyes.

And so they headed to Karlín, to the apartment of the Field Chaplain.

The first to speak up to Švejk was the short fat one. Just then they were in Small Side, down under the arcades.

"Where are you from?" asked the short fat one.

"From Prague."

"And won't you run away from us?"

The beanstalk mixed himself into the conversation. It is a very peculiar phenomenon, that if short fat ones are mostly good-natured optimists, extruded beanstalks are usually on the other hand skeptics.

And therefore the beanstalk said to the short one: "If he could, he'd run away."

"And why would he be running away," asked the short fatso, "one way or the other he's free, out of the garrison prison. It's here in the packet I'm carrying."

"And what's in that packet for the Field Chaplain?" asked the beanstalk.

"That I don't know."

"There you see, you don't know and you talk."

They walked across the Charles' Bridge in absolute silence. In Charles' street, the short fat one spoke again up to Švejk:

"Do you know, why we're escorting you to the Field Chaplain?"

"To confession," said nonchalantly Švejk, "tomorrow they're going to hang me. It is always done like that and it is called comforting the soul."

"And why are they going to, you know, like…" asked carefully the beanstalk, while the fat one cast a consoling look at Švejk.

They both were tradesmen from the country, fathers of families.

"I don't know," answered Švejk, smiling good-naturedly, "I don't know of anything. It's apparently my fate."

"Perhaps you were born on an unlucky planet," like an expert and with sympathy remarked the little one. "Where I'm from, in Jasenná, near Josefov[190], back during the Prussian[191] War they also hanged someone. They came for him, didn't tell him anything and in Josefov they hanged him."

"I think," said the skeptical beanstalk, "that they don't hang a man for no reason at all, that there always has be some cause for it, so that it can be justified."

"When there isn't a war," remarked Švejk, "then they go about justifying it, but in wartime one man isn't considered. Is he to fall at the front, or be hanged at home. On foot, same as following the cart."

"Listen, aren't you some kind of a political case?" asked the beanstalk. From the cadence of his question it was discernible, that his sympathy was beginning to lean toward Švejk.

" Political I'm too much," gave a smile Švejk.

"Aren't you a national socialist[192]?" Now began the short fat one to be cautious. He mixed himself into it. "What business is it of ours," he said, "there are lots of people everywhere and they're watching us.

95

At least if we could in a passageway somewhere take these prongs off our rifles, so it wouldn't be so conspicuous. Won't you run away from us? That would mean unpleasant consequences for us. Am I not right, Toník?" he turned to the beanstalk, who said in a low voice:

"The prongs we could take off. He's our kind, after all."

He had ceased to be a skeptic and his soul filled with sympathy toward Švejk. So they searched for a suitable passageway, wherein they removed the bayonets, and the fat one allowed Švejk to walk next to him.

"Dying for a smoke, right?" he said, "I wonder if…" He wanted to say: "I wonder if they will give you a smoke before they hang you," but didn't finish the sentence, as he felt, that it would be tactless.

They all had a smoke and the escorts began telling Švejk about their families in the Hradec Králové region, about wives, children, about a tiny piece of a field, about one cow.

"I'm thirsty," said Švejk.

The beanstalk and the short one looked at each other.

"We would stop somewhere for one too," said the short one, sensing the beanstalk would agree, "But we've got to go somewhere, where we wouldn't be conspicuous."

"Let's go to Kuklík[193]," was suggesting invitingly Švejk, "your rifles you'll stack in the kitchen, the pubkeeper Serabona[194] is a Sokol[195], him you don't have to fear. — They have violin and accordion music there," continued Švejk, "and in there go street girls and various other good company that is forbidden from showing up at the Rephouse[196]."

The beanstalk and the short one looked one more time at each other and then the beanstalk said:

"So there we'll go, it's still a long way to Karlín."

Along the way Švejk was telling them a variety of jokes and in good mood they entered the Kuklík, and did exactly, as Švejk had advised. The rifles they hid in the kitchen and they walked into the pub, where the violin and accordion were filling the room with the sounds of a popular song "At Pankrác, on that little hill, there stands a nice alley of trees…"

Some miss, who was sitting on the lap of a burned-out young man with a crisp part in his smoothly-combed hair, sang in a raspy voice: "I had a girl all talked up, but someone else is romancing her…"

At one of the tables, there was sleeping a drunken sardine vendor, now and then he'd wake up, bang his fist on the table and mumble: "It won't work," then he'd fall back to sleep.

On the other side of the pool table under a mirror there were sitting three other young ladies and were shouting at a railway conductor: "Young man, treat us to some vermouth." Over by the musicians, two were arguing, that some Mares was yesterday picked up by the patrol. One saw it with his own eyes and the other insisted, that she went with a soldier, to sleep with, to the U Valšů[197] hotel.

Right by the door there was a soldier sitting with several civilians and telling them about his injury in Serbia. He had a bandaged hand, pockets full of cigarettes, that he had gotten from them. He was saying, that he can't drink any more, and one of the company, a bald old geezer, kept challenging him: "Just drink, soldier boy, who knows if we'll ever meet again. Should I have them play something for you? Do you like 'A Child Was Orphaned'?"

This was in fact the bald old geezer's tune and indeed within a few moments the violin and accordion started to ululate, at which time tears entered the old geezer's eyes and he sang with a trembling voice: "When the babe began to reason, it was asking for its mommy, it was asking for its mommy…"

From another table came the sound of "Keep that to *themsleves*. *They* go get stuffed. *They* hang it up on a nail! *They* peel away from here with that orphan."

And for the final trump began the hostile table to sing: "Parting, oh sad parting, my heart is altogether broken, broken…"

"Franta," they called to the injured soldier after they finished singing, having drowned out 'The Orphaned Child', "leave them be already and come and sit with us. Piss on them already and send those cigarettes here. Why should you entertain them, the old stuffings."

Švejk and his escorts watched with great interest all of it.

Švejk immersed himself in the memories, as he often used to sit here before the military service. How there used come here the police inspector Drašner[198] for a police inspection and the prostitutes were afraid of him and composed songs about him with the opposite content. How this one time they all sang in unison:

> During the reign of Mister Drašner,
> There was quite a rumble here.
> Tough Mary was oh so drunk,
> And Drašner she feared not.

Right then strode in Drašner with his entourage, frightful and relentless. It was, as if it gets shot into a flock of quails. Plainclothes patrolmen marshaled all of them into a cluster. Even he, Švejk, was back then in the cluster, because given his bad luck he told inspector Drašner, who ordered him to show his identification: "Do *they* have an authorization for this from the police headquarters?"

Švejk was remembering also a poet, who used to sit under the mirror and in the general bustle of the Kuklík, the singing and in the midst of the accordion sounds he would write little poems and read them out to the prostitutes.

By contrast, Švejk's escorts had no similar reminiscences. It was for them something quite new. They were beginning to like it. The first of the two to find complete satisfaction here was the short fat one, since such people, aside from their optimism, have a great tendency to be Epicurean[199]. The beanstalk for a while wrestled with himself. And just as he had lost his skepticism, he began to slowly lose his sense of aloofness and remaining prudence.

"I will have a dance," he said after the fifth beer, when he saw the couples doing the stomp dance.

The short one devoted himself completely to pleasure seeking. Next to him was sitting a miss, talking obscenely, and his eyes just sparkled.

Švejk was drinking. The beanstalk finished dancing and returned with his partner to the table. Then they were singing, dancing, kept on drinking, patting their female companions. And in the atmosphere of love for sale, of nicotine and alcohol, was circling inconspicuously an old slogan:

"After us let the flood come!"

Past the noon there sat down beside them some soldier and was offering, that for a tenner he'll give them phlegmon[200] and blood poisoning. He has on him a syringe and will inject into their foot or hand kerosene*. They will be laid up for at least two months, and if they keep feeding the wound with saliva, for perhaps half a year, and they will have to be released from military service for good.

The beanstalk, who had already lost all mental balance, had in the bathroom the soldier inject kerosene under the skin of his leg.

---

* It is a means, rather well proven, of getting oneself into a hospital. But the odor of kerosene, which stays in the swelling, gives one away. Gasoline is better, because it evaporates faster. Later they were injecting ether along with the gasoline, and still later came other improvements.

When the day was leaning toward evening, Švejk suggested, that they get on the way to the Field Chaplain. The short fatso, who started to babble already, was tempting Švejk to wait still a little. The beanstalk was also of the opinion, that the Field Chaplain can wait. Švejk, however, wasn't enjoying himself at the Kuklík anymore, and therefore he threatened, he'd go on by himself.

So they went, but Švejk had to promise, that they would all stop somewhere yet again.

They stopped past Florenc[201] in a nice little coffeehouse, where the fat one sold his silver watch, so that they could continue to revel.

From there on Švejk was already leading them both under the arms. It gave him a terrible lot of work. Their legs kept buckling under them and they still wanted to go somewhere. The short fat one would have almost lost the packet for the Field Chaplain, so Švejk was forced to carry it himself.

Švejk had to be constantly alerting them, when there was approaching an officer or some noncom. After a superhuman effort and exertion Švejk managed to drag them up to the building on the King Boulevard, where the Field Chaplain resided.

By himself he fixed for them the bayonets on to their rifles and forced them with a poke under the ribs to escort him, and not the other way around.

On the second floor, where there was a calling card on the door of the apartment, "Otto Katz, Field Chaplain", there came to open for them some soldier. From the room were coming the sounds of voices and clanking of bottles and glasses.

"*We—dutifully—report—Field Chaplain—Sir,*" said laboriously the beanstalk, saluting the soldier "*bringing in—one—packet—and one man.*"

"Crawl inside," said the soldier, "where did you get so messed up? The Field Chaplain is also…" The soldier spat.

The soldier left with the packet. They waited in the hallway for a long time, until the door opened and through it didn't walk in, but flew into the hallway the Field Chaplain. He had only a vest on, and in his hand was holding a cigar.

"So you're here already," he said to Švejk, "and they escorted you. Eh — do you have matches?"

"I dutifully report, Field Chaplain, Sir, that I don't."

"Eh — and why don't you have matches? Every soldier is supposed to have matches, so that he can light up for himself. A soldier, that doesn't have matches, is...What is he?"

"He is, I dutifully report, without matches," answered Švejk.

"Very good, he is without matches and cannot light up for anybody. So that's the one thing, and now the second. Don't your feet stink, Švejk?"

"I dutifully report, Sir, that they don't."

"So that's the second thing. And now the third. Do you drink booze?"

"I dutifully report, that I don't drink booze, only rum."

"All right, take a look over here at this soldier. Him I borrowed for today from Senior Lieutenant Feldhuber, he's his spotshine[202]. And he doesn't drink anything, he's a t-t-teetotaler, and that's why he'll go with a marchy[203]. B-because for such a man I've got no use. He is no spotshine, he is a cow. It too drinks only water and lows like an ox. — You are a teetotaler," he turned to the soldier, "you should be ashamed, you idiot. You deserve a couple of slaps."

The Field Chaplain turned his attentions to those, who brought Švejk and who in an effort to stand up straight were tottering, in vain leaning on their rifles.

"You got d-drunk," said the Field Chaplain, "you got drunk on duty and for that I will have you lo-locked up. Švejk, you will take the rifles from them and escort them to the kitchen and will guard them, until the patrol comes to take them away. I will immediately telepho-pho-pho-phone the garrison."

And so the words of Napoleon: "In the military, the situation changes with every blink of an eye", were even here fully borne out.

In the morning those two were escorting him under bayonets and they feared, lest he might run away from them, then he himself brought them in, and in the end, he had to guard them himself.

At first they did not quite realize this turnabout had occurred, and did so only when they were sitting in the kitchen and saw Švejk standing by the door with a rifle and a bayonet.

"I'd like something to drink," sighed the short optimist, while the beanstalk got again a fit of skepticism and said, that it was all a lousy betrayal. He took to loudly blaming Švejk for bringing them into this position, and he reproached him, that supposedly he had promised, that tomorrow he will be hanged, and that it was all clear now, that it is a joke even about the confession, even about the hanging.

Švejk kept silent and paced along the door.

"Dumb oxen we were!" screamed the beanstalk.

In the end having heard all the accusations Švejk declared:

"Now at least you see, that military service is no bowl of honey. I am doing my duty. I got into this the same way like you, but as they say on the streets, Lady Luck gave me a smile."

"I'd like something to drink," repeated desperately the optimist.

The beanstalk got up and walked to the door with a wobbly gait.

"Let us go home," he said to Švejk, "come on, colleague, don't act the idiot."

"Get away from me," answered Švejk. "I must guard you. We don't know one another now."

In the doorway appeared the Field Chaplain: "I, I just can no way get through to the garrison on the phone, so go home and re-remember that drinking on duty is fo-forbidden. March!"

To credit the Field Chaplain, let it be said that he wasn't calling the garrison, because he didn't have a telephone in his home and had been talking into a bare bulb stand.

2

For third day already had Švejk been Otto Katz's personal servant, and in that time he had seen him only once. On the third day came the military servant of Senior Lieutenant Helmich for Švejk to come and pick up the Field Chaplain.

On the way he informed Švejk, that the Field Chaplain had argued with the Senior Lieutenant, broken the upright piano, that he is soused to the gills and doesn't want to go home.

Senior Lieutenant Helmich, he said, is also drunk and threw the Field Chaplain out into the hallway and he is sitting on the floor by the door and is snoozing.

When Švejk arrived at the location, he shook the Field Chaplain, and when he growled and opened his eyes, Švejk saluted and said: "I dutifully report, Field Chaplain, Sir, that I'm here."

"And what do you want — here?"

"I dutifully report, that I am to come to get you, Field Chaplain, Sir."

"So you're to come to get me — and where will we go?"

"To your apartment, Field Chaplain, Sir."

"And why am I to go to my apartment — you mean I'm not in my apartment?"

"I dutifully report, Field Chaplain, Sir, that you are in a hallway in a stranger's building."

"And — how — did — I — get here?"

"I dutifully report, that you were visiting."

"Visi — ting — I was n-not. —You — are — mi-mistaken."

Švejk lifted the Field Chaplain and stood him against the wall. The Field Chaplain was swinging from side to side and slumping up against him, while saying: "I'll fall, that'll be on you. — I'll fall," he repeated one more time, grinning idiotically.

At last Švejk managed to press the Field Chaplain against the wall, who in the new position started again to doze.

Švejk woke him up. "What do you want?" said the Field Chaplain, making a futile attempt to slide down the wall and sit on the ground. "Who are you, anyhow?"

"I dutifully report," answered Švejk, holding the Field Chaplain again up against the wall, "that I'm your spotshine, Field Chaplain, Sir."

"I don't have any spotshine," said with great effort the Field Chaplain, making another attempt to collapse onto Švejk, "I'm no field chaplain. — I'm a pig," he added with the sincerity of a dedicated drinker, "let me go, mister, I don't know you."

This tussle ended with Švejk's total victory. Švejk took advantage of his victory in such a way, that he pulled the Field Chaplain down the stairs and into the courtyard passageway, where the Field Chaplain was putting up resistence, so he wouldn't be pulled out into the street. "I don't know you, mister," he kept insisting during the struggle, straight into Švejk's eyes. "Do you know Otto Katz? That's me. — I was at the Archbishop's," he hollered, while hanging onto the gate in courtyard passageway. "The Vatican[204] is interested in me, do you understand?"

Švejk shed the "I dutifully report" and spoke to the Field Chaplain in a purely familiar tone.

"Let go, I'm telling you," he said, "or I'm gonna whack you across that paw. We're going home and that's it. No more talk."

The Field Chaplain let go of the gate and slumped up against Švejk: "Then let's go somewhere, but I won't go to Šuha's[205], there I owe."

Švejk both pushed him and carried him out of the courtyard passageway and it was a drag hauling him along the sidewalk in the direction of his home.

"What kind of gentleman is that?" asked somebody from among

the onlookers on the street.

" That's my brother," answered Švejk, "he got leave, so he came to visit me and from joy he got drunk, because he thought, that I was dead."

The Field Chaplain, who caught the last words, while humming to himself some motif from an operetta, which nobody could recognize, arose to face the audience: "Whoever among you is dead, let him register at the Corps Command[206] within three days, so that his corpse can be fully sprinkled with holy water."

And he fell silent, striving to fall nose-first onto the sidewalk, as Švejk was dragging him under his arm home.

Having his head forward and his feet behind, which he flailed like a cat with a broken back, the Field Chaplain kept murmuring to himself: "Dominus vobiscum — et cum spiritu tuo. Dominus vobiscum."

At a cab stand, Švejk sat the Field Chaplain up against a wall and went to negotiate with the carriage drivers over transport.

One of the drivers declared, that he knows that mister very well, that he had driven him only once and that he will never drive him again.

"He puked all over my cab," he expressed himself forthrightly, "and didn't even pay for the ride. I drove him around for over two hours before he found, where he lives. Only a week later, after I'd been to see him about three times, he gave me for all of it five crowns."

After a long negotiation did one of the cab drivers make up his mind, that he would take them.

Švejk turned to the Field Chaplain, who was asleep. The firm black hat (since he usually went about in civilian clothes) somebody meanwhile removed from his head and carried it away.

Švejk woke him up and with the help of the cab driver transported him into the cab. In the cab the Field Chaplain fell into complete dull apathy and took Švejk for Colonel Just of the 75th Infantry Regiment[207] and several times in succession repeated: "Don't be angry, buddy, that I address you in the familiar form[208]. I'm a pig."

For a moment it seemed, that by the rattling of the cab over the cobblestones he was regaining his ability to reason. He sat up straight and started singing some excerpt from an unknown song. It could also be, it was his imagination:

> I'm remembering the golden times
> When he rocked me in his lap.
> We were living at the time
> Near Domažlice in Merklín.

After a while, however, he fell again into complete dull apathy, and turning to Švejk, he asked, squinting one eye: "How are you doing today, ma'am? — Will you go anywhere to spend the summer?" he said after a short pause, and seeing everything double, he asked: "You would already have an adult son?" while pointing his finger at Švejk.

"Sit!" Švejk screamed at him, when the Field Chaplain tried to climb up onto the seat, "don't think, that I won't teach you what's proper."

The Field Chaplain fell silent and was staring out of the cab with little piggy eyes, not understanding what was actually happening to him.

He had totally lost his sense of reality, and turning to Švejk, he said wistfully: "Ma'am, give it to me first class." He made an attempt to drop his pants.

"You button up right away, you swine!" barked Švejk, "all the cabmen already know you, you had puked once already, and now this. Don't think, that you'll end up owing again, like the last time."

The Field Chaplain melancholically rested his head into the palms, and started to sing: "Nobody likes me anymore..." He interrupted his singing immediately, however, and remarked: *"Excuse me dear friend, you are an idiot, I can sing what I want."*

He apparently wanted to whistle some melody, but instead, such a mighty whoa gushed over his lips that the carriage came to a stop.

When at Švejk's command they continued on their way, the Field Chaplain started to light up his cigarette holder.

"It won't burn," he said desperately, having used up a whole box of matches, striking one after another, "You're blowing them out!"

However, he immediately lost his train of thought and started to laugh. "That's funny, we're alone in the street car, aren't we, my dear colleague." He started searching through his pockets.

"I've lost the fare-card!" he shouted, "stop, the fare-card must be found!"

He waved his hand in resignation: "Let them go..."

Then he babbled: "In most occurring cases... Yes, all right... In all cases... You are mistaken... The second floor?... That's an excuse... Never mind me, but regarding you, dear madam... I'd like to pay... I've had black coffee..."

Half dreaming, he began to argue with some imagined enemy, who is denying him the right to sit in a restaurant at the window. Then he started to think the carriage was a train, and leaning out, he screamed into the streets in Czech and German:

"Nymburk, change trains!"

Švejk pulled him toward himself and the Field Chaplain forgot about the train and started to imitate various animal sounds. He lingered the longest on the rooster and his cock-a-doodle-do was triumphantly resounding from the cab.

For a while, he was actually quite lively and restless, and kept trying to fall out of the cab, abusing all the people they passed, calling them street punks. He then threw a handkerchief out of the cab and yelled for the driver to stop, saying he had lost his luggage. He began to narrate: "In Budějovice there was a military drummer. — He got married. — A year later he died." He broke into laughter: "Isn't that a good joke?"

The whole time Švejk had been dealing with the Field Chaplain with ruthless strictness.

During the various attempts of the Field Chaplain to play little games, like falling out of the cab, or ripping out the seat, Švejk gave him one punch under the ribs after another, which the Field Chaplain received with unusual apathy.

Only once did he attempt to rebel and jump out of the cab, having declared, that he won't ride any farther, that he knows, that instead of going to Budějovice, they're riding to Podmoklí[209].

Within a minute had Švejk snuffed out his rebellion entirely and forced him to return to the first position on the seat, making sure that he would not fall asleep. The gentlest thing, that he uttered during the course of it, was: "Don't sleep, you croaking stiff."

The Field Chaplain was suddenly gripped by a fit of melancholy and began to shed tears, questioning Švejk, whether he had a mother.

"I am, folks, all alone in this world!" he screamed from the cab, "take me under your care!"

"Don't embarrass me," Švejk admonished him, "stop it, everybody will say that you're soused."

"I've had nothing to drink, my friend," answered the Field Chaplain, "I am totally sober."

Suddenly however he stood up, saluted:

"*I dutifully report, Colonel, Sir, I am drunk.* — I'm a filthy porker," he repeated ten times in a row with a desperate, sincere hopelessness.

And turning to Švejk he was begging and pleading persistently: "Throw me out of this automobile. Why are you taking me along with you?"

He sat down and growled: "Around the moon circles are being formed. — Do you believe, Captain, Sir, in the immortality of the soul? Can a horse get to heaven?"

He began to laugh loudly, but after a moment he grew sad and was apathetically staring at Švejk, uttering: "Permit me, mister, I've seen you somewhere before. Haven't you been to Vienna? I remember you from the seminary."

For a while he amused himself by declaiming Latin verses: "*A golden age first arose that did not need judges.* — Can't go any farther," he said, "throw me out. Why don't you want to throw me out? I won't get hurt. — I want to fall on my nose," he stated in a resolute voice.

"Mister," he continued again in a pleading voice, "dear friend, give me a head slap."

"One or several?" asked Švejk.

"Two."

"Here they come…"

The Field Chaplain counted out loud the head slaps, which he was receiving, with a blissful look on his face.

"It's doing me a lot of good," he said, "it's on account of the stomach, it gets the stomach going and works up an appetite. Slap my mug now! — Heartfelt thanks!" he exclaimed, when Švejk quickly obliged him, "I'm completely satisfied. Rip my vest, please!"

He was expressing the most varied wishes. He wished Švejk to sprain his ankle, to choke him for a while, to cut his nails, to pull out his front teeth.

He was displaying longings for martyrdom, requesting that he tear off his head, put it in a bag and throw it into the Vltava.

"Those little stars around my head would suit me well," he said with enthusiasm, "I'd need ten of them."

Then he started talking about horse races and quickly switched to ballet, which he didn't stick with long either.

"Do you dance the czardas?" he asked Švejk, "do you know the bear dance? Like this…"

He wanted to hop and fell on Švejk, who started punching him and then deposited him on the seat.

"I want something," shouted the Field Chaplain, "but I don't know what. Don't you know, what I want?" He hung his head in total resignation.

"What is it to me, what I want," he said seriously, "and you, mister, it's none of your business, either. I don't know you. How dare you to stare at me? Do you know how to fence?"

He became for a minute more aggressive and made an attempt to knock Švejk off the seat.

Afterward, when Švejk calmed him down, shamelessly letting him feel his physical superiority, the Field Chaplain asked: "Is today Monday or Friday?"

He was also curious, as to whether it was December or June, and showed a great ability to pose the most varied questions: "Are you married? Do you enjoy eating Gorgonzola[210]? Did you have bedbugs at home? Are you doing well? Has your dog had distemper?"

He became talkative. He was narrating, that he owes someone for riding boots, a whip and a saddle, that years ago he had gonorrhea and that he was treating it with potassium permanganate.

"There wasn't the time or thought for anything else," he said hiccupping, "may be, that it seems to you to be a rather bitter pill. But say, uh, uh, what am I to do, uh? You just have to forgive me for it already. — "Autotherm," he continued, forgetting what he was talking about a moment ago, "is a term designating vessels, which keep drinks and meals at original temperature. What do you think, dear colleague, about which game is fairer: ferbl or one-and-twenty[211]? — Really, I've seen you already somewhere before," he exclaimed, trying to hug Švejk and kiss him with drooling lips, "we used to go to school together. — You good-natured guy," he was saying gently, caressing his own leg, "how you've grown since the time, when I saw you last. The joy of seeing you makes up for all the suffering."

He got into a poetic mood and started talking about the return into the sunshine of happy faces and warm hearts.

Then he knelt down and prayed the "Hail Mary", at the same time laughing broadly.

When they stopped in front of his apartment, it was very hard to get him out of the carriage.

"We're not there yet," he yelled, "help me. They're kidnapping me. I wish to ride farther." He was in the true sense of the word pulled out of the cab like a boiled tender gastropod out of its shell. At one moment it seemed. that they'd rip him in two, because his feet got entangled under the seat.

But laughed loudly as they did, that he tricked them. "You'll rip me in two, gentlemen,"

Then he was dragged through the courtyard passageway over the stairs to his apartment and in the apartment thrown down like a bale of hay onto the sofa. He declared, that he would not pay for the automobile, which he did not call for, and it took over a quarter of an hour, before they managed to explain to him, that it was a horse-drawn cab.

Even then he didn't agree, objecting that he rides only in a fiacre[212].

"You want to fool me," was proclaiming the Field Chaplain, winking at Švejk and the driver meaningfully, "we went on foot."

And suddenly in a fit of magnanimity he threw his money pouch to the cabman: "Take it all, *I can pay*. I couldn't care less about a krejcar[213]."

To be correct, he should have said that he couldn't care less about thirty six krejcary, because there weren't any more than that in the pouch. Fortunately the cabman subjected him to a thorough search, while talking about face slaps.

"So hit me then," responded the Field Chaplain, "do you think, that I couldn't take it? I can take five of yours."

In the vest of the Field Chaplain the cabman found a tenner. He left, cursing both his fate and the Field Chaplain, for having delayed him and ruining other fares.

The Field Chaplain was slowly falling asleep, because he was continuously building up some plans. He wanted to undertake all kinds of things, to play piano, attend dancing lessons and fry for himself little fishes.

Then he was promising Švejk his sister, which he didn't have. He also wished, that he be carried to his bed and laid down, and in the end he fell asleep, having declared, that he wants the humanity in him to be recognized, an equally valuable unit as the pig.

3

When in the morning Švejk stepped into the Field Chaplain's living room, he found him lying on the sofa, thinking strenuously, how it could be, that someone doused him in such a strange manner, that his pants got stuck to the leather sofa.

"I dutifully report, Field Chaplain, Sir," said Švejk, "that in the night you…"

With but a few words he explained to him, how terribly mistaken he is, thinking that he'd been doused. The Field Chaplain, whose head felt unusually heavy, was in an uneasy mood.

"I can't remember," he said, "how I got from the bed to the sofa."

"There you haven't been at all, as soon as we arrived, we deposited you onto the sofa, any farther it wouldn't work."

"Was I doing silly things? Was I actually acting up at all? Wasn't I perhaps drunk?"

"Beyond recognition," answered Švejk, "totally, Field Chaplain, Sir, there came over you a tiny little delirium. I hope you will feel better when you change and wash up."

"I feel, as if somebody has beaten me up," was complaining the Field Chaplain, "then I've got thirst. Wasn't I fighting yesterday?"

"It wasn't quite the worst, Field Chaplain, Sir. Thirst is the consequence of yesterday's thirst. A man can't get over that so soon. I knew a cabinet maker, he got drunk for the first time on New Year's Eve of the year 1910 and on January first in the morning he had such a thirst and he felt so ill, that he bought himself a herring and was drinking again and he's kept it up daily already for four years and nobody can help him, because on Saturday he always buys for himself the herring for the whole week. It is a sort of merry-go-round, as used to say an old master sergeant of the 91st Regiment."

The Field Chaplain was afflicted by a perfect hangover and total depression. at that moment, whoever might have heard him, had to be convinced, that he was attending lectures of Dr. Alexandr Batěk[214] "Let Us Declare a Life or Death Struggle against the Demon of Alcohol, Which Murders the Best of Men, Who Are Our Best" or that he was reading his "Hundred Sparks of Ethics."

He, it's true, changed it a little. "If", he said, "a man would drink some noble drinks, like arak, maraschino, or cognac, but this time, yesterday, I drank borovička[215]. I marvel that I can lap it up like that. Its taste is repulsive. If it at least had been cherry brandy. People will think up all kinds of swine filth and drink it like water. That kind of borovička is neither tasty, nor has color, burns in the throat. And if it had been at least genuine, a distillate from juniper, like the one I drank once in Moravia[216]. But this borovička was made from some wood alcohol and oils. Take a look at how I'm burping. — Booze is poison," he decided, "it must be unadulterated original, genuine, and not something from the Jews, manufactured at a factory the cold way. It's the same with rum. Good rum is a rarity. — If there were some genuine nut liquor here," he sighed, "that would fix my stomach. The kind of nut liquor Captain Šnábl in Bruska[217] has."

He started frisking himself and looking through his money pouch.

"All I have is thirty six krejcary. What if I were to sell the sofa," he pondered, "what do you think? Will anybody buy a sofa? I'll tell the landlord, that I loaned it out or that somebody stole it from us. No, I'll keep the sofa. I'll send you to Captain Šnábl, for him to lend me a hundred crowns. He won at cards the day before yesterday. If you don't succeed there, then you'll go to Vršovice, to the garrison[218], to Senior Lieutenant Mahler. Should you fail there, you'll go to Hradčany to Captain Fišer. You'll tell him that I have to pay for the horse's fodder, the money for which I spent on drink. And if you don't succeed even there, we will pawn the upright piano, regardless of what may happen. I will write a few generic lines of introduction. Don't let them brush you off. You'll tell them that I'm in need, that I'm absolutely without any money. Make up anything you want, but don't come back with empty hands, or I'll send you to the front. Ask of Captain Šnábl where he buys that nutty liquor and buy two bottles."

Švejk fulfilled his mission excellently. His simple-heartedness and honest face evoked full trust, that whatever he was saying was true.

Švejk considered it appropriate not to tell Captain Šnábl, Captain Fišer and Senior Lieutenant Mahler that the Field Chaplain needed money for horse fodder, but to prop up his appeal by the declaration, that the Field Chaplain must pay alimonies. He got money everywhere.

When he was displaying the three hundred crowns, having returned honorably from the expedition, the Field Chaplain, who had in the meantime washed and changed, was very surprised.

"I took it all in one sweep," said Švejk, "so that tomorrow or the day after tomorrow we wouldn't have to be concerned about money again. It went pretty smoothly, but I had to get down on my knees in front of Captain Šnábl. He's some sonofabitch. But when I told him that we are to pay alimonies…"

"Alimonies?" repeated the horrified Field Chaplain.

"Yep, alimonies, Field Chaplain, Sir, disposition payments to the girls. You said I should think something up and I couldn't come up with anything else. Where I come from, a cobbler was paying alimonies to five girls at once and he was totally desperate from it all and he was borrowing for it and everybody gladly believed that he was in a horrible position. They asked me what kind of girl it is, and I said that she's very pretty and not yet fifteen years of age. So they wanted her address."

"You sure executed that mess nicely, Švejk," the Field Chaplain sighed heavily and started pacing around the room.

"Another big embarrassment," he said, grabbing his head, "I've got such a headache."

"I gave them the address of an old deaf woman on our street," explained Švejk. "I wanted to execute it thoroughly, because an order is an order. I didn't let them brush me off — and I had to think of something. Next, they're waiting in the hallway for the upright piano. I brought them in to take it to the pawn shop for us, Field Chaplain, Sir. It won't be so bad, when the upright is gone. There'll be more room in here and we'll have more money piled together. And we can be carefree for a few days. If the landlord should ask what we did with the upright, I'll say that the wires in it got torn up and that we sent it to the factory for repairs. I already told the resident custodian, so that it won't be suspicious, when they carry it out and load it in their wagon. I also have a buyer for the sofa already. He's an acquaintance of mine, a trader in old furniture and he'll come here past noon. Nowadays, a leather sofa brings good money."

"You haven't perpetrated any other mess, Švejk?" asked the Field Chaplain, still holding his head in his hands and showing desperation in his face.

"I've brought, I dutifully report, Field Chaplain, Sir, instead of two bottles of nutty liquor, the kind that Captain Šnábl buys, five bottles, so that we'd have some stock on hand, and have something to drink. May they step in for the upright piano, before they close the pawn shop on us?"

The Field Chaplain waved his hand hopelessly and a short while later, they were already loading the upright on a cart.

When Švejk returned from the pawn shop, he found the Field Chaplain sitting in front of an open bottle of the nutty liquor and bitching that the schnitzel he got for lunch wasn't cooked well enough.

The Field Chaplain was at it again. He was declaring to Švejk, that starting tomorrow he will lead a new life. That drinking alcohol is vulgar materialism and that one needs to live a spiritual life.

He spoke philosophically for about half an hour. When he opened the third bottle, there came by the trader of old furniture and the Field Chaplain sold him the sofa for next to nothing, and invited him for a chat, and was very dissatisfied, when the trader excused himself, that he still had to go to buy a night stand.

"Too bad I don't have one," the Field Chaplain said reproachfully, "one doesn't think of everything."

After the departure of the trader of used furniture, the Field Chaplain got into friendly amusement with Švejk, with whom he drank up another bottle. A part of the conversation was filled with the Field Chaplain's personal relationship with women and cards.

They kept at it a long time. Even the evening caught Švejk and the Field Chaplain still absorbed in friendly conversation.

In the night, however, the relation changed. The Field Chaplain returned to the state of yesterday, mistook Švejk for somebody else and told him: "Not at all, don't leave, do you remember that red-haired cadet from the supply train?"

This idyll continued until Švejk told the Field Chaplain: "I've had enough of this, now you'll crawl in bed and saw logs, understand!"

"I'm crawling, darling, crawling — how could I not crawl," babbled the Field Chaplain, "remember when we were attending the *tenth grade*[1] together and I used to do your Greek language homework? Your family has a villa in Zbraslav[219]. And you can ride the steam boat on the Vltava. Do you know what the Vltava is?"

Švejk forced him to take off his shoes and undress. The Field Chaplain obliged, while protesting to unknown persons.

"See, gentlemen," he said, addressing the wardrobe and the ficus plant, "see how my relatives treat me. — My relatives are strangers to me," he decided suddenly, depositing himself in bed. "If heaven and earth were to conspire against me, I don't acknowledge them…"

And throughout the room resounded the snoring of the Field Chaplain.

4

---

[1] "kvinta" was the fifth year of an eight-year Gymnasium (secondary school), following five years of elementary school. "Kvinta" marks the tenth year of schooling, but also encodes a specific place in the classical Central European secondary system, which included Latin, Greek, and modern languages.

Within the time-frame of these days is also to be found Švejk's visit at the apartment of his old cleaning lady missis Müller. In the apartment Švejk found missis Müller's female cousin, who told him, while weeping, that missis Müller had been arrested in the evening of the same day, when she drove Švejk to enter military service. The old woman had been tried by the military courts and they had taken her, since they couldn't prove anything against her, to the concentration camp in Steinhof[220]. A post card from her had already arrived.

Švejk took the domestic relic and read:

Dear Aninka!
We have it really good here, we are all healthy. The neighbor on the bed next to me has spotted ▮▮▮▮ and there are here also cases of small ▮▮. Other than that, everything is all right.
We have plenty of food and we collect potato ▮▮▮▮ for soup. I have heard that Mr. Švejk already ▮▮, so somehow search out where he lies, so that after the war we can have his grave decked with sod. I forgot to tell you, that in the attic, in the dark corner in a box, there is a little ratter doggie, a puppy. But it's been I don't know how many weeks that he hasn't gotten anything to eat, since the time when they came for me for ▮▮▮▮▮▮. So I think it's too late and that the doggie is also in the truth ▮▮.

And stamped across the whole card in pink letters was: *Censored. I & R Concentration Camp Steinhof.*

"And in truth the little dog was already dead," started sobbing missis Müller's cousin, "and also, you wouldn't even recognize your apartment. I have seamstresses renting there. And they've turned it into a ladies salon. There are pictures from fashion magazines all over the walls. Dainty flowers in the windows."

Missis Müller's cousin was not to be consoled.

Constantly weeping and wailing, she expressed finally her fear, that Švejk had run away from the military and wants to corrupt her too and bring a disaster upon her. In the end she spoke to him as if to a degenerate adventurer.

"This is very funny," said Švejk, "I'm really enjoying it. Just so that *they* know, missis Kejřová, *they* are absolutely right, that I had gotten out. But I had to kill fifteen *sergeants at arms* and *master sergeants*. But don't *they* tell anybody…"

And Švejk left his home, that didn't accept him, having declared:

"Missis Kejřová, at the laundry I've got some collars and shirt-fronts, so *they* pick it up for me, so that, when I come back from the military service, I'll have something to wear as a civilian. *They* also watch out, that moths don't get into my clothes in the wardrobe. And as for those little ladies, who sleep in my bed, let them know I'm sending greetings."

After that Švejk went to check out The Chalice. When missis Palivec saw him, she declared, that she won't pour for him, that he had probably run away.

"My husband," she started rehashing the old story, "was so careful, and he's sitting there, the poor soul, locked up for nothing whatsoever. And such people as you are roaming the world, running away from military service. They were already in here last week looking for you again. — We are more careful than you," she said ending her discourse, "and we're in misfortune. Not everybody is as lucky as you."

Present during the discourse was an older man, a locksmith from Smíchov[221], who approached Švejk and said to him: "Please, mister, wait for me outside, I must talk to you."

In the street he reached an understanding with Švejk, whom he also thought by the reference of missis pubkeeper Palivec to be a deserter.

He shared with him, that he has a son, who had also run away from the military service and is at his grandma's at Jasenná near Josefov.

Disregarding the fact, that Švejk kept assuring him, that he is not a deserteer, the old man pressed a tenner into his hand.

"That's first aid," he said, dragging him along to the wine-bar at the corner, "I understand you. Me you don't have to fear."

Švejk returned late in the night home to the Field Chaplain's, who was not home yet.

He came only toward morning, woke Švejk up and said: "Tomorrow we're going to serve a field Mass. Start making black coffee with rum. Or better yet, start making grog."

11

ŠVEJK RIDES WITH THE FIELD CHAPLAIN TO SERVE A FIELD MASS

1

The preparations for putting people to death have always taken place in the name of God or some other supposedly higher being, which humankind had created in its imagination.

Before the old Phoenicians would cut the throat of some prisoner of war, they performed as glorious of a divine service, as did several thousand years later new generations before hauling off to war and exterminating their enemies with both fire and sword.

The cannibals of the Guinea[222] islands and Polynesia[223], before they ceremonially devour their prisoners of war, or useless people like missionaries, explorers, agents of various commercial firms, or simply the curious, sacrifice to their gods, performing the most varied religious acts. Because the culture of the chasuble has not penetrated yet to their environs, they decorate their buttocks with wreaths made of the colorful feathers of forest birds.

Before the Holy Inquisition would burn its victims at the stake, it performed the most glorious of divine services, the holy High Mass with singing.

During the executions of the guilty, there always play a role priests, annoying with their presence the delinquent.

In Prussia a pastor would lead the poor condemned soul under the ax, in Austria a Catholic priest to the gallows, in France under the guillotine[224], in America to the electric chair, in Spain[225] to a chair, on which by an ingenious apparatus he was strangled, and in Russia a bearded Orthodox priest leading the revolutionary and so forth.

Everywhere during such occasions they waved the one on the crucifix, as if they wanted to say: They will only chop your head off, or hang you, or strangle you, zap you with fifteen thousand volts, but what this one must had suffered.

The great slaughter of the World War could not proceed without a priestly blessing. Field chaplains of all armies prayed and served field Masses for the victory of the side, whose bread they ate.

During the executions of mutinous regular army soldiers a priest would show up. During the executions of Czech Legionnaires[226] one could see a priest.

Nothing has changed since the time, when the highwayman Adalbert[227], to whom they gave the moniker "Saint," played his role with a sword in one hand and a cross in the other during the killing and extermination of the Baltic Slavs.

People in the whole of Europe have been going to slaughter like cattle, being led there aside the butcher emperors, kings and other potentates and military leaders, by priests of all denominational confessions, blessing them and having them falsely swear their allegiance that "on earth, in the air, at sea," and so forth...

Twice would Field Masses be served. First, when a detachment was going away to take a position at the front, and then again near the front line, before bloody clashes, crushing slaughter. I remember, that once during such a field Mass an enemy airplane dropped a bomb right on the field altar and nothing was left of the field chaplain but some bloody rags.

Afterward they wrote about him as a martyr, while our airplanes were preparing similar glory for the field chaplains on the other side.

We had a crude sort of fun with it and on the makeshift cross, where they buried the remnants of the field chaplain, appeared overnight this cemetery sign:

> What can befall us is what befell you also.
> You kept promising us heaven, old boy, for sure.
> Then it fell on you during the Holy Mass from heaven
> Only a stain is left of you on this spot.

2

Švejk made the glorious grog, surpassing the grogs of the old sailors. Such grog could be drunk by the pirates of the eighteenth century and they would be satisfied.

Field Chaplain Otto Katz was elated. "Where did you learn to cook such a good thing?" he asked.

"When I wandered years ago," answered Švejk, "in Bremen[228], from a degenerate sailor, who used to say that grog has to be so strong, that if somebody fell into the sea, he must be able to swim across the English Channel[229]. After drinking weak grog he'll drown like a puppy."

"After drinking such grog, Švejk, we'll have an easy time serving field Masses," the Field Chaplain mused, "I think I should say a few words of parting beforehand. A field Mass is not easy fun, like serving a Mass in the garrison prison or preaching to those hoodlums. In this case, one really has to have all his five senses together. We do have the field altar. It's a collapsible, pocket edition. — "Jesusmaria, Švejk," he grabbed himself by the head, "but what dumb oxen we are. Do you know where I hid that collapsible field altar? In the sofa, which we sold!"

"Yeah, that is a disaster, Field Chaplain, Sir," said Švejk, "granted, I do know that trader in old furniture, but the day before yesterday I ran into his wife. He's now sitting doing time on account of some stolen wardrobe and our sofa is with a teacher in Vršovice. That field altar is gonna be a problem. It will be best if we drink up the grog and go try chasing it down, because I think that without a field altar the Mass cannot be served."

"All we're missing is really only the field altar," the Field Chaplain said broodingly, "other than that everything is ready at the training ground. The carpenters have already built a platform there. The Břevnov monastery[230] will lend us the monstrance. I'm supposed to have my own chalice, but where is it now…"

He started thinking: "Let's say that I've lost it. — Then we'll get the sports trophy cup from Senior Lieutenant Witinger from the 75th Regiment. Years ago he used to run races and he won it running for Sport-Favorit[231]. He was a good runner. He used to do the 40 kilometers, Vienna — Mödling[232] in 1 hour 48 minutes, as he always brags. I already made a deal with him yesterday. I'm a dumb beast, always postponing everything until the last moment. Why didn't I, the nitwit, take a look inside that sofa."

Under the influence of the grog made according to the recipe from the degenerate sailor, he started berating himself in ungodly manner and expressed in the most varied sentences where it was, that he actually belonged.

"So we should already go to look for the field altar now," Švejk challenged, "it is morning already."

"I still have to put on my uniform and drink one more grog."

Finally they set off. On the way to see the wife of the trader in old furniture, the Field Chaplain was telling Švejk, that the day before he had won a lot of money by the grace of God, and if all turned out well, he would redeem the upright piano from the pawn shop.

It was a thing similar to pagans promising some sacrifice.

From the half-awake wife of the used furniture trader they learned the address of the teacher in Vršovice, the new owner of the sofa. The Field Chaplain displayed unusual generosity. He pinched her cheek and tickled her under the chin.

They went to Vršovice on foot, since the Field Chaplain declared that he needed to stroll in the fresh air to chase away unpleasant thoughts.

In the Vršovice apartment of the mister teacher, an old pious man, an unpleasant surprise awaited them. Having found the field altar in the sofa, the old gentleman believed it was a divine occurrence and he gifted it to the local church for its sacristy, having secured a provision that on the reverse side of the altar they would add an inscription:

"Gifted to honor and praise God, by Mr. Kolařík, teacher, Anno Domini 1914." Having been caught in his underwear, he was exhibiting great hesitancy.

From the conversation with him it was apparent, that he ascribed to the discovery the meaning of a miracle and an instruction from God. When he bought the sofa, he said, some inner voice told him:

"Take a look, what's in the sofa, in the drawer." He supposedly also saw some angel in a dream, who outright ordered him: "Open the drawer of the sofa." He obeyed.

And when he saw the miniature collapsible three-part altar, with a built-in recess for the tabernacle, he knelt in front of the sofa and for a long time prayed fervently and exalted God and took it for an instruction from heaven to adorn the church in Vršovice.

"We're not interested in that," said the Field Chaplain, "you should have turned such a thing, which didn't belong to you, over to the police and not to some damn sacristy."

"On account of this miracle," added Švejk, "*they* may have some difficulties. *They* bought a sofa, and not any altar, which belongs in the military inventory[233]. Such an instruction from God can cost *them* dearly. *They* shouldn't have listened to any angels. A man in Zhoř, tilling a field once, also dug up a chalice, that was part of booty from a sacrilegious theft and was hidden there for better times, when the theft would be forgotten, and he too thought it was an instruction from God and he, instead of melting it down, went to the parish priest with the chalice, saying that he wanted to gift it to the church. And the parish priest thought pangs of conscience had stirred in in him, sent for the mayor, the mayor sent for the state policemen and he was sentenced, though innocent, for sacrilegious theft, because he kept blathering something about a miracle. He wanted to save himself and so he also kept talking about an angel and mixed into it even Virgin Mary and gotten ten years. The best you can do is to come with us to the local priest to have him return the government property. A field altar is no cat or sock you can gift anybody you want."

The old man's whole body trembled and as he was dressing his teeth chattered: "I have really neither intended nor entertained any evil or wrong. I thought that through such a divinely guided occurrence I might help to adorn our poor temple of the Lord in Vršovice."

"At the expense of the military inventory, of course," Švejk said firmly and harshly, "thank God for these divinely guided occurrences. Some guy Pivoňka from Chotěboř also once thought it was a divine dispensation, when a halter with somebody else's cow attached wandered into his hand."

The poor old man was so confused by all of these pronouncements, that he stopped defending himself altogether, caring only to dress up and dispense with the whole matter as fast as possible.

The Vršovice parish priest was still asleep, and having been awakened by noise, he started to curse and swear, because being still half asleep he thought, that he was supposed to go out and give someone the last sacrament.

"They should leave me in peace and forget that extreme unction," he growled, dressing up reluctantly, "these people decide to die when I am in my best sleep. And one is then to haggle with them over money."

So in the hallway they met. He, the representative of the Lord God among civilian Catholics in Vršovice, and the other, the representative of God on Earth of the military inventory.

Overall, though, it was a dispute between a civilian and a soldier.

If the parish priest claimed that the field altar did not belong in a sofa, the Field Chaplain mentioned that it belonged accordingly even less in the sacristy of a church, where all, who go there, are civilians.

Švejk was at the same time making various remarks that it had been all too easy to enrich a poor church at the expense of the military inventory. The word "poor", he pronounced in quotes.

In the end they went to the sacristy of the church and the parish priest gave up the field altar with this receipt:

I received a field altar, which accidentally ended up in the temple of Vršovice[234].

Field Chaplain Otto Katz

This glorious field altar came from a Jewish firm, Moritz Mahler of Vienna, which used to make all kinds of holy mass accessories as well as religious objects, like rosaries and pictures of saints.

The altar consisted of three sections, appointed with very fake gild, just like the entire glory of the Holy Church.

It also was impossible to find out without imagination what the pictures painted on all its sections actually represented. What is certain is, that it was an altar, which could be used equally by some pagans on the Zambezi[235], or by shamans of the Buryats[236] or the Mongols[237].

Provided with loud colors, from afar it looked like those charts intended for examining *color-blind*[238] people at the railroad.

Only one figure stood out. Some naked man with a halo and a greenish body like the bishop's nose on a goose that already reeks and is in decay.

Nobody was doing anything to that saint. To the contrary, on both sides he had two winged creatures, that were supposed to represent angels. But the viewer had the impression that the saint naked man was screaming with fright over the company he was surrounded by. That is, the angels looked like fairy-tale monsters, something between a winged wildcat and an apocalyptic monster.

Opposite to it was a picture that was supposed to represent the Trinity of God. There was nothing about the dove the artist could, generally speaking, screw up. He painted some bird, which could have been either a dove or a White Wyandotte[239] hen.

But on the other hand, God the Father looked like a Wild-West robber, who was being introduced to the audience in a movie version of some suspenseful blood-and-gore story.

The Son of God was in contrast a merry young man with a nice tummy, covered by something that looked like a swimsuit. The whole created the impression of a sportsman. He held the cross in his hand with much elegance, as if it were a tennis racket.

From a distance though, it all blended and created an impression of a train rolling into railway station.

The third picture was altogether impossible to appraise as to what it represented. Soldiers were always arguing and trying to decipher this picture-puzzle. Somebody even thought that it was a landscape from the Posázaví[240].

There was, however, a caption underneath: Holy Mary, mother of God, have mercy on us.

Švejk luckily loaded the field altar into a cab, he himself took seat next to the cabman on the coach box, the Field Chaplain rested his feet in the cab comfortably on the Trinity of God.

Švejk chatted with the driver about military service.

The cabman was a rebel. He made various remarks about the victory of Austrian arms, such as: "They sure rocked you back on your heels in Serbia," and the like. When they crossed the food-tax line, the attendant asked what they were carrying.

Švejk answered:

"The Trinity of God and the Virgin Mary with the Field Chaplain."

At the training ground in the meantime, the marching companies had been impatiently waiting for the Field Chaplain. And waiting for a long time. For they still went to Senior Lieutenant Witinger's to fetch the sports chalice and then for the monstrance, ciborium and other appurtenances for the Mass to the Břevnov monastery, including a bottle of consecrated wine. All of this shows, that it is not that easy to serve a field Mass.

"We slap it together whichever way we can," Švejk told the cabman.

And he was right. The thing is that when they finally reached the training ground and were standing by the platform with the wooden railing and table, on which the field altar was to be set, it became apparent that the Field Chaplain had forgotten about the altar-boy.

For the altar boy he always used to have an infantryman from the regiment, who however preferred to get himself transferred to the telephone and rode off to the front.

"It doesn't matter, Field Chaplain, Sir," said Švejk, "I too can manage it and stand in."

"Do you know how to be an altar-boy?"

"I've never done it," answered Švejk, "but anything can be tried. Nowadays there is a war, and in war people do things they hadn't even dreamt of before. I can manage to put together some silly 'et cum spiritu tuo' to your 'dominus vobiscum' too. And then I think it shouldn't be that hard to pace around you like a cat around a bowl of hot porridge. And to wash your hands for you and pour wine from little jugs…"

"All right," said the Field Chaplain, "but don't pour me any water. Better pour wine into your second little jug right away as well. And besides, I'll always tell you whether you're to go right or left. If I whistle faintly once, that means to go to the right, twice to the left. You don't have to bother to drag the missal around much either. It's fun, after all. Don't you have stage fright?"

"I'm not afraid of anything, Field Chaplain, Sir, not even of serving as an altar-boy."

The Field Chaplain was right when he said: It's fun, after all.

Everything went tremendously smoothly.

The Field Chaplain's sermon was very terse.

"Soldiers! We've gathered here before your departure to the battle field to turn our hearts to God, so that he would give us victory and preserve us in good health. I won't be delaying you long and wish you all the best."

"*At ease*," hollered an old colonel on the left flank.

Field Mass is called field, because it is subject to the same principles as the military tactics are in the field. During the long maneuvers of troops during the Thirty Years War, the field Masses too were unusually long.

Given modern tactics, whereby the movements of the troops are quick and smart, the field Mass must also be quick and smart.

This one had just been underway ten minutes, and those, who were nearer the altar, were extraordinarily wondering, why in the midst of the Mass the Field Chaplain was whistling here and there.

Švejk had the signals down really sharp. He'd walk to the right side of the altar, again he was on the left, and kept saying nothing but "et cum spiritu tuo".

It looked like an American Indian dance around a sacrificial rock, but it made a good impression and alleviated the boredom of the dusty, sad training ground with an alley of plum trees in the back, and the latrines, the scent of which substituted for the mystical fragrance of frankincense of Gothic cathedrals.

All were tremendously entertained. The officers around the colonel were telling one another jokes and so everything went along in absolute order. Here and there among the troops could be heard: "Give me a drag".

And like a sacrificial smoke rising from the companies to heaven were blue puffs of tobacco smoke. All noncoms were smoking, when they saw that even the Colonel lit up.

At last *"To prayer"* rang out, a swirl of dust arose and the gray rectangle of uniforms bent its knees before the sports chalice of Senior Lieutenant Witinger, which he had won for Sport-Favorit in the race

Vienna — Mödling.

The chalice was full and the general judgment, accompanying the Field Chaplain's motions was that, which was sweeping through the ranks: "He sure slurped that up!"

That performance was repeated twice. Then one more time "*To prayer*", to which the band added for good measure "Preserve for us, oh Lord," fall in formation and dismissed.

"Pick up that junk," the Field Chaplain told Švejk, pointing to the field altar, "so that we can take it all and drive it back to where it belongs!"

So they rode with their cabman, returned everything honestly, except for the bottle of consecrated wine.

And when they were home, having referred the unhappy cabman to the Command Headquarters, regarding compensation for the long rides, Švejk said to the Field Chaplain: "I dutifully report, Field Chaplain, Sir, does the altar-boy have to be of the same confession as the one he assists?"

"Of course," answered the Field Chaplain, "otherwise the Mass wouldn't be valid."

"Then there's been, Field Chaplain, Sir, a big mistake," Švejk let himself be heard, "I'm of no confession. I just have such bad luck."

The Field Chaplain looked at Švejk, was silent for a while, then he patted him on the shoulder and said: "You can drink up the consecrated wine, which was left in the bottle, and think that you've again joined the Church."

12

A RELIGIOUS DEBATE

Sometimes it would happen, that for days at a time Švejk did not see the cultivator of military souls. The Field Chaplain performed his duties between carousing, and would come home only very rarely, dirty, unwashed, like a tomcat, when eager to mate he makes his outings across the rooftops.

Upon return, if able to express himself coherently, he would still chat with Švejk, before falling asleep, about lofty goals, zeal, the joy of thinking.

Sometimes he'd try to speak in verse, quote Heine[241].

Švejk served one more field Mass with the Field Chaplain at the sappers'[242], to which had been mistakenly invited yet another field chaplain, a former catechism teacher, an unusually pious man, looking at his colleague in amazement, when he offered him a swig of cognac from Švejk's field flask, something the latter always carried to perform such religious acts.

"It's a good brand," said Field Chaplain Otto Katz, "have a drink and go home. I'll take care of it myself because I need to be under the open sky, somehow I have a headache today."

The pious field chaplain left, shaking his head, and Katz acquitted himself, as usual, very well in his role.

At that time it was wine spritzer, that was being changed into blood of the Lord, and the sermon was longer, while every third expression he used was and so forth and certainly.

"Today, soldiers, you will be riding off to the front, and so forth. Do turn to God now, and so forth, certainly. You don't know what will happen to you, and so forth, and certainly."

And the so forth and certainly kept thundering from the altar, alternating with God and all the Saints.

In his zeal and lofty rhetoric, the Field Chaplain even tried to pass off Prince Eugene of Savoy as a Saint, who would protect them, when they're building bridges over rivers.

Nevertheless, the Field Mass ended without any scandal, pleasantly and entertainingly. The sappers had been entertained very well.

On the way back, they didn't want to let them on the streetcar with the collapsible altar.

"Don't make me whack you over your head with this saint," Švejk remarked to the conductor.

When they made it home at last, they discovered that somewhere along the way they had lost the tabernacle.

"It doesn't matter," said Švejk, "the first Christians used to serve the Holy Mass even without a tabernacle. If we were to report it somewhere, an honest finder would want a reward from us. If it were money, then there would be likely no honest finder to be had, although there still are such people. With our regiment in Budějovice there was a soldier, such a good-natured dumb beast, he once found six hundred crowns in the street and turned them in at the police station and in the newspaper they wrote him up as an honest finder and it brought him such shame. Nobody wanted to talk to him, everybody kept telling him: 'You stupid idiot, what a silly thing you have done. Come on, until the day you die you will regret it, if you have a bit of honor left in your body.' He had a girl and she stopped talking to him. When he came home on leave and went dancing, his friends threw him out of the pub on account of it. He started to waste away, let it get to him and in the end he let himself be run over by a train. Another time, a tailor in our street found a golden ring. People warned him not to turn it in at the police station, but he wouldn't let them talk him out of it. They welcomed him unusually kindly, saying that there had already been reported a loss of a golden ring with a cut diamond, but then they looked at the stone and said to him: 'Man, but this is glass, not a diamond. So how much did they give you for the diamond? We know all about honest finders like you.' In the end, the explanation was that another man had lost a golden ring with a fake diamond, some family memento, but the tailor did time sitting three days, nonetheless, because in the excitement he committed an insult of the patrolman. He received the lawful reward of 10 percent, 1 crown and 20 halers, because that junk was worth only 12 crowns, and he threw the lawful reward into that mister's face, and he sued him for insulting his honor and the tailor was fined ten crowns to boot. Afterward he would say everywhere he went, that every honest finder deserved twenty five lashes and to have his ass kicked until he turned blue, be thoroughly thrashed in public, so that people would remember all this and act accordingly. I don't think that anybody will bring back our tabernacle, even though it has the mark of our regiment on the back, because nobody wants anything to do with military matters. They would rather throw it in the water somewhere, to avoid any difficulties. Yesterday

I spoke at the Golden Wreath[243] pub with a man from the country, he is already fifty six years old, and he went to the District Administrator's Office in Nová Paka[244] to ask why they had requisitioned his gig. On the way back, after they threw him out of the District Administrator's Office, he watched a supply train that had just arrived and stopped in the square. Some young man asked him to watch his horses for a moment, because they were bringing food for the troops, and he never showed up again. When they got moving, he had to go with them and made it all the way to Hungary, where he too asked somebody else somewhere to stand by the wagon, and only that way he saved himself, when they would have dragged him all the way to Serbia. He came back all dumbfounded and never again wants to have anything anymore to do with military matters."

In the evening, they received a visit from the pious field chaplain, who had that morning also wanted to celebrate the field Mass for the sappers. He was a man fanatic, who wanted to get everybody closer to God. When he had been a catechist, he would develop a religious sense in the children by slapping their heads and once in a while, in various magazines, they'd publish brief items about him: "A brutal catechist," "A catechist, who gives out head slaps". He was convinced that a child would internalize catechism best with the help of the switch system.

He limped a bit with one leg, which was a consequence of having been looked up by the father of one of his pupils, whom the catechist had slapped a few times across the back of the head, because the pupil had been manifesting certain doubts about the Trinity of God. He had received three head slaps. One for God the Father, the second one for God the Son, and the third for the Holy Ghost.

Today he had come to steer his colleague Katz onto the right path, and to speak to his soul, which he began with these remarks: "I'm amazed that there's no crucifix hanging in your home. Where do you pray your divine office? Not even one picture of a saint adorns the walls of your living room. What is it you have hanging over your bed?"

Katz flashed a smile: "That is 'Susanna in the bath'[245] and the naked broad underneath is my old flame. On the right is a Japanese decorative artifact, representing a sexual act between a geisha and an old Japanese samurai. Really, something very original? My breviary is in the kitchen. Švejk, bring it here and open it to the third page."

Švejk left and from the kitchen came three times in quick succession the sound of the cork being pulled out of wine bottles.

The pious catechist was crushed, when three bottles appeared on the table.

"It's consecrated light wine, dear colleague," said Katz, "very good quality, Riesling. The taste is similar to Moselle[246]."

"I'm not drinking," said in stiff-necked tone the pious chaplain, "I came to talk about your soul."

"But you will, dear colleague, get very dry throat," said Katz, "have a drink and I'll listen. I am a very tolerant man and capable of listening to differing opinions."

The pious chaplain took a gulp and his eyes bugged out.

"Demons' grade of good wine, dear colleague, isn't that true?"

The fanatic replied harshly: "I see that you swear."

"That's a habit," answered Katz, "sometimes I catch myself that I'm even blaspheming. Pour for mister chaplain, Švejk. I can assure you, that I also say heavenly-lord-god and crucifix and damn. I think that when you will have served in the military as long as I have, you'll get the hang of it too. It is nothing at all hard or difficult and to us spiritual shepherds, it is very familiar: heaven, God, the cross and the exalted sacrament, doesn't that sound nice and expert? Drink up, dear colleague."

The former catechist took a sip mechanically. It was apparent, that he would have liked to say something, but couldn't. He was collecting his thoughts.

"Dear colleague," Katz continued, "keep your head up, don't sit there looking so sad, as if they were about to hang you in five minutes. I heard that once on a Friday by mistake you ate a pork chop at a restaurant, because you thought it was Thursday, and that in the bathroom you stuck a finger down your throat so that it would come out, because you thought that God would blot you out. I'm not afraid to eat meat during a fast and I'm not even afraid of hell. Pardon me, drink up. There, don't you feel better already? Or is it that you have a progressive view of hell and go along with the spirit of the times and with the reformists? That is, in place of the common cauldrons with sulfur for poor sinners Papin's[247] pressure cookers, high pressure cauldrons, sinners fry in margarine, electrically driven spits, for millions of years sinners are being driven over by road-building steam rollers, the sinners' gnashing of teeth is provided by dentists with special apparatuses, the wailing is being captured by the gramophones and the record plates are sent up to paradise for the amusement of the righteous. In paradise are engaged cologne[248] sprayers, the philharmonic plays Brahms[249] for so long, until you prefer hell or purgatory instead. The cherubs have in their butts airplane propellers, so that they don't have to toil so hard with their wings. Drink up, dear colleague, Švejk, pour him cognac, it seems to me, that he's not feeling well."

When the pious chaplain had recovered from Katz' salvo, he whispered:

"Religion is a rational speculation. He, who doesn't believe in the existence of the Holy Trinity…"

"Švejk," Katz interrupted him, "pour the mister Field Chaplain one more cognac, so that he comes to his senses. Tell him something, Švejk."

"Once there was near Vlašim[250], I dutifully report, Field Chaplain, Sir," said Švejk, "a dean and he had, since his housewife ran away with a boy and all his money, a housekeeper. In his old age this dean started studying St. Augustine[251], of whom they say that he is one of the holy fathers, and reading, he came across the statement that who believes in the existence of antipodes is to be cursed. So he called in his housekeeper and said to her: 'Listen, you told me once that your son is a machinist, who left for Australia[252]. That would mean that he is among antipodes, and Saint Augustine orders, that everybody, who believes in antipodes, be damned.' 'Gentle Sir,' replied the woman, 'but my son sends me letters and money from Australia.' 'That is satanic deceit,' retorted the dean, 'according to Saint Augustine some Australia does not exist, it's only the Antichrist seducing you.' On Sunday he publicly cursed them and kept hollering, that Australia didn't exist. So right away they drove him from the church straight to the madhouse. If you ask me, there are a few more that belong in there. At the Ursulines'[253] convent they have a vial of milk of Virgin Mary, with which she nursed the baby Jesus, and at the orphanage[254] near Benešov[255], when they brought in water from Lourdes[256], the orphans got the runs from it like the world has never seen before."

The pious field chaplain now started seeing black spots dancing in front of his eyes and he only came to with another shot of cognac, which went straight to his head.

His eyes squinting, he asked Katz: "You don't believe in the Immaculate Conception of the Virgin Mary, don't believe that the thumb of John the Baptist[257], being preserved and protected at the Piarists'[258] monastery, is genuine? Do you even believe in the Lord God? And if you don't, why are you a field chaplain?"

"Dear colleague" answered Katz, slapping him on the back in a familiar manner, "as long as the State doesn't consider it to be good, that soldiers, before they set out to die in battle, don't need God's blessing for it, the position of field chaplain is a fairly well remunerated employment, in which one doesn't overwork himself. For me, it was better than running around the training grounds, or going off on maneuvers... In those days, I used to receive orders from my superiors, and today, I do what I want. I represent somebody, who doesn't exist, and I myself play the role of God. If I don't want to forgive somebody his sins, then I don't forgive him, even if he begged me on his knees. However, one would find damn few of those."

"I love the Lord God," the pious chaplain said, beginning to hiccup, "I love Him very much. Give me little wine. — I respect God," he then continued, "I respect and honor Him very much. I don't respect anybody as much as Him."

He banged his fist on the table so hard, the bottles skipped: "God is an exalted character, something unearthly. He is honest in His matters. It is a sunshiny phenomenon, nobody can uproot that belief of mine. I respect Saint Joseph[259] as well, I respect all the Saints, with the exception of Saint Serapion[260]. He has such an ugly name."

"He should apply for a name change," remarked Švejk.

"I like Saint Ludmila[261] and Saint Bernard[262]," continued the former catechist, "he saved many pilgrims at Saint Gotthard[263]. He's got a bottle of cognac around his neck and he searches out people buried in the snow."

The entertainment took off in another direction. The pious chaplain started talking nonsense: "I honor the innocents, their Holy Day is December 28th. Herod[264] I hate. — When the hens sleep, then you can't get fresh eggs."

He started laughing and began to sing "Holy God, Holy, Mighty."

However, he interrupted it immediately, and turning to Katz, asked him sharply, getting up:

"You don't believe that August 15th is the Holy Day of the Assumption of the Virgin Mary?"

The merriment was now going at full throttle. Still more bottles appeared, and every so often Katz would pipe up: "Say that you don't believe in the Lord God, or else I'm not going to pour another for you."

It seemed that the times of the first persecuted Christians were returning. The former catechism teacher sang some song of martyrs in the Roman arena and hollered: "I believe in the Lord God, I won't deny Him. Keep your wine. I can send out for it myself."

In the end they deposited him in bed. Before he fell asleep, he declared, raising his right hand for an oath: "I believe in God, the Father, the Son, and the Holy Ghost. Bring me the breviary!"

Švejk stuck into his hand some book lying on the bedside table, and so the pious chaplain fell asleep with the Decameron by G. Boccaccio[265] in his hand.

13

ŠVEJK GOES TO PROVIDE THE LAST RITES

The Field Chaplain Otto Katz sat lost in thought over a circular, which he had just brought from the garrison. It was a classified memorandum from the Ministry of Military Affairs:

"The Ministry of Military Affairs is abolishing, for the duration of the war, the regulations which are in force regarding the provision of the last rites for the enlisted men of the Army and establishes the following rules for military clergymen[266]:

§ 1: At the front the last rites are abolished.

§ 2: It is not allowed for seriously ill or wounded soldiers to leave for the rear for the sake of the last anointing. Military clergymen are obligated to turn such people immediately over to the proper authorities for further prosecution.

§ 3: In military hospitals in the rear it is still possible to administer the last anointing to soldiers en masse, on the basis of expert opinion of military physicians, provided the last rite doesn't in itself have the characteristic of inconveniencing the given military institution.

§ 4: In exceptional cases, the Command of military hospitals in the rear can allow individuals to receive the last anointing.

§ 5: Military clergymen are obligated, when request-ed by the Command of military hospitals, to administer the last rites to those being nominated by the Command."

Afterwards the Field Chaplain read one more time the order informing him, that he was to go to the military hospital[267] in Charles' square the next day, to provide the last rites for the seriously wounded.

"Listen, Švejk," Field Chaplain called, "isn't that swine filth?" "As if in the whole of Prague I were the only field chaplain. Why don't they send there that pious chaplain that slept over here the last time. We're to go to provide the last rites at Charlie's. I've already forgotten how it's done."

"Then we'll buy a catechism booklet, Field Chaplain, Sir, it will be in there," said Švejk, "it's like a tourist guide for spiritual shepherds. In the Emmaus monastery there worked a gardener's helper, and when he wanted to join the order of laymen and get a frock, so he wouldn't have to tear his own clothes, he had to buy a catechism and learn how a sign of the cross is made, who was the only one spared from original sin and what is it to have a clean conscience, and other such trifles, and then he sold half the cucumbers from their cloister garden on the sly, and left the monastery in shame. When I next ran into him, he told me: 'I could have been selling those cucumbers even without the catechism.'"

When Švejk brought the purchased catechism, the Field Chaplain, paging through it, said: "See, the last anointing can be administered only by a priest, and only with oil sanctified by a bishop. So you see, Švejk, you yourself cannot provide the last anointing. Read for me the part about how the last anointing is given."

Švejk read: "It is administered in this way: The priest anoints the sick person's individual senses, praying concurrently: 'Through this holy anointing and His exceedingly gracious mercy, God has forgiven you whatever sins you have caused by sight, hearing, smell, taste, speech, touch and walk.'"

"I would like to know, Švejk, what sins a man can commit by touch, can you explain that to me?"

"Many things, Field Chaplain, Sir, he can touch the inside of somebody else's pocket or, at dancing parties, but you understand what spectacles take place there."

"And by walking, Švejk?"

"When he starts hobbling to make people take pity on him."

"And by smell?"

"When he doesn't like some stinking sonofabitch."

"And by taste, Švejk?"

"When he's got the taste for somebody's blood."

"And by speech?"

"That goes with the hearing already, Field Chaplain, Sir. When somebody blabs a lot and another is listening to him."

After these philosophical contemplations the Field Chaplain stopped and said: "Then we need oil sanctified by a bishop. Here you have ten crowns and buy a vial. They apparently don't have such oil at the army supply depot[268]."

So Švejk set out on a journey in search for oil sanctified by a bishop. Such a thing is worse than looking for the life-giving water in the fairy tales by Božena Němcová[269].

He went to several drugstores, and as soon as he said: "I'd like a vial of oil sanctified by a bishop, please," in some of them they started to laugh and elsewhere they hid terrified under the counter. At the same time Švejk had an unusually serious look on his face.

He then decided to try his luck at pharmacies. At the first one, they had him escorted out by the laboratory technician. At the second one, they threatened to phone the security station and at the third one, the head pharmacist told him, that the firm Polák on *Long Boulevard*[270], a purveyor of oils and lacquers, would definitely have the desired oil in stock.

The Polák firm on *Long Boulevard* was indeed an agile firm. It didn't let go of any buyer without having satisfied his wish. Should he want copaiba balsam, they poured him turpentine and that did just as well.

When Švejk arrived and expressed a desire for ten crowns worth of oil sanctified by a bishop, the boss told his shop clerk: "Mister Tauchen, *they* pour for him ten decagrams of hemp oil number three."

And the shop clerk, wrapping the vial in paper, told Švejk, strictly business-like: "This is top quality, should you want brushes, lacquers or varnish, do turn to us. We will take care of you reliably, honestly and thoroughly."

In the meantime, the Field Chaplain was brushing up in his catechism booklet on what in the seminary had not stuck in his memory. He really liked the unusually clever sentences, at which he genuinely laughed:

"The term 'last anointing' originates from the fact that this anointing is usually the last of all anointments that the Church gives to a man."

Or: "The last anointing can be received by any Catholic Christian, who has fallen dangerously ill and already come to his senses."

"The sick is to receive the last anointing, if possible, while still in possession of a good memory."

Then an army messenger arrived with a package, in which the Field Chaplain was informed, that the next day at the hospital, during the administering of last rites, there would also be present members of the Association of Noblewomen[271] for the Religious Education of Soldiers.

This Association consisted of hysterical nags and distributed among soldiers in the hospitals pictures of saints and a story book about a Catholic private dying for the lord Emperor. On the cover of the story book was a color picture representing a battle ground. Everywhere were strewn the carcasses of people and horses, turned-over munition wagons, and cannons with their gun carriages flipped up. On the horizon a village was burning and shells were bursting, and in the foreground lay a dying soldier with his leg ripped off, above whom was an angel bending over and giving him a wreath with an inscription on the ribbon: "This very day you will be with me in paradise." And the dying man smiled blessedly, as if they were bringing him ice cream.

After Otto Katz read through the contents of the package, he spat and thought: "Tomorrow is going to be one of those days."

He knew that rabble, as he called it, from the temple of Saint Ignatius[272], since years ago he used to give sermons to the troops there. Back then, he still put a lot into his sermons and the Association would sit behind the Colonel. Two longish females in black dresses with rosaries once approached him after a sermon and for two hours talked about the religious education of soldiers, until he got ticked off and told them: "Forgive me, my ladies, the Captain is waiting for me to join him for a game of ferbl."

"So now we have the oil," Švejk said festively upon his return from the Polák firm, "hemp oil number three of top quality, we can grease the whole battalion with it. It's a solid firm. They also sell varnish, lacquers and brushes. We still need a little bell."

"What for a little bell, Švejk?"

"We have to ring on the way, so people will take their hats off to us as we're going with the Lord God, Field Chaplain, Sir, with that hemp oil number three. That's the way it's done, and there have already been a lot of people locked up, who weren't paying any attention to it, because they didn't take their hats off. In Žižkov[273], a parish priest once beat up a blind man, because he didn't take his hat off on such an occasion, and he was locked up on top of it, because in court they proved that he wasn't deaf and dumb, but only blind, so he must have heard the tinkling of the bell and he caused people to feel offended, although it happened at night. It is like on the holy day of Corpus Christi. At other times people wouldn't even notice us, but now they'll be taking their hats off to us. If then, Field Chaplain, Sir, you don't have anything against it, I'll bring one right away."

Having received permission, Švejk brought a little bell in half an hour.

"It's off the gate of Křížek's roadside inn," he said, "it cost me five minutes of fear and I had to stall, because people kept trickling in and out."

"I'm going to the coffeehouse, Švejk, should anybody come, let him wait."

The Fateful Adventures of the Good Soldier Švejk

In about an hour arrived a graying, older gentleman with erect body posture and a stern look.

His whole appearance reeked of belligerent tenacity and anger. His eyes cast looks as if he had been sent by fate to destroy our miserable planet and obliterate its traces in the universe.

His speech was rough, dry and stern: "At home? That he's gone to some coffeehouse? That I'm to wait? Fine, I'll wait until morning. He's got enough for some coffeehouse, but to pay his debts, no way. Priest, phooey you demon!"

He spat on the kitchen floor.

"Mister, don't spit here in our place," said Švejk, watching the stranger with interest.

"And I'll spit one more time, see, like this," said stubbornly the stern gentleman, spitting on the floor for the second time, "how come he's not ashamed? Military clergyman, for shame!"

"If you are an educated man," said Švejk, putting him on notice, "then quit the habit of spitting in somebody else's apartment. Or do you think that, because there's a World War, you can dare to do anything? You are to behave properly, and not like a bum. You are to act gently, speak decently and not carry on like a rascal, you civilian jerk."

The stern gentleman got up from the chair, started shaking with agitation and screamed: "How dare you say that I am not a decent man, what am I then, tell me…"

"You are a little shithead," answered Švejk, looking straight into his eyes, "you're spitting on our floor, as if you were in a streetcar, on a train, or in some other enclosed public space. I've kept wondering, why there hang those signs everywhere, that spitting on the ground is forbidden, and now I see, that it's on account of you. They must know you very well everywhere."

The stern gentleman's face started changing colors and he was striving to answer with a flood of epithets aimed at both Švejk and the Field Chaplain.

"Are you done with your speechifying," Švejk asked calmly (when the last "both of you are hoodlums; so the master, so also is his knave" were uttered) "or do you want to add to it somehow, before you'll be flying down the stairs?"

Because the stern gentleman had exhausted himself to such an extent, that no valuable epithet came to his mind, and therefore he fell silent, Švejk took it to mean, that waiting for further addenda would be in vain.

So he opened the door and placed the visitor in the doorway facing the hall, and for such a kick would not have been ashamed even the best player on an international championship soccer team.

And following the stern gentleman's body down the staircase was carried Švejk's voice: "The next time you go somewhere for a visit to be among decent people, I suggest you behave properly."

The stern gentleman kept pacing under the windows for a long time and was waiting for the Field Chaplain. Švejk opened a window and observed him.

Finally the visitor's patience paid off and the Field Chaplain escorted the stubborn man into the living room and sat him down in a chair opposite him.

Švejk, maintaining silence, brought in a spittoon and placed it in front of the guest.

"What is it you're doing, Švejk?"

"I dutifully report, Field Chaplain, Sir, that there has already been a slight unpleasantness with this gentleman on account of spitting on the floor."

"Leave us, Švejk, we have something to resolve between the two of us."

"I dutifully report, Field Chaplain, Sir, that I'm leaving you."

He went into the kitchen and in the living room a very interesting conversation was taking place.

"You came for the money to cover the draft, if I'm not mistaken?" the Field Chaplain asked of his guest.

"Yes, and I hope…"

The Field Chaplain let out a sigh.

"A man comes often into a situation where all he has left is hope. How beautiful is that little phrase 'keep your hope', one part of that three-leafed clover, that elevates man from the chaos of life: faith, hope, and love."

"I hope, dear Field Chaplain, that the amount…"

"Certainly, honorable Sir," the Field Chaplain interrupted him, "I can repeat one more time, that the word 'to hope' strengthens man in his struggle with life. Even you are not losing hope. How beautiful it is to hold a certain ideal, to be an innocent, pure creature, someone, who lends money against a draft and has the hope that it will get repaid on time. To keep hoping, incessantly hoping, that I will pay you the 1,200 crowns, when in my pocket I have less than a hundred."

"Then you...," stuttered the guest.

"Yes, I then...," answered the Field Chaplain.

The face of the guest regained the expression of belligerent tenacity and anger it had displayed earlier.

"Sir, this is fraud," he said, getting up.

"Calm down, honorable Sir..."

"This is fraud," the guest bellowed stubbornly, "you have taken advantage of my trust."

"Sir," said the Field Chaplain, "you will certainly benefit from a change of air. It is too stuffy in here. — Švejk," he yelled into the kitchen, "this gentleman wishes to go out into the fresh air."

"I dutifully report, Field Chaplain, Sir," resounded from the kitchen, "that I have already thrown the gentleman out once."

"Repeat," was the announced order, which was executed quickly, smartly and cruelly.

"It's a good thing, Field Chaplain, Sir," Švejk said as he returned from the hallway, "that we got rid of him, before he committed some breech of the peace here. In Malešice[274] there was once a pubkeeper, an avid reader of the Scriptures, who had quotes from the Holy Writ for everything, and when he had to whack somebody with a blackjack, he would always say: 'He, who spares the rod, hates his son; but he, who loves him, chastens him betimes, I'll get you for fighting in my pub.'"

"You see, Švejk, that's how it ends up with a man, who doesn't honor a priest," the Field Chaplain said with a smile. "Saint John Chrysostom[275] said: 'He, who honors the priest, honors Christ, he, who persecutes the priest, persecutes Christ the Lord, whose representative is that very priest.' — We have to be perfectly prepared for tomorrow. Let's make fried eggs and ham, cook up some Bordeaux[276] punch and then, let's meditate, because as it says in the evening prayer: 'Turned away by the mercy of God are all the snares of the enemies of this dwelling.'"

In this world there exist some very persistent people, among which belonged the man, who had already been thrown twice out of the Field Chaplain's apartment. Just when the dinner was ready, somebody rang the doorbell. Švejk went to open the door, then came back shortly and reported: "He's here again, Field Chaplain, Sir. I've locked him in the bathroom, for the time being, so that we could dine contentedly."

"That's not the right thing to do, Švejk," Otto Katz said. "a guest enters the house, God's in the house. During the feasts of ancient times they amused themselves with mutant freaks. Bring him in here, and let him entertain us."

Švejk returned in a while with the amazingly persistent man, who stared morosely off into distance.

"Take a seat," the Field Chaplain invited him kindly, "we're just finishing our dinner. We had lobster, salmon and now still fried eggs and ham. It's easy for us to feast, when people lend us money."

"I hope that I'm not here to be the butt of jokes," said the sullen man, "today I'm here for the third time already. I hope that now everything will get explained."

"I dutifully report, Field Chaplain, Sir," remarked Švejk, "that he's almost the perfect diehard, like some guy Boušek from Libeň. Eighteen times in one night they threw him out of Exner's[277], and each time he came back in, saying that he had forgotten his pipe there. He crawled in through a window, through a door, from the kitchen, over a wall into the pub, through the cellar into the taproom and he would have dropped in down the chimney, had the firemen not picked him off the roof. So persistent was he that he could have become a government minister, or a member of the Parliament. They've done everything for him they could."

The persistent man, as if not caring what was being said, stubbornly repeated: "I want to have a clear picture and I wish to be heard out."

"That will be permitted of you," the Field Chaplain said, "speak, honorable Sir. Speak as long as you want, and we will, in the meantime, continue our feast. I hope that it won't hinder your narration. Švejk, bring more to the table."

"As is known to you," said the persistent man, "a war rages. I lent you that sum before the war, and if it weren't for the war, I wouldn't insist, that it be paid up. But I've had sad experiences."

He pulled a notebook from his pocket and continued: "I have it all written down. Senior Lieutenant Janata owed me 700 crowns, and had the audacity to fall at the Drina[278]. First Lieutenant Prášek was captured on the Russian front, and he owes me around two thousand crowns. Captain Wichterle[279], owing me the same amount, let himself get killed by his own soldiers near Rawa Ruska[280]. Senior Lieutenant Machek[281] was taken prisoner in Serbia, owing me 1,500 crowns. There are more people like that. This one falls in the Carpathians[282] with my draft unrepaid, that one goes into captivity, another drowns on me in Serbia, this one dies in Hungary in a hospital. Now you understand my fears, that this war will annihilate me, if I am not energetic and inexorable. You may raise the objection that, in your case, no direct danger looms. Take a look."

He pushed his notebook under the field chaplain's nose. "You see: Field Chaplain Matyáš in Brno died in an isolation hospital a week ago. I could pull my hair out. He didn't pay me my 1,800 crowns, and goes into some quarantined cholera building to give the last rites to a man, who was none of his business."

"That was his duty, dear Sir," said the Field Chaplain. "I too am going tomorrow to administer last rites."

"And also in a choleric building," remarked Švejk; "you can come along, so that you'd see what it means to sacrifice oneself."

"Field Chaplain, Sir," the persistent man said, "trust me, I'm in a desperate situation. Is the war being fought in order to wipe all of my debtors off the face of the Earth?"

"When they draft you in the military and march you into the field," remarked Švejk again, "then the Field Chaplain and I will celebrate a Holy Mass, in order for the heavenly God to grant, that the first grenade would condescend to bust you up."

"Sir, this is a serious matter," the perfect diehard said to the Field Chaplain, "I ask that your servant not mix himself into our affairs, so that we can immediately bring it to an end."

"Excuse me," Field Chaplain, Sir," piped up Švejk, "condescend to really order me that I not mix myself into your affairs, otherwise I'll keep defending your interests, as becomes a real soldier and is proper for him. That gentleman is completely right, he wants to leave here on his own. I too don't like any scenes, I'm a social man."

"Švejk, this is beginning to bore me," said the Field Chaplain, as if not noticing the guest's presence. "I thought that the man would entertain us, would tell us some jokes, but he requests, that I order you not to mix yourself in it, even though you already had to deal with him twice. In the evening, when I stand before such an important religious act, when I'm supposed to turn all of my senses to God, he is bothering me with some asinine story about miserable 1,200 crowns, distracting me away from searching my conscience, away from God, and he wants me to tell him one more time, that I won't give him any money. I don't want to talk to him any longer, lest this sacred evening be spoiled. You yourself tell him, Švejk: Mister Field Chaplain won't give you anything."

Švejk fulfilled the order, having yelled it into the guest's ear.

The persistent guest, however, remained seated.

"Švejk," the Field Chaplain urged, "ask him, how much longer he thinks he's going to stay here gawking?"

"I won't move from here, until I am reimbursed," the perfect diehard said stubbornly.

The Field Chaplain stood up, went to the window and said: "In that case, I am relegating him to you, Švejk. Do with him what you want."

"Let's go, mister," said Švejk, having grabbed the unpleasant guest by the shoulder, "third time's lucky."

And he repeated his earlier performance quickly and elegantly, while the Field Chaplain drummed a dirge with his fingers on the window pane.

The evening devoted to meditation passed through several phases. The Field Chaplain was drawing closer to God so piously and ardently, that at twelve o'clock at night the sound of his singing could still be heard coming out of his apartment:

> When we were marching,
> all the girls were weeping…

Singing along with him was also the good soldier Švejk.

*

Desiring the last anointing in the Military Hospital were two men. One old major and the other a bank manager reserve officer. They both had caught a bullet in the belly in the Carpathians and were on beds next to each other. The reserve officer felt, it was his duty to have the last rites for the dying, because his superior strongly desired he have the last anointing. He believed, that not to have the last anointing would be a breach of subordination. The pious major was doing it out of smart calculation, thinking that a prayer of faith would heal a sick man.

However, the night before their last anointing, they both died, and when the Field Chaplain and Švejk arrived in the morning, they were lying under bed sheets with their faces turned black, like all those, who die of asphyxiation.

"We were in our glory, Field Chaplain, Sir, and now they've spoiled it for us," expressed his anger Švejk, when at the office they were informed that those two no longer needed anything.

It was true, that they had been in their glory. As they rode in the cab, Švejk kept ringing and the Field Chaplain held in his hand the vial of oil, wrapped in a cloth napkin, with which he solemnly blessed any passers-by, who took off their hats.

Truly, there weren't many of them, although Švejk strove to create a huge racket with his bell.

Behind the cab ran several innocent babes, one of whom sat down on the back bumper, whereupon his cohorts cried out in unison:

"Follow the carriage, follow the carriage!"

Švejk kept ringing his bell in the midst of it all, the cabman slashing his whip to the back, on Vodičkova street some resident custodian, a member of a Marian congregation[283], caught up with the cab jogging, had herself blessed on the go, crossed herself, then spat: "You're riding with the Lord God, as if all the demons were driving the cab! One could catch consumption!" and out of breath she returned to her old spot.

The most disturbed by the sound of the bell was the mare pulling the cab, as apparently it must have reminded her of something from the past, because she kept turning and looking back and every so often, she'd attempt to do a dance on the cobble stones.

So this was the great glory Švejk was talking about. The Field Chaplain went into the office in the meantime, to take care of the financial side of the last anointing, and he had already calculated for the accounting master sergeant, that the military owed him about one hundred and fifty crowns for the sanctified oil and the journey.

What followed next was a dispute between the officer in command of the hospital and the Field Chaplain, during which the Field Chaplain banged his fist on the desk several times and expressed himself thusly: "Don't think, mister commander, that last anointing is free of charge. When an officer of the Dragoons[284] is ordered to a stud farm to be with his horses, then he gets his per diem paid too. I truly regret that these two didn't live to get the last anointing. It would have been fifty crowns more expensive."

Švejk in the meantime waited down at the guard house with the vial of sanctified oil, which stirred real interest among the soldiers.

One was of the opinion, that the oil might well be used to clean their rifles and prongs.

Some very young soldier from Czech-Moravian Highlands[285], who still believed in the Lord God, begged them not talk about such things and said not to bring the Holy Mysteries into the conversation. We have to Christianly hope.

An old reservist looked at the greenhorn and said: "Nice hope that is, that shrapnel will tear your head off. They bamboozled us. At one time there came to us some member of the Parliament and told us about God's peace arching over the Earth, and how the Lord God doesn't wish for a war and wants that everybody live in peace and tolerate one another like brothers. And look at him, the dumb ox, as soon as the war broke out, in all the churches they pray for the success of arms and they speak of the Lord God like he's a chief of the general staff[286], who directs and conducts the war. I've already seen too many burials out of this hospital, and cut-off legs and arms they cart away from here."

"And they bury the soldiers naked," said another soldier, "and they dress up another live one in that uniform again and so it goes nonstop."

"Until we win," remarked Švejk.

"This old pipe wants to win something," piped up a sergeant in a corner. "To position with you, into the trenches, drive you into bayonet attacks for all it's worth, wires, saps and mortars. Lying around in the rear, anybody can handle that, and nobody wants to fall."

"I also think that it is very nice to get run through with a bayonet," said Švejk, "and it's not bad either to get a round in the belly, and it's nicer yet, when a grenade breaks a man up and he sees that his legs even with the belly are somehow detached from him, and he thinks it so strange, that he will die from it before somebody can explain it to him."

A very young soldier sighed sincerely. He pitied his own young life, that he was born in such a stupid century, to be cut like a cow at slaughter. Why then is all this?

One of the soldiers, a teacher by profession, as if he were reading his thoughts, remarked: "Some learned men explain war by the emergence of spots on the sun. As soon as such a spot emerges, then something terrible always comes. The conquest of Carthage[287]..."

"*They* keep *their* educated bullshit," the sergeant interrupted him, "and go sweep out the room, today it's your turn. What do we care about some stupid sun spot? If there were even twenty of them, that couldn't buy me anything."

"The spots on the sun have a really great significance," Švejk mixed in, "there once emerged such a spot and the very same day I got beaten up at Banzets' in Nusle. Since then, whenever I'd go somewhere, I always searched in the newspaper to see, whether some spot hasn't emerged. As soon as it has, good-bye, Mary, I didn't go anywhere and only just like that I waited it out. When back then that Mount Pelée[288] volcano destroyed the whole island of Martinique[289], a professor[290] wrote in the *National Politics*, that he'd been long alerting readers to a large spot on the sun. But the *National Politics* didn't arrive at the island in time, and so they really over there on that island paid for it."

In the meantime the Field Chaplain was meeting in the office upstairs with one lady of The Institute for the Noblewomen for the Religious Education of Soldiers, an old, unpleasant hag, who since early that morning had been going around the hospital, handing out everywhere pictures of the saints, which the sick and wounded would pitch into the spittoons.

During her rounds she kept upsetting everybody with her stupid prattle, that they should feel sincerely sorry for their sins and truly repent, so that way after they died God would give them eternal salvation.

She was pale, when she spoke to the Field Chaplain. How the war, instead of ennobling, turned the soldiers into animals. Downstairs the patients stuck their tongues out at her and told her that she was a mummer and a heavenly goat. *"That is really horrible, mister Field Chaplain. The people have turned coarse."*

And she started speaking of her vision of the religious education of the soldier. He fights courageously for his lord Emperor only when he believes in God and has religious affection, as then he is not spooked by death, because he knows that paradise awaits him.

This motor-mouth said a few more similar idiocies and it was apparent, that she was determined not to let go of the Field Chaplain, who excused himself quite without elegance.

"We're going home, Švejk!" he called into the guard house. On the return trip they were not making any glory.

"Next time let whomever wants to go to provide the last rites," said the Field Chaplain, "it's as if a man has to haggle over money for each soul he wants to save. All they have is their accounting, the riffraff."

Spotting the vial of 'sanctified' oil in Švejk's hand, he frowned: "We'll do best, Švejk, when you shine my and your shoes with it."

"I'll try to grease the lock with it, too," added Švejk, "It screeches terribly when you're coming home in the night."

Thus ended the last anointing, that never took place.

14

ŠVEJK AS A MILITARY SERVANT UNDER SENIOR LIEUTENANT[1] LUKÁŠ

1

Švejk's good luck and happiness was not of long duration. Merciless fate tore asunder the friendly relationship between him and the Field Chaplain. If the Field Chaplain had been likeable until that event, what he now did has the potential to tear the likable visage off him.

The Field Chaplain sold Švejk to Senior Lieutenant Lukáš, or better said, he lost him playing cards. That way in earlier times in Russia they used to sell serfs. It happened so unexpectedly. There was a nice social gathering at Senior Lieutenant Lukáš's and the game played was one-and-twenty.

The Field Chaplain lost everything and in the end he said: "How much are you going to lend me against my military servant? Tremendous idiot and an interesting figure, something non plus ultra[2]. You have never had such a military servant."

"I will lend you a hundred crowns," Senior Lieutenant Lukáš offered, "if by the day after tomorrow I don't get them back, you'll send me this rarity. My spotshine is an irritating man. He constantly sighs, writes letters home, and all the while he steals everything he comes across. I have already beaten him, but it's of no use. I slap him across the head every time I run into him, but it doesn't help. I have knocked out a couple of his front teeth, but still haven't straightened the guy out."

"Then it's a deal," said carelessly the Field Chaplain, "either a hundred crowns the day after tomorrow, or Švejk."

He lost even the hundred crowns and went home sad. He knew with certainty, and also didn't doubt it in any way, that by the day after tomorrow, he wouldn't be able to chase down the hundred crowns and that he had lousily and villainously sold Švejk.

"I could have asked for two hundred crowns," he mused petulantly, but changing to the streetcar line that was to carry him home shortly, he was attacked by feelings of recrimination and sentimentality.

---

[2] Latin: *"nothing further beyond"*; meaning *"the highest"*, *"unsurpassed"*

"This is not nice of me," he thought to himself, as he rang the doorbell by the door of his apartment, "how will I be able to look into his stupid, good-natured eyes?"

"Dear Švejk," he said, when he was at home, "today something unusual happened. I had such bad luck at cards. I kept hopping[291] everything and I had an ace in my hand, then I got a ten, and the banker had a jack in the hand and he too made it to one-and-twenty. I licked off an ace or a ten several times, but I always had the same count as the banker. I blew through all my money."

He paused. "And in the end, I lost you. I borrowed a hundred crowns against you, and if I don't bring them back by the day after tomorrow, you won't belong to me anymore, but to Senior Lieutenant Lukáš. I'm really sorry about it..."

"A hundred crowns, that much I still have," said Švejk, "I can lend them to you."

"Give them to me," the Field Chaplain revived, "I'll take them to Lukáš right away. I really wouldn't like saying goodbye to you."

Lukáš was very surprised when he saw the Field Chaplain again.

"I'm coming to pay my debt to you," said the Field Chaplain, looking around triumphantly, "deal me in too."

"I'll hop it," the Field Chaplain said when it was his turn. "I was over" he announced "only by an eye."

"I'll hop it again," he said the second time around, "I'll hop — blind."

"Twenty takes," the banker announced.

"I got all of nineteen," the Field Chaplain proclaimed softly, giving the banker the last forty of the one hundred crowns, which Švejk had lent him to redeem himself out of his new serfdom.

Returning home, the Field Chaplain became convinced, that this was the end, that nothing could save Švejk, it was foreordained, that he serve under Senior Lieutenant Lukáš.

And when Švejk opened the door for him, he said "All is in vain, Švejk. Nobody can defend himself against fate. I lost you and the one hundred crowns of yours, too. I've done everything, which was in my power, but fate is stronger than I. It has cast you into the talons of Senior Lieutenant Lukáš and the time will come, that we'll have to part."

"Was there a lot in the bank?" Švejk asked calmly, "or were you only seldom the forehand? When the cards are not coming your way, it is very bad, but sometimes it's just as lousy, when the game goes your way too well. In Na Zderaze[292] street, there lived some tinsmith named Vejvoda and he always played mariáš[293] in a pub behind the Centennial Coffeehouse[294]. This one time too, the demon had whistled the lure in his ear, he says: 'And how about casting a oner for a nickel.' So they played a nickel oner and he held the bank. They all tropped[295] out and so the ante grew to a tenner. Old Vejvoda wanted to let the others also get something and he kept saying: 'Little one, bad one, come home.' You cannot imagine the bad luck he had. The little bad one wouldn't and wouldn't come, the bank grew, and already a hundred was in it. None of the players had enough to hop it, and Vejvoda was already all in sweat. You could hear nothing else, but this: 'Little one, bad one, come home.' They kept upping the stakes by a tenner and they kept falling in the bank. A master chimney sweep got ticked off and went home to get more money, when there was already more than a hundred and a half in there, and he hopped it. Vejvoda just wanted to get rid of it, and as he later told the story, he wanted to draw his hand up to maybe thirty, just so that he wouldn't win, and instead of that, he got two aces. He acted as if he had nothing, and purposefully said: 'Sixteen takes.' And the master chimney sweep had all in all fifteen. Isn't that bad luck? Old Vejvoda was all pale and unhappy, all around they were already bitching and whispering that he uses sleight of hand, that he'd been beaten up once already for cheating at the game, although he was the most honest player, and they poured one little crown in there after another. There were already five hundred crowns. The pubkeeper finally broke down. He just had money put aside ready to pay the brewery, so he grabbed it, took a seat, threw in at first two hundred crowns at a time, closed his eyes, turned the chair around for good luck and said that all of what is in the bank, he's hopping it. 'Let's play,' he says, 'with open cards'. Old Vejvoda would have given anything to lose now. They all marveled when he turned a card and a seven showed up, and he kept it. The pubkeeper smiled under his mustache, because he had one-and-twenty. A second seven came to old Vejvoda, and he kept that one too. 'Now, you will get an ace or a ten,' the pubkeeper said with malicious pleasure, 'I'm betting my neck, Mister Vejvoda, that you'll be trop.' There was astounding silence, Vejvoda turns next one over, and what appears, but a third seven. The pubkeeper turned pale as chalk, that was his last money, he went into the kitchen and after a little while, a boy, his apprentice, runs in yelling that we should go and cut the pubkeeper down, that he's hanging on the window handle. So we cut him down, revived him, and the game went on. Nobody had any money anymore, it was all in the bank in front of Vejvoda, who only kept saying: 'Little one, bad one, come home' and for the love of the living God wanted to go trop, but because he had to turn his cards over and lay them on the table, he couldn't cheat and go over on purpose. They were all completely dazed already over his good luck, so what they did, since they didn't have money, they would just keep putting in their markers. It took several hours and in front of old Vejvoda were piling thousands and thousands. The master chimney sweep already owed the bank over a million and half, a coalman from Zderaz about a million, the custodian from the Centennial coffeehouse 800,000 crowns, and a medic over two million. Just the pinka[296] pile held another 300,000 on all little scraps of paper. Old Vejvoda kept trying every which way. He kept going to the bathroom, and always gave it to somebody else to stand in for him, and when he came back, they would report to him, that he got paid, that another one-and-twenty came his way. They sent out for new cards, and again it was in vain. When Vejvoda stopped at fifteen, then the second one would have fourteen. They all looked angrily at old Vejvoda and the one cursing and swearing the most was a paver, who had put in all of eight crowns. He openly proclaimed that a man such as Vejvoda shouldn't walk the face of the Earth and should be brutally kicked, thrown out and drowned like a puppy. You cannot imagine the desperation of old Vejvoda. Finally, he got an idea. 'I'm going to the bathroom,' he said to the chimney sweep, 'take over for me, master chimney sweep'. And just like that, without a hat, he ran right to Myslíkova street[297] for the patrolmen. He found the patrol and informed it that in such and such pub they're playing a hazardous card game. The patrolmen asked him to go up ahead, that they would follow him right away. So he returned and they informed him, that so far the medic had lost over two million and the custodian more than three. They said the pinka now had markers for over five hundred thousand crowns. A little while later the patrolmen burst in, and the paver yelled out: 'Save yourself, all who can,' but it was in vain. They confiscated the bank, led all to the police station. The coalman from Zderaz resisted, so they brought him in in a košatinka. In the bank there were marks for over half a billion and fifteen hundred in cash. 'I've never laid my eyes on anything like it,' said the police inspector, when he saw such dizzying amounts, 'this is worse than Monte Carlo[298].' They all stayed there, except for old Vejvoda, until morning. Since Vejvoda was the informer, they let him go and promised that he'd get the legal reward of one third of the confiscated bank, about more than one hundred sixty million, but by morning he had gone mad and in the morning he was walking around Prague ordering burglar-proof safes by the dozen. That's what you call bad luck at cards."

Švejk then went to make grog, and the way it ended up was that the Field Chaplain, when in the night Švejk managed to transport him with effort to bed, shed a tear and whined:

"I've sold you, buddy, shamefully sold you. Curse me, beat me, I won't flinch. I threw you away. I can't look you in the eyes. Tear me, bite me, destroy me. I don't deserve anything better. Do you know what I am?"

The Field Chaplain, burying his tear-stained face into a pillow, said in a low, gentle, soft voice: "I am an unscrupulous scoundrel," and he fell deep asleep, as if they'd thrown him in water.

The next day, the Field Chaplain, avoiding again Švejk's gaze, left early in the morning and returned only in the night with some fat infantryman.

"Show him, Švejk," he said, again avoiding his gaze, "where everything is, so that he can orient himself, and instruct him, how grog is made. In the morning, report to Senior Lieutenant Lukáš."

Švejk and the new man spent the night pleasantly, making grog. Toward the morning, the fat infantryman was barely able to stand on his feet and was humming a strange medley of various national folk songs, which he got comingled: "Around Chodov[299], a little water runs, my most beloved draws red beer there. Mountain, mountain, you are high, maids strolled down the road, on the White Mountain[300] a little farmer is plowing."

"I don't worry about you," said Švejk, "with such talent, you'll manage to hang on with the Field Chaplain."

So it happened that morning, that Senior Lieutenant Lukáš saw for the first time the honest and sincere face of the good soldier Švejk, who reported to him: "I dutifully report Senior Lieutenant, Sir, that I'm that Švejk lost by the Field Chaplain playing cards."

2

The institution of military officers' servants is of ancient origin. It seems that Alexander of Macedonia already had his spotshine. It is certain, however, that in feudal times the knights' mercenaries fulfilled this role. What was Sancho Panza³⁰¹ to Don Quixote³⁰²? I am surprised, that the history of military servants has not yet been written by anyone. We would find in there, that the Duke of Almavira³⁰³ ate his military servant during the siege of Toledo³⁰⁴ due to hunger without any salt, which the duke himself writes about in his memoirs, saying that his servant's meat was delicate, tender, and supple, in taste similar to something between meat of chicken and donkey.

In an old Swabian³⁰⁵ book on the military arts, we find detailed guidelines for military servants. The spotshine of old times was to be pious, virtuous, truthful, modest, valiant, courageous, honest, and diligent. In short, he was to be the paradigm of a man. In this new era, a lot has changed pertaining to this archetype. The modern pipe³⁰⁶ isn't usually pious, or virtuous, or truthful. He lies, bamboozles his master, and turns the life of his officer very often into genuine hell. He is a sly slave, thinking up the most varied insidious tricks to make his master's life bitterer. Among this new generation of spotshines cannot be found such self-sacrificing creatures, which would let themselves be eaten by their master without salt, as the Duke of Almavira's noble Fernando did. On the other hand we see that officers, wrestling for life or death with their servants of the new era, use the most diverse means to hold onto their authority. It tends to be a certain type of rule by terror. In the year 1912 there was a trial in Graz³⁰⁷, in which an outstanding role was played by a captain, who had kicked his spotshine to death. He was freed back then, because he had done it only for the second time. In the opinions of these gentlemen, the life of a spotshine has no worth. It is merely an object, in many cases, a punching bag, a slave, a maidservant for all work. It's no wonder then, that such a position demands of the slave to be crafty and sly. His position on our planet can be compared only to the suffering of the waiter apprentices of old times, who were trained to be conscientious by slaps to the head and torture.

There occur cases, however, when a spotshine rises to become a favorite and here he becomes the terror of the company, the battalion. All noncoms try to bribe him. He decides the leaves, he can put in a good word, so that at the command report it turns out well.

These favorites would be during the war awarded large and small silver medals for courage and gallantry.

At the 91st Regiment I knew several of them. One spotshine got a large silver one, because he was an excellent cook of the geese he used to steal. Another one got a small silver one, because he used to receive beautiful shipments of food supplies from home, so that his master during the time of the greatest hunger overstuffed himself so much, that he couldn't walk.

And his master formulated the recommendation for awarding him medals thusly:

"For, in battles, he shows extraordinary courage and valor, kept disregarding his own life and wouldn't abandon his officer, not moving away from him even by one step, while under the heavy fire of the charging enemy."

And he was actually somewhere in the rear plundering henhouses. The World War has changed the relationship of the spotshine to his master and has made him the most hated creature among the troops. The spotshine always had a whole can of food when one was being distributed for five men. His field flask was always full of rum or cognac. All day this creature chewed on chocolate, gobbled up officers sweet biscuits, smoked his officer's cigarettes, whipped up meals and cooked for hours on end and wore an extra uniform blouse.

The officer's servant was in intimate contact with the official army messenger and granted him plentiful left-overs from his table and from all those privileges he had. To complete the triumvirate he would take in the accounting master sergeant. This threesome, living in immediate contact with their officer, knew all the operations and war plans.

The best informed about when it will begin, was the unit, whose sergeant was the buddy of the officer's servant.

When he said: "At two-thirty-five we'll be hauling our ass out of here," then at exactly two-thirty-five the Austrian soldiers started disengaging from the enemy.

The officer's servant also had the most intimate of relationships with the field kitchen and gladly hung by the cauldron and ordered food for himself, as if he were at a restaurant and had a menu in front of him.

"I want a rib," he'd tell the cook, "yesterday you gave me a tail. Also, add a piece of liver to the soup for me, you know that I don't feed on spleen."

And the spotshine was at his most magnificent when he created panic. During a bombardment of the positions, his heart would drop into his pants. At that time, he would be with his and his master's luggage in the safest covered trench and hide his head under a blanket, so that a grenade couldn't find him, and he had no greater wish than for his master to be wounded, and with him he would get to the rear, fade into the background, really deep.

He cultivated panic constantly with certain secretiveness. "It seems to me, that they are breaking down the telephones," he would relay confidentially among the units. And he was happy, when he could say: "They've already broken them down."

Nobody liked to retreat as much as he did. At that moment he would forget, that swishing above his head were grenades and shrapnel, and he would make his way tirelessly with the luggage to the staff headquarters, where the horse-drawn transport wagons were waiting. He was fond of the Austrian military supply trains and he was unusually fond of riding in them. In the worst cases he would make use of even two-wheeled ambulance gigs. When he had to go on foot, he made the impression, that he was the most devastated human. In such case he left his master's luggage in the trenches and would drag only his own possessions.

Should such a case happen, that his officer ran away to avoid capture and he himself remained there, the officer's servant in no case forgot to drag into captivity his master's luggage, as well. It became his property, to which he clung with all of his soul.

I saw once a captured officer's servant, who walked from Dubno[308] all the way to Darnitsa[309] on the other side of Kiev[310]. In addition to his backpack and the backpack of his officer, who had run away to avoid capture, he had with him also five hand suitcases of various shapes, two blankets and a pillow, aside from some luggage he carried on his head. He complained that the Cossacks had stolen from him two more suitcases.

I'll never forget the man, who was killing himself dragging it so through the whole of Ukraine[311]. He was a live shipping wagon and I cannot comprehend, how he was able to carry and drag it for so many hundreds of kilometers and then ride with it all the way to Tashkent[312], looking after it and die on his luggage from spotted typhus in a prisoner-of-war camp.

Nowadays are officers' servants dispersed throughout this whole Republic of ours and they tell yarns of their heroic deeds. They charged the enemy at Sokal[313], Dubno, Niš[314], and Piave[315]. Every one of them is a Napoleon: "I told our Colonel to call the Staff Headquarters, that it can now begin already."

Most were reactionaries and the troops hated them. Some were informers and it was for them a special pleasure to be able to watch, as somebody was being tied up.

They evolved into a special caste. Their selfishness knew no limits.

3

Senior Lieutenant Lukáš was the archetypical active duty officer of the decrepit Austrian monarchy. The cadet school prepared him well to be an amphibian. He spoke German when socializing, wrote in German, read Czech books, and when he taught at the school of one-year volunteers[316], all Czechs, he'd tell them in confidence: "Let us be Czechs, but nobody has to know about it. I am also a Czech."

He viewed Czechness as some sort of a secret organization, which it is better to detour far around.

Otherwise he was a kind man, who didn't fear his superiors and he took good care of his company during maneuvers, as is decent and proper. He'd always find for it comfortable deployment in barns and often, from his modest pay, he'd have them roll out for his soldiers a barrel of beer.

He liked when on the march the soldiers sang songs. They had to sing, both when going to and coming from their exercises. Walking alongside his company, he would sing along with them:

> And when it was midnight,
> The oats would jump from the sack,
> Zhoom-tar-ee-ah, boom!

He was popular with the troops, because he was unusually just and it was not his habit to torture anybody.

The noncoms trembled before him and he'd turn the most brutal master sergeant into a genuine lamb in a month.

It's true that he knew how to scream, but he never swore or cursed. He used choice words and sentences. "You see," he would say, "I really don't like punishing you, boy, but I can't help it, because on discipline depends the capability of the troops, prowess, and without discipline the army is a reed swaying in the wind. If you don't have your uniform in order and the buttons are not sewn on well and are missing, it is apparent, that you've forgotten your obligations, which you have to the army. It could be that it seems incomprehensible to you, why you should be locked up because yesterday, during uniform inspection, you were missing one button on the blouse, such a tiny, minuscule thing, which in civilian life is totally overlooked. And see, neglect of your appearance in the military must immediately be punished. And why? It is not about your being short a button, but about your having to get used to order. Today you won't sew on a button and you start being lackadaisical. Tomorrow it will already seem too difficult to disassemble your rifle and clean it, the day after tomorrow you'll forget your bayonet in a pub somewhere and in the end you'll fall asleep at your post, because with that unfortunate missing button you started to live the life of a slacker. That's the way it is, boy, and that's why I'm punishing you, so that I can spare you even worse punishment for acts that you might commit later, forgetting slowly, but surely your duties. So, I'm locking you up for five days and I hope, that on bread-and-water you will think over that this punishment is not revenge, but means of education, seeking reformation and improvement of the punished soldier."

He should have been a captain long since and his caution regarding the nationalities question didn't help him, because he approached his superiors with real directness, refusing to be servile in military service.

That was what he had preserved of the character of a farmer in the Czech south[317], where he was born in a village in the midst of black forests and ponds.

Though he was just toward his troops and didn't torment them, there was in his character a peculiar trait. He hated his servants, because he always had the luck to get the most irritating and vile spotshine.

He'd hit them in the mouth, slap them across the head and tried hard to train them up by reproofs and deeds, not regarding them as soldiers. He wrestled with them hopelessly for a number of years, he replaced them constantly and in the end he sighed: "Again I've gotten a vile dumb beast." He viewed his military servants as a lower species of animal life.

He liked animals to an unusual degree. He had a Harz canary[318], an Angora cat and a stable pinscher. All his servants he'd gone through treated his animals no worse, than Senior Lieutenant Lukáš treated them, when they did something vile.

They'd torment the canary by starving it, one servant even knocked one of the Angora cat's eyes out, the stable pinscher was beaten up by them on sight and in the end, one of Švejk's predecessors led the poor creature to a knacker[319] in Pankrác, where he had him put down, not regretting giving up ten crowns out of his own pocket. He then simply informed the Senior Lieutenant that the dog had run away from him during a stroll, and the next day he was already marching with the company to the training ground.

When Švejk went to report for duty with Lukáš, the Senior Lieutenant led him to the living room and said to him: "You were recommended by Field Chaplain Katz and it's my wish, that you don't disgrace his reference. I've already had a dozen servants and none has stayed long enough to even warm up. I'm letting you know, that I am strict and that I punish horribly every vile deed and every lie. I want you to always speak the truth and without grumbling carry out all my orders. If I say: 'Jump into the fire,' then into that fire you must jump, even if you don't feel like it. What are you staring at?"

Švejk had been looking with interest to the side at the wall, where there was hanging a cage with a canary in it, and now, fixing his good-natured eyes on the Senior Lieutenant, he answered him in a pleasant, good-natured tone: "I dutifully report, Senior Lieutenant, Sir, there is a Harz canary over there."

And having had interrupted thus the flow of the Senior Lieutenant's speech, Švejk stood in military fashion, and not even blinking, he was gazing straight into his eyes.

The Senior Lieutenant wanted to say something sharp, but observing the innocent expression on Švejk's face, he only said: "The Field Chaplain recommended you as an astounding idiot and I think that he was not mistaken."

"I dutifully report, Senior Lieutenant, Sir, that the Field Chaplain really wasn't mistaken. When I was on active duty, I was discharged for idiocy, and notorious idiocy at that. They let two of us from the regiment go on that account, myself and Captain von Kaunitz. He, if you excuse me, Senior Lieutenant, Sir, when he walked down the street, he would dig into the left nostril of his nose with a finger of his left hand and with the other hand in the right nostril at the same time, and when he came with us to exercises, he would always stand us in a parade-march formation and say: 'Soldiers, eh, remember, eh, that today is Wednesday, because tomorrow will be Thursday, eh.'"

Senior Lieutenant Lukáš shrugged his shoulders like a man puzzled and unable to immediately find the words to express a certain thought.

He strolled from the door to the window on the opposite side passing Švejk and back again, while Švejk, depending on where at that moment the Senior Lieutenant was located, was doing eyes-*right* and *eyes-left* with such an emphatically innocent face, that the Senior Lieutenant lowered his gaze, and looking at the carpet, said something, that had no bearing on Švejk's remark about the idiotic Captain: "Yes, at my place I've got to have order and cleanliness and I must not be lied to. I love honesty. I hate a lie and I punish it mercilessly, do you understand me well?"

"I dutifully report, Senior Lieutenant, Sir, that I do understand. Nothing is worse, than when a man lies. Once he starts getting entangled, then he's lost. In a village on the other side of Pelhřimov[320], there was some teacher Marek and he kept going after the daughter of a gamekeeper named Špera, and he let Marek know through somebody else, that if he keeps meeting his daughter in the forest, he would use his rifle to shoot him in the butt with bristles and salt. The teacher sent to Špera a message, that it wasn't true, but once again, when he was to meet the girl, the gamekeeper caught him and already wanted to perform the operation on him, but he was trying to talk himself out it, saying that he was there gathering little flowers, and then again, that he was trying to catch some beetles, and he was getting further and further entangled, until in the end he swore, as he was all spooked, that he was there to lay down snares for the hares. So the dear gamekeeper packed him up and led him to the police station, from there it went to court and the teacher would have almost gone to jail. Had he only told the bare truth, he would have had just gotten the bristles with salt. I'm of the opinion, that it is always best to confess, to be open, and when I've already done something, to come and say: 'I dutifully report, that I've done such and such.' And as concerns honesty, it is always a very nice thing, because with it man always gets the farthest. Like when there are those speed-walking races. As soon as he starts cheating by running, he's disqualified. That happened to my cousin. An honest man is esteemed, honored everywhere, satisfied with himself and feels as if born again, when he goes to sleep and he can say: 'Today I was again honest.'"

During this talk Senior Lieutenant Lukáš had been already long sitting in the chair, looking at Švejk's shoes, and thought to himself: "My God, but I too spout often such idiocies and the only difference is the form I serve them up in."

Nevertheless, not wanting to lose his authority, he said, when Švejk finished:

"Under my command, you have to shine your shoes, have your

uniform in order, buttons sewn on correctly and you must have the appearance of a soldier, and not some civilian bum. It is curious that none of you can carry on as a military man. Only one of all my military servants had a combat appearance, and in the end he stole my dress uniform and sold it in the Jewtown[321] market."

He fell silent and continued, explaining to Švejk all his duties, wherein he didn't fail to put main stress on the fact, that he must be loyal, say nothing anywhere about what happens at home.

"There are ladies, who visit me," he pointed out, "sometimes one of them will stay overnight, when I don't have duty in the morning. In such case, you bring us coffee to bed, when I ring, do you understand?"

"I dutifully report, that I understand, Senior Lieutenant, Sir, if I were to come near the bed unexpectedly, then it could perhaps be unpleasant for a lady. I once brought a young lady home and my cleaning woman brought, just as we were having enormous fun, coffee to bed. She panicked and drenched my whole back and still said: 'May God give you a good morning.' I know what is decent and proper, when a lady is sleeping somewhere."

"Good, Švejk, toward ladies we always have to maintain unusual tact," said the Senior Lieutenant, who was getting into a better mood, because the talk had turned to a subject, which filled his free time between the garrison, the training ground and playing cards.

Women were the soul of his apartment. They created a home for him. There were several dozen and many of them would try to decorate his apartment during their stay with various nick-knacks.

A wife of a coffeehouse owner, who lived with him for two whole weeks before her husband came for her, embroidered a charming cloth table-runner, monogrammed all of his underwear with his initials and would have perhaps even finished embroidering the wall tapestry, if her husband hadn't destroyed their idyll.

One dame, for whom her parents came after a three-week stay, wanted to turn his bedroom into a ladies' boudoir, and arranged various trinkets, little vases everywhere, and over his bed she hung the picture of a guardian angel.

From all the corners of the bedroom and dining room one could sense the touch of a female hand, which penetrated even into the kitchen, where could be seen the most varied kitchen tools and implements, the magnificent gift from one missis factory-owner in love, who brought along besides her passion an apparatus for cutting any kitchen vegetables and cabbage, an apparatus for grating buns and scraping liver, pots, baking pans, frying pans, wooden mixing spoons and God-knows what else.

However, she left a week later, because she couldn't reconcile herself to the thought, that the Senior Lieutenant had besides her about twenty other lovers, which left certain imprints on the performance of the noble stud in uniform.

Senior Lieutenant Lukáš also kept up an extensive correspondence, had an album of pictures of his lovers and a collection of various relics, because for the past two years he'd exhibited a tendency toward fetishism. So he had several ladies garters, four charming pairs of female panties with embroidery, three fine, thin ladies' negligees, batiste kerchiefs, even a corset and several stockings.

"I'm on duty today," he said, "I'll come back late in the night, look after everything and put the apartment in order. The last servant, due to his villainy, rode off today to position with a marchy."

Having given still more instructions regarding the canary and the Angora cat, he left not having failed to throw in a few words about honesty and order, while still in the doorway.

After his departure Švejk put everything in the apartment in the best of shape, so that when Senior Lieutenant Lukáš returned home in the night, Švejk was able to report:

"I dutifully report, Senior Lieutenant, Sir, that everything is in order, only the cat got into mischief and devoured your canary."

"How come?" thundered the Senior Lieutenant.

"I dutifully report, Senior Lieutenant, Sir, I knew that cats don't like canaries and that they mistreat them. So I wanted to get them mutually acquainted, and in case the beast wanted to venture something, I intended to dust her fur so hard, that she'd never forget till the day she died, how she's to behave toward a canary, because I like animals very much. In our building there lives a hat maker and he had so trained a cat, that before that, she ate three canaries and now not even one, and that canary can even sit on her. So I wanted to try it too and pulled the canary out of the cage and gave it to her to sniff, and she, the monkey, before I became aware, bit its head off. I really didn't expect such low-down thing from her. If it were a sparrow, Senior Lieutenant, Sir, I would say nothing, but such a nice canary, a Harz one. And how eagerly she devoured him, even the feathers, and all along purred from the very joy. Cats, it is said, aren't musically educated and can't stand it when a little canary is singing. I really gave that cat a piece of my mind, but God forbid, I didn't do anything to her and waited for you, until what you decide, that should to happen to her for it, the mangy bitch."

While relaying this, Švejk was gazing so sincerely into the Senior Lieutenant's eyes, that the same, having at first stepped up to him with certain brutal intention, backed away, sat down in a chair and asked:

"Listen, Švejk, are you really such a God's dumb beast?"

"I dutifully report, Senior Lieutenant, Sir," Švejk answered festively, "I am! — Since I was little I've had such bad luck. I always want to fix something, do good, and nothing ever comes out it other than some unpleasantness for me and the people around me. I really wanted to have the two get acquainted, so they would understand each other, and it's not my fault that she devoured him and that was the end of the relationship. In the U Štupartů[322] building, a cat devoured years ago even a parrot, because it was laughing at her and meowing like her. But cats have a tough life. If you order me, Senior Lieutenant, Sir, to execute her, then I'll have to slam the door on her and yank her by the tail, otherwise she might never die."

And Švejk, maintaining the most innocent face and a likable, good-natured smile, expounded for the Senior Lieutenant, how cats get executed, which due to the content would certainly have driven the association against tormenting animals into a madhouse.

As he did so, he exhibited expert knowledge, so that Senior Lieutenant Lukáš, forgetting his wrath, asked:

"You know how to handle animals? Do you have a feel and love for animals?"

"I love dogs best of all," said Švejk, because it is a lucrative trade for one, who knows how to sell them. I couldn't do it well, because I've always been honest; and yet people would come after me, saying that I had sold them some half-dead scrag instead of a pure-blooded healthy dog, as if all dogs must be pure-blooded and healthy. And each right away wanted a pedigree, so I had to get pedigrees printed up. I had to make some mutt from Košíře, which was born in a brick yard, into the most pure-blooded nobleman from the Bavarian[323] kennel Armin von Barheim. And really, people were immediately glad, that it turned out so well, that they have a pedigreed dog at home, and that I was able to offer, let's say, a mutt from Vršovice as a dachshund, and they only marveled, why such a precious dog, which had come all the way from Germany, is hairy and doesn't have crooked legs. That's the way it's done in all the kennels, Senior Lieutenant, Sir, if you could only see the fraud with those pedigrees, which is perpetrated in the big kennels. The dogs that could say of themselves: 'I'm a pure-blooded critter,' are few. Either the mother forgot herself with some mutant, or his grandmother did, or he had more than one daddy and inherited something from each of them. From this one the ears, from that one the tail, from another the hair on his snout, from the third one the nose, from the fourth limping legs, and from the fifth one his size, and when he has had twelve of such fathers, then you can imagine, Senior Lieutenant, Sir, what such a dog looks like. I once bought such a dog, the ugliest mongrel[324], which having taken after his fathers was so ugly, that all the other dogs avoided him, and I bought him out of pity, since he was so forlorn. And he would constantly sit at home in a corner, used to be sort of sad, until I had to sell him as a stable pinscher. The hardest part of the job for me was to change his color, so that he would be salt-and-pepper. So he got with his master as far as Moravia, and since that time I haven't seen him.

Senior Lieutenant began to be very interested in this cynology exposition, and so Švejk was able to continue without any obstacle:

"Dogs can't color their hair by themselves, as the ladies do, that always has to be taken care of by the one, who wants to sell them. When a dog is such an ancient, that he's all gray, and you want to sell him as a year old puppy, or even try to pass him, the grandpa, off for a nine-month old, then you buy cracking-silver, dissolve it and paint him black, so that he looks like new. In order for him to gain strength, you feed him like a horse with arsenic trioxide and clean his teeth with sand paper, the kind that they clean rusty knives with. And before you take him on a leash to sell to some buyer, you pour plumb brandy into his yap, so the dog would get a little drunk, and he's right away lively, joyful, he barks joyously and makes friends with everybody like a drunken city council member. But what the main thing is, is this: people have to be, Senior Lieutenant, Sir, talked to, talked to for so long, until the buyer is totally baffled into a stupor from it. If somebody wants to buy a little ratter and you don't have anything at home but some hunting dog, then you must be able to talk the man into changing his mind, so that instead of a little ratter he will take away that hunting dog, and if by chance you only have at home a little ratter, and somebody comes to buy a mean German mastiff for a watch dog, you must so confuse him, that he will carry away that midget little ratter in his pocket, instead of a mastiff. When long ago I used to trade animals, a lady came, saying that her parrot had flown away into the garden, and just then some little boys were playing Red Indians in front of her villa, and that they caught the parrot for her and pulled out all his tail feathers and adorned themselves like cops[325]. And that parrot fell sick from the shame, that he had no tail and the veterinarian finished him off with some powder pills. So she wanted then to buy a new parrot, some decent one, she said, no vulgar one, which only knows how to swear and curse. What was I supposed to do, when I had no parrot at home and knew of none. I only had a mean bulldog at home, totally blind. So, Senior Lieutenant, Sir, I had to talk to her from four o'clock in the afternoon until seven in the evening, before instead of a parrot she bought that blind bulldog. It was worse than some kind of a diplomatic situation, and when she was leaving, I said: 'Just let the boys try to pull his tail out,' and I've never spoken to her again, because on account of that bulldog she had to move out of Prague, because he had bitten everyone in the whole building. Do you believe, Senior Lieutenant, Sir, that it is very hard to get a proper animal?"

"I like dogs very much," said the Senior Lieutenant, "some of my buddies, who are at the front, have dogs with them and they wrote to me, that the war in the company of such a loyal and devoted animal passes very well for them. You know very well then all the kinds of dogs and I hope, that if I had a dog, you would take care of him properly. What kind, in your opinion, is the best? I'm thinking namely about a dog as a companion. I once had a sort of a stable pinscher, but I don't know…"

"In my opinion, Senior Lieutenant, Sir, the stable pinscher is a very pleasant dog. True, not everybody likes it, because he's got bristles and such hard hair on the snout, that he looks like a released convict. He's so ugly, that he's even beautiful, and nevertheless, he's smart. Some stupid St. Bernard can't even come close. He's even smarter than a fox-terrier. I used to know one…"

Senior Lieutenant Lukáš looked at his watch and interrupted Švejk's talk:

"It's already late, I have to go to sleep. Tomorrow I'm on duty again, so you can devote the whole day to finding some stable pinscher."

He went to sleep and Švejk laid down on a sofa in the kitchen, and still for a while read the newspaper, which the Senior Lieutenant had brought from the garrison.

"There you see," Švejk said to himself, following with interest the digest of the day's events, "the Sultan[326] decorated Emperor Wilhelm with a war medal, and I still don't have even a small silver one."

He paused in thought and jumped up: "I would have almost forgotten…"

Švejk went to the room of Senior Lieutenant, who had already fallen into a deep sleep, and woke him up:

"I dutifully report, Senior Lieutenant, Sir, that I don't have any order regarding the cat."

And the still half asleep Senior Lieutenant in semi-dreaming state turned over to the other side of the bed and muttered: "Three days of confinement to the barracks!" and kept sleeping.

Švejk quietly left the room, pulled the unlucky cat from underneath the sofa and told her: "You have three days of confinement to the barracks, fall out!"

The Angora cat crawled under the sofa again.

4

Švejk was just getting ready to go to look for some stable pinscher, when a young lady rang the doorbell and wished to speak to Senior Lieutenant Lukáš. Next to her lay two heavy suitcases and Švejk still caught a glimpse of the cap in the stairwell, as the helper was descending the stairs.

"He's not home," said toughly Švejk, but the young lady was already in the hallway and categorically ordered Švejk: "Carry the suitcases into the bedroom!"

"Without the permission of the Senior Lieutenant it's impossible," said Švejk, "mister Senior Lieutenant ordered me to never do anything without him."

"You've gone mad," exclaimed the young lady. "I have arrived to visit the Senior Lieutenant."

"I know absolutely nothing about that," answered Švejk, "mister Senior Lieutenant is on duty, he'll return only late in the night and I got an order to find a stable pinscher. I know nothing of any suitcases or any lady. Now I'll lock the apartment, so I beg you kindly to leave. I've been notified of nothing and I can't leave any stranger, a person I don't know, here in the apartment. Just like once in our street they left a man behind at the confectioner Bělčický's, and he opened the wardrobe and fled. — I don't mean anything bad about you by that," continued Švejk, when he saw that the young lady had a desperate look on her face and was weeping, "but you definitely cannot stay here, I'm sure you'll recognize that, because the whole apartment has been entrusted to me and I am responsible for every little detail. Therefore I'm asking you one more time very kindly, not to exert yourself for nothing. As long as I don't get an order from the Senior Lieutenant, I don't do even for my own brother. I am really sorry, that I have to speak to you like this, but in the military there has to be order."

In the meantime, the young lady had recovered a little bit. She pulled a calling card out of her purse, wrote several lines in pencil, inserted them into a small envelope and said dejectedly: "Take this to the Senior Lieutenant, while I'll wait here for an answer. Here you have five crowns for the trouble."

"That won't do any good," answered Švejk, offended by the intransigence of the unexpected guest, "keep your five crowns, they're here on the chair, and if you want, come along to the garrison, wait for me, I'll hand your little note in and bring you the answer. But for you to wait here in the meantime, that's definitely impossible."

After those words he pulled the suitcases into the hallway, and rattling the keys like some chateau warden, he said meaningfully by the door:

"We're locking up."

The young lady walked hopelessly out into the hall, Švejk closed the door and went up ahead. The female visitor pitter-pattered behind him like a little doggie and caught up with him only when Švejk went into a tobacco shop to buy cigarettes for himself.

She walked now alongside him and was trying to establish a conversation:

"You will hand it in for sure?"

"I will, since I said so."

"And will you find the Senior Lieutenant?"

"That I don't know."

They again walked side by side mutely, only after a considerable while did his female companion start talking again:

"You think then, that you won't be able to find mister Senior Lieutenant?"

"I don't think that."

"And where do you think he could be?"

"I don't know."

Thereby was the conversation interrupted, until it was continued

again with a question from the young lady:
"Have you lost the letter?"
"So far I haven't lost it."
"Then you'll certainly hand it over to mister Senior Lieutenant?"
"Yes."
"And will you find him?"
"I've already said that I don't know," answered Švejk, "I wonder, how can people be so curious and incessantly ask about one thing. It is as if I were to stop every other man on the street and ask him what date it is."

Thereby was finished for good the attempt to reach an understanding with Švejk and the rest of the journey to the garrison went by in total silence. Only when they already stood by the garrison, Švejk invited the young lady to wait, and engaged in talk about the war with the soldiers at the gate, from which the young lady surely must have derived an absolutely tremendous joy, because she began pacing nervously on the sidewalk and wore a very unhappy face, when she saw, that Švejk continued his expositions with such a stupid expression, as can also be seen in a photograph published at that time in the Chronicle of the World War[327]: "The Austrian heir to the throne[328] is seen conversing with two pilots, who have shot down a Russian airplane."

Švejk sat down on a bench at the gate and was relaying, that on the Carpathian battle front the army's offensives had failed, that on the other hand the commander of Przemyśl, General Kusmanek[329], had arrived in Kiev and we had left eleven bridgeheads behind us in Serbia and the Serbians won't be able to keep running after our soldiers for long.

He then delved into a critique of all the individual known battles and discovered a new El Dorado of military strategy, that a platoon, when it is besieged on all sides, must surrender.

When he's had his fill of talk, he judged it appropriate to walk out and tell the desperate lady, that he'd be right back and not to leave and go anywhere, and he went upstairs to the office, where he found Senior Lieutenant Lukáš, who was just then deciphering a trench schematic for a lieutenant and was admonishing him, that he couldn't draw and had no idea whatsoever of geometry.

"See, this is the way to draw it. If given a straight line we are to draw a straight line perpendicular to it, we have to draw a line that forms a right angle with the first. Do you understand? In that case you'll direct the trenches correctly and you won't direct them toward the enemy. You'll stay six hundred meters away from him. But the way you were drawing it, you would ram our position into the enemy line and would stand with your trenches perpendicular above the enemy, and you need an obtuse angle. That's so simple after all, isn't that true?"

And the reservist lieutenant, a the treasurer of some bank in civilian life, stood over the plans for the trenches all in despair, didn't understand anything and really sighed with relief when Švejk stepped up to the Senior Lieutenant:

"I dutifully report, Senior Lieutenant, Sir, that some lady has sent you this note and is waiting for an answer." As he spoke, he was winking meaningfully and confidentially.

What he read did not impress the Senior Lieutenant favorably:

Dear Heinrich! My husband is persecuting me. I absolutely must visit you and stay a couple of days. Your servant is a vulgar, dumb beast. I am unhappy. Yours Katy.

Senior Lieutenant Lukáš sighed, led Švejk next door to an empty office, closed the door and started pacing among the desks. When he finally stopped by Švejk, he said: "That lady writes, that you are a dumb beast. What is it you've you done to her?"

"I have done nothing to her, I dutifully report, Senior Lieutenant, Sir, I have behaved very decently, but she wanted to settle in the apartment right away. And because I had not received any order from you, I would not leave her behind in the apartment. On top of it, she arrived with two suitcases as if coming home."

The Senior Lieutenant sighed again loudly, which Švejk also echoed after him.

"What's that?" yelled menacingly the Senior Lieutenant.

"I dutifully report, Senior Lieutenant, Sir, that it is a hard case. In Vojtěšská[330] street two years ago, a young lady moved in to the upholsterer's apartment, and he couldn't drive her out and had to kill both her and himself with gas and the fun was over. Dealing with women is troublesome. I can see through them."

"A hard case," echoed after Švejk the Senior Lieutenant and never had he uttered such a bare truth. Dear Jindřich[331] was certainly in an ugly situation. A wife persecuted by her husband decides to come to him for a few days on a visit, just when missis Micková from

Třeboň[332] is supposed to come, to repeat for three days that, which she provides every quarter of the year, when she takes a trip to Prague to do her shopping. Then the day after tomorrow a young lady is to come. She'd given him a definite promise, that she would let herself be seduced, when she had taken all week making up her mind, because no sooner than a month later, she is to be wedded to an engineer.

The Senior Lieutenant was now sitting on the desk with his head bowed, was quiet and kept thinking, but so far hasn't thought up anything, until finally he took a seat at the table, took an envelope, paper, and wrote on the official letterhead:

Dear Katy! On duty until the 9th hour in the evening. I will come at ten. Please, I want you to feel in my place as if you were in your own household. As regards Švejk, my servant, I have already given him orders to oblige you in every way. Yours Jindřich.

"You will," said the Senior Lieutenant, "hand this letter to the gentle lady. I'm ordering you to behave toward her deferentially and with tact and fulfill all her wishes, which for you must be commands. You must behave gallantly and serve her honestly. Here you have one hundred crowns, which you'll account for to me, because she may send you to fetch something, you'll order lunch, dinner for her and so forth. Then you'll buy three bottles of wine, a pack of Memphis[333] cigarettes. There. Nothing more for the time being. You can go and one more time, take this to heart, you have to do for her whatever you see in her eyes."

The young lady had already lost all hope that she would see Švejk again, and therefore she was very surprised when she saw him, walking out of the garrison and aiming toward her, carrying a letter.

Having saluted, he gave her the letter and reported: "According to the order of the Senior Lieutenant, I am, gentle lady, to behave toward you deferentially and with tact and serve you honestly, and do for you whatever I see in your eyes. I am to feed you and buy for you whatever you wish. I got for it from the Senior Lieutenant one hundred crowns, but out of that I must buy three bottles of wine and a pack of Memphis cigarettes."

When she finished reading the letter, she recovered her decisiveness, which found its expression in ordering Švejk to get her a fiacre, and when that was fulfilled, she ordered him to sit next to the fiacre driver on the coach box.

They rode home. Once they were in the apartment, she played the role of the lady of the house to the hilt. Švejk had to carry the suitcases over to the bedroom, beat the dust out of the carpets in the yard and a minute cobweb behind the mirror threw her into a state of great wrath.

Everything seemed to suggest that she wanted to dig herself in for a long time, at this fought for and captured position. Švejk was sweating. After he finished beating the carpets, she remembered, out of the blue, that the curtains had to be taken down and have the dust shaken out of them. Then he was ordered to wash all the windows in the bedroom and the kitchen. Following that, she began rearranging the furniture, which she did nervously, and when Švejk was done dragging it all from corner to corner, she didn't like it and was mixing ideas and thinking up a new arrangement.

She turned everything in the apartment inside out and slowly her energy for rearranging the nest became depleted and finally the plundering was coming to an end.

She still took clean linen out from the chest of drawers, changed the pillow and feather-down comforter cases by herself and it was apparent, that she was doing this with a great love for the bed, an object, which induced in her sensuous quiver of her nostrils.

Then she sent Švejk to fetch lunch and wine. And before he returned, she changed into a see-through morning-gown, which made her unusually seductive and attractive.

During lunch she drank up a bottle of wine and smoked up many Memphis cigarettes and lay down in the bed, while Švejk was in the kitchen enjoying his commissary ration bread, which he was dunking in a glass of some sweet booze.

"Švejk," was the sound coming from the bedroom, "Švejk!"

Švejk opened the door and saw the young lady in a charming position on the pillows.

"Come on in!"

He stepped up to the bed and now, with a peculiar smile, she took the full measure of his husky figure and strong thighs.

Pulling away the fine fabric, which has been veiling and hiding everything, she said sternly: "Take off your shoes and pants. Come…"

So it happened, that the good soldier Švejk could truthfully report to the Senior Lieutenant, when he returned from the garrison: "I dutifully report, Senior Lieutenant, Sir, that I fulfilled all the wishes of the gentle lady, and served her honestly according to you order."

"Thank you, Švejk," said the Senior Lieutenant, "did she have a lot of those wishes?"

"About six," answered Švejk, "but now she's sleeping as if she were dead, killed by the ride. I did everything for her that I saw in her eyes."

5

While the masses of troops, pinned down in the forests by the Dunajec[334] and Raba rivers, stood in the rain of grenades and big caliber guns were ripping up whole companies and pounding them into the Carpathians and the horizons on all the battlefields were lit with the fires of burning villages and towns, Senior Lieutenant Lukáš and Švejk were stuck in an unpleasant idyll with a dame, who had run away from her husband and assumed the role of the lady of the house.

When she left for a stroll, the Senior Lieutenant held a war council with Švejk on how to get rid of her.

"It would be best, Senior Lieutenant, Sir," said Švejk, "if that husband of hers — whom she ran away from and who is looking for her, as you reported, that it was in that letter, which I brought to you — knew about where she was, so that he'd come for her. To send him a telegram, that she's located here with you and that he can pick her up. There was such a case last year at a villa in Všenory[335]. But at that time, the woman herself sent the telegram to her husband and he came for her and slapped both of them around. Both were civilians, but in this case, he won't dare to strike an officer. After all, you are absolutely not a bit guilty, because you didn't invite anybody, and when she ran away, she did it on her own. You'll see that such a telegram will render good service. Even if any slaps should be thrown…"

"He is very intelligent," interrupted him Senior Lieutenant Lukáš, "I know him, he trades hops wholesale. I definitely have to talk to him. Send the telegram I will."

The telegram he sent was very terse, business-like: "The current address of your spouse is…" The address of Senior Lieutenant Lukáš's apartment followed.

So it happened that lady Katy was unpleasantly surprised, when through the door barged the trader in hops. He appeared both judicious and careful when lady Katy, not having lost in that moment her composure, introduced them to each other: "My husband — Senior Lieutenant Lukáš." Nothing else came to her mind.

"Please sit down, Mister Wendler," offered affably Senior Lieutenant Lukáš, pulling a cigarette case out of his pocket, "wouldn't you like one?"

The intelligent trader of hops took politely a cigarette, and releasing the smoke out of his mouth, he said deliberately: "Will you be going to a front-line position soon, Senior Lieutenant?"

"I have requested a transfer to the 91st regiment in Budějovice, where I'll probably go to as soon as I'm done with the one-year volunteer school. We need a lot of officers and nowadays there's a sad phenomenon of young people, who having a legitimate claim to the entitlement of one-year volunteer, don't claim it. They would rather remain common infantrymen, than strive to become cadets."

"The war has greatly damaged the hops trade, but I think that it can't last long," remarked the trader of hops, looking alternately at his wife and the Senior Lieutenant.

"Our situation is very good," said Senior Lieutenant Lukáš "nowadays no one doubts anymore, that the war will end with the victory of arms of the Central Powers. France, England and Russia are too weak against the Austro-Turko-German granite. True, we've suffered slight setbacks at some fronts. However, as soon as we break through the Russian front between the Carpathian ridge and the central Dunajec, there's no doubt whatsoever that it will mean the end of the war. Likewise, the French face the threat of losing the whole of eastern France in very short time and invasion of German troops into Paris[336]. It is absolutely certain. Besides that, our movements in Serbia continue very successfully and the departure of our troops, which is in fact only a shift in deployment, is being interpreted by many altogether differently, than how it demands absolute cool-headedness in war. As soon as possible we will see that our calculated movements in the southern theater of war will bear fruit. Be so kind and take a look..."

Senior Lieutenant Lukáš took the hops trader gently by the shoulder and led him over to the map of the theater of war hanging on the wall, and showing him the individual points, expounded:

"The Eastern Beskids[337] are an excellent base for us. In sections of the Carpathians, as you can see, we have great support. A mighty blow on this line, and we won't stop until in Moscow[338]. The war will be over before we know it."

"And what about Turkey?" asked the hops trader, pondering at the same time, how to start in order to get to the crux of the matter, on account of which he had arrived.

"The Turks are holding up well," answered the Senior Lieutenant, leading him back to the desk, "the Speaker of Turkish Parliament[339], Hali Bey[340], and Ali Bey[341] have arrived in Vienna. Marshall Liman[342], the nobleman of Sanders, was appointed supreme commander of the Turkish Dardanelles[343] army. Goltz Pasha[344] has come from Constantinople[345] to Berlin[346] and our Emperor decorated Enver Pasha[347], Vice-Admiral Usedom Pasha[348], and General Cevat Pasha[349]. Relatively a lot of decorations in such a short time."

They all sat for a while in silence facing each other, until the Senior Lieutenant judged it fitting to interrupt the embarrassing situation with these words: "When did you arrive, Mister Wendler?"

"This morning."

"I am very glad that you found me and caught me at home, because after noon I always go to the garrison and have night duty. Because the apartment is actually empty all day long, I was able to offer your gentle wife hospitality. She's not bothered by anybody here during her stay in Prague. For the sake of old acquaintance…"

The hops trader coughed: "Katy is certainly a strange dame, Senior Lieutenant, accept my most heart-felt thanks for everything, which you have done for her. She takes to her head to go to Prague out of the clear blue, that she has to cure her nervousness, I'm on the road, come home and the house is empty. Katy's gone."

Trying to affect the most pleasant demeanor, he shook his finger at her threateningly, and forcibly smiling, he asked the wife: "You probably thought apparently, that since I was on the road you could travel, too? But it didn't cross your mind…"

Senior Lieutenant Lukáš, seeing that the flow of the conversation was veering into unpleasant difficulties, again led the intelligent hops trader to the map of the theater of war, and pointing to the underlined places, said: "I forgot to alert you to one very interesting circumstance. To this big southwest-facing arc, where this group of mountains forms a great bridgehead. Here is where the offensive of the allies is directed to. By closing this railway, which connects the bridgehead with the main defense line of the enemy, must be severed the contact between the right flank and the Northern Army on the Vistula[350] River. Is that clear to you now?"

The hops trader answered, that everything was clear to him, and being apprehensive in his tact, lest what he says be taken as a hint, returning to his place he mentioned: "Due to the war, our hops have lost their markets abroad. France, England, Russia, and the Balkans are now lost for hops. We still ship hops to Italy[351], but I'm afraid that Italy will also get mixed up in it. But then, when we finally win, it is we, who will dictate the prices for our goods."

"Italy is maintaining strict neutrality," consoled him the Senior Lieutenant. "that is…"

"Then why doesn't she admit, that she is bound by the Triple Alliance treaty with Austria-Hungary and Germany?" asked the instantly enraged hops trader, all of whose troubles suddenly flooded into his head, the hops, his wife, the war, "I expected that Italy would march into the field against France and against Serbia. Then the war would have been already over. The hops in my warehouses are already rotting, domestic closed trades are few, exports equal zero, and Italy is maintaining neutrality. Why did Italy, as late as 1912, renew the Triple Alliance with us? Where is the Italian foreign minister, the Marquis of San Giuliano[352]? What is that gentleman doing? Is he sleeping or what? Do you know the annual sales revenue I had before the war and what I have today? — Do not think that I don't follow the events," he continued, looking furiously at the Senior Lieutenant, who was calmly releasing from his mouth rings of cigarette smoke, that were chasing one after the other and smashing against it, which Katy was watching with great interest, "why did the Germans go back to the border, when they were near Paris already? Why are there artillery battles raging between the Meuse[353] and the Moselle? Do you know that in Combres[354] and Woëwre[355] near Marchéville, there were burned out three breweries, where I had been sending to them annually over five hundred bales of hops? And even the Hartmansweiler[356] brewery in the Vosges[357] burned down, and leveled to the ground is the huge brewery in Niederaspach[358] near Mühlhausen[359]. Right there you have a loss of 1,200 bales of hops annually for my company. The Germans have fought the Belgians six times over the Klosterhoek[360] brewery, there you have a loss of 350 bales of hops annually."

He couldn't speak any longer being so upset, just got up, marched over to his wife and said:

"Katy, you're going immediately home with me. Get dressed. — All those events upset me so," he said after a while in an apologetic tone, "I used to be completely calm at one time."

And when she'd left to dress, he said quietly to the Senior Lieutenant:

"It's not the first time she's acted up. Last year she rode away with a substitute teacher and I found them only all the way in Zagreb[361]. I closed a deal on that occasion at the municipal brewery in Zagreb for six hundred bales of hops. Aye, the south was altogether a gold mine. Our hops used to go as far as Constantinople. Today we're half ruined. If the government limits production of beer in this country, it will deliver the last blow to us."

And lighting an offered cigarette, he said desperately: "Warsaw[362] alone used to take 2,370 bales of hops. The biggest brewery there is the Augustinian. Their representative used to visit me every year. It is enough to drive one to desperation. Fortunately, I don't have any children."

This logical conclusion of the annual visit of the representative of the Augustinian brewery from Warsaw caused the Senior Lieutenant to smile gently, which the hops trader caught, and therefore continued talking: "The Hungarian breweries in Sopron[363] and Nagykanizsa[364] used to take from my company for their export beers, which they shipped as far as Alexandria[365], annually an average one thousand bales of hops. Nowadays they refuse to order anything on account of the blockade. I'm offering them hops thirty percent cheaper, and they don't order even one bale. Stagnation, downturn, misery and domestic cares on top of it."

The hops trader fell silent and the silence was interrupted by lady Katy, ready to leave: "How are we going to deal with my suitcases?"

"They will come for them, Katy," said contentedly the hops trader, rejoicing in the end, that everything had ended without an outburst or an offense inducing scene, "if you still want to take care of some shopping, it is high time that we went. The train leaves at two-twenty."

They both said their friendly goodbyes to the Senior Lieutenant, and the hops trader was so glad, that it was all over with, that while parting in the hallway, he told the Senior Lieutenant: "Should you, God forbid, get wounded in the war, come to us to recuperate. We will take the most diligent care of you."

Having returned to the bedroom, where Katy had dressed for the journey, the Senior Lieutenant found 400 crowns and this note on the sink:

Mister Senior Lieutenant! You did not stand up for me in front of that monkey, my husband, an idiot of the first order. You allowed him to drag me away like some thing, which he had forgotten at the apartment. At the same time, you dared to make the remark, that you had offered me hospitality. I hope that I didn't cause you any larger expenses than the enclosed 400 crowns, which I beg you to share with your servant.

Senior Lieutenant Lukáš stood for a while with the note in his hand and then he slowly ripped it into pieces. With a smile he looked at the money lying on the sink, and seeing, that being upset she had forgotten a decorative hair comb on the vanity, when she was fixing her hair in front of the mirror, he deposited it among his fetishistic relics.

Švejk returned after noon. He had gone to look for a stable pinscher for the Senior Lieutenant.

"Švejk," said the Senior Lieutenant, "you're lucky. The lady, that was staying with me, is already gone. Her husband took her away with him. And for all the services you extended to her, she left 400 crowns on the sink for you. You have to thank her nicely, or rather her spouse, because it was his money she took with her on the trip. I will dictate the letter for you."

He dictated to him:

"Most Honored Sir! Condescend to relay my most heart-felt thanks for the 400 crowns, which your gentle spouse bestowed on me as a gift for the services I extended to her during her visit in Prague. All that I did for her, I did willingly, and therefore cannot accept this sum and I am sending it… — Well, just go on writing, Švejk, why are you fidgeting so? Where did I stop?"

"And I am sending it…," said Švejk in a quivering voice, full of tragic essence.

"All right then: I am sending it back with the assurance of my deepest respect. Respectful greetings and a kiss for the gentle lady's hand. Josef Švejk, officer's servant of Senior Lieutenant Lukáš. Done?"

"I dutifully report, Senior Lieutenant, Sir, what's still missing is the date."

"December 20th, 1914. And so now write on the envelope, take those 400 crowns and carry them to the Post Office, and send them to this address."

And the Senior Lieutenant Lukáš began merrily whistling an aria from the operetta The Divorced Lady.

"One more thing, Švejk," the Senior Lieutenant asked as Švejk was leaving for the Post Office, "what's with the dog that you went to look for?"

"I've got one in mind, Senior Lieutenant, Sir, he's a tremendously pretty animal. But it will be hard to get him. I hope to bring him perhaps tomorrow nevertheless. He bites."

6

Senior Lieutenant Lukáš didn't catch that last word, and yet it was so important. "The sonofabitch was biting everything like there was no tomorrow," Švejk wanted to repeat one more time, but in the end thought to himself: "What business of the Senior Lieutenant's is it actually. He wants a dog, so he'll get one."

It isn't a light matter to say: "Bring me a dog!" Owners of dogs are very careful about their dogs, and it doesn't have to be just a pure-blooded dog. Even that mutt that doesn't do anything else, except warm the feet of some dear old woman, is loved by the owner, who won't let anybody hurt him either.

A dog himself has to have the instinct, especially if he's pure-blooded, that one beautiful day he will be stolen from his master. He lives constantly in fear that he will be stolen, that he has to be stolen.

A dog will, for example, get a certain distance away from his master during a walk, is at first cheerful, frolicking. He plays with other dogs, climbs on them immorally, they on him, he sniffs cornerstones, raises his little leg at every opportunity, even over the grocer-woman's basket of potatoes, in short he has such a joy of life, that the world seems to him to be beautiful as it does to a youth after his successful high-school graduation.

But suddenly you notice his cheerfulness is fading, that the dog is beginning to feel that he's lost. And only now that genuine despair is coming over him. He runs horrified up and down the street, sniffs, whines and in absolute desperation pulls his tail between his legs, turns his ears backward and zips down the middle of the street to some unknown destination.

If he could talk, he'd be screaming: "Jesusmaria, somebody is going to steal me."

Have you ever been in a kennel and seen there such frightened canine apparitions? All these have been stolen. The big city has bred a peculiar species of thieves, who make a living exclusively by stealing dogs. There are small breeds of parlor doggies, midget size, little ratters, quite a minuscule glove, they fit into the pocket of an overcoat, or in a lady's muff, where they are carried along. Even from there they will pull your poor thing out. A mean spotted German mastiff, that is furiously guarding a villa in some suburb, they will steal at night. A police dog they'll steal from right under a detective's nose. You're leading your dog on a leash, they will cut it and already they're gone with your dog and you're staring like an idiot at the empty leash. Fifty percent of the dogs, which you pass in the street, have changed masters several times, and often, years later, you'll buy your own dog, that was stolen from you as a puppy, when you'd taken it out for a walk. The greatest danger of being stolen looms for dogs when they're taken out to perform their number one and two physical needs. Especially during the latter most of them disappear. That's why every dog during this act looks around carefully.

There are several systems of stealing dogs. Either directly, something in the manner of a pick-pocket, or fraudulently enticing the unlucky creature to come to you. The dog is a loyal animal, but in a classroom reader or in a nature science textbook. Let even the most loyal dog sniff fried horsemeat sausage, and he's doomed. He'll forget the master alongside whom he's marching, he'll turn and follow you, while from his snout saliva is drooling and in the premonition and with the hunch of great joy over the sausage he'll wag his tail affably and flare his nostrils like the most high-spirited stallion, when they're taking him to a mare.

*

In the Small Side by the Castle Steps[366] there is a small beer tap-room[367]. One day there sat there in the back in semidarkness two men. One a soldier and the other a civilian. Leaning to each other they whispered mysteriously. They looked like conspirators from the times of the Venetian Republic[368].

"Every day at eight o'clock," whispered the civilian to the soldier, "the maidservant walks with him to the corner of Havlíček's square[369] toward the park. But he is a sonofabitch, he bites everything like there's no tomorrow. He won't let anybody pet him even once."

Leaning still closer to the soldier, he whispered in his ear:
"Not even a fat smoked sausage he'll eat."
"Fried one?" asked the soldier.
"Not even a fried one."
They both spat.
"What then does the sonofabitch eat?"
"God knows what. Some dogs are spoiled and pampered like an archbishop."

The soldier and the civilian clanked their steins and the civilian whispered further:

"Once a black spitz, whom I needed for a kennel above Klamovka[370], also wouldn't take a fat smoked sausage from me. I kept going after him for three days, until I couldn't stand it anymore and asked the woman that used to go with the dog for a stroll, what is it the dog actually eats, that he is so pretty. The woman was flattered and said that he likes pork cutlets best. So I bought a schnitzel for him. I'm thinking that's even better. And see, that sonofabitch didn't even look at it, because it was veal. He was used to pork meat. So I had to buy him a pork cutlet. I let him sniff it and I'm off running, the dog after me. The woman screamed: 'Spot, Spot,' but dear Spot paid no attention. He ran after the cutlet all the way around the corner, there I slipped a chain around his neck and the next day he was already in the kennel above Klamovka. Under his neck he had a few white hairs, a tuft, they painted it over in black and nobody recognized him. But the other dogs, and there have been many, all went for the fried horsemeat fat smoked sausage. You too would do best, if you just asked her what that dog prefers to feed on the most; you are a soldier, you are well-built and she is likely to tell you. I've already asked her, but she looked at me like she wanted to skewer me, and said: 'What is it to you.' She's not too pretty, she's a monkey, she'll talk to a soldier."

"Is it a real stable pinscher? My Senior Lieutenant wants none other."

"A dandy stable pinscher. Salt-and-pepper, really pure-blooded, just as you are Švejk and I am Blahník. What I'm after is what he eats, that's what I'll give him and I'll bring him to you."

The two friends clinked their steins again. When Švejk was still making his living selling dogs until the war, Blahník used to supply them for him. He was an experienced man and it was rumored about him, that on the sly he bought questionable dogs from a carrion collector and then resold them. He had once even had rabies and the Pasteur Institute[371] in Vienna was like his second home. Now he viewed it as his duty to selflessly help the soldier Švejk. He knew all the dogs in the whole city of Prague and its vicinity, and the reason he spoke so softly was that he didn't want to reveal himself to the pubkeeper, because half a year ago he carried from the pub, tucked under his coat, his puppy, a dachshund, whom he gave milk to suck out of a baby bottle, so the silly puppy apparently took him for its mommy and didn't as much as make a sound under his coat.

As a matter of principle, he stole only pure-blooded dogs and could be an expert witness in court. He supplied all kennels and private persons any way it could be managed, and when he walked down a street, then dogs would growl at him, since he had stolen them once upon a time, and if he stood somewhere by a shop window, often some vengeful dog would raise its little leg behind his back and sprinkle on his pants.

*

At eight o'clock in the morning of the next day, the good soldier Švejk could be seen pacing at the corner of Havlíček's square and the park[372]. He was waiting for the maidservant with the stable pinscher. At last his wait was over and right past him flew a bearded dog, bristled up, sharp haired, with wise black eyes. He was cheerful like all dogs, that have just finished doing their business, he frolicked for a while. Then, something caught his attention, and he rushed toward the sparrows breakfasting on horse dung in the street.

Then past Švejk walked the one, who was charged with his care. She was an older girl with her hair neatly braided into a little wreath. She was whistling at the dog and twirling a chain and an elegant whip.

Švejk addressed her:

"Pardon me, miss, which way does one go to Žižkov?"

She stopped and looked at him, to see whether he meant it sincerely, and Švejk's good-natured face told her, that this soldier boy perhaps did want to go to Žižkov. The expression on her face softened and she willingly told him the way he'll get to Žižkov.

"I've only recently been transferred to Prague," said Švejk, "I'm not from around here, I'm from the countryside. You too aren't from Prague?"

"I'm from Vodňany."

"Then we're not far from one another," answered Švejk, "I'm from Protivín."

This knowledge of the topography of the Czech south, gained some time ago during maneuvers in that region, filled the heart of the girl with the warmth of local fellowship.

"So you know the butcher Pejchar in the square in Protivín?"

"How could I not know him."

"That is my brother."

"Everybody likes him very much over there among us," said Švejk, "he is very nice, helpful, he's got good meat and gives honest weight."

"Aren't you Jareš's?" asked the girl, beginning to sympathize with the anonymous soldier boy.

"I am."

"And which Jareš? The one from Krč[373], near Protivín, or the one from Ražice?"

"From Ražice."

"Does he still deliver beer?"

"Still."

"But he's got to be way over sixty?"

"He was sixty eight this year in the spring," Švejk replied calmly, "now he got himself a dog and really enjoys his route. The dog sits on his wagon. He's a dog just like that one over there, that's chasing the sparrows. A nice doggie, very nice."

"That's ours," explained his new acquaintance, "I'm in service here with mister Colonel. You don't know our Colonel?"

"I do, he's some would-be intellectual," said Švejk, "we had a colonel like that in Budějovice too."

"Our master is strict, and when people were saying the last time that they really beat us up in Serbia, he came home rabid and knocked all the plates down in the kitchen and wanted to fire me."

"So that is your doggie," Švejk interrupted her, "it's a pity that my Senior Lieutenant can't stand dogs, I like dogs very much." He paused and then suddenly exclaimed: "Not all dogs will eat everything, though."

"Our Fox is terribly picky, at one time he didn't want to eat meat at all, only now he does again."

"What does he like best to eat?"

"Liver, cooked liver."

"Veal or pork?"

"It's all the same to him," Švejk's fellow countrywoman smiled, viewing his last question as an unsuccessful attempt at a joke.

They strolled still for a little while, then they were joined too by the stable pinscher, who was attached to a chain. He behaved toward Švejk in a very familiar way and tried to at least rip his pants with his muzzle, was jumping up on Švejk and suddenly, as if he sensed what Švejk was thinking, he stopped jumping and walked sad and stunned, looking at Švejk askance, as if he wanted to say: So it is awaiting me too now?

Afterward she still told him that she walked with the dog every evening at six o'clock, that she didn't trust any guy from Prague, that she had advertised herself in the newspaper once and the only one, who answered, was a locksmith proposing marriage and he talked her out of 800 crowns for some invention and disappeared. In the countryside people are much more honest. If she were to marry, she would wed only a country man, but only after the war. She viewed wartime weddings as stupidity, because usually such a woman ends up as a widow.

Švejk gave her hope several times, that he would come back at six, and left to inform his friend Blahník that the pinscher eats liver of any kind.

"I'll treat him to beef," decided Blahník, "I've already hooked a St. Bernard with beef liver. He belonged to the factory owner Vydra[374], a tremendously loyal animal. Tomorrow I'll bring the dog in good order."

Blahník kept his word. When in the forenoon Švejk was done tidying up the apartment, barking was heard on the other side of the door and Blahník dragged into the apartment the resisting stable pinscher, whose hair stood on end even more than nature had bristled him up. He rolled his eyes wildly and cast such a contemptuous look that was reminiscent of a hungry tiger in a cage, in front of which is standing a fattened up visitor of the zoo. He chattered his teeth, growled, as if he wanted to say: I'll rip you apart, devour you.

They tied the dog to the kitchen table and Blahník described the process of the theft.

"I passed him by on purpose, holding the cooked liver in paper. He started sniffing and jumping up on me. I didn't give him anything and kept going. The dog after me. By the park I made a turn into Bredovská street[375] and there I gave him the first piece. He was devouring it while walking, so he wouldn't lose sight of me. I turned the corner into Jindřišská street[376], where I gave him a new portion. Then I, when he got his fill, put him on a chain and I dragged him all across Wenceslas square to Vinohrady, all the way to Vršovice. On the way, he came up with some wonderful tricks. When I crossed the streetcar tracks, he lay down and didn't want to move. Perhaps he wanted to get himself run over. I've also brought a blank pedigree with me, which I bought at the Fuchs' stationer[377]. You know how to forge pedigrees, Švejk."

"It must be written by your hand. Write down that he comes from Leipzig[378], from the von Bülow kennel. The father, Arnheim von Kahlsberg, the mother, Emma von Trautensdorf, after her father,

Siegfried von Busenthal. The father received the first prize at the Berlin exhibition of stable pinschers in the year 1912. The mother decorated with the gold medal by the Nüremberg[379] society for the breeding of noble dogs[380]. How old do you think he is?"

"By his teeth, about two years."

"Write down that he's one and a half."

"He's not been clipped right, Švejk. Look at his ears."

"That can be fixed. We'll trim them for him as the case may be when he's used to us. Now he would just get angrier."

The stolen one growled rabidly, panted, writhed and then he lay down with his tongue sticking out, tired, he waited to see what would happen to him next.

Slowly, he grew calmer, only once in a while he would give out a sad whimper.

Švejk put in front of him the rest of the liver, which Blahník handed over to him. He wouldn't even peek at it and only cast that hard-to-get look at them and looked at both of them with an expression that seemed to say: I've been tricked once already, you eat it yourselves.

He lied there in resignation and pretended that he was dozing. Then all of a sudden, something got into his head, he got up, stood on his hind legs, and started begging with his front paws. He was capitulating.

This touching scene had no effect on Švejk.

"Down," he shouted at the wretch, who lay down again, whining sorrowfully.

"What name should I give him on the pedigree?" asked Blahník, "his name was Fox, so something similar, so that he'd understand it right away."

"So we'll we call him maybe Max, look Blahník, how he's perking up his ears. Up, Max!"

The unfortunate stable pinscher, whom they had robbed of both home and name, stood up and awaited further orders.

"I would think we'll untie him," Švejk decided, "we'll see what he's going to do."

When he was untied, his first trip was to the door, where he barked three short times at the door handle, relying apparently on the magnanimity of these bad people. Seeing though, that they had no sympathy for his desire to get out, he made a little puddle by the door, convinced that they'd throw him out, as they used to once upon a time, when he was young, and the Colonel had been training him, brusquely, in the military style, to be housebroken.

Instead of that Švejk remarked: "He's a smart one, he's got a big chunk of the Jesuit in him," he struck him with his belt and dunked his snout into the puddle so, that he couldn't lick himself clean fast enough.

He whined over the humiliation and started running around the kitchen, sniffing desperately at his own trail, then clear out of the blue he went to the table, gobbled up the rest of the liver presented on the floor, lay down by the stove and fell asleep after the whole adventure.

"What do I owe you?" Švejk asked Blahník, when he was saying goodbye to him.

"Don't even talk about it, Švejk," said softly Blahník, "for an old friend I'll do anything, especially when he's serving in the military. God be with you, boy, and don't ever take that dog across Havlíček's square, lest something unfortunate happens. Should you need yet another dog, you know where I live."

Švejk let Max sleep for a long time and in the meantime he bought him a quarter kilo of liver at the butcher's, cooked it and waited until Max wakes up, having put next to his nose a piece of the warm liver.

Max started licking himself in his sleep, then he stretched, sniffed over the liver and gobbled it up. Then he went to the door and repeated his attempt with the door handle.

"Max!" Švejk called him, "come to me!"

He went with distrust, Švejk took him in his lap, stroked him and for the first time Max wagged the remnant of his clipped tail in a friendly way and gently snatched Švejk's hand, held it in his mouth, and looked wisely at Švejk, as if he wanted to say: There is nothing that can be done here, I know that I have lost.

Švejk continued to stroke him and started narrating to him in a tender voice:

"So there was once upon a time a doggie, his name was Fox and he lived with a colonel. The maidservant would take him for a stroll and at one time a man came and he stole Fox. Fox ended up in the military service with a Senior Lieutenant and they gave him the name Max.

"Max, give me your paw! So you see, you dumb beast, that we will be good buddies, if you behave and are obedient. Otherwise, your military service will be as tough as a leather belt."

Max jumped down from Švejk's lap and started to merrily pester him. By the evening, when the Senior Lieutenant returned from the garrison, Švejk and Max were the best of buddies.

Looking at Max, Švejk thought philosophically: "When you look at it from all sides, every soldier too is actually stolen from his own home."

Senior Lieutenant Lukáš was very pleasantly surprised, when he saw Max, who also exhibited great joy upon seeing again a man with a saber.

As to the question where he's from and how much he cost, Švejk informed him with absolute calm, that the dog had been given to him as a gift by a friend, who had just been called up to his unit.

"Alright, Švejk," said the Senior Lieutenant, playing with Max, "on the first of the month you'll get fifty crowns from me for the dog."

"I can't accept, Senior Lieutenant, Sir."

"Švejk," the Senior Lieutenant said sternly, "when you entered into service, I explained to you that you have to obey my every word. When I'm telling you that you'll get fifty crowns, then you have to take them and drink them up. What will you do with the fifty crowns, Švejk?"

"I dutifully report, Senior Lieutenant, Sir, that I will drink them up as ordered."

"And should I, Švejk, perhaps forget, I order you to report to me, that I am to give you fifty crowns for the dog. Understand? Does the dog have fleas? Better give him a bath and brush him down. Tomorrow I've got duty, but the day after tomorrow, I will go for a stroll with him."

While Švejk was bathing Max, the Colonel, his former owner, was at home cursing and swearing up a storm and threatening that he would make whoever stole his dog face a military court, have him shot, hanged, locked for twenty years and chopped up.

"*Let the demon from hell screw this bum,*" resounded from the apartment of the Colonel so loudly, the windows rattled, "I'll soon be finished with such assassins!"

Over both Švejk and Senior Lieutenant Lukáš there hovered in the air a catastrophe.

15

THE CATASTROPHE

Colonel Friedrich Kraus, also having the nobility predicate von Zillergut, after some little village in the Salzburg area[381], which his forefathers had picked clean and frittered away in the 18th century, was remarkably asinine. When relating a story, he would speak only positive things, asking all the while, whether all present understood the most primitive expressions: "Then a window, gentlemen, yes. Do you know what a window is?

Or: "A path, along the both sides of which there is ditch, is called a road. Yes, gentlemen. Do you know what a ditch is? A ditch is an excavation, on which work a greater number of people. It is a depression. Yes. The work is done with hoes. Do you know what a hoe is?"

He suffered an explanation mania, which he would engage in with such spirited animation, like some new inventor talking about his life's work.

"A book, gentlemen, is made of multiple variously cut paper sheets, of differing formats, which are imprinted and assembled together, bound and glued. Yes. Do you know, gentlemen, what glue is? Glue is an adhesive."

He was so blatantly stupid that officers avoided him by taking a detour far around, so they didn't have to hear him say, that a sidewalk runs parallel to a roadway and that it is an elevated, paved lane alongside the front of the house. And the front of the house is that part, which we see from the street or from the sidewalk. The back part of the house we cannot see from the sidewalk, of which we can convince ourselves immediately by stepping into the roadway."

He was willing to demonstrate that interesting point right away. Luckily though, they ran him over. Since that time, he's turned even more stupid. He would stop officers and get engaged with them in endlessly long conversations about omelets, the sun, thermometers, doughnuts, windows and postage stamps.

It was really amazing, that the idiot was able to advance relatively quickly and have very influential people behind him, like the commanding general, who always rooted for him even given his total military incompetence.

On maneuvers, he would execute some genuine spectacles with

his regiment. He never made it anywhere on time and would lead his regiment in columns against machine guns, and years ago, during imperial maneuvers in the Czech south, he got totally lost with his regiment and ended up with it all the way into Moravia, where he walked it about for several days, until after the maneuvers were over and the soldiers had been already lying around back in the garrison. He got away with it.

His friendly relations with the commanding general and other no-less-idiotic military bigwigs of old Austria yielded him several decorations and orders of merit, by which he was unusually honored, and he viewed himself as the best soldier under the sun and theoretician of strategy and all military science.

During regimental parade reviews he would engage the soldiers in talk and always ask them one and the same:

"Why is the rifle adopted by the military called the manlicher gun[382]?"

At the regiment his nickname was the *manlicher idiot*[383]. He was unusually vengeful, destroyed subordinate officers when he didn't like them, and when they wanted to get married, then he would send up the chain of command bad recommendations for their requests.

He was missing half of his left ear, which an antagonist had cut off in his youth in a duel on account of simple statement of the truth, that Friedrich Kraus von Zillergut is a notorious idiot."

Should we analyze his mental abilities, we would gain the conviction, that they were not any better than those, which made the bulldog-faced Hapsburg František Josef renowned as the notorious idiot.

The same flow of his speech, the selfsame inventory of utter naiveté. At one banquet in the officers' club the Colonel Kraus von Zillergut out of the clear blue proclaimed, when the talk had turned to Schiller[384]: "So get this gentlemen, yesterday I saw a steam plow driven by a locomotive. Imagine gentlemen, by locomotive, not one, but two locomotives. I see smoke, get closer, and it was a locomotive, and on the other side another one. Tell me, gentlemen, isn't that laughable? Two locomotives, as if one wouldn't be enough."

He fell silent and after a while remarked: "Should the gas run out, the automobile must stop. I saw that yesterday, too. Then they keep blathering about inertia, gentlemen. It's not going, is standing, it won't move, doesn't have gas. Isn't it laughable?"

In his dullness he was unusually pious. He had at home in his apartment a domestic altar. He'd often go to confession and communion at St. Ignatius and since the outbreak of the war he prayed for the success of Austrian and German arms. He mixed Christianity with his dreams of Germanic hegemony. God was to help appropriate the wealth and territory of the vanquished.

He always got terribly upset, when he read in the newspaper, that again they had brought in prisoners of war.

He would say: "What for bring in prisoners of war? They all should be mowed down by guns. No mercy. Dance among the corpses. Burn up all the civilians in Serbia to the last one. Snuff out the children with bayonets!"

He was no worse, than the German poet Vierordt[385], who published verses during the war to encourage Germany to hate and kill, with an iron soul, millions of French devils:

> All the way to the clouds and above the mountains
> Piling up are human bones and smoldering flesh…

*

Having finished teaching at the one-year-volunteer school, Senior Lieutenant Lukáš decided to take Max out for a stroll.

"I take the liberty of bringing to your attention, Senior Lieutenant, Sir," said with concern Švejk, "that you have to be careful with that dog, so that he won't run away on you. He might get a pang of homesickness for his old home and he could take off, if you were to untie him from the leash. And also I wouldn't recommend you to take him across Havlíček's square, there walks about a mean butcher's dog from the Marian Picture[386] that bites tremendously. If he sees a strange dog in his territory, he immediately gets jealous, fearing the new dog will eat something of his. He is like that beggar at Saint Haštal[387]."

Max merrily jumped around and was getting under the Senior Lieutenant's feet, wrapped his leash around the saber and expressed unusual joy to be going out for a stroll.

They walked out into the street and Senior Lieutenant Lukáš with the dog aimed toward Příkopy street[388]. He was to meet a lady at the corner of Panská[389]. He was absorbed in official thoughts. What was he to lecture on to the one-year-volunteers at the school the next day? How do we state the height of a hill? Why do we always state the height as above the sea level? From heights above the sea level, how do we determine the simple height of a hill from its foot? Damn, why does the Ministry of Military Affairs put such things into the school program? But this stuff is for the artillery. And there are maps of the General Staff after all. If the enemy is at spot elevation 312, it's not enough to think ordinarily about why the height of the hill is stated as from the sea level, or to calculate yourself how high the hill is. We look at the map, and we've got it.

He was disturbed out of those thoughts by a stern "*Halt!*" just as he neared Panská street.

Simultaneously with the "*Halt!*" the dog was trying to yank himself free, with the leash included, and barking joyfully hurled himself at the man, who had said the stern "*Halt!*"

In front of the Senior Lieutenant there stood Colonel Kraus von Zillergut. Senior Lieutenant Lukáš saluted and stood in front of the Colonel apologizing, that he hadn't seen him.

Colonel Kraus was known among the officers for his passion for stopping and detaining soldiers.

He viewed saluting as something, on which depended success of the war and upon which was built all of military might.

"The soldier is supposed to insert his soul into saluting," he would say. It was the most beautiful example of corporal mysticism.

He took care, that he, who renders honor, salutes according to the regulation down to the subtlest detail, exactly and solemnly.

He laid in wait for all, who passed by him. From infantrymen, all the way to lieutenant colonels. Infantrymen, who saluted on the fly, as if they were saying, while casually touching the bill of their caps "How's it going," these he himself would bring to the garrison for punishment.

For him "I didn't see you" had no currency.

"A soldier," he would say, "must be seeking his superior out in a crowd and think of nothing else, than that he must meet all his duties, which are prescribed for him in the service regulations. When he falls on the battlefield, before his death arrives he is to salute. He, who doesn't know how to salute, or acts as if he doesn't see, or salutes carelessly, is a beast."

"Senior Lieutenant," said in a terrifying voice Colonel Kraus, "lower ranks must always render honor to the higher. That hasn't been abolished. Secondly: Since when have officers become accustomed to walking down the promenade with stolen dogs? Yes, with stolen dogs. A dog, which belongs to another, is a dog stolen."

"This dog, Colonel, Sir…" objected Senior Lieutenant Lukáš.

"…belongs to me, Senior Lieutenant," interrupted him roughly the

Colonel. "That is my Fox[390]."

And Fox or Max remembered his old master, and the new one he totally expelled out of his heart, and having torn himself loose was jumping up on the Colonel and expressing such joy, which only a high-school sophomore in love would be capable of, when he discovers his idol has sympathy for him.

"Walking with stolen dogs, Senior Lieutenant, is incompatible with an officer's honor. Didn't know? An officer cannot be buying a dog not having ascertained that he can buy it without repercussions," kept thundering Colonel Kraus, stroking Fox-Max, who out of villainy started growling at the Senior Lieutenant and baring his teeth, as if the Colonel said, having pointed to the Senior Lieutenant: "Get him!"

"Senior Lieutenant," continued the Colonel, "do you consider it right to ride a stolen horse? Haven't you read my ad in the Bohemie or the Tagblatt that my stable pinscher had disappeared on me? You have not read an ad, which your superior has placed in the newspapers?"

The Colonel slapped his hands together.

"Really, these young officers! Where's the discipline? A colonel places ads, and a senior lieutenant doesn't read them."

"If I could, you old fart, slap you a few times," Senior Lieutenant Lukáš thought to himself, staring at the colonel's sideburns, reminiscent of an orangutan.

"Come along for a minute," the Colonel said. And so they walked and were conducting a very pleasant conversation:

"At the front, Senior Lieutenant, Sir, a thing like this could not happen to you for the second time. Strolling in the rear with stolen dogs is certainly very unpleasant. Yes! Strolling with the dog of your superior. At a time when daily we lose on the battlefields hundreds of officers. And ads go unread. I could advertise for a hundred years that I lost a dog. Two hundred years, three hundred years!"

The Colonel blew his nose loudly, which was in his case always a sign that he was greatly upset, and said: "You can just keep on strolling," he turned around and was walking away, cracking angrily his riding whip across the tips of his officer's overcoat.

Senior Lieutenant Lukáš crossed to the sidewalk on other side and even there he heard again "*Halt!*" The Colonel had just intercepted an unfortunate infantryman, a reservist, who had been thinking of his mom at home, and failed to see him.

The Colonel dragged the soldier with his own hands to the

garrison for punishment, calling him a sea-pig.

"What will I do to this Švejk?" the Senior Lieutenant thought to himself. "I'll smash his mouth, but that's not enough. Even pulling narrow strips of skin off his body is not enough for that hoodlum. Disregarding that he was to meet with a dame, he set off toward home.

"I'll kill him, the shameless rube," he said to himself, while boarding a streetcar.

*

In the meantime was the good soldier Švejk engrossed in a conversation with a messenger from the garrison. The soldier had brought some papers for the Senior Lieutenant to sign and was waiting now.

Švejk treated him to coffee and they were telling each other that Austria will blow it.

They carried on the talk as if this was self-evident. It was an endless stream of statements, wherein each word would certainly be defined in a court of law as high treason and both would be hanged.

"The lord Emperor must be stupid from it all," Švejk proclaimed, "he was never smart, but this war is sure to finish him off."

"He's stupid," proclaimed with certainty the soldier from the garrison, "he's as stupid as a log. He perhaps doesn't even know there is a war. Maybe, they were ashamed to tell him. If his signature is on that proclamation to those nations of his, then it must be a fraud. They surely had it printed without his knowledge, he can't think about anything anymore."

"He's finished," Švejk added expertly, "he craps in his pants and they have to feed him like a little kid. The last time, one of the guys in the pub was telling us, that he's got two wet nurses and that the lord Emperor is at the breast three times a day."

"If only it would happen already," sighed the soldier from the garrison, "and they had given us a whooping, so that Austria would finally be left untroubled."

And they both continued their conversation, until finally Švejk condemned Austria for good with the words: "Such an idiotic monarchy shouldn't even exist in this world," to which, in order to sort of augment this statement in a practical way, the other added: "As soon as I get to the front, I'll bug out."

When both then continued to express the Czech man's opinion of the war, the soldier from the garrison repeated what he had heard in Prague that day, that near Náchod[391] artillery could be heard and that the Russian Czar would be in Krakow as soon as possible.

Then they talked about the fact, that grain was being transported from us to Germany, that German soldiers get issued cigarettes and chocolate.

Then they recalled the times of past wars and Švejk seriously attempted to prove that when long ago they used to throw reeking stink-pots into a besieged castle, it was no bowl of honey either to fight in such stench. That he had read, how they had once laid siege to a castle somewhere for three years and the enemy had done nothing else, but toyed daily with those under siege in this manner.

He would certainly have said more of something interesting and enlightening, if their talk hadn't been interrupted by the return of Senior Lieutenant Lukáš.

Having cast a horrible, crushing look at Švejk, he signed the papers, and having dismissed the soldier, beckoned Švejk to follow him into the living room.

The eyes of the Senior Lieutenant emitted menacing lightning bolts. Having sat down in a chair, he pondered, while watching Švejk, when should he commence the massacre.

"First I'll punch his mouth a few times," the Senior Lieutenant thought to himself, "and then I'll bust his nose and rip off his ears and the rest remains to be seen."

And across from him were staring at him sincerely and good-heartedly a pair of amiable, innocent eyes of Švejk's, who dared to interrupt the quiet before the storm with these words:

"I dutifully report, Senior Lieutenant, Sir, that you've lost your cat. She devoured the shoe polish and took the liberty to croak. I threw her into the cellar, but the next one over. Such a well-behaved and pretty Angora cat you'll never find again."

"What will I do to him?" flashed through the mind of Senior Lieutenant, "forchristhelord, he has such a stupid expression on his face."

And the good-hearted, innocent eyes of Švejk kept right on radiating softness and tenderness, combined with demeanor of absolute mental balance, that everything was all right and nothing happened, and if something did happen, that was alright too, since at least something was happening at all.

Senior Lieutenant Lukáš jumped up, but, he didn't strike Švejk, as he had originally intended. He waved his fist under his nose and screamed: "You have, Švejk, stolen a dog!"

"I dutifully report, Senior Lieutenant, Sir, that I know of no such recent case, and I take the liberty, Senior Lieutenant, Sir, to remark, that you went with Max for a stroll after noon, and so I couldn't have stolen him. To me it looked striking right away, when you came back without the dog, that something must have happened. That's called a situation. In Spálená street, there is a bag maker named Kuneš and he couldn't go with a dog for a walk, so that he wouldn't lose him. Usually he forgot the dog somewhere in a pub, or somebody stole him from him, or borrowed him and didn't return…"

"Švejk, you cattle beast, *himllaudon*[392], shut your trap! Either you're a cunning scoundrel, or you are a stupid camel and an idiotic dodo. You're all about examples, but I'm telling you, don't play with me. Where did you bring that dog from? How did you come to him? Do you know that he belongs to our mister Colonel, who took him back when we ran into each other by chance? Do you know that this is a huge scandal? So tell the truth, did you steal the dog or not?"

"I dutifully report, Senior Lieutenant, Sir, that I didn't steal him."

"Did you know the dog was stolen?"

"I dutifully report, Senior Lieutenant, Sir, that I did know that dog was stolen."

"Švejk, jesusmaria, Lord-God-in-heaven, I'll shoot you dead, you dumb beast, you cattle beast, you ox, you shithead sonofabitch. Are you that idiotic?"

"Right, I dutifully report, Senior Lieutenant, Sir."

"Why did you bring me a stolen dog, why did you plant that beast in my apartment?"

"To make you happy, Senior Lieutenant, Sir."

Švejk's eyes looked good-naturedly and tenderly into the face of Senior Lieutenant, who sat down and groaned: "Why is God punishing me with this dumb beast?"

The Senior Lieutenant was sitting in his chair in quiet resignation and had a feeling, that he didn't have enough strength not only to give Švejk a slap across his head, but to roll himself a cigarette either, and he himself didn't even know, why he's sending Švejk for the Bohemie and the Tagblatt, for Švejk to read the Colonel's ad about the stolen dog.

With the newspapers already opened to the classifieds, Švejk returned. He was all beaming and joyously reported: "It's in there, Senior Lieutenant, Sir, the Colonel describes the stolen stable pinscher so nicely, it's just a pleasure, on top of all that, he's giving a hundred-crown reward to whomever brings the dog to him. That is a very decent reward. Usually they give a reward of fifty crowns. Someone named Božetěch from Košíře[393], made a living doing just that. He'd always steal a dog, then search in the classifieds to see, who had gone astray, and right away he'd go over there. Once he stole a nice black spitz, but because the owner didn't report it in the classifieds, he tried and placed an ad in the newspaper himself. He spent whole tenner advertising, until finally one man responded, that it was his dog, that he had gone astray and he thought it would be futile to look for him. That he didn't believe in people being honest anymore. Now, however, he sees, how after all there can still be found honest people, which tremendously pleases him. He said it was against his principles to reward honesty, but that as a memento he would give him his book on growing flowers both at home and in little backyard gardens. Dear Božetěch took the black spitz by the hind legs and thrashed the gentleman over the head with it, and since that time he has foresworn advertising. He would rather sell a dog to a kennel, when nobody wants to report and claim him in the classifieds."

"Go lie down, Švejk," ordered the Senior Lieutenant, "you're capable of acting silly until the morning." He too went to sleep and in the night he dreamt about Švejk, that Švejk had also stolen a horse from the heir to the throne, brought it to him, and that the heir to the throne recognized the horse during a parade review, when he, the unfortunate Senior Lieutenant Lukáš, rode the horse at the head of his company.

In the morning the Senior Lieutenant felt as if they slapped him about his head after a night on the town. An unusually heavy and some sort of mental nightmare haunted him. He still fell to sleep toward the morning, exhausted by the horrible dream, and was awakened by persistent knocking on the door, in which emerged the good-natured face of Švejk with the question, when was he to wake up mister Senior Lieutenant.

The Senior Lieutenant groaned in the bed: "Out, you cattle beast, this is something horrific!"

When he was then up already and Švejk brought him breakfast, the Senior Lieutenant was surprised by a new question from Švejk: "I dutifully report, Senior Lieutenant, Sir, wouldn't you wish for me to procure a new doggie for you?"

"You know, Švejk, I'd like to send you to face a field court," said the Senior Lieutenant with a sigh, "but they would acquit you, because they would never have seen such a colossally idiotic thing in their lives. Look at yourself in the mirror. Don't you get sick from the dumb expression on your face? You are the stupidest freak-of-nature that I have ever seen. Well, tell the truth, Švejk. Do you like the way you look?"

"I dutifully report, Senior Lieutenant, Sir, that I don't, I look somehow crooked or something. Well, this is not a polished mirror. Once, at that Chinaman Staněk's[394], they had a convex mirror, and when somebody would take a look at himself, then he wanted to hurl. The mouth like this, the head like a slop sink, the gut like a drunken canon's, in short, a strange figure. The regional governor passed by, took a look at himself and immediately they had to take the mirror down."

The Senior Lieutenant turned away, gave a sigh and judged it more reasonable to, rather than with Švejk, busy himself with his coffee with milk.

Švejk was already putzing around in the kitchen and Senior Lieutenant Lukáš heard Švejk's singing:

> Grenevil[395] is marching through the Powder Gate[396] for a stroll,
> His sabers are flashing, pretty girls are weeping...

Then from the kitchen was resounding another song:

> We soldiers, we are masters,
> Us the girls love on their own,
> We get paid, we have it good everywhere...

"You sure have it made, you churl," thought to himself the Senior Lieutenant and spat.

In the doorway suddenly emerged Švejk's head: "I dutifully report, Senior Lieutenant, Sir, that they're here for you from the garrison[397], you are to go immediately to see the Colonel, there's a messenger here."

And confidentially he added: "Perhaps it's on account of that doggie."

"I've already heard," said the Senior Lieutenant, when the messenger in the hallway wanted to report to him.

He said it with distress in his voice and leaving, he shot a devastating look at Švejk.

*

It was not just a report, it was something worse. The Colonel was sitting in an armchair looking very gloomy, when the Senior Lieutenant entered his office.

"Two years ago, Senior Lieutenant, Sir," said the Colonel, "you wished to be transferred to the 91st Regiment in Budějovice. Do you know where Budějovice is? On the Vltava, yes, on the Vltava, and the Ohře[398], or something similar, flows into it. The town is very, I should say, friendly, and if I'm not mistaken, it has an embankment. Do you know what an embankment is? It is a wall built above the water. Yes. However, that's beside the point. We conducted maneuvers there."

The Colonel fell silent, and looking into an ink well, he quickly changed the subject: "That dog of mine turned bad while with you. He won't eat anything. See, there's a fly in the ink well. It is peculiar, that even in winter, flies fall into the ink well. What disorder."

"So spit it out already, you miserable old fart," thought to himself the Senior Lieutenant.

The Colonel stood up and walked across the office several times.

"I've been thinking it over for a long time, Senior Lieutenant, Sir, what should I actually do to you, so that this could never be repeated, and I remembered that you wished to be transferred to the 91st Regiment. The Supreme Command[399] informed us not long ago, that at the 91st Regiment there's now a great shortage in the officers corps, because the Serbians slaughtered them all. I guarantee you with my word of honor, that within three days you will be with the 91st Regiment in Budějovice, where they're forming march-battalions. You don't have to thank me. The military needs officers who…"

And not knowing anymore what to say next, he looked at his watch and spoke: "It is half past ten, high time to go to the regimental report."

Thus was the pleasant conversation ended and the Senior Lieutenant felt much better, when he walked out of the office and went to the school for one-year volunteers, where he announced that in a few days he will be riding to the front, and will therefore organize a going away party in Nekázanka[400].

Having returned home, he said toward Švejk meaningfully:

"Do you know, Švejk, what a march-battalion is?"

"I dutifully report, Senior Lieutenant, Sir, that a march-battalion is a marchbattie, and that marchy is a marchgang. We always shorten it."

"Then, Švejk," said in festive voice the Senior Lieutenant, "I am informing you, that you will soon be riding with me in a marchbattie, since you like such short forms. But don't think that, at the front, you'll be acting out similar idiocies as you do here. Does this make you happy?"

"I dutifully report, Senior Lieutenant, Sir, that I am tremendously happy," answered the good soldier Švejk, "it will be something exquisite, when we both fall together for the lord Emperor and his family…"

AFTERWORD
To The First Volume: "In The Rear"

Having finished the first volume of this book, *The Fateful Adventures of the Good Soldier Švejk (In the Rear)*, I am announcing that two more parts will be issued in quick succession: At the Front and in Captivity[401]. In these next volumes, both soldiers and people will again speak and act as they do in reality

Life is no school of polished behavior. Everybody speaks as he is capable. The Master of Ceremonies, Doctor Guth[402]. speaks differently than the pubkeeper Palivec does at The Chalice. This novel is not meant to be a text used to refine someone so he might enter the salons of society. Nor is this a book to inform socialites of which expressions they might use in polite society. It is but a historical snapshot of a certain time.

When there is a need to use a strong expression, which was actually uttered, I do not hesitate to relay it in the very way it happened. I view the use of euphemisms, or the dotting out of a word, as the most asinine hypocrisy imaginable. These very words are even used in the world's parliaments.

It was said correctly, once upon a time, that a well-reared man could read anything. Only the biggest, dirty-minded swine, and other cunning vulgarians, stumble over that, which is natural. In their most miserable, fraudulent pseudo-morality, they refuse to grasp the true content. Instead, in frantic indignation, they throw themselves at individual words.

Years ago, I read a review of some novel. The critic was upset over the fact that the author wrote: "He blew and wiped his nose."

He said this crass statement was contrary to everything esthetic and exalted, and to all that our literature is supposed to give to the nation.

That is just one little example of the vile, dumb beasts that are born under the sun.

People, who become disconcerted over a strong expression, are cowards, because it is really life that shocks them, and such weak people are the very greatest agents of harm to both culture and character. They would have us be a nation of oversensitive folks, masturbators of false culture, of the type of Saint Aloysius[403], of whom it is said in a book by the monk Eustach[404], that when Saint Aloysius heard how a man with flatulence released his winds, there he began to weep, and it was only by prayer that he consoled himself and found peace.

Such people say publicly that they are offended, but with unusual fondness they will make a circuit of public bathrooms, just to read the vulgar inscriptions on the walls.

By using several strong expressions in my book, I have simply demonstrated how people actually speak.

We cannot demand that the pubkeeper Palivec speak as gently as missis Laudová[405], Doctor Guth, missis Olga Fastrová[406], and a whole number of others, who would love the best to make the whole Czechoslovak Republic a huge salon with parquet floors, where people would come in tails and gloves and refined language would always be used, and salon manners would be exercised, under the veil of which the lions of the salons indulge themselves in the worst vices and eccentricities.

*

I use this opportunity to advise the reader that the pubkeeper Palivec is alive. He withstood the war by serving his sentence in a hard-labor prison, and he has remained the same man as when he had the trouble over the picture of the Emperor František Josef.

He also came to visit me, when he read that he was in the book, and he bought over twenty copies of the first installment of the serial issue and has distributed them among his acquaintances, thereby helping to spread the book far and wide.

He is sincerely happy that I wrote about him and described him as a well-known foul-mouth.

"Nobody will ever make me change," he told me. "all my life I've spoken vulgar, as I meant it, and I'll keep on talking like that. I won't, on account of some silly cow, put a napkin over my trap. Today I'm famous."

His self-confidence has really risen. His fame is based on several strong expressions. That is enough for him to be satisfied, and had I perhaps wanted to advise him, having reproduced his speech faithfully and precisely, as I have described it, that he shouldn't speak that way, which was not my intention, I definitely would have offended that good man.

With unstudied natural expressions, he simply and honestly expressed the resistance of the Czechs to Byzantine ways and he himself didn't even know it. It was in his blood, that disrespect for the Emperor and decent expressions.

*

Otto Katz is also alive. He is a real figurine of a field chaplain. He hung it all up on a nail after the change of the regime, resigned from the Church, works nowadays as a manager at a factory that produces bronze and paints in northern Bohemia[407].

He wrote me a long letter, in which he threatens that he'll set things in order with me. A certain German paper published the translation of one chapter, in which he is described as he really was. So I visited him and it turned out very well with him. At two o'clock in the morning he could not stand on his feet, but he was preaching and saying: "I am Otto Katz, Field Chaplain, you plaster heads."

*

Today, there are a great many people of the type of the late Bretschneider, the state detective of old Austria, still walking around in this Republic. They are unusually interested in what is being said, and who is saying it.

*

I do not know whether I will manage to express with this book what I wanted. Just the circumstance, that I heard one man cussing at another by saying: "You're as stupid as Švejk," does not attest to that. However, should the word Švejk become a new epithet in the flowery wreath of abuse, I have to be content with this as my contribution to the enrichment of the Czech language[408].

Jaroslav Hašek

Endnotes

[1] The Czech title of Book One is "V zázemí". Morphologically, the word "zázemí" is formed from the prefix "za-"(*behind*) and "země" (*land, ground*), and in military-administrative usage of Hašek's time denoted the rear area: the zone behind the front, where armies were supplied, policed, treated, and governed. In the architecture of the novel, Book One is explicitly the rear, followed by second volume "Na frontě" (*At the Front*). Hašek underlines this himself in his Afterword to the first book. In there the author promised to follow with the next volume "V zajetí" (*In Captivity*). Instead, he produced "Slavný výprask" (*The Illustrious Thrashing*) and the unfinished "Pokračování slavného výprasku" (*The Illustrious Thrashing Continued*).

Here the nuance of Czech vocabulary is crucial. The language distinguishes between "zázemí" and "týl". Týl, inherited from Old Slavic and cognate with Russian "тыл" (tyl), denotes the strict military rear echelon, immediately behind the line of battle, the zone of reserves, supply depots, and field hospitals. It corresponds closely to the English journalistic idiom "behind the lines," with its trench warfare imagery of billets and relief camps. "Zázemí", by contrast, is a newer Czech formation, bureaucratic in tone, denoting the broader hinterland of institutions and administration. It is this word that Hašek uses: not the operational rear, but the civilian and bureaucratic back-world of police, courts, hospitals, gendarmes, and garrison chaplains.

Cecil Parrott's nomenclature, which has for decades passed through academic discourse as if it were canonical, labeled Book One *Behind the Lines*. The phrase has strong resonance in English reportage and memoirs of the First World War: billets, rest camps, casualty clearing stations, entertainments and training areas just beyond the trenches. It is vivid, idiomatic, and steeped in trench culture. But Book One of *Švejk* does not take place there. Its chapters unfold in the police headquarters, before court doctors, in an asylum, in billets with Senior Lieutenant Lukáš, and in the world of a chaplain's military servant, punctuated by medical examinations, arrests, interrogations, and garrison life. The whole design of the first volume is urban, bureaucratic, and institutional. To call this world "behind the lines" imports the atmosphere of the trenches that Hašek deliberately withholds until the later books.

The phrase "in the rear," by contrast, is dry, technical, and bureaucratically precise, exactly what "v zázemí" denotes. Etymologically it comes through Old French "arrière" from Latin "retro" (*behind*), entering English military vocabulary in formations like "rear guard" and by extension "the rear" as the back area of an army. It lacks the picturesque trench associations of "behind the lines," and thus better fits the flat official tone Hašek uses when naming the first part of his novel.

The logic here is the same as with the titles of Books Three and Four. Just as Parrott's "licking" introduced a metaphor foreign to Czech *výprask*, so his "behind the lines" imported English trench-reportage color foreign to Czech "zázemí". In both cases The Centennial Edition of the "Chicago version" resists this drift and lets the Czech word's own register and imagery direct the English. For Book One, the choice "In the Rear" reproduces the bureaucratic blandness Hašek intended, situates the narrative exactly where he places it, and preserves the novel's deliberate structural progression from the administrative rear to the fighting front.

[2] In the Czech original, Lukáš is referred to as "nadporučík", a Czech word for the rank, or - twice as often in Book One alone - as "obrlajtnant" (*Upper Lieutenant)*, the Czech corruption of the German "Oberleutnant". Austro-Hungarian k.u.k. infantry used only "Leutnant" and "Oberleutnant", while there are and have been sometimes three levels of the lieutenant rank in a number of countries across the globe. Lukáš's level was the higher of the two lieutenant ranks in the Austro-Hungarian army. His rank is missing in the U.S. and British military forces and a number of others. It sits between the U.S. 1st Lieutenant (or UK Lieutenant) and Captain (or Lieutenant J.G. and Lieutenant of the U.S. Navy). But Lukáš's rank ought to be understood by any English language reader anywhere. That is not necessarily easy to achieve, especially in the U.S. as there is no universal draft and the basic knowledge of military nomenclature is becoming less common. It seemed reasonable to convey Lukáš's 'lieutenant' kind of rank as 'Senior Lieutenant' aligning him with the uppermost of the customary lieutenant ranks anywhere, regardless of the military service branch, the historic period or language.

[3] Napoléon was emperor of France from 18 May 1804 to 6 April 1814. He gradually assembled power after the French Revolution, aided by his unique military talent and many battlefield successes. He conquered and ruled over most of Western and Central Europe and held power in Egypt for a couple of years. A failed campaign in Russia in 1812 weakened his position and laid the foundations for his ultimate defeat at Waterloo in 1815.

Several battles during the Napoleonic wars are mentioned in *The Good Soldier Švejk*: Leipzig, Aspern and Waterloo. Napoleon emerged victorious from the only major battle he was involved in on Czech territory. By Austerlitz (now Slavkov u Brna), Napoleon's army defeated Austrian and Russian forces on 2 December 1805. Many historians regard this battle as his greatest military achievement ever. [honsi.org]

[4] Macedonia ["Macedon" in antiquity] was an ancient kingdom with its origin in the northern part of the Greek peninsula. During the reign of Philip II of Macedon and his son Alexander the Great, it became an enormous empire, stretching all the way to the river Indus. The capital at the time (400 BC to 300 BC) was Pella. Macedonia is the first of more than eight hundred geographical references in *The Good Soldier Švejk*, and it appears already in the third sentence! It is also the first of a number of references to ancient history, whether Roman or Greek. [honsi.org]

[5] Prague is the capital and largest city of Czech Republic. It is located on the river Vltava and the population is about 1.2 million. After 1648 Prague has been largely spared from warfare and, as a result, the old city center is very well preserved. The city can thus offer intact architecture from several eras, and is considered one of the most beautiful in Europe. The inner city area has been on UNESCO's World Heritage List since 1992.

Prague was already an important city in the Middle Ages and reached its summit during the reign of Charles IV, who was also Holy Roman Emperor. After Bohemia came under Habsburg rule from 1526 onwards, it gradually lost its importance and had, by the outbreak of World War I, been reduced to being one of several Austrian regional capitals.

At the outbreak of World War I, the city was much smaller than today, consisting of the districts I. Staré město, II. Nové město, III. Malá Strana, IV. Hradčany, V. Josefov, VI. Vyšehrad, VII. Holešovice-Bubny, and VIII. Libeň. The city was officially called Královské hlavní město Praha (*the Royal Capital Prague*).

The numbering of the districts differed from today's; Malá Strana, for instance, was Prague III, whereas it is now part of Praha I. The population count in 1910 was approximately 224,000; with suburbs included, it was 476,000. More than 90 per cent reported Czech as their everyday language. The rest were predominantly German speakers. In 1922, several adjoining districts were incorporated into the now Czechoslovak capital. The new administrative unit became known as Velká Praha. [honsi.org]

[6] Kingdom of Bohemia was a historical kingdom that existed from 1198, and from 1526 to 1918 it was a political entity (crownland) ruled by the Habsburg Empire. Some of the Habsburg emperors were also crowned as kings of Bohemia. Emperor Franz Joseph I refused to be crowned, which caused considerable resentment among Czechs.

The emperor's executive in the kingdom was the Statthalter (governor), who resided in Prague. The official languages were Czech and German. The kingdom was dissolved in 1918 and its territory became the most influential region in the newly proclaimed Czechoslovakia. [honsi.org]

[7] [The Republic of] Czechoslovakia was a historic state in Central Europe. It was established on 28 October 1918 as a consequence of the collapse of Austria-Hungary at the end of World War I.

Czechoslovakia consisted of the regions of Bohemia, Moravia, Slovakia, Carpathian Ruthenia, and a small part of Silesia. In the inter-war years, the state enjoyed a functioning democracy with a strong industrial base. The infamous Munich agreement of 1938 forced the country to cede to Germany the regions that were mainly populated by German speakers, and on 15 March 1939 the rest of the Czech lands were occupied by the Nazis and Slovakia became a German client state.

After the defeat of Germany, the country was restored with a democratic government, but in February 1948 the communists took power in a coup and a one-party state was established. In 1989, democracy was restored, but the state was peacefully split into the Czech Republic and Slovakia on 1 January 1993. [honsi.org]

[8] Ephesus was in ancient times an important port on the western coast of Asia Minor with around 250,000 inhabitants. The city was the economic center of Ionian Greece and later one of the most important cities of the Roman Empire. The city was home to one of the seven wonders of the world: the Temple of Artemis. [honsi.org]

[9] [Franz] Ferdinand was a nephew of Emperor Franz Joseph I and, from 1896 to 1914, heir to the throne of Austria-Hungary. He was murdered in Sarajevo on 28 June 1914 together with his wife Duchess Sophie, an event that eventually led to the outbreak of World War I. His full name was Franz Ferdinand Carl Ludwig Joseph Maria von Österreich-Este. He owned Konopiště castle by Benešov where the family spent much of their time.

Franz Ferdinand's political views were relatively liberal; he opposed preventive warfare against Serbia, and he advocated making Austria-Hungary a three-pillar federal state where the Slav nations were put on an equal footing with Germans and Hungarians. [honsi.org]

[10] Průša was the owner of Drogerie Průša at Tylovo náměstí (*Tyl's square*) in Vinohrady. Jaroslav Hašek worked here as an apprentice from March 1898 (or later) until September 1899. Exactly when he started is not known, but it happened after he had been dismissed at drogerie Kokoška.

The pharmacist was born in Votice in 1862, was married to Mathilde (b. 1872) and they had the son Rudolf. The family moved to Vinohrady in 1893.

Otherwise we know little about him but newspaper adverts reveal that his store existed at least until 1915, the year Průša died. In 1916 Čech reported that his widow had been the victim of fraud, but that the culprit had been arrested and sentenced to 5 months in prison. From the death protocols it transpires that Průša died from a brain stroke, that he suffered from diabetes and lived at Vinohrady čp. 603 when he passed away.

Adverts from a chemist's Fr. Průša appeared already in 1890 but then from Kamenice nad Lipou. That said there is no doubt that this Průša is the same person as police registers reveal that the son Rudolf was born in the very Kamenice in 1893.

Průša is the first of countless examples of how the author pulled in fragments from his own experiences to create the backdrop for the novel. Even Průša who appears to be a fictional person, is drawn from real life. This is probably the case with most of the apparently fictional figures in the novel. Their role might have been distorted or mystified but the names were rarely thought up. [honsi.org]

[11] Konopiště is a village and castle by Benešov that was owned from 1887 to 1914 by Archduke Franz Ferdinand, then Austrian heir to the throne. [honsi.org]

[12] Sophie was a Bohemian noble lady, married to the heir to the Austrian and Hungarian thrones, Archduke Franz Ferdinand. She was killed in Sarajevo together with her husband. The Habsburg imperial family never accepted Sophie due to her non-royal background. Therefore, the children of Sophie and Franz Ferdinand had no right to succession to the throne.

Her full name was Sophie Maria Josephine Albina Gräfin Chotek von Chotkowa und Wognin. [honsi.org]

[13] Bosnia-Hercegovina was (and is) the political entity consisting of Bosnia and Hercegovina. The area was annexed by Austria-Hungary in 1908. This led to widespread dissatisfaction among Serbs and is arguably the main reason for the grievances that led terrorists to plot and carry out the murder of Archduke Franz Ferdinand six years later. [honsi.org]

[14] In the increasingly apostate western society, in which once common Biblical concepts were widely understood, I was gently alerted that an explanation is in order here. Even the original Czech expression "být už na pravdě Boží" is marked as "*outdated*" in the *Academic dictionary of contemporary Czech*, published by the *Institute for the Czech Language of the Academy of Sciences of the Czech Republic*. And it wasn't even included in the *Dictionary of Standard Literary Czech Language (1960–1971)*. The

term is a euphemism for "to be dead" according to the dictionary entry. No wonder it's not understood. It is actually a euphemism for "passed away". (The only equivalent for that expression I know of is "odebrat se na onen svět", "*to repair/betake oneself into that [other] world*".) The difference being that "passing away" implies dual nature of human life and life after death. Specifically, the immortal soul passes from the material body, which starts decomposing, into the presence of God. (30% of Czechs are atheists and 41% "non-religious" for a combined score that puts them in the third place behind Sweden, bested by the Swedes by mere 1%, and ahead of the Brits by 3%. The list is headed by China with 90%.)

Now to the point of why such a euphemism for "being dead" or "passed away", depending on your world-view:

> "Jesus saith unto him, I am the way, and the truth, and the life; no one cometh unto the Father, but by me." John 14:6

> "I was greatly delighted to find some of your children walking in truth, just as we have been commanded by the Father." 2 John 1:4

Followers of Jesus strive to walk in truth given to them by Him. Once they pass away, they have reached the goal and are fully in the truth of the Lord Himself. [Translator's note]

[15] The italicized '*They*' or '*they*' and their morphological variants indicate, that they are used instead of 'you', when addressing a stranger or showing respect to age, position, or maintaining distance. [Translator's note'

[16] Nusle was from 1898 a town in the Prague conurbation that grew rapidly during the industrial revolution. In 1922 it became part of greater Prague. The capital Prague (so-called *Great Prague)* was established on January 1, 1922 by annexing 37 municipalities and settlements. In addition to Nusle, all these, mentioned in Book One, are among them: Podolí, Vinohrady, Dejvice, Motol, Karlín, Vršovice, Smíchov, Žižkov, Malešice, and Košíře. [honsi.org]

[17] Franz Joseph I was emperor of Austria and after Ausgleich *(The Compromise)* in 1867 also crowned king of Hungary. His reign lasted from 1848 to 1916 and is the fourth longest in European history. He ascended the throne when he was 18 years old, after the revolution of 1848. He was regarded as very conservative during his first period in power. The young emperor was initially unpopular and in 1853 he survived an attempt on his life. The next year he married his cousin, Empress Elisabeth (Sisi). They had four children.

The emperor-king suffered a number of personal tragedies: the oldest daughter died when she was two, his brother Maximilian was executed in

Mexico, his son and heir Crown Prince Rudolf committed suicide, Sisi was murdered, and in 1914 his nephew Archduke Franz Ferdinand was shot in Sarajevo. The emperor was rather unpopular among Czechs because he refused to be crowned as king of Bohemia. [honsi.org]

[18] It is found in the fourth stanza of the 1854-1918 version of the Astro-Hungarian anthem, "Mit vereinter Kräfte Walten, Wird das Schwere leicht vollbracht" (nationalanthems.info), i.e. *"Done with united forces, the hard will be accomplished easily"*. [Translator's note]

[19] Lucheni was a French-born anarchist of Italian descent, who lived most of his life in Switzerland. He murdered Empress Elisabeth of Austria-Hungary in Geneva in 1898. He was given a life sentence (Switzerland had abolished the death penalty) and later committed suicide in prison. [honsi.org]

[20] Elisabeth was Empress of Austria, Queen of Hungary, also called Sisi (later Sissi), and married to Emperor Franz Joseph I. Her full name was Elisabeth Amalie Eugenie, Herzogin in Bayern.

Elisabeth was the second eldest daughter of duke Maximilian Joseph of Bayern of the royal Bavarian Wittelsbach dynasty, one of eight siblings. Only 17 years old she married her cousin Emperor Franz Joseph I in what could be described as a dynastically arranged marriage. The couple had four children, but mostly lived separate lives. After Ausgleich (the Vienna Accord of 1867 that put Hungary on an equal footing with Austria and in practical term led to the creation of the Dual Monarchy), she was crowned queen of Hungary on 8 June 1867.

The empress/queen was very popular and has over the years acquired a status as a legend. She has been the focus of countless books, films, plays, and animations. [honsi.org]

[21] The Russian equivalent of emperor and empress, who used to rule Russia until 1917:

Nicholas was a Tsar (Emperor) of the Romanov dynasty and the last monarch of Russia. His reign lasted from 1894 to 1917, when on March 15 he was forced to step down after the February Revolution. He was from September 1915 commander-in-chief of Russia's armed forces after replacing his cousin Nicholas Nikolaevich. On July 17th 1918 he and his family were executed by the Bolsheviks, an event which is regarded as one of the most significant political murders in recent history.

Nicholas was regarded a weak and inept ruler, but has since 1990 seen a certain postmortem rehabilitation. He was officially buried in 1998 and in 2000 he was declared a saint by the Russian-Orthodox church.

A paradox is that Jaroslav Hašek in 1916 and 1917 advocated czarist rule and even proposed that a Romanov prince ascend the Czech throne after the foreseen victory in the war and the subsequent break-up of Austria-Hungary. [honsi.org]

Alexandra was Empress of Russia from 1894 to 1917, married to Tsar Nicholas II. She was executed together with her family in Yekaterinburg (Екатеринбу́рг). [honsi.org]

[22] *A two-wheeled wagon with a wicker chest, used by police to transport drunkards and rioters. Košatinka also had a lid. The people of Prague also called this cart "an etui", i.e. "a pencil case".* [svejkmuseum.cz]

[23] Switzerland was neutral during World War I and was, as today, a federal republic. As a curiosity, it must be mentioned that the Habsburg family hailed from Switzerland. During World War I, Lenin lived in Switzerland. From 1917, he was to play an important role in the events leading to Russia's withdrawal from the war.

In addition, Switzerland was at times during the war a place of refuge for Professor Masaryk and other Czechs who worked for national independence. [honsi.org]

[24] Gavrilo Princip [mentioned indirectly] was one of the assassins who took part in the plot to kill Archduke Franz Ferdinand in Sarajevo on June 28th 1914. Princip and his accomplices were trained by and acted on orders from the Serbian nationalist group The Black Hand, a group that had it's origin in the Serbian armed forces. Their principal goal was to join all Serb-populated territories in a greater Serbia.

It was Princip who fired the lethal bullets after several attempts had failed in the preceding minutes. Princip unsuccessfully tried to commit suicide and was immediately arrested.

The trial started in Sarajevo on October 12th 1914, and on the 28th, the verdict fell. Some of the conspirators were handed death sentences, but Princip was convicted to life imprisonment as he was too young for capital punishment.

He died in jail in Terezín already in 1918. Thus, he never lived to see the greater Serbia that Yugoslavia, in many ways, became. [honsi.org]

[25] [John Moses] Browning was an American firearms designer. He made pistols, rifles, shotguns and machine guns. Archduke Franz Ferdinand was killed with a Belgian-made Browning semi-automatic pistol (FN Model 1910). [honsi.org]

[26] Even though his name is not mentioned directly there is no doubt that Švejk had King Carlos I in mind. He was king of Portugal from 1889 until he was

murdered by republican activists in 1908. The Portuguese state went bankrupt twice during his lifetime, including once during his reign, in 1902.

The king had indeed, as Švejk said, become quite fat in his later years. He was however killed by rifle shots, and not with a Browning. [honsi.org]

[27] "státní policie", Staatspolizei (officially k.k. Staatspolizei) was the domestic civilian intelligence service of Cisleithania, whose main task was surveillance of potential enemies of the state. In the context of *The Good Soldier Švejk* we understand it to be the Prague branch. The Department was created in 1893 following civil unrest and the unit reported directly to the "Statthalter" (*Governor*). In Prague their servicemen and agents were operating from the premises of c.k. policejní ředitelství (*I&R Police Headquarters*). In their service were among others two young lawyers, Slavíček and Klíma. Head of the unit was Viktor Chum.

Jaroslav Hašek had intimate knowledge of the state police, originating from his period as an anarchist activist (from 1904). His most celebrated encounter with them was after his famous hoax at U Valšů on November 24th 1914 where he registered as a Russian trader, ostensibly to test the vigilance of the Austrian security service. He was let off with only 5 days in jail which he served immediately.

During the war the eyes of the State Police again fell on Jaroslav Hašek. It happened after the author on June 17th 1916 published a story in Čechoslovan where he lets a tomcat soil pictures of the emperor. This led to charges of high treason and an arrest order was issued. Several of the other stories he wrote also aroused interest at home. They were translated to German for the benefit of the investigators and led to a lively exchange between the police headquarters in Prague and Vienna. [honsi.org]

[28] Victor Hugo was a French author and politician who published poetry, drama and novels. In France he is regarded as one of the country's leading poets. His most famous novel is probably "Les Misérables". Hugo was also a political activist and was forced into exile for a number of years. After his return in 1870 he was elected member of the Senate. He was also known as an advocate of human rights. [honsi.org]

[29] Palivec put forward Victor Hugo in defense of his vulgar language. Indirectly he referred to a passage in Les Misérables where the famous "*word of Cambronne*", which is connected to Napoléon's old guard in the battle of Waterloo, is quoted. General Cambronne is said to have given this simple answer to General Colville when the latter insisted he surrender: *Shit*! [honsi.org]

[30] Věznice Pankrác (*Pankrác Prison*), officially c.k. penitentiary for men in Prague, was at the time a large penitentiary for men, and "pankrác" is almost synonymous with "prison" in Czech slang. The prison is named after the Pankrác district where it is located. Construction started in 1885 and was complete in 1889. It was at the time a modern prison with good conditions for the inmates. In Austrian times the prison mostly housed dangerous male criminals but also saw the odd political prisoner. The prison later became the scene of executions and 1,580 persons were killed; 1,087 of them during the Nazi occupation. During Communist rule starting 1948 another few hundred were executed. [honsi.org]

[31] The Czech "lazar" is a common noun meaning a wretched, helpless, or half-dead person — a bedridden invalid. It derives from Lazarus the beggar in the parable of Luke 16:20–25, whose ulcerated, prostrate condition gave rise to the word in several European languages. It does not refer to Lazarus of Bethany in John 11 (the man Jesus resurrects), and carries no implication of revival. Hašek uses "lazar" in the folk-lexical sense: someone lying like a sick, exhausted, or nearly lifeless man. [Translator's note]

[32] "Karlák", rendered as *Charlie's* here, is the Czech vernacular shorthand for "Karlovo náměstí", i.e. Charles' square.

[33] "Mladočeši" (*Young Czechs*) - officially Národní strana svobodomyslná (*National Liberal Party*), was a Czech political party that existed from 1874 to 1918. The party reached its zenith after 1890. Due to their, for the time radical, demands on universal suffrage and greater autonomy for the Czech lands of Austria-Hungary, they received considerable support in their homeland, but correspondingly greater opposition from Vienna. Thereafter the Social Democrats and the Agrarian Party made inroads into their electoral base, and the party lost much of its influence. The leading politician in the history of the party was Karel Kramář. The party's official newspaper was Národní listy, to which Jaroslav Hašek contributed many short stories. At the 1911 election to Reichsrat (*Imperial Council*), i.e. bi-cameral Parliament, they received 9.8 per cent of the votes in Bohemia and had 14 representatives. [honsi.org]

[34] Krumlov was until 1920 the name of Český Krumlov, a town not far from the Austrian border. The district of Krumlov was located in the recruitment area of Infantry Regiment No. 91, so Jaroslav Hašek would have known many fellow soldiers from there.

The medieval structure of the town has been preserved and it is on the world heritage list of UNESCO. It has become a major tourist attraction.

According to the 1910 census, Krumlov had 8,716 inhabitants, of whom

1,295 (14 per cent) reported using Czech as their everyday language. The *judicial district* was okres Krumlov, administratively it reported to hejtmanství *(administrative district)* Krumlov.[honsi.org]

[35] The Vltava is the longest river in Bohemia. From its sources in Šumava, it passes Český Krumlov, České Budějovice and Prague, before emptying into the Labe (Elbe, in German) by Mělník. The river's length is 430 km, and the catchment area is 28,090 km². In foreign languages the German name Moldau is frequently used. First attested in Latin as Albis, the name Elbe means "river" or "river-bed" and is nothing more than the High German version of a word albī found elsewhere in Germanic; compare Old Norse river name Elfr, Swedish älv "river", Norwegian elv "river", Old English river name elf, and Middle Low German elve "river-bed". [honsi.org]

[36] Zliv is a village in South Bohemia, situated 10 km north west of Budějovice and 4 km west of Hluboká.

During the summer of 1896 (or 1897), Hašek's mother Kateřina took the children on a trip to the area around Protivín to visit relatives. Both his parents were from this area. They visited Zliv, Mydlovary, Hluboká, Budějovice, Putim, Skočice, Krč, Protivín, Ražice, and Vodňany. All of these places appear in *The Good Soldier Švejk* and some of them even in the short stories.

In the spring of 1915 Jaroslav Hašek reportedly appeared in Zliv again, now on an unauthorized "excursion" from the Budějovice garrison. [honsi.org]

[37] Mydlovary is a village in South Bohemia, 16 km north west of Budějovice and the birthplace of Josef Hašek, the father of Jaroslav Hašek. He was born in house number 8. The budding satirist visited Mydlovary during his childhood (1896 or 1897) and couldn't have been far away in 1915.

The fact that his father was born in Mydlovary is significant. This meant that Jaroslav Hašek had right of domicile here so he, just like his literary hero, was drafted into Infantry Regiment No. 91. [honsi.org]

[38] The Prince at Hluboká probably refers to Adolf Joseph Schwarzenberg (1832-1914), the 8th Prince of Schwarzenberg and a major landowner in South Bohemia. Another candidate is his son Johann II (1860-1938) as both were alive at the time the event is said to have taken place ("years ago"). They also held the title Duke of Krumlov, another of the Schwarzenberg estates. [honsi.org]

Hluboká is a small town in South Bohemia, 15 km north of Budějovice. It was one of the favorite haunts of German-Roman emperor Charles IV, who often visited when he resided in Budějovice. Nowadays Hluboká is best known for its Windsor-style chateau which until 1938 belonged to the House of Schwarzenberg. [honsi.org]

[39] Ražice is a village in the Písek district in South Bohemia. It is an important railway junction between Písek, České Budějovice and Plzeň.

Jaroslav Hašek knew the village very well and mentions it both in *The Good Soldier Švejk* and in some of his stories. [honsi.org]

[40] "Krajský soud Písek" (*Písek Regional Court*) was an institution that was part of the judiciary of Austria, and also remained functional in Czechoslovakia until 1945.

The court in Písek hosted the 2nd trail of the infamous Hilsner affair (or Polná affair) in which the young Jew Leopold Hilsner was accused of ritual murder. His death-sentence was confirmed in Písek on November 14th 1900 but was converted to life imprisonment by Emperor Franz Joseph I and in 1918 he was set free during a general amnesty. Future president Professor Masaryk put his academic career at stake during his defense of Hilsner, and an article he wrote in on the case was confiscated. The verdict at Písek was quashed only as late as 1998. [honsi.org]

[41] Rudolf was crown prince and heir to the thrones of Austria-Hungary and the only son of Emperor Franz Joseph I and Empress Elisabeth. He committed suicide together with his lover Maria Vetsera at Mayerling castle outside Vienna.

Rudolf suffered from severe mood changes and there is still some debate over whether it really was suicide. The death certificate mentions "spiritual confusion." The drama of Mayerling has been filmed many times, including in a French/British production from 1968 with Omar Sharif in the role as Rudolf.

The free-thinking crown price lived a dissolute life, got dependent on morphine after treatment for VD and infected his wife with gonorrhea, which made her sterile. Rudolf was politically liberal and associated with the organization Free Thought. His political views prevented him from being included in the influential circles of the court, his father keeping him at distance. [honsi.org]

[42] Johann Orth was Archduke of the House of Habsburg and Prince of Tuscany. His real name was Johann Salvator, but he took the common name Orth in 1889 after having reneged on his imperial privileges. This happened after a conflict with the court as Salvator wanted to marry the dancer Ludmilla Schubel, a lady well below his rank. He took the new name after a castle he owned in Salzkammergut. Orth was a good friend of Crown Prince Rudolf and shared his liberal political views. After breaking with the court he was

forced to leave the country. Already having obtained a ship captain's certificate he tried his luck in merchant shipping. In 1890 he left for London where he bought a cargo vessel and embarked on a freight mission to Argentina and Chile. Around July 12th 1890 the ship went missing near Cabo Tres Puntas.

His full name was Giovanni Nepomuceno Salvatore Maria Giuseppe Giovanni Ferdinando Baldassares Lodovico Carlo Zenobio Antonino d'Asburgo-Lorena. [honsi.org]

[43] [The Mexican Emperor] Maximiliano I was an archduke of the House of Habsburg, and brother of Emperor Franz Joseph I. He was installed as Emperor of Mexico by the French in 1863, but was executed in 1867 at Cerro de las Campanas in Querétaro after a rebellion led by the liberal Benito Juárez.

His full name was Ferdinand Maximilian Joseph von Österreich. [honsi.org]

[44] "c.k. policejní ředitelství" (*I&R Police Headquarters*) refers to the Prague Police Headquarters. It was (and is) a huge complex, located between Ferdinandova, Karoliny Světlé and Bartolomějská streets. It is still (2018) the HQ of the Prague's police.

The Police HQ was organized in five departments where the State Police (Staatspolizei), Department III (public order), and Department IV (safety) are the ones that are relevant in the context of *The Good Soldier Švejk*. Department III is directly mentioned in the novel, although the author most probably has the State Police Department in mind. In 1913 the following of our acquaintances from the novel were employed: Slavíček and Klíma (State Police) and Police Commissioner Drašner (Department IV). Head of the 1st Department was Rudolf Demartini, a person who may have inspired Mr. Demartini, the fat gentleman at c.k. Zemský co trestní soud (*I&R Regional as Criminal Court*). [honsi.org]

[45] "U Brejšky" was a restaurant in Spálená street in Praha II. that in its original form existed from 1884 until around 1920. It was known as a meeting place for journalists; Egon Erwin Kisch and others wrote about the phenomenon of "news exchange" in Prager Tagblatt in 1925. Both Czech and German newspapermen frequented the place. Immediately after opening the restaurant had installed a telephone station (No. 180), a rare sight in 1884.

The restaurant served beer from Plzeň and was also known for its good food. Not only was it popular among journalists: visitors from the province also enjoyed it here. On the first floor it offered meeting rooms and accommodation. U Brejšky (*At Brejška's*), aka. U Brejšků (*At Brejškas'*) or

209

Brejškova restaurace (*Brejška's Restaurant*) was altogether one of the most best known and popular taverns in all of Prague, as indicated by the endless amount of newspaper clips. The restaurant was named after the original owner, Karel Brejška. [honsi.org]

[46] Montmartre was a was a night coffeehouse and entertainment establishment in the center of Prague that recently (as of 2010) was re-opened after a hiatus of 70 years. The name is taken from the famous Paris district of Montmartre. The coffeehouse is decorated with period photos, and Jaroslav Hašek plays a prominent role.

Montmartre was opened in 1911 by the well-known actor and artist Josef Waltner. From the beginning, it became a popular meeting place among artists, intellectuals and the bohemian set. Apart from Jaroslav Hašek it was also frequented by the likes of Zdeněk Matěj Kuděj, Max Brod, Egon Erwin Kisch, Franz Werfel and Franz Kafka. Hašek wrote four short stories where Montmartre was involved, and Kisch also immortalized the coffeehouse through his writing. [honsi.org]

[47] Columbus was a discoverer and merchant of Italian origin, known for the European "discovery" of America in 1492.

Columbus' egg describes a brilliant idea or discovery that seems simple or easy after the fact. The expression refers to a popular story of how Christopher Columbus, having been told that discovering the Americas was no great accomplishment, challenged his critics to make an egg stand on its tip; and, after they gave up, he did it himself by tapping the egg on the table so as to flatten its tip. [honsi.org]

[48] *The text "Hej, Slované" was written by the Slovak evangelical priest Samuel Tomášik in 1834 and set to a traditional Polish tune (today's Polish anthem). At the All-Slavic Congress in Prague in the revolutionary year 1848, the composition "Hej, Slované" was presented and accepted as the anthem of all Slavs:* [svejkmuseum.cz]

> Hey Slavs, our Slavic speech
> still lives,
> as long as our faithful hearts
> are beating for our nation.
> Slavic spirit lives, lives
> it will live for ages.
> Thunder and hell, vain your
> rages are against us.
> God entrusted us with the gift of language,
> our thunderous God.
> So none can snatch it from us,

> none in the world.
> Let there be as many people,
> as the devils in the world.
> God is with us, the one, who is against us,
> Perun* will sweep away.
> And let above us
> arise a terrible storm.
> The rock is cracking, the oak is breaking.
> Let the earth shake!
> We're still standing firmly,
> like walls of a castle.
> The black earth will swallow the one,
> who resigns treacherously! [lyricstranslate.com]

[49] A card game played with German suited cards.

[50] In Switzerland and in the Tirol of Austria, archeologists found parts of skeletons of dogs, whose descendants were found all over Europe in later years. One special variety was the so called "Stallpinscher" (*Stable Pinscher*), which lived on farms in Bavaria and Baden-Württemberg. He was a rough coated and sturdy guy. No one can really say when this little fellow appeared for the first time. He was mainly used as a guard dog, protecting mail carriages on their long ways through the woods. This small Pinscher was making long distances, loyally trotting along the horses. [schnauzer.at]

[51] A French term for the method of preparing fish the minute it has been killed – the fish is plunged into a boiling court bouillon, i.e. "*short broth*", which turns the skin a metallic blue color. [lovefrenchfood.com]

[52] Golgotha was an execution ground outside Jerusalem where Jesus was crucified between two rebels. The name is a Greek form of the Aramaic version Gûlgaltâ, which means «skull», and the name might refer to natural formations that resemble a skull or a place where many skulls are found. Golgotha is believed to have been near Jerusalem, but the location has not been confirmed. [honsi.org]

[53] Lombroso was an Italian psychologist, criminologist, and anthropologist of Jewish origin, baptized Ezechia Marco Lombroso. He was a pioneer of anthropological criminology which promoted the claim that criminality was inherited. Lombroso rejected the hitherto classical view that the criminal instinct was part of human nature. His political anthropology criminology maintained that criminal behavior is in the genes and could be enhanced by physical defects. The physical shape could indicate whether a person was a

---

* Perun – Slavic God of thunder

criminal, which he gave many examples of in the illustrations in his books.

Lombroso never wrote any book with the title About Criminal Types so the book that Hašek refers to in *The Good Soldier Švejk* is often believed to be L'uomo delinquente (*Criminal Man*), his best known publication. Still, there are only a handful of drawings in this book, at least in the first edition, so it may be that Hašek drew inspiration from some of Lombroso's other works. That said, during Lombroso's lifetime five distinct editions appeared and in these more illustrations were added.

The book was never translated into Czech so Hašek probably read a German version. [honsi.org]

[54] *"Národní politika" (National Politic), a newspaper published in the years 1883 - 1945 referred to by the nickname čubička (a little bitch). "Among the newspapers, National Politics is the pike!" claimed its slogan, rhyming in the original Czech. It might be true, since it survived even the Nazi occupation. Why it was called čubička, Břetislav Hůla writes in his explanations as follows: "Because of the lack of principles, the servitude to government power, and the submissiveness of the property-rich classes, this paper was commonly called 'čubička' among the people, which showed contempt for the entire way, in which this paper was managed." Although Hůla was a witness of that time, his version could be reflecting the time when his annotations were created, i.e. sometime in the fifties of the 20th century. It is therefore possible that the moniker čubička is derived precisely from extensive advertising section, which was full of advertisements for the sale of various domestic animals, mainly dogs. And they were definitely watched not only by Švejk, who made living selling dogs, but also by Jaroslav Hašek when he ran his own dog shop.* [svejkmuseum.cz]

The Czech original reads: "...kupuji si odpoledníčka Národní politiky, čubičky", i.e. "*I buy the small afternoon edition of National Politics*, **čubičky**. Here's a fine example of the wonderful consequences of the richness of the Czech (and in general, Slavic) morphology. The word "čubičky" represents two forms of the word: 1. the nominative case of the plural of "čubička", i.e. "little bitches", or the possessive case of the singular "čubička", i.e. "of the little bitch/little bitch's". The latter would mean that Švejk is specifying the newspaper, the afternoon edition of which he buys.

I believe that if Hašek wanted the word to refer to the content of the advertisements Švejk peruses, he would had written "ty čubičky", i.e. "those little bitches (they advertise). Perhaps Hašek consciously wrote it in such a way that it could be interpreted either way. He was not an ox. More like a fox. He knew what he was doing. [Translator's note]

[55] Jan Nepomucký, a.k.a. John of Nepomuk, was a Czech priest and martyr, who was blinded, tortured, and drowned in the Vltava. Today there is a statue of him at the point at Karlův most where he was thrown off. He was canonized in 1729 and is now a patron saint. He is buried in *Saint Vitus Cathedral* in Prague. [honsi.org]

[56] Museum is in this context almost certainly refers to the main building of the Museum království Českého (*Museum of the Czech Kingdom*), now Národní muzeum (*National Museum*) in Prague. It is located at the southern end of Václavské náměstí. The building was erected between 1885 and 1891. [honsi.org]

[57] *A slang term for carriages designed to transport arrested, detained or imprisoned persons. There are several versions of why it was named Anton. First: the carriages were painted green, and according to Břetislav Hůla's explanation, the first coachman was Antonín Douša, who was called Anton, and the first "passenger" was the prostitute Antonie "Tonka" Vyšínová, who rolled up her skirt when boarding and shouted: "So, Tonka, climb onto the green Anton". Another version assumes that it is apparently based on the Berlin prison in Antonstrasse, where criminals were transported in such a car.* [svejkmuseum.cz]

[58] The Criminal Court for Prague, a Department of c.k. zemský soud (k. k. Landesgericht, *Imperial Royal Regional Court*), the highest judicial instance in the Kingdom of Bohemia. It was located in the enormous judiciary complex between Spálená street, Karlovo square and Vodičkova street. The court also contained a prison. Today this building houses the City Court of Prague. [honsi.org]

[59] Roman Empire was a civilization that developed from the city state of Rome, founded on the Italian peninsula in the 8th century before Christ. Through its life span of 1200 years, the Roman civilization changed from being a monarchy to a republic to become an empire. It came to dominate the western part of Europe and the area around Mediterranean Sea by conquest and integration. The empire collapsed through foreign invasions in the 5th century, known as the end of the Roman Empire and start of medieval times.

The Roman Empire left a lasting cultural legacy and is together with ancient Greece regarded the cradle of European civilization. Formal remnants of the empire lasted until the age of Napoléon in guise of the Holy German-Roman Empire where several Habsburg rulers were nominal heads. Czech king Karel IV was also Roman Emperor. [honsi.org]

[60] Jerusalem was at the time of Pontius Pilate capital of the Roman province of Judea. [honsi.org]

[61] Pontius Pilate (died after 36 A.D) was a Roman prefect (governor) of Judea (26–36 A.D.) under the emperor Tiberius who presided at the final trial of Jesus and gave the order for his crucifixion. [britannica.com]

> King James Version
> Matthew 27
>> 19 When he was set down on the judgment seat, his wife sent unto him, saying, Have thou nothing to do with that just man: for I have suffered many things this day in a dream because of him.
>> 20 But the chief priests and elders persuaded the multitude that they should ask Barabbas, and destroy Jesus.
>> 21 The governor answered and said unto them, Whether of the twain will ye that I release unto you? They said, Barabbas.
>> 22 Pilate saith unto them, What shall I do then with Jesus which is called Christ? They all say unto him, Let him be crucified.
>> 23 And the governor said, Why, what evil hath he done? But they cried out the more, saying, Let him be crucified.
>> 24 When Pilate saw that he could prevail nothing, but that rather a tumult was made, **he took water, and washed his hands before the multitude, saying, I am innocent of the blood of this just person**: see ye to it.
>> 25 Then answered all the people, and said, His blood be on us, and on our children.
>> 26 Then released he Barabbas unto them: **and when he had scourged Jesus, he delivered him to be crucified.** [famous-trials.com]

[62] By "a *pepper*", "paprika" in Czech, the author meant the traditional Hungarian "paprikash" dish. [Translator's note]

[63] "Plzeň" (*Pilsen*) was one of the most important industrial centers in Austria-Hungary. It was the monarchy's primary weapons forge and Škoda delivered the bulk of the heavy artillery to the army, and even supplied Germany.

The city is nowadays best known for having given name to the Pilsner beer that has been brewed since 1842 and has now become a somewhat imprecise term for pale, bottom-fermented beers. The best known brands that are made in the city today are Pilsner Urquell and Gambrinus.

Jaroslav Hašek visited Plzeň in the summer of 1913 together with Zdeněk Matěj Kuděj. The two writers sought out Karel Pelant, editor of the weekly Směr (*Direction*). He owed Hašek money for a couple of short stories but tried his best to avoid meeting the two. In the end they tricked him into appearing at U Salzmannů and the editor ended up paying the restaurant bill for his guests after an almighty party.

The two stayed there for a couple of days and visited an impressive number of pubs. Plzeň was the final destination of a trip that had started in Prague and gone via Loděnice, Beroun, Nový Jáchymov, Rakovník, Zbiroh and Rokycany. Most of it was done on foot and Kuděj describes the trip in his book Ve dvou se to lépe táhne (*It's Easier to Pull When There are Two*) (1923-24). Hašek mentions the editor in the story O upřímném přátelství (*Of Sincere Friendship*), albeit without mentioning his name (nor does Kuděj).

On 13 September 1913 Hašek would be back, now as part of a cabaret. The other members of the group were Emil Artur Longen, Xena Longenová and Jan Leitzer.[honsi.org]

[64] "U Teissiga" (*At Teissig's*) was a restaurant located across the street from the massive City Court complex (former *I&R Regional as Criminal Court*) and owned by Karel Teissig. He had been running the restaurant at least since 1895. Address books confirm that the restaurant was operating as late as 1940. Teissig had previously managed the still existing (2025) U kotvy (*At the Anchor*), two houses down the street. [honsi.org]

[65] "Státní návladnictví" (*State prosecutor's office*) is a term that is rarely used in modern Czech, and is now mostly referred to as Státní zastupitelství, (literally *Office of the Representative of the State* i.e. *State Prosecutor's Office*), a wording that was used even during the lifetime of the author. Their main seat for Bohemia was at Malostranské náměstí in the building of the Regional High Court, and their Prague office was located in the same building as the *I&R Regional as Criminal Court*. It is surely those premises that the author had in mind. [honsi.org]

[66] "Karlovo náměstí" (*Charles' Square*) is the center of Nové město (*New Town*) and is one of the largest city squares in Europe. Today it appears more like a park than a square. It was founded by King Charles IV in 1348.

The square is right in the area where Jaroslav Hašek grew up and this is reflected in the number of places here that are mentioned in the novel: c.k. zemský co trestní soud (*I&R Regional as Criminal Court*), Černý pivovar (*Black Brewery*), Vojenská nemocnice na Karlově náměstí (*Military Hospital at Charles' square*), U mrtvoly (*At the Corpse*), Kostel svatého Ignáce (*Church of Saint Ignatius*). Both the gymnasium and Obchodní akademie (*Commercial Academy*), where Hašek studied, are located off the square. [honsi.org]

[67] Domicile certificate was a proof of the right of a person to reside in a specific community (town, village, settlement) undisturbed, receive care in

poverty, and elder care. Stemming from an 1849 law, the right was bestowed upon a person by birth (receiving the parents' or unwed mother's domicile right), marriage (whereby the wife gained the domicile right in her husband's community), or by entering into a relationship with the community either by an express decree of the local authority or the community having tolerated for four uninterrupted years the presence of the person without the right to domicile, or by an order to permanently reside in a community (in case of civil servants, officers, clergy and public teachers). [scanzen.cz]

[68] "U Bansethů" was the name of two restaurants in Nusle, owned by Alois Banseth. Which of the two public houses the author had in mind is uncertain. The original U Bansethů also arranged public meetings on its premises, for instance on February 26th 1906 where anarchists took part, and among them Jaroslav Hašek was very likely to be found. On this occasion the anarchist Čeněk Körber (1875-1951) caused such uproar that the meeting was abandoned. The pub also hosted meetings by Česká strana národně sociální (*Czech National Social party*), Sokol, Volná myšlenka (*Free Thought*) and Mladočeši (*Young Czechs*). Particularly the first seemed to have met a lot here, and in Strana mírného pokroku v mezích zákona (*Party of Moderate Progress Within the Bounds of the Law*) Jaroslav Hašek describes one of their meetings where he provoked and caused disorder. [honsi.org]

[69] "podolský kostelík" is almost certainly the parish church "kostel sv. Michala" (*Church of Saint Michael*) in Podolí, south of Vyšehrad. [honsi.org]

[70] Kladno is an industrial city west of Prague and was a vital hub of the labor movement even under Austria-Hungary. It was from here that a failed Communist coup and general strike was organized in December 1920. Jaroslav Hašek was designed by the Comintern to play a role in it but arrived a few days after the coup had been put down. [honsi.org]

[71] Rotter was a renowned dog breeder and policeman, stationed in Kladno in 1909 and 1910. During his period of service here he became the first ever to introduce police dogs in k.k. Gendarmerie (*I&R State Police*). [honsi.org]

[72] Česká radikální strana was not the name of any particular political party but it is quite obvious that Švejk had either Strana radikálně pokroková (*Radically Progressive Party*) or Státoprávně radikální strana (*Radically State-Rights Party*) in mind. The former party existed from 1897 to 1908 and campaigned for extensive political reforms, whereas the latter was formed in 1899 and their main goal was extended state rights for the Czech lands.

In 1908 the two parties merged and founded Česká strana státoprávně pokroková Czech (*State-Rights Progressive Party*). From 1914 the party openly campaigned for an independent Czech state and suffered persecution as a result. It cannot be ruled out that the label "radical" stuck even with the new party and that it was indeed them Švejk had in mind. [honsi.org]

[73] "Parliament" refers to Reichsrat (*Imperial Council*), i.e. bi-cameral Parliament, in Vienna. From 1867 until 1918 it was the national assembly of Cisleithania, i.e. the Austrian part of the Dual Monarchy. The Council consisted of a Herrenhaus (*House of Lords*) and a Abgeordnetenhaus (*House of Commons*).

The last election to the Abgeordnetenhaus was held in June 1911, and that year the House had 516 deputies of which 232 were Germans, 108 Czechs and 83 Poles. The remaining seats were occupied by Ukrainians, Slovenes, Italians, Romanians, Croats, Serbs and a lone Zionist.

Several of the politicians mentioned in *The Good Soldier Švejk* served as deputies at the outbreak of the war: Professor Masaryk, Kramář, Klofáč, Jos. M. Kadlčák, and a certain agrarian politician Josef Švejk. The parliament was suspended at the outbreak of war in 1914 and was only reconvened on 30 May 1917. During the period of suspension, Masaryk had fled abroad, Kramář sentenced to death (later converted to 15 years) and Klofáč interned without a trial. During the general amnesty in July 1917, the last two were released and allowed to resume their political careers, including taking up their seat in Reichstag. [honsi.org]

[74] [Doctor Antonín] Heveroch was a notable Czech psychiatrist and neurologist who was, among other things, known for his studies on dyslexia and epilepsy. His book On Freaks and Striking People was according to František Langer among Jaroslav Hašek's favorites. [honsi.org]

[75] The madhouse was some mental hospital in Prague which is not explicitly located. Still, we can with near certainty conclude that the author had Kateřinky in mind. This is an institution where he himself spent a few weeks in February 1911. [honsi.org]

[76] Virgin Mary was the mother of Christ and the principal saint of the Catholic Church. In the New Testament she is featured in the gospels and in the deeds of the Apostles. At the Ecumenical Council of Ephesus in 431, the Council Fathers bestowed upon her the title Theotokos, 'Mother of God'. The Quran portrays her as selected by God above all women in the world; she is mentioned in seven chapters in the Quran, one of them with her name as the title. She features in numerous works of art, where she is usually just called 'Madonna' - 'Our Lady'. [honsi.org]

[77] The Pope is the bishop of Rome and head of the Roman Catholic Church, based in the Vatican. The Pope from 1904 until August 20th 1914 was Pius X, who was succeeded by Benedict XV. Hence, Pius still occupied the seat at the time Švejk was at the madhouse (July 1914). [honsi.org]

[78] [English King] seems to refer more to the king as a title and is not necessarily a reference to George V who was King of Great Britain, Ireland and the Commonwealth from 1910 to 1936. The title king of England hadn't formally existed since 1707, but then as now it was common to interchange the terms England, Great Britain and United Kingdom.

King George belonged to the House of Saxe-Coburg, a noble family originating from Germany. He was cousin of both Emperor Wilhelm II and Tsar Nicholas II. He bore considerable physical resemblance to the Russian tsar. In 1917 the Royal House was renamed House of Windsor, one of several examples of politically motivated name changes during World War I. [honsi.org]

[79] Saint Wenceslaus (Czech "Václav") was the prince of Bohemia from 921 until his death. He was murdered by his brother Boleslav, canonized soon afterward, and became the patron saint of the Czech people. His feast day, September 28th, is a Czech national holiday.

Wenceslas Square (Václavské náměstí) is named after him. The large equestrian statue at its upper end, in front of the National Museum, was unveiled in 1912.

The two English forms Wenceslas and Wenceslaus refer to the same historical person: Wenceslaus is used when speaking of the saint, while Wenceslas is the established English form in the name of the square.

Václav remains one of the most common Czech male names. [honsi.org]

[80] Saint Cyril and his brother Methodius were Greek missionaries, who together started the Christianization of the Slavic peoples. The brothers first developed the Glagolitic script, an alphabet for the Slavic peoples, which included the unique sounds of Slavic tongues: their work laid the foundation for the Cyrillic alphabet named after Cyril, which is used in places like Ukraine, Russia, Bulgaria and Serbia. They translated the Bible and liturgical books to what is now called Old Church Slavonic. The two brothers are often referred to as the "Apostles to the Slavs". Because of their tireless work for the Slavic peoples, in the Orthodox Church they hold a title "Equal to the Apostles". Fifty years after their death Pope John IX 914-328) canonized them. In 1880, Pope Leo XIII brought their feast day to the Roman Catholic Church. [carpatho-rusyn.org]

[81] *Giant Mountains*, Krkonoše in Czech, is a mountain range on the border between Poland and the Czech Republic, and in 1914 it was the border between Austria-Hungary and Germany. The name is very old, was mentioned by Ptolemy, and may be of Indo-European origin. The interpretation of the name has been preserved, and the Latin name was Gigantei montes. These are the highest mountains in Czech lands; the highest peak, Sněžka reaches 1,602 meters above sea level. [honsi.org]

[82] Otto was a Czech publisher best known for publishing Ottův slovník naučný (*Otto's Educational Dictionary*). He also published literature, text books and magazines. Among the latter were Zlatá Praha and Světozor which Jaroslav Hašek contributed to. The head office of the publishing house J. Otto was located at Karlovo náměstí No. 34 and they also had a branch office in Vienna.

Otto's son studied at Obchodní akademie at the same time as Jaroslav Hašek (1899-1902). Otto also ran a foundation that enabled poor students to attend the academy. [honsi.org]

[83] A long and wide robe presented by a person of rank and worn as a mark of distinction in India and Middle East. [merriam-webster.com] [collinsdictionary.com]

[84] Královy lázně (*Royal Spa*) was a public bath at the end of Karlův most (*Charles' Bridge*) and is listed at the address Karoliny Světlé 43. This is confirmed by Baedeker Österreich 1913 that refers to it as Königsbad.

Some baths north of the bridge are also shown, called Gemeindebad (*Municipal Bath*). This was more likely an open-air bath and to judge by the description in the novel, Švejk is almost certainly talking about the more luxurious indoor Royal Spa.

Břetislav Hůla refers to the bath as Karlovy lázně (*Charles' Spa*) and this corresponds to the entry in the address book of 1936. It is not known when exactly the renaming took place. [honsi.org]

[85] Karlův most (*Charles' Bridge*) is the oldest and most famous bridge in Prague and the second oldest bridge in Czech Republic after the one in Písek. It connects the Malá Strana (*Lesser Town*) and Staré město (*Old Town*). As a landmark and tourist attraction it belongs to the most famous in the country.

Construction was started in 1357 under Charles IV's reign and the bridge is named after him. Around 1700 it was given the shape known today and the baroque statues were erected in this period. The bridge has repeatedly been threatened by high water levels but escaped the great flood of 2002 without damage, but in 1890 it was partly destroyed. [honsi.org]

[86] *'Where Is My Home'* was written as a part of the incidental music to the comedy Fidlovačka aneb žádný hněv a žádná rvačka (*Fiddling Fair, or No Anger and No Brawl*). It was first performed by Karel Strakatý at the Estates Theatre in Prague on 21 December 1834. The original song consists of two verses. Although J. K. Tyl is said to have considered leaving the song out of the play, not convinced of its quality, it soon became very popular among Czechs and was accepted as an informal anthem of a nation seeking to revive its identity within the Habsburg Monarchy. Soon after Czechoslovakia was formed in 1918, the first verse of the song became the Czech part of the national anthem, followed by the first verse of the Slovak song "Nad Tatrou sa blýska". [m.wikisource.org]

[87] Who the song refers to, is somewhat unclear. It has long been believed that the person in question was General Alfred I. Fürst zu Windisch-Graetz. He was a famous commander, who brutally suppressed the revolutions of 1848, both in Prague and Vienna. The song in question however refers to events during the Second Italian War of Independence in 1859, and on this occasion the old field marshal was not involved. On the other hand, his nephew and son-in-law was on duty: Karl Vinzenz (1821-1859), colonel and commander of Infantry Regiment No. 35 (Pilsen), and he even fell at Solferino on 25 June 1859. On July 18th his body was brought back to Prague, and the event received extensive press coverage. [honsi.org]

[88] In the original German, 'Gott erhalte Franz den Kaiser', meaning God Save Francis the Emperor, was the national anthem of Austria-Hungary. It was sometimes known as the "Kaiserhymne". It was a personal hymn for Emperor Francis II of the Holy Roman Empire. The words of the song were written by Lorenz Leopold Haschka in 1797, and in that same year, the music was composed by the famous musician Joseph Haydn. The melody would later be used in other songs, such as "Deutschlandlied", the German national anthem. By the time Švejk sang the anthem, it was the 1854 text version of the Austrian Imperial Anthem, written by Johann Gabriel Seidl. [simple.wikipedia.org]

[89] *This old military song was certainly one of Hašek's most popular. After all, it appears in the novel a total of three times. According to witnesses, as reported by Václav Pletka, the original text began with "Když jsme táhli k Ostroměři..." Ostroměř is located near Sadová, which was the infamous site of the Prussian-Austrian battle of 1866. It is therefore possible that the song originated just that very year.* [svejkmuseum.cz]

[90] An old Marian pilgrimage song. The melody is played from 8 a.m. to 6 p.m.,

every full hour by the carillon at the place of pilgrimage on Loretánské náměstí (Loreta square) *in Prague, only a few hundred meters up from Prague Castle.* [svejkmuseum.cz]

[91] Karlín is a district in Prague that stretches along the southern bank of the Vltava. It borders the urban districts Praha II., Žižkov and Libeň. Until 1922 it was a separate town.

"Ferdinandova kasárna" [*garrison*] (also "Karlínská kasárna") was located here and served as the headquarters of Infantry Regiment No. 91 from 1906 until August 1914. Karlín was an industrial town where large plants like Daňkovka were located. Another important institution in town was Invalidovna. During World War I, it was used as a military hospital, and it was until 2013 the site of VÚA (*The Central Military Archive*).

Karlín *administrative district* had a population of 69,184 where the largest communities apart from the town itself were Troja, Kobylisy and Vysočany. According to the 1910 census, Karlín had 24,230 inhabitants, of whom 20,694 (85 per cent) reported using Czech as their everyday language. The judicial district was Karlín, administratively it reported to *administrative district* Karlín. [honsi.org]

[92] Ward for the indigent.

[93] Salmova ulice is the author's way of writing Salmovská ulice, a short and curved street in Praha II, not far from U kalicha (*At the Chalice*). At the time there was a police station at the corner of Ječná ulice. The street is named after Franz Altgraf von Salm-Reifferscheid who at the end of the 18th century laid out a large garden behind house No. 506. Interestingly enough, an advert from 1891 was placed by a certain wood trader Josef Švejk who lived in No. 14. He put beech planks up for sale.[honsi.org]

[94] Nero was Roman Emperor from 54 AD. Some contemporary chronicles portray Nero as a tyrant, and an early persecutor of Christians. These stories originate from Tacitus, Svetonius and Cassius Dio. Other contemporary sources claim that Nero really was very popular in his lifetime.

The first part of his time as Emperor was characterized by stability and prosperity, much thanks to his advisers, among them the philosopher Seneca. But Nero initiated many expensive building projects which eventually led to an economic crisis.

In 66 AD Nero added the title of "Imperator" to his name. The empire experienced insurgencies because of the economic problems. After the people had rebelled in 68 AD he was deposed by the Senate. Nero though that the Senate would execute him, so he took his own life.

As Emperor he used the official name Nero Claudius Caesar Augustus Germanicus, but was born Lucius Domitius Ahenobarbus.

In *The Good Soldier Švejk*, the term "throw...to the lions" is used. It originates from Tacitus's writing and refers to the persecutions of Christians after the Great Fire of Rome in 64 AD. According to Tacitus, Nero blamed the Christians for the fire and subjected them to brutal executions, including being thrown to wild animals in the arena.[honsi.org]

[95] Vršovice is from 1922 a district in Prague, now contained entirely within the capital's 10th district but at Švejk's time it was still a separate town.

Jaroslav Hašek lived in Vršovice with his wife Jarmila in 1911 and 1912, and it was here in the house no. 363 (Palackého třída, now Moskevská) that his son Richard was born on May 2nd 1912. The author was registered at this address on December 28th 1911, but already on July 29th 1912 he was listed in Vinohrady. His wife had also moved, to her parents in Dejvice. The split must obviously have happened very soon after their son was born.

[honsi.org]

[96] Marathon is the former name of Marathónas, a small town north of Athens that has been widely known through the marathon run. According to legend a messenger ran to Athens with the news of victory at the battle of Marathon in 490 BC, then collapsed and died.

The marathon run was introduced during the first Olympic Games in 1896 in Athens. In the beginning the distance varied slightly until it was fixed at the current 42,195 meters in 1921. In 1914 the distance was 40.2 kilometers. The first official run in Bohemia took place on August 25th 1908 between Smíchov and Dobříš. It was arranged by SK Slavia and the distance was 40 km.

Today marathon is a big sport with hundreds of runs annually around the world. The largest take place in New York with more than 50,000 finishers (2013). Within the former Austria-Hungary there are annual runs in, among others, Prague, Vienna, Budapest and Bratislava. Every year there is also a classic marathon along the presumed original route. [honsi.org]

[97] Emauzský klášter (*Emmaus Monastery*) is a Benedictine monastery in Prague, located south of Karlovo náměstí (*Charles' square*). It was founded by Emperor Charles IV in 1347. The above-mentioned Father Albán served as abbot here from 1908 until 1918, and during the war part of the monastery was converted to a hospital for soldiers.

After the proclamation of Czechoslovak independence on October 28th 1918, the abbot and the German monks left the country after being subjected to harassment from crowds and militia groups. This was caused by accusations in the press, one of them being that they had spied for Germany.

The monastery was badly damaged during an Allied bombing raid in 1945 and was reconstructed in a somewhat different style after the war. It was confiscated by both the Nazis (1941) and the Communists (1950), but was returned to the Benedictine order in 1990. [honsi.org]

[98] Name's day has its origins in the Catholic tradition. In the church calendar, specific saints are assigned to individual days of the year. On that day, not only the life and deeds of this saint are celebrated, but also his namesakes'. In Christian communities, a name's day may even be a more significant day than a birthday. Several saints can bear the same name, so Christians of the same name can celebrate the feast on different days, depending on which of the saints they have taken as their patron. The date of the holiday usually depends on the date of the saint's death. The situation is made even more complicated by the fact that traditional church calendars may differ from the calendar of John Paul IV. There are also cases where the faithful celebrate more than one holiday, because they took more than one name, for example, during confirmation or a religious name when entering the order. Modern name's day celebrations are freed from their Catholic origins and become only the feast of the given name. The basis for the date of the name-day celebration is the classic civil calendar. It differs considerably from the old church calendar. As a rule, each name appears only once in the calendar, and it is also expanded to include new, modern and rare names. Holidays as Christian celebrations of specific saints are honored mainly in Catholic and Orthodox countries, but even classical name celebrations are primarily a European domain. [svatky.centrum.cz]

[99] Královské Vinohrady (*Royal Vineyards*) is a former city and now a district of Prague, southeast of the center. Administratively it is split between Prague 2, 3 and 10. After 1968 the official name has been Vinohrady, and this short form was common already during Austrian rule. This is also the name the author uses throughout. In 1922 Vinohrady became part of the capital.

Vinohrady achieved status of "royal town" in 1879 and grew quickly to become the third largest city of the Kingdom of Bohemia.

Jaroslav Hašek lived at various locations in Vinohrady from 1896 to 1908 and for shorter periods later. On 23 May 1910 he married Jarmila Mayerová here, in kostel svaté Ludmily (*church of Saint Ludmila*). His famous "party" Strana mírného pokroku v mezích zákona (*Party of Moderate Progress Within the Bounds of the Law*) held many of their election meetings here, mainly before the elections of 1911, where he, according to legend, stood as

223

a candidate. [honsi.org]

[100] Bendlovka (also Bendovka) is almost certainly an alternative term for Bendova kavárna (*Benda's coffeehouse*), a former tavern in Nové město (*New Town*) that Jaroslav Hašek knew well. A well-documented incident involving the author took place here on December 31st 1908. According to police reports, Jaroslav Hašek was involved in a brawl at the coffeehouse during the small hours of the morning. He and a Croatian technical student Rudolf Giunio refused to pay the bill; an argument erupted and glasses were broken. When the patrolman Antonín Slepička arrived to take them to the police station, the two refused and even physically attacked the policeman. Reinforcements had to be called, and the two troublemakers were taken to Salmova street police station to sober up. They were released the next morning. [honsi.org]

[101] "U mrtvoly" (*At the Corpse*) has not been identified with certainty, but was in all probability a coffeehouse at Karlovo náměstí (*Charles' square*), at the corner of Resslova ulice. The building, which among others housed Pivovar U Šálků (*Brewery At Šáleks'*), was demolished in 1939. There was a coffeehouse in the building, with an entrance at *Charles' square*, but the pictures do not reveal any name.

The address book from 1910 has an entry for coffeehouse "Rubáš" here, and this provides a hint: "Rubáš" means *shroud* and "mrtvola" means *carcass/dead body*. [honsi.org]

[102] *judicial district* Hluboká refers to "okres" (*the judicial district*) named after its seat Hluboká. The district belonged to hejtmanství (*administrative district*) Budějovice as Švejk clearly states. The district counted 26 municipalities that were almost exclusively inhabited by Czechs: Bavorovice, Břehov, Čejkovice, Češnovice, Dasný, Dobřejice, Dříteň, Hluboká, Hosín, Hrdějice, Chlumec, Chotýčany, Jaroslavice, Jeznice, Česká Lhota, Lišnice, Munice, Mydlovary, Nakří, Opatovice, Pištín, Plastovice, Purkarec, Velice, Nová Ves, Volešník, Vyhlavy, Zbudov, Zliv.

Mydlovary plays a particularly prominent role because this is where Jaroslav Hašek had right of domicile and was thus under jurisdiction of the recruitment region of Infantry Regiment No. 91. [honsi.org]

[103] Ječná ulice (*street*) is a busy street in Praha II., leading from Karlovo náměstí (*Charles' square*) to IP Pavlova [street]. The family of Jaroslav Hašek lived in no. 7 for a while in 1884, the year after he was born. [honsi.org]

[104] Spálená ulice is a street in Praha II. leading from Karlovo náměstí north

towards Národní třída (then Ferdinandova třída). The name means "Burnt Street".

This street was also the home of U Teissiga and U Brejšky, restaurants that are mentioned in the novel. [honsi.org]

[105] Europe was at the outbreak of World War I far less fragmented than today, not the least because of Austria-Hungary that covered areas that now belong to 13 different states. Germany and Russia were also much larger than they are today.

The great war turned Europe upside down. The empires of Germany, Austria-Hungary, Turkey and Russia all collapsed and the human and material losses were enormous. The total death toll is estimated to around 15 million. Only Spain, Netherlands, Switzerland, Sweden, Denmark and Norway managed to preserve their neutrality. [honsi.org]

[106] Black and yellow and the eagle were the colors and the symbol of the Habsburg Empire.

[107] k.u.k. Militärgericht Prag (*I&R Military Court Prague*) was the military court of the Prague-based 8th Army Group. The court was located at Hradčany in the same building complex as the garrison prison and the military hospital. The *I&R Land Defense Court* was also located here. An article in Prager Tagblatt also mentions a brigade court, but it is not clear how these administrative subdivisions worked. To judge by newspapers reports from 1914 Hauptmann G. Heinrich led the Court. The address book of 1912 lists Major Josef Plzák as the highest ranking officer. His assistant was Senior Lieutenant Vladimír Dokoupil. [honsi.org]

[108] Dominating the city from a high hill on the west bank of the Vltava River, Hradčany, the castle district, was then the seat of provincial and imperial power. It was a powerful cluster of edifices containing the central headquarters of the government and military, plus courts, a prison, a palace, a cathedral and the ancient tombs of saints and Czech Kings. Today, it enjoys a similar status and its spires still reach to the clouds and loom above all. [Translator's note]

[109] "Kostel svatého Apolináře" (*Church of Saint Apollinaire*) is a church in Nové město (*New Town*) located only a few hundred meters from U kalicha (*At the Chalice*). It was built in the 15th century and named after Apollinaris of Ravenna. [honsi.org]

[110] Free Thought (*Volná myšlenka*) was an association of freethinkers, an anticlerical and atheist movement that appeared in many countries in the 19th century. The best-known freethinker internationally was Francesc Ferrer i

Guàrdia (1859-1909).

The Czech organization was founded in 1904 and provisionally dissolved in 1915. The best-known representative of the Czech organization was Machar, chairman from 1909. The organization also published a monthly periodical of the same name. Their most immediate goal was the separation of state and church.

Karel Pelant (1874–1925) was one of the founders of the Czech section, and this was a person Hašek knew well. Zdeněk Matěj Kuděj describes a meeting between the two in Plzeň in 1913 that was arranged because Pelant, at the time editor of the weekly Směr (*Direction*), owed Hašek money for a few stories he had written.

Pelant also appears in *The Party of Moderate Progress Within the Bounds of the Law* and is listed as the publisher of the Freethinkers' monthly. [honsi.org]

[111] Besides being the headgear of the monarch, the crown was also the empire's chief monetary unit. [Emmett Michael Joyce]

[112] Dejvice is an urban area and cadastral district in western Prague between the center and the airport. It is administratively part of Prague 6, and is regarded as one of the more exclusive parts of the capital. The district became part of Prague in 1922 and Vítězné náměstí (*Victory square*) is regarded its focal point.

In 1913 Dejvice was still a separate administrative unit, although it was part of the Prague conurbation.[honsi.org]

[113] The St. Bernhard dogs are considered the largest of all dog breeds and may weight up to one hundred kilo and reach a height of one meter. It was originally bred by the sanctuary at Great St Bernard Pass and used for rescue duties in the mountains. One hundred years ago the dogs were much smaller than today, but because of the increased weight they are not longer suitable as avalanche- and rescue dogs.

Great St Bernard Pass is a mountain pass in the western Alps that has given name to the mentioned dog bread. The highest point is 2,469 meters above sea level and the pass connects Switzerland and Italy. It is named after Bernard of Aosta, better known as Saint Bernhard. [honsi.org]

[114] Leonberger dogs are written about in Svět zvířat (*Animal World*) at the time when Jaroslav Hašek was editor of this weekly. The author had good knowledge of dog-breeding, something that is reflected in the many references to dogs throughout the novel and otherwise in his literary output.

Leonberg is a town in Swabia that gave its name to the mentioned dog breed. This is a very large and fury dog breed, that appeared through breeding in 19th century. It can weigh up to 80 kilos (175 lbs). [honsi.org]

[115] Mimosa was a night coffeehouse in Staré město (*Old Town*) that no longer exists. In the 1910 address book, another coffeehouse is listed at number 496/31: U Hvězdičky tři zlaté.

From February 1913, adverts reveal that Mimosa was now established on the premises. The owner was Antonín Růžička, providing live music, dancing, entertainment, food, and Pilsner Urquell on tap. The establishment also advertised around-the-clock opening hours.

In February 1917, Čech reported that the establishment had been forced to close down on demand from the police. [honsi.org]

[116] Brno is the largest city and capital of Moravia, the other part of the Czech lands; not a foreign city.

[117] Angora is the historical name of Ankara, the capital of Turkey. Ankara is the second largest city in the country and has been capital since 1923. The Angora cat is a breed of domestic cats originating from central Asia Minor.

Pictures of Angora-cats appeared on the pages of the animal magazine Svět zvířat during the time Jaroslav Hašek edited the periodical (1909-1910). At the same time he wrote a story about the Angora tomcat Bobeš, a cat that could talk. The story's title was O domýšlivém kocouru Bobešovi (*About the conceited tomcat Bobeš*) and was printed in Svět zvířat on March 1st 1910.

The Angora Cat also appears in altogether six (or more) pre-war stories. One of them is Má drahá přítelkyně Julča (*My dear friend Julie*) that was printed in three issues of Zlatá Praha (Golden Prague) in April/May 1915. This story is also set during Hašek's time as animal trader at Košíře and contains themes known from the novel (Brehm and Klamovka are mentioned). The story O nejošklivějším psu Balabánovi (*About the ugliest dog Balabán*) (Svět zvířat, 1913) also contains a reference to an Angora cat. Another talking cat Markus features in another story, there is also a cat Lili in the story about Professor Axamit. [honsi.org]

[118] The detective may have been inspired by Josef Kalous, a policeman in Nusle who is listed in the address book of 1910.

In 1913 Karikatury (*Caricatures*) printed a story by Jaroslav Hašek called The detective Mr. Kalous. It was signed Richard Mayer, one of the many pseudonyms that Hašek used. [honsi.org]

[119] Raba is a river in Galicia which empties into Vistula east of Kraków, in the

south of current Poland. In 1914 the entire river flowed on Austrian territory.

The event referred to in the novel is by near certainty the situation on the Galician battlefield in late November 1914. On the 26 November, during the advance on Kraków, the Russian 3rd Army led by Radko Dimitriev crossed the river, some units having reached and crossed it the evening before by Mikluszowice. According to Russian reports the Austro-Hungarian army retreated in disorder and suffered from low morale. They took up new defensive positions west of the river, on the line Dobczyce - Niepołomice, and by the end of the month they had retreated to Wieliczka, only 13 kilometers south-east of Kraków.

This situation persisted until December 8th when the Russians were pushed eastwards towards Dunajec during the battle of Limanowa. It was during the advance on Kraków that Czech volunteers in the Russian army, Česká družina (*Czech Battalion*), first were in action against k.u.k. Heer. Wieliczka was also the westernmost point the imperial Russian army ever reached. [honsi.org]

[120] Galicia was until 1918 an Austrian "Kronland" (*Crownland*) north of the Carpathians. As a political unit it was known as Königreich Galizien und Lodomerien from 1846 until 1918. The population at the time was mixed: Poles, Germans, Jews and Ukrainians were the largest groups. Galicia enjoyed a large degree of autonomy and Polish had status as official language within the administration. The "polonization" of the region enjoyed support even from the Emperor. The administrative capital was Lwów which was a Polish enclave in an otherwise Ukrainian dominated region.

In September 1914 Russia occupied most of Galicia, and by the 12th the I&R Army had withdrawn behind the river San. By late November the enemy had advanced much farther west and even threatened Kraków. From May 2nd 1915 and throughout the summer most of Galicia was reconquered by the Central Powers. It was during these offensives that Jaroslav Hašek took part as a soldier from July 11th to September 24th.

From 1918 the region became part of Poland, and in 1939 it was partitioned between Germany and the Soviet Union. From 1945 it was split between Poland and the USSR, and from 1991 between Poland and Ukraine.

Apart from his stay during the war the author knew Galicia well from his wanderings after the turn of the century. He traveled in the "Kronland" both in 1901 and 1903; more precisely in and around Kraków and Tarnów. He wrote several stories set in the region, two of them with Jewish themes from a town he named Zapustna (not identified). [honsi.org]

[121] What the author meant by "rakouské ministerstvo vojenství" (*Austrian Ministry of Military Affairs*) was the Kriegsministerium (*War Ministry*), the common ministry of war of Austria-Hungary, one of the three ministries shared by the two constituent parts of the Dual Monarchy. The Minister of War from 1912 until 1917 was Alexander von Krobatin. He was regarded as one of the hawks, who wanted to settle scores with Serbia at the slightest pretext. He gave audience to civilians two hours every week.

The War Ministry was not responsible for k.k. Landwehr and Honved, the territorial armies of the two parts of the Empire. The formal status Švejk held concerning the ministry is unclear. He was classified as one of the Landsturm (*Land Defense*) reservists who were only called up in great danger to the motherland. [honsi.org]

[122] Kraków is a city in southern Poland and the second largest in the country with more than 800,000 inhabitants (2023). It has a beautiful and well preserved historic center that is on UNESCO's World Heritage list.

Until 1918 Kraków was part of Cisleithania and even enjoyed the status as a separate crown land within Galicia.

Kraków never experienced fighting during World War I, but in late November 1914 the situation was critical as Russian forces reached positions only 13 kilometers east of the city. They were however pushed back to the river Dunajec during the battle of Limanowa in early December.

Jaroslav Hašek visited the area in the summer of 1901 and again two years later. On July 28th 1903 the Kraków police inquired with their colleagues in Prague whether "the 20 year old Jaroslav Hašek had Heimatrecht [right of domicile] in Praha". The exact content of the letter is not known but is referred to by Břetislav Hůla in a document dated February 1st 1949. The reason for the detention is not stated.

A letter from the Frýdek police dated August 6th 1903 sheds more light on the circumstances. Here it is recorded that Hašek stated that he was a reporter for a newspaper, had worked for Banka Slavia until May 28th 1903 and had traveled across Galicia and Hungary since. His mother had on behalf of the paper sent him 24 crowns on August 1st. On that day he was still in Kraków but five days later the money had been spent. The police also reveals that his clothing was in a bad state and also infested with insects. The reason for his arrest was breach of passport regulations. The newspaper in question was Národní listy and in July they indeed published two of his stories. Both are set in the area around Kraków although the city is not mentioned explicitly. The stories indicate that he had arrived in the city from the south, via

Zakopane.

This information fits well with Hašek's story Justice in Russia. According to this tale he had arrived from Zakopane and was arrested after having crossed over to Russian Poland without his documents in order. In 1905 Světozor published the story *Among tramps* where Hašek described his stay in the city prison. This story was even printed in the Czech-American newspaper Dennice novověku (Cleveland, Ohio) in May the same year. [honsi.org]

[123] Hungary (Magyar Királyság) here refers to the historical Kingdom which, from 1867 to 1918, was in an imperial-royal union with Austria; together they constituted Austria-Hungary. The kingdom roughly comprised modern Hungary, Slovakia, Burgenland, Transylvania and those parts of present-day Ukraine that lie west of the Carpathians. The head of state was King I. Ferenc József (i.e. Franz Josef). In addition, Croatia was a nominal kingdom under Hungarian rule with considerable autonomy.

The population in 1910 was slightly above 21 million, of whom less than half were ethnic Hungarians. The capital during this period was Budapest. The kingdom was also known as Lands of the Holy Hungarian Crown of Saint Stephen, and after 1867 as Transleithania (the land beyond the Leitha). Hungary shared borders with Austria, Romania and Serbia.

After the 1867 Ausgleich (*The Compromise*), Hungary used its newly gained autonomy to impose a policy of Magyarization on its minorities, causing widespread resentment among the kingdom's other nationalities. The Treaty of Trianon in 1920 stripped Hungary of roughly two-thirds of its territory and population, but the kingdom continued to exist formally until 1946, albeit without a king. Since then, Hungary has been a republic. [honsi.org]

[124] Windischgrätz may refer to general Alfred I Fürst zu Windisch-Graetz (ref. Břetislav Hůla, 1951). He was a famous Austrian commander who brutally suppressed the revolutions of 1848, both in Prague and Vienna.

The song in question however refers to events during the Second Italian War of Independence in 1859, and on this occasion the old field marshal was not involved. On the other hand, his nephew and son-in-law was on duty: Karl Vinzenz (1821-1859), colonel and commander of Infantry Regiment No. 35. He was killed during the battle by Solferino on 25 June 1859. On 18 July his body was brought back to Prague, and the event received extensive press coverage. [honsi.org]

[125] Piedmont was in 1914 as today a province of Italy. It is located in the north-western part of the country and borders France and Switzerland. The capital is Torino *(Turin)*.

The song refers to events during the Second Italian War of Independence in 1859. On April 27th war erupted between Austria and the kingdom of Sardinia (that Piedmont was part of). At the start of the war, before Sardinia's ally France had come to her aid, Austrian forces crossed into Piedmont. They crossed the border river Ticino on April 29th, and occupied Novara, Montara, Vercelli and the surrounding land west of the river. The four bridges the song mentions may refer to the river Ticino or the river Sesia to the west (which was as far as the invaders got). By early June the Austrian forces had withdrawn east of Ticino and all of Piedmont was again under allied control.

The war ended in victory for Sardinia and France, and as a result Austria had to cede most of Lombardy. The decisive battle took place at Solferino on June 24th 1859, mentioned in the same song. The ceasefire was effectuated on July 12th (l'armistizio di Villafranca). [honsi.org]

[126] Solferino is a small town in Italy, slightly south of Lake Garda. During the second war of Italian independence Austria lost the decisive battle here against France and Sardinia on June 24th 1859. Austria was forced to cede Lombardy and this outcome paved the way for the unification of Italy.

Henry Dunant took part in the battle and moved by witnessing the sufferings of the soldiers he was later to found the Red Cross. This was the last major battle in history where the monarchs commanded their armies directly. Emperor Franz Joseph I withdrew as Austrian commander-in-chief after this battle. [honsi.org]

[127] Infanterieregiment Nr. 18 was recruited from the Hradec Králové district and took part in nearly every war the Habsburg empire fought since the regiment was founded in 1682.

The theme of the song is the battle of Solferino that decided the outcome of the Second Italian War of Independence in 1859. During the battle only the regiment's 4th battalion was involved, the other battalions were fortunate enough to be assigned border duty.

In 1914 the bulk of the regiment's soldiers were Czechs (75 per cent), the rest Germans. [honsi.org]

[128] Austria-Hungary was a political unit that existed from June 8th 1867 to October 21st 1918 in the form of a personal union between Austria and Hungary. By area and population (about 52 million) it was one of the largest states in Europe. Austria-Hungary was a multi-ethnic state with 11 official languages and even more ethnic groups. It was a constitutional monarchy with freedom of worship and universal suffrage, although with authoritarian leanings. This was first and foremost the case in Hungary where the ethnic

minorities had a far weaker position than in the Austrian part of the empire.

With its mixed population Austria-Hungary was vulnerable to internal strife, which was particularly evident in times of crisis. There were also large differences in economic and social development between the various parts of the monarchy. The present Czech Republic and Austria had mostly reached an advanced stage of industrial development, whereas the Balkans, parts of Hungary and Galicia were relatively backward agrarian societies with considerable illiteracy.

Until Ausgleich (*The Compromise*) in 1867 the Habsburg state was known as the Austrian Empire. Hungary took advantage of defeat by Prussia the previous year to force through a redistribution of power that put them on equal terms with Austria. These privileges granted to the Hungarians provoked great resentment among the other peoples of the empire, particularly the Slavs. [The Czechs felt particularly aggrieved, as the Czech crownlands produced a vastly disproportionate share of Cisleithania's industrial output and national income — far exceeding their share of the population — yet received no corresponding political influence under the 1867 settlement.]

The state was also called the Dual Monarchy or the Danube Monarchy. Emperor Franz Joseph I was emperor of Austria and king of Hungary respectively. The river Leitha formed in part the boundary between the two parts of the monarchy, which therefore were unofficially referred to by the Latin terms Cisleithania (*the lands on this side of the Leitha*) and Transleithania (*the land beyond the Leitha*). [honsi.org]

[129] "odvodní komise" (*Draft Commission*) refers in this context to Reserve Draft Examination Board No. 1, a temporary body which was tasked with carrying out medical examinations of Landsturm (*Land Defense*) recruits who in peace time had either been declared "waffenunfähig", *unfit* for armed service, or had been "superarbitriert" (judged by a higher board to be medically unfit), and dismissed from the armed forces after initially having started their military service.

Commission No. 1 was responsible for recruits who lived in Prague and had Heimatrecht (*Right of Domicile*) in the city. In addition it examined residents of Prague with right of domicile elsewhere, if these were born from 1878 to 1883. Jaroslav Hašek belonged to the latter group (right of domicile Mydlovary, born 1883) and necessarily also Švejk. As a soldier in Infantry Regiment No. 91 his right of domicile must have been in *Army Replenishment District No. 91*.

The commission started the examinations on October 1st 1914 when those born from 1892 to 1894 were called in. Among this group more than half were deemed fit for service. From November 16th to December 31st it was the turn of those born from 1878 to 1890. Among this group far fewer were passed as "Tauglich" (*fit for duty*), less than one third. This latter group is the most interesting for us as it was here where Jaroslav Hašek fit in. Everything indicates that Švejk also belonged to this group and was thus born between 1878 and 1883. On January 20th 1915 it was announced that Austrian citizen who were passed fir for duty had to report at their *Replenishment Command* on February 15th.

The examinations took place in the garden restaurant at Střelecký island, in the southern part of the island. The restaurant was in 1914 a popular destination. [honsi.org]

[130] Brass pin bearing the Emperor's Franz (Frank) Josef initials FJ. Hence "frankie".

[131] Belgrade was in 1914 the capital of the Kingdom of Serbia and after the war it became capital of Yugoslavia. Its position was very exposed, right on the border with Hungary which at the time ruled Vojvodina and Banat [a fertile plain extending through Hungary, Romania, and Serbia] on the opposite banks of the rivers Sava and Danube. The current urban district of Zemun west of Sava at the time belonged to Hungary. The first shots of the world war were fired against Belgrade from river boats (monitors) on July 29th 1914.

In late November the city was abandoned, and k.u.k. Wehrmacht duly entered on December 2nd 1914. But facing a Serbian counter-attack their position became untenable and the occupiers were forced out by the 15th. Belgrade didn't succumb again until October 9th 1915 when Serbian resistance collapsed after Bulgaria and Germany came to the aid of Austria-Hungary. Belgrade was liberated on November 1st 1918 by Serbian and French forces. [honsi.org]

[132] Pražské úřední noviny (*Prague official newspaper*) actually functioned as the collective designation for the publications of c.k. Místodržitelství/k.k. Statthalterei (*I&R Governorate*), which included Pražské noviny, Prager Zeitung (i.e. Czech and German versions of the *Prague Newspaper*), and Prager Abendblatt (*Prague Evening Sheet*). [honsi.org]

[133] Mucius Scaevola was a known figure from ancient Rome who through his bravery is supposed to have saved the city during the Etruscan siege of 508 BC. He was sent to the enemy's camp to murder king Porsena but was captured. To show the king how little physical sufferings meant to a Roman

soldier he held his hand in the fire without showing any signs of pain. The king released Mucius and offered peace. It has not be established if this story has a factual background but is in any case based on the writing of Roman historian Titus Livius.

Mucius and his burnt hand often appears as symbolism in stories about heroic deeds that the press of the Dual Monarchy printed during the war, particularly during the summer of 1915. References can also be found in the Czech press, even before the war. Among the papers who printed these stories in 1915 were Neue Freie Presse and Pester Lloyd. One such story appeared in June 1915 and was printed in several newspapers, including Pester Lloyd. It refers to an attack on Italian coastal defenses by Porto Corsini on May 24th 1915, led by admiral Miklos Horthy. The admiral is better known as the inter-war and World War II Hungarian dictator who led his country to war as an allied of Nazi Germany. [honsi.org]

[134] *Prague Daily, German language liberal democratic newspaper. It was published between 1877 and 1939, when the publication was stopped after the German Nazi occupation of Czechoslovakia. The most prominent contributors were Franz Kafka, Max Brod, Egon Erwin Kisch and occasionally Grete Reiner, the first translator of Hašek's novel. According to the quote from the novel, the reader might think that Prager Tagblatt was somehow chauvinistic toward the Czechs, but the opposite is true. The editors did not resent Jaroslav Hašek. After his death on January 3, 1923, an obituary and Brod's German translation of the first chapter of the novel were published in the Tagblatt on January 5, 1923.* [svejkmuseum.cz]

[135] Lynch (Charles or William) are both the probable candidates for the etymological origin of the term "lynching". Both lived in the 18th century, were judges and the circumstance was the American war of independence (1776-1783). In the US the term was later mostly used in connection with abuses directed against blacks. Austrian newspapers used the term "Lynchjustiz" already before 1840, mostly in connection with cases in the US (but not exclusively there).

It has not been possible to find anything in Prager Tagblatt that relates to the quote from the novel and fatal lynching was unusual among civilians in Austria-Hungary, even during the war. Arbitrary justice was however widespread at the front. It was used against both the enemy population and own subjects who were suspected of co-operating with the enemy. The victims were mostly Ukrainians and South Slavs. [honsi.org]

[136] Members of the alliance against Austria-Hungary, Germany and Turkey:

France, the United Kingdom and Russia. These nations were later joined by Japan, Italy and the United States. Serbia, Montenegro, and Belgium ended up entering the conflict on the side of the Entente, although not originally members of it.

[137] German daily in Prague that became increasingly chauvinistic during the war. It was renamed Deutsche Zeitung Bohemia (*German Newspaper Bohemia*) after the outbreak of war. Before the war, they seemed more balanced, and Hašek even advertised dogs in this paper. [honsi.org]

[138] "posádková věznice" (*Garrison prison*) is the author's term for "c.a k. vojenská věznice v Praze"/k.u.k. Militärgefängnis von Prag, a prison that was part of the garrison complex at Hradčany (*Castle District*). It shared the building with k.u.k. Militärgericht Prag (*I&R Military Court, Prague*) and the k.k. Landwehrgericht (*Landwehr Court*). The building is located behind Loreta, and was opened in 1896 and is still in use but not publicly accessible. Its function as a prison and brutal interrogation center was revitalized during the Nazi and Communist dictatorships.

In 1906, there were two Stabsprofusen (*Garrison Staff Wardens*) employed at the prison, but none of them fit the description of Stabsprofus Slavík, Korporal (*Corporal*) Říha, or Feldwebel (*Sergeant Major*) Řepa. The two were Jan Frkal and Josef Bureš, and they lived on the premises. Whether any of them was a model for the literary figures is impossible to say, and it cannot be determined if the author had anything to do with the garrison prison at all, so we must assume that the inspiration for those figures came from elsewhere. On the other hand, it is possible that Jaroslav Hašek had heard some story from former inmates of the prison. The description of the conditions in the prison and the brutality of the warders all in all appears strongly exaggerated.

It seems that the author was unfamiliar with the organization of the prison and adjoining buildings. There is contradictory information on where Švejk actually was: at Vojenská nemocnice (*Military Hospital*) Hradčany or in a sick bay within the prison. One passage indicates that the author believed that the military hospital was part of the prison, which it clearly was not. In chapter nine, the reader gets the impression that the garrison actually WAS the prison, which it was not (at most, "garrison" was a colloquial term for the garrison prison).

In 1923, a series of publications called "Documents from our national revolution" started to appear. Here one witness, A. Matějovský, gives some insight into the conditions at the prison. He was arrested after having distributed the so-called "Tsar Nicholas II's manifesto" in 1914 and given a

10-year term. He spent the first 16 months at Hradčany before being transferred to Arad. His description of the prison is completely at odds with what Švejk experienced. The staff behaved impeccably towards the prisoners and gave them a friendly send-off to Arad, where the conditions were much worse. Matějovský was released in 1917 during the general amnesty issued by the new emperor, Karl I. [honsi.org]

[139] Radetzky was a famous Czech nobleman and Austrian field marshal. He was Austria's most prominent commander in the first half of the 19th century and distinguished himself during the war in Italy in 1848/49, where his armies emerged victorious in the battles of Custoza, Santa Lucia and Novara. He served in Austria's army for 72 years, under five emperors, participated in 17 field operations, and was decorated 146 times.

In 1848 Johann Strauss the Elder composed the famous Radetzky march, which even today is played at the end of the Vienna New Year Concerts. [honsi.org]

[140] "Malá Strana" (*Lesser Town*) is, in the strictest sense, a topographical name: "strana" denotes the side, slope, or flank of the Castle hill (hradní stráň), not a "town," "district," or "quarter." Its literal and structurally faithful English equivalent is therefore *Small Side*.

The familiar English rendering "Lesser Town" does not translate the name. It emerged in the 19th century from Anglophone guidebooks and travel literature that preferred a more urban-sounding category. In doing so, they conflated the place name Malá Strana with the historically distinct administrative term Menší město pražské (*the Smaller Town of Prague*), which refers to one of Prague's medieval municipal units but is not the same as the topographical name.

Using "Lesser Quarter" is simply an English attempt to imitate French and Italian municipal vocabulary, where "quartier" or "quartiere" means "neighborhood." But Prague is not Paris or Rome, and "strana" is neither a town nor a quarter. Thus the English conventions reflect Victorian normalization rather than Czech usage:

• Malá Strana — *Lesser Town* (topographical name)

• Menší město pražské—*Smaller Town of Prague* (administrative term)

The native Czech understanding of "strana" as "side" belongs to an everyday, concrete semantic register rather than to urban or administrative nomenclature. This is further confirmed by idiomatic usage: "jít na malou stranu" ("*to go to the small side*") is a polite euphemism for going to the washroom to urinate. The expression draws on the same spatial notion of "side" and would be unintelligible if "strana" were understood as a town, district, or quarter.

To avoid perpetuating this long-standing Anglophone domestication and to preserve the structure and imagery of the Czech name, the translation uses "Small Side" in the main text. [Translator's note.]

[141] This is not a typographical error, but an attempt to replicate "dezentér", the common corruption of the Czech word "dezertér" (*deserter*). The rendition "deserteer" is later used also for the related "dezentýrovat", i.e."dezertovat" ("*to desert*").

This form ("deserteer"—both as a verb and a noun) is used again in Book One, and recurs in later volumes, to preserve the bent Czech military slang reported by Hašek. [Translator's note]

[142] A marching battalion, or march-battalion, is a battalion that is formed to move to the battlefield. [Translator's note]

[143] Epilepsy.

[144] Giordano Bruno was an Italian astronomer and philosopher who was burned as a heretic in 1600. Finally, in the year 2000 the Papal Cultural Council and a theological commission declared his execution as illegal. [honsi.org]

[145] Galileo was an Italian scientist, best known for his work in the fields of astronomy and physics. He is regarded as the founder of experimental natural sciences.

The trial that is mentioned in *The Good Soldier Švejk* was conducted in 1633 as a result of Galilei's book Dialogo sopra i due massimi sistemi del mondo (*Dialogue concerning the two chief World Systems*). The systems being discussed in the book is the heliocentric (Copernicus) and the geocentric (Ptolemy).

The book caused anger in clerical circles and Galilei was put before a papal court. Here he withdrew his theories and thus avoided being sentenced to death by burning. He was found guilty of heresy and ordered to abjure (*recant*), sentenced to life imprisonment, albeit soon converted to house arrest. During interrogation when he was forced to retract his heliocentric world view, he allegedly said about the earth: "*and yet it moves*" (Eppur si muove). It is this statement that the author refers to in connection with Švejk being arrested by Wachtmeister Flanderka in Putim.

Only in 1835 did the Catholic Church withdraw the ban of the book, but the final rehabilitation of the author only followed in 1992. [honsi.org]

[146] Břevnov is a district in western Prague, between Střešovice and Motol.

Administratively it is part of Prague 6. It is best known for its monastery. [honsi.org]

In 1907 Břevnov obtained city status and that year even His Imperial Highness Emperor Franz Joseph I visited!

[147] Smelly, surface ripened round cheese.

[148] The Czech "šarže", i.e. "*rank*", is being used here as a term for "non-commissioned officers", applied to them by the non-officer troops, who are below them in ranking.

[149] K.u.k. Heer (*I&R Army*) - short for Kaiserliche und Königliche Heer (*The Imperial and Royal Army*) - also called k.u.k. Armee or Gemeinsame Armee, was the largest and most important body in k.u.k. Wehrmacht (*I&R Armed Forces*), being the common army of both constituent parts of the Dual Monarchy. Together with the k.k. Landwehr (*Austrian national guard*) and the Honvéd (*Hungarian national guard*) it made up the Landstreitkräfte (*terrestrial forces*). These and the k.u.k. Kriegsmarine (*navy*) made up the total armed forces of the Dual Monarchy.

The common army consisted of infantry, cavalry, artillery, supply-troops and technical troops. The period of service was until 1912 three years, then two. During the war, losses were replaced by so-called march battalions, one of which Švejk was later to be assigned to. The common army existed from 1867 to 1918 and suffered disastrous losses in World War I, the only full-scale war it ever participated in. At various times it fought on four fronts; Serbia, Galicia, Romania and Tyrol and after the heavy losses in 1914 it became increasingly dependent on German support. [honsi.org]

[150] The Czech "poddůstojník", literally "underofficer" is "non-commissioned officer" in the US and UK, commonly referred to by the official acronym "NCO".

[151] The Slovak spa town of Piešťany is famous for the medicinal geothermal water and sulfuric mud with extraordinary therapeutic effects on inflammatory disorders. [slovakia.travel]

[152] Vojenská nemocnice Hradčany (*Military hospital at Hradčany*) refers to a part of the k.u.k. Militärspital Nr. 11 (*I&R Military hospital No. 11*) in Prague. It was located in the same barrack complex as the garrison prison, the military court, and other army institutions. The main military hospital in Prague was Vojenská nemocnice na Karlově náměstí (*Military hospital at Charles' square*).

The Chief Staff Doctor in 1916 was Dr. Krejčí, as revealed when newspapers reported on a visit by Countess Coudenhove, the wife of Bohemia's governor. The visit took place on April 10th 1916, too late to fit chronologically with the visit of Baroness von Botzenheim, but nevertheless there are interesting similarities. [honsi.org]

[153] Socrates was a Greek philosopher, one of the all time greats, and regarded as one of the founders of Western philosophy. The outspoken philosopher was late is his life accused and convicted of impiety and having corrupted the youth. He was sentenced to either exile from Athens or to take his own life by a method of his own choice. He chose the latter by emptying a chalice of poison. [honsi.org]

[154] The famous outlaw Babinský.

[155] England was in 1914 center of the British Empire, the largest colonial power the world has ever seen. The empire entered the war on August 4th, through the alliance with France and Russia (the Entente), provoked by the German attack on Belgium. The declaration of war on Austria-Hungary followed on August 12th.

There was only limited fighting between British and Austro-Hungarian forces as the former mostly operated on the Western Front, in the Middle East, in the colonies and on the seas. By the end of 1914 almost all the German colonies had been conquered. The British Empire's economic power and its control of the seas were crucial to the outcome of the war. Particularly effective was the naval blockade of the Central Powers. [honsi.org]

[156] Wilhelm II was Emperor of Germany and King of Prussia from 1888 until 1918, member of the house Hohenzollern. Forced to abdicate in 1918 after the defeat in World War I, he lived the rest of his life in the Netherlands. Tsar Nicholas II and the king of England were both his cousins. He was also related to the royal houses of Spain, Norway, Romania and Greece.

It has not been possible to verify that bottles of Kriegslikör (*war-time liqueur*) with labels where Emperor Franz Joseph I and Wilhelm hold hands existed, but in any case similar propaganda material abounded. A color post-card with this theme was actually printed and had the title In Treue fest (*Firm in fidelity*)*. The postcard was in circulation in 1916 and perhaps already in 1914.

Gott strafe England was likewise a common slogan from the end of 1914 onwards, so even if the bottle that Švejk was given is not hundred per cent pinpointed, similar items that may have inspired the author were plentiful.

 * the motto of the Kingdom of Bavaria.

[157] Czech children's game ditty.

[158] The person the narrator had in mind was probably Otakar Filip. He was a Czech journalist, author, and illustrator, and long time editor of local news in official newspapers that were published in Prague both under Austria-Hungary and Czechoslovakia. The book that is referred to he actually wrote, albeit with a title that differs somewhat from the one given in the novel. It was published in 1910 and contained 242 pages. That he was editor in chief of Československá Republika isn't entirely true; he was one of the board of editors. Filip specialized in reports and literature about Prague and published several books.

The full title of the book Jaroslav Hašek refers to was: Osmdesátiletý mocnář: Význačné události a zajímavé obrazy ze života jeho veličenstva císaře a krále Františka Josefa I (*The eighy year old monarch: significant events and interesting pictures from the life of His Majesty Emperor and King Franz Josef I*).

On August 18th 1915, ironically on the very day that Jaroslav Hašek was awarded the small silver medal for bravery, an advert for a patriotic book appeared in his home town. It was titled *The supreme protector of Czech children, His Highness Emperor and King Franz Josef I* and written by none other than our editor Filip! [honsi.org]

[159] Československá Republika (*Czechoslovak Republic*) was an official government daily newspaper of inter-war Czechoslovakia. It was published under this name from 1919 to 1932; In that year it was renamed Pražské noviny (*Prague Newspaper*)and continued publishing until the end of 1938. It was a direct successor to Pražské úřední noviny (*Prague Official Newspaper*) and was even located in the same offices. The mentioned editor Filip had been working for the paper also during the old regime. From 1932 to 1938, it continued publishing but now using the name Pražské noviny. The government's newspaper group also issued Úřední List Československá Republika *(The Official Government Newspaper Czechoslovak Republic)* and the evening paper Prager Abendblatt (in German).

Jaroslav Hašek also wrote a satirical article in Rudé Právo (*Red Law*) where editor Filip and his newspaper are treated in more detail: *What I would advise the Communists if I were the Chief Editor of the official Government newspaper Československá Republika*. The article was dated April 7th 1921 and printed on May 8th, around the time when the passages in the novel was written. In the article, he claims that some Svátek was editor-in-chief; in the novel, the author of the book about the Emperor (i.e. Filip) has this role. According to the 1924 address book, the chief editor was Josef Hevera, and another of the names mentioned in the Rudé Právo article, Adolf Zeman, was indeed on the editorial board. The article furthermore suggests that Jaroslav Hašek was still a Communist at heart.

The newspaper wrote about Hašek from time to time, mainly after he became famous, and on January 5th 1923, they printed an obituary. Shortly after his return from Russia, they printed adverts for his appearance at the theater (*The Red Seven*), where he related stories from his stay in Russia. [honsi.org]

[160] Latin for "by united forces".

[161] Cone-shaped Austrian soldier's helmet.

[162] Inflammation of a mucous membrane, especially one chronically affecting the human nose and air passages. [merriam-webster.com]

[163] Siam is the former name of Thailand and roughly the area that corresponds to the modern state. Siam was never colonized but lost some territory to European imperial powers in the 19th century. The capital was always Bangkok.

The term Siam elephant mostly refers to white (albino) animals that were regarded as holy. It was even on the flag of Siam until 1916. Thus Siam elephant is not an animal breed. [honsi.org]

[164] Eugen of Savoy was an Austrian prince and field commander. The full name of the French born prince was Eugène-François de Savoie. He gets most of the credit for the successful military operations against the Ottomans from the siege of Vienna in 1683 to the peace treaty of Sremski Karlovci in 1699. [honsi.org]

[165] Klíma was a lawyer and high commissioner in the State Police whose career was very similar to that of Mr. Slavíček (read about him in the next paragraph). In Czechoslovakia he continued to serve in the police but was like his colleague "exiled" to Slovakia. In 1927 he fell ill with complications from the Spanish flu, was sent abroad for recuperation, but died soon after, at the age of 48. He was succeeded as Bratislava police chief by Mr. Slavíček. [honsi.org]

Slavíček was a police officer, lawyer and civil servant in the State Police where he was employed from 1900 until 1918. He held a degree in law from Charles University and joined the police when he was 26. His career progressed rapidly within the security police where he also came across Jaroslav Hašek, for instance after the famous episode at U Valšů on 24 November 1914. He was promoted to commissioner in 1909, to high commissioner in 1913 and in 1915 became the head of the State Police in Prague. He was investigated by the new Czechoslovak authorities in 1919, but was allowed to continue in the police, albeit in "exile" in Bratislava, current capital of Slovakia. Here he played a major part in organizing and "demagyarizing" the police in Slovakia. From 1923 he was stationed in Košice. From 1927 he was back in Bratislava as Police Director (head of the police). Two years later he suddenly died from a stroke, at the age of 55. [honsi.org]

[166] Motol is a district in western Prague that became part of the capital in 1922. In 1910 it was a small village of 21 houses and 273 inhabitants. In the context of *The Good Soldier Švejk* is however meant Motolské cvičiště (Motol exercise ground). During World War I it was the scene of several executions, where the best known victim was reservist Kudrna from Infantry Regiment No. 102 who was executed on May 7th 1915. [honsi.org]

[167] "vězeňská kaple" (*prison chapel*) possibly refers to Vojenský kostel sv. Jana Nepomuckého (*the Military Church of St. John of Nepomuk*) at Hradčany. The church belongs to the same building complex as the military hospital, the garrison prison, and the military court. It is easily accessible across the courtyard between the buildings. It shares the address with Voršilské kasárny (*Ursuline Barracks*).

Another place the author might have had in mind is a chapel on the premises of the Zemská trestnice pro ženy (*Land Penitentiary for Women*) next door. This was not an army institution, but that would not necessarily have stopped the author from including it in the plot. It also fits the description in the novel more accurately as a house chapel (of the garrison) and a prison chapel is mentioned. [honsi.org]

[168] Kohn was professor of church law and theology, and between 1892 and 1904 archbishop of Olomouc. He was of Jewish descent but his grandfather had converted to Catholicism. The family was Czech-speaking and of humble origins but thanks to grants the gifted and diligent young man got a good education and he was consecrated as a priest in 1871. After serving in various parishes, holding positions at the University of Olomouc and at the city's archdiocese, he was finally elected archbishop in 1892. He was the first non-noble holding the seat in 300 years, and his election was therefore popular among the population, particularly the Czechs.

Kohn gradually fell out with parts of the Catholic Church hierarchy, he was for instance not well thought of in Vienna due to his common and Jewish background. Kohn notes in his autobiography that Eduard Taaffe, the Minister-President in Cisleithania made the following comment about his election as archbishop: Und hat er sich schon getauft lassen? (*And has he already had himself baptized?*) [honsi.org]

[169] Machar was a Czech poet and satirist. He was, like Jaroslav Hašek, strongly anti-Austrian, anti-clerical and a master in the use of colloquial Czech. He was for a while one of the favorites of Professor Masaryk, member of his Realist Party and contributed to the party newspaper Čas (*Time*). After the war he fell out with the president and oriented himself towards the political far right. The friendship with Archbishop Kohn that the author refers to is probably based on events in 1903 at the height of the so-called Rectus affair when controversy around Kohn reached a critical point. Machar defended the archbishop in a newspaper article in Die Zeit, printed on May 5th 1903. He also visited the now deposed Kohn in Ehrenhausen in 1909. Both these events were widely reported in the press and Jaroslav Hašek was surely well informed about the case. [honsi.org]

[170] "obchodní akademie" (*business academy*) is a generic term, but we must assume that Otto Katz studied at one of the two commercial academies in Prague. Because he was Jewish, it is at a first glance logical to assume that his mother tongue was German and he therefore studied at the German academy. On the other hand, the Field Chaplain was no doubt bilingual, so the Czech academy must also be considered.

Českoslovanská akademie obchodní (*Czechoslavonic Commercial Academy*) in Resslova ulice is all in all the likelier candidate. Hašek himself studied here, and this weighs heavily in favor of the latter when guessing which commercial academy the future field chaplain studied at. It should also be noted that some Otto Katz actually graduated from this academy in 1881, and the author may well have been aware of him. Augustin Knesl claimed that this person was the model of Hašek's literary field chaplain.

Another Otto Katz graduated from the German academy in 1896, but in 1906 he lived in Trieste, so it is less likely that Hašek knew him.

Jaroslav Hašek studied here from 1899 to 1902 and left with good grades. Here he met some of his best friends, first and foremost Ladislav Hájek, but also Karel Marek, a person who probably lent his name to the literary (*One-Year Volunteer*) Marek.

It was this education that enabled Hašek to serve as a one-year volunteer in k.u.k. Heer (*I&R Army*). The institution was on the list of establishments that gave its graduates the right to one year of military service instead of the compulsory three (from 1912, two).

In 1909, Jaroslav Hašek wrote the story Obchodní akademie for Karikatury. Here the head teacher, "Jeřábek", in real life Jan Řežábek, is mercilessly pilloried, and the piece was censored and was only printed the next year in a revised version. Jeřábek was even assigned qualities that readers of *The Good Soldier Švejk* will recognize in Colonel Kraus. In addition, the academy is mentioned multiple times in *The Party of Moderate Progress Within the Bounds of the Law*. [honsi.org]

171 North America denotes a geographical area, the American continent north of the Panama Canal. There are many definitions but the simplest one describes the area north of the Panama Canal and includes the Caribbean Islands. The largest states are the United States, Canada and Mexico. The former two both took part in World War I; US entered the war in 1917, Canada already in 1914 as part of the British Empire. [honsi.org]

172 Argentina was until 1916 governed by a conservative elite, and was at the time a relatively wealthy republic. General male suffrage was introduced in 1912. The country was neutral in the world war and benefited greatly economically. A dispute with Germany occurred because some Argentinian ships were sunk, but it never came to any formal declaration of war.

The country's capital is Buenos Aires and the official language is Spanish. The population is almost entirely of European descent, predominantly through immigration from Spain and Italy. [honsi.org]

173 South America is the southernmost of the two continents that make up America. In 1914 it consisted of the same countries as today, it was only in Guyana that colonies remained. The other countries except Brazil (and the three mentioned colonies) had Spanish as official language.

During World War I all the states except Brazil preserved their neutrality. The Brazilians entered the war on the side of the Entente in 1917 and sent auxiliary personnel to the western front and the navy took over patrolling duties in the south Atlantic. Fighting around the continent only took place at sea and were limited to 1914 when British and German naval forces clashed. The German Pacific Fleet (on their way home) was destroyed by the Falkland Islands on 8 December 1914. [honsi.org]

174 Alban Schachleitner was a Benedictine monk, who later emigrated to Germany and became a Nazi. [honsi.org]

175 Konsistoř (*The Consistory*), also called the Curia, is a religious council that advises, for instance, the archbishop or the pope. In this case, it is surely the archbishop's consistory at Hradčany, i.e. Knížecí arcibiskupská konsistoř (*Princely Archbishop's Consistory*). In 1907, the council's address was the archbishop's palace itself, and they held meetings every Wednesday. [honsi.org]

176 This most probably refers to Arcibiskupský seminář, (*Archbishop's

Seminary), an institution for education of Catholic priests that still exists. At the time of Jaroslav Hašek the Seminary was located in Klementinum, but in 1929 was moved to Dejvice where it is still housed. [honsi.org]

[177] Dům za Vejvodovic (*house behind Vejvodas'*) most probably refers to a brothel owned by Čeněk Bartoníček in Vejvodova street No. 10, just a few steps east of U Vejvodů. Bartoníček was in the address book of 1913 listed as owner of the brothel at this address. This is also the only house of pleasure that fits the description in the novel.

In the address book from 1910 a man who carried this name was listed as a "coffee-house" owner in Lužická street No. 29 in Malá strana (*Lesser Town*). This café was entered as a brothel in 1913 but with František Stránský as owner. Bartoníček thus seems to have sold and re-established himself east of the Vltava. Police registers reveal that he lived in Lužická ulice, Praha III/124 already from 1901 and he is registered in Vejvodová ulice from 24 November 1910.

The house itself, also known as Bílý kříž (the white cross) was in 1910 owned by Josef Sobička. To judge by the address books there was no "café" in Vejvodova 10 in 1910 so Bartoníček seems to have started the establishment from scratch. [honsi.org]

[178] "U Vejvodů" (*At Vejvodas'*) is a house and a restaurant in Staré město (*Old Town*) in Prague and one of the oldest of its kind. It has existed at least since 1560. In 1717 Jan Václav Vejvoda bought the property and the building is named after him. Early in the 20th century Karel Klusáček took over and rebuilt it to become what it was known as until 1990. The house was also for a period the home of a cinema as well as hosting Umělecká beseda (*Artistic Forum*).

U Vejvodů still exists as a large restaurant which serves Czech food and Pilsner Urquell. The place is totally changed after the renovation in the 1990's, but is still very popular and relatively affordable considering the location. [honsi.org]

[179] *Ferbl is a gambling card game partly similar to poker. It originated in Austrian Styria and was also played in the Czech lands during the reign of Maria Theresa. A ban dated 1746 mentions it under the name Farbeln*, fables. *The name is derived from the German Färbeln,* coloring. *Other names of this game in German-speaking countries are Einundvierzig* (forty-one) *according to the highest possible point total, Spitz, Zwei auf- zwei zu, and Zwicken. Ferbl is intended for 3 to 7 players. It is played with a deck of 32 cards of four suits that start with a seven and ends with an ace. It can be played with*

245

German (double-headed or single-headed) or French cards.
[svejkmuseum.cz]

[180] Bare-butt spanking game.

[181] Saint Francis de Sales, was a French bishop and theologian, later to be canonized. He was a distinguished Counter-Reformist, notable for his stand against Calvinism. He is the patron saint of the deaf, writers and journalists. [honsi.org]

[182] A sleeveless outer vestment worn by the officiating priest at mass. [merriam-webster.com]

[183] Infantry Regiment No. 28 was one of 102 infantry regiments in the *I&R Army*. It was founded as early as 1698 and was one of the oldest in the entire Army. The Regiment thus took part in many campaigns and they particularly distinguished themselves by Custozza on June 24th 1866. They also participated in battles during the Napoleonic Wars, for instance at Aspern and Leipzig.

It was a predominantly Czech regiment (95 percent), recruited from *Army Recruiting District No. 28*, Prague. They had moved here from Kutná Hora in 1817. Apart from the capital it recruited from Žižkov, Smíchov, Královské Vinohrady, Kladno, Slaný, Kralupy, etc.

The Regiment's home barracks were the Bruské kasárny in Malá Strana (*Lesser Town*). In 1914 only the 2nd battalion and the Recruitment District Command were located here. The rest of the regiment had since 1912 been garrisoned in Tyrol: The Staff and the 3rd Battalion in Innsbruck and the 1st and 4th Battalions in Schlanders (It. Silandro) and Malè respectively. The Regimental Commander in 1914 was Colonel Ferdinand Sedlaczek.

After the outbreak of WWI, the three battalions from Tyrol were sent to the Eastern front and took part in the invasion of Russian Poland, including the battle by Komarów on August 28th 1914. The rest of the year and until April 1915 they were fighting north of and in the Carpathians, for instance by Limanowa in December where they suffered severe losses.

Easter Saturday April 3rd 1915 would become the most controversial day in the history of the Regiment. At the front section north of Bardejov the bulk of the Regiment surrendered after having been partly cut off by numerically superior Russian forces during a surprise attack in the early hours. On April 8th Major General Josef Krautwald, Commander of III Corps of the 3rd Army, reported that the Regiment had surrendered to a single Russian battalion without firing a shot, that the newly arrived 8th March Battalion was the main culprit, but that the old core of the regiment was reliable. He claimed that he had received this information from the Regiment's Commander, a claim that the commander Schaumeier later contested. On April 10th, the Commander of 3. Armee, general Svetozar Boroević von Bojna, decided to dissolve the Regiment temporarily, effective the next day. He also informed Archduke Friedrich who on April 16th presented the case to the Emperor. He in turn issued a brief order dated April 17th 1915. It rubber-stamped the decision to temporarily dissolve the Regiment, ordered its standard to be deposed in the Army Museum in Vienna, and that the decision be made public within the army. On April 22nd Emperor Franz Joseph I's decree was indeed read out to the troops. [honsi.org]

[184] *Macau, also spelled Makaua, Macaua or Macao, is a shedding-type card game from Hungary. It is played almost all over the world, but always with the region's own rules. In Poland, Macao is played with French cards in a set of 52 cards. In the USA it is a juvenile UNO game played with special cards. In Russia it is 101 or Чешский дурак, Czech fool - played with French-type cards in a deck of 36 cards (from 6 - A). In Germany and Austria the game is called Mau-mau and is played with German cards 32 piece deck. In the Czech Republic it is also played with German cards and it is called Prší!* (It's raining!) *The name of the game Macao comes from the name of the former Portuguese colony of Macau (Macao), which now belongs to China as a region with special administration.* [svejkmuseum.cz]

[185] The Czech "baťák", rendered here as "*battie*", is a short version of the slang term "maršbaťák", rendered as "*marchbattie*", i.e. march battalion; the preceding hyphenated "*march-battalion*" is a rendition of the "maršbatalión" version of the Chechicized German term for "march battalion".

[186] Slovakia was in 1914 part of Austria-Hungary and was governed from Budapest. It was also referred to as Upper Hungary. From Ausgleich (*The Compromise*) in 1867 onwards Slovakia was subjected to increased Magyarization, with oppression and discrimination, economically as well as culturally. Schools were closed and the Slovak language suppressed. During this period international names like Bjørnson, Seton-Watson and Tolstoy came to the aid of the Slovak cause. The biggest city was Pozsony (Ger. Pressburg), after the war renamed Bratislava.

From November 1914 to the spring of 1915 Russian forces occupied a smaller part of Slovak territory, but were finally pushed out in early May 1915. In 1918, Slovakia together with Bohemia, Moravia, Ruthenia and a small part of Silesia formed the new state of Czechoslovakia. [honsi.org]

[187] Libeň is an urban district and cadastral area in the north-eastern parts of

Prague. It was granted town rights in 1898 but was included in Prague only three years later and administratively it became Praha 8. [honsi.org]

[188] "Policejní komisařství XIII." was the District Police Station in Libeň, Prague's Police District number 13. It was located in Stejskalova ulice 185 and the station's head in 1906 was chief commissioner Josef Roubal. [honsi.org]

[189] k.k. Landwehr (*I&R Land Defense*) was the territorial army in Cisleithania, a force that was created in 1868 after Ausgleich (*The Compromise*). Their Hungarian counterpart was Honved. Landwehr reported to Ministerium für Landesverteidigung (*Ministry of National Defense*) and was rather a regular fighting force than a pure territorial army/reserve force. Their units were not associated with k.u.k. Heer (*I&R Arm*y), had their own barracks and infrastructure, even their own military academies. The term of service was two or three years, and the arrangement with one-year volunteers functioned roughly like in the common army. [honsi.org]

[190] Josefov is a fortress and former garrison town in eastern Bohemia, near the border with Poland. It is now part of Jaroměř. [honsi.org]

[191] Prussia was until 1947 a geographical and political unit, and had been a separate kingdom from 1701 til 1871. Prussia was the leading state in Germany until 1945. The area is today split between Germany, Poland and Russia. The capital was Berlin.

The Prussian War, more commonly known as the German war, was a month-long armed conflict between Prussia and Italy on one side and Austria and their mainly south German allies on the other. The war took place in 1866 and ended quickly with a Prussian victory. The deciding battle was fought by Hradec Králové (Königgrätz) on July 3rd 1866. The Austrian defeat had far-reaching political repercussions. Hungary exploited the defeat to demand parity within the monarchy, thus the war led directly to the creation of Austria-Hungary. [honsi.org]

[192] "Česká strana národně sociální" (*Czech National Social Party*) was a political party that was founded in April 1897 as a break-away group from the Social Democrats and some defectors from Mladočeši (*Young Czechs*). The split came about mainly because the mother party advocated working within Cisleithania as a whole, whereas the splinter group advocated state rights for the Czech Lands. The relatively large number of Jews in the mother party also played a part in provoking the break. Their political platform was roughly based on reform socialism, radical nationalism, and anti-militarism. They were also strongly anti-clerical, anti-German, promoted use of the

Czech language in the public sector. The party was often referred to as "Czech Radicals".

The party chairman from 1898 to 1938 was Klofáč. In 1914 the party was banned and the leaders were arrested, and two party members were executed (editor Kotek and Slavomír Kratochvíl) in November 1914. Klofáč was interned soon after the outbreak of war. However, he was never prosecuted and was released in 1917.

The party's own press printed the first three stories about Švejk in 1911 (Karikatury, Josef Lada), and their principal mouthpiece České Slovo was one of the main promoters of *The Good Soldier Švejk* after the author's death. Hašek was also shortly employed by this paper both in 1908 and 1912 and also contributed in other periods. He was a personal friend of several of the newspapermen who served the party press, and Hašek as a nationalist and socialist was no doubt ideologically close to the party.

In 1918 the party was renamed the *Czechoslovak Socialist Party* and in 1926 even the *National Socialist Party*. Their best known public profile after the war was without doubt Edvard Beneš, the 2nd president of Czechoslovakia from 1935 to 1938, and again from 1939 to 1948 (from 1939 to 1945 in exile), who joined in 1923. The party was during the inter-war years member of the five-party ruling coalition. It was brutally persecuted during Nazi rule and in 1948 it was swallowed up by the communists and became their puppet party. It reappeared after the 1989 Velvet Revolution but with a dwindling number of votes, high debts, and frequent name changes, the party is now for all practical purposes non-existing. [honsi.org]

[193] "Na Kuklíku" (*At the Kuklík*) was a restaurant in Prague at Petrské square. Newspaper adverts from 1877 revealed that the pub existed and that they also brewed their own beer. Towards the end of the 1880s brewing appears to have ceased, but the restaurant business continued. According to the 1900 census Gustav Holan was the landlord.

Vilém Srp was granted a license in 1901 and in 1923 was still the owner. That year a newspaper report revealed that treasures worth Kč 50,000 had been hidden in the loft but had been stolen at a time when the landlord couple were ill. The culprits were caught and sentenced. [honsi.org]

[194] Serabona is a name which origin is unclear but the connection to the mentioned pub is obvious. Landlord at Na Kuklíku (*At the Kuklík*) from 1901 was Vilém Srp, and there is even a picture of him on a postcard from 1906. Here the pub is called U Serabono (*At Serabono*) and the address confirms that it is the same place as Kuklík. [honsi.org]

It is possible that Serabono was a former owner; pubs were often named after the original owners. It may hypothetically even be a nickname of Vilém Srp, or the name could have an entirely different origin.

[195] Sokol (*Falcon*) is a still existing patriotic gymnastics movement founded in Prague in 1862 by Miroslav Tyrš and Jindřich Fügner. It soon became an important part of the Czech national consciousness and also took root among other Slavic peoples in Austria-Hungary and even in Russia, Serbia and Bulgaria.

Throughout the time of the monarchy the authorities kept a close eye on the movement that had strong support from parties that advocated Czech state rights, namely Česká strana národně sociální (*Czech National Social Party*) and Mladočeši (*Young Czechs*). On November 24th 1915 the two Prague-based umbrella organizations of Sokol, Česká Obec Sokolská (*Czech Falcon Community*) and Svaz Slovanského Sokolstva (*Union of Slavic Falcons*), were dissolved at the order of the Ministry of Interior.

Local organizations were however allowed to function. The official reason for the crackdown was pro-Serbian and pro-Russians activities, anti-Austrian propaganda, and contact with the North American Sokol organization that was very hostile to the ruling dynasty. Sokol leader Scheiner had been arrested already on May 25th. Many Sokol members were indeed active in the Czech resistance movement during the war. Sokol reached its pinnacle during the First Republic, but was of course banned by both the Nazis and the Communists.

On January 6th 1923 members of Sokol carried Jaroslav Hašek's coffin to his grave at Lipnice. [honsi.org]

[196] "Reprezenťák" is the colloquial term of the concert hall and entertainment complex in Prague, now officially called Obecní dům (*Municipal House*). The Czechoslovak independence was proclaimed here on October 28th 1918. [honsi.org]

The *Municipal House* (originally named *The Municipal House of the Royal Capital City of Prague*, also called, for example, *The Municipal House at the Powder Gate* or *The Representative House of the Capital City of Prague*), no. 1090, is one of the best-known Art Nouveau buildings in Prague. It stands on Republic Square (*orientation no. 5*), next to the *Powder Gate*, opposite the House At the Hyberns. It serves primarily representative purposes and cultural events (concerts, exhibitions). [cs.wikipedia.org]

[197] "U Valšů" was a coaching inn and hotel in Prague's Old Town. It had an illustrious history and is mentioned in newspapers like Fremden-Blatt as early

as 1861. It was still operating in 1917 but seems to have ceased soon after. In 2021 the building housed a theater. [honsi.org] *The taproom of this pub was filled with prostitutes, beggars and vagabonds, and in its stables there used to be lodgers - for 4 to 10 krejcary they slept here on the sly.* [pepikov.cz]

[198] Drašner was a policeman in the IV. Department of c.k. Policejní ředitelství (*I&R Police Headquarters*) in Prague. He was employed in the police force at least from 1902 and records shows that he held the mentioned position in 1913. Čech informs that he had been promoted already in 1911. By 1918 he had been promoted to head commissioner. He continued to serve in the 4th Department also in Czechoslovakia.

A photo from Milan Hodík confirms that Drašner was alive as late as 1937. This is confirmed by newspaper articles from January 1939 that also indicate that he had recently retired.

On November 7th 1948 Břetislav Hůla noted that he planned to visit Drašner to ask for advice on navigating police archives, indicating that the pensioned policeman was still alive.

Newspapers reveal that Drašner was very active in controlling prostitution in Prague and he also investigated cases of human trafficking. He was a well known figure among the prostitutes and was in general held in high esteem by them although some also feared him.

Drašner was married to Cecilie (b. 1880), and in 1905 their first child was born. The girl however died already in 1909. In 1913 no further children are registered in the police protocols. [honsi.org]

[199] Epicurus was a Greek philosopher who maintained that the connection between good and evil is equivalent to the physical sensation of pleasure and pain. A well-known quote: "Do not fear death because when you exist death does not and when death does you do not". This laid the foundation of the Epicurean philosophical school: obtain maximum pleasure when you still can. [honsi.org]

[200] Inflammation of soft tissue that spreads under the skin or inside the body. It's usually caused by an infection and produces pus. The name phlegmon comes from the Greek word phlegmone, meaning inflammation or swelling.

Phlegmon can affect internal organs such as your tonsils or appendix, or can be under your skin, anywhere from your fingers to your feet. Phlegmon can spread rapidly. In some cases, phlegmon can be life-threatening. [healthline.com]

[201] Florenc is a self-administering city quarter of Prague, east of the center towards Karlín. Today it is a traffic hub, with the Prague's enormous bus

terminal and metro station. The name Florenc appeared in the 15th century, and is believed to be named after Italian workers, who settled here. [honsi.org]

[202] A rendition of "pucflek", the Czech spelling of the German term "Putzfleck", from putzen = to clean, polish, wipe, brush down, groom, trim; and der Fleck = spot, stain. Previous, British English translations rendered "pucflek" into "batman = an orderly of a British military officer". That term originated from "the French bât = packsaddle" [merriam-webster.com], "a saddle designed to support loads on the backs of pack animals". [merriam-webster.com] As you'll read on, Švejk relates a story, in which the spotshine fits that description perfectly. [Translator's note]

[203] A rendition of "marška", short version of "marškumpačka", which is *a slang term for a "march company" - a unit created for transport to the battlefield, where it was transformed into a field company or served to replenish losses in existing field companies.* [svejkmuseum.cz]

[204] Vatican is the center of the Roman-Catholic Church, and the name of the associated micro-state located in the middle of Rome. Here it is probably to mean The Holy See as an institution rather than the Vatican State. The Pope from 1904 until August 20th 1914 was Pius X, who was succeeded by Benedict XV. [honsi.org]

[205] "U Šuhů" was a brothel in Benediktská 9. According to Chytilův úplný adresář království českého (*Chytil's Complete Address Book of Czech Kingdom* (1913) it was owned by Jan Schuha whom the establishment presumably was named after.

Feldkurat Katz and tinsmith Pimpra were not the only notabilities who frequented Šuha. In his diary Franz Kafka discretely mentions a visit on 28 September 1911 when he was served by a "Jewess with a narrow face". He also describes the interior in some detail. The brothel's hostess is described in rather unflattering terms. [honsi.org]

[206] Korpskommando (*Corps Command*) here refers to the VIII. Korpskommando, one of a total of 16 Army Groups in Austria-Hungary. The Corps, with headquarters in the Lichtenstein Palace in Malá Strana (*Lesser Town*), recruited from south, west, and central Bohemia. Together with 9. Armeekorps (Litoměřice), it covered all of Bohemia. [honsi.org]

[207] Infantry Regiment No. 75 was one of 102 Austro-Hungarian infantry regiments. It was founded in 1860 and had its baptism of fire in 1866 at the second battle of Custozza.

Infantry Regiment No. 75 was a predominantly Czech regiment, recruited from Heeresergänzungsbezirk Nr. 75 *(Army Replenishment District No. 75)*, Jindřichův Hradec (Ger. "Neuhaus"). The *Army Replenishment District Command* and the 3rd Battalion were located here in 1914. The Staff and the other three battalions had been garrisoned in Salzburg from March 1912. In Salzburg, they raised some attention with their Czech songs and are said to have caused a boom in the local interest in football.

Already on 5 August 1914, the regiment departed for the front against Russia. The regiment received particular attention after the battle of Zborów on July 2nd 1917. On this day many of the regiment's soldiers were taken prisoners by their own countrymen from the Legions. This led to accusations of treason and the case was debated in Reichsrat *(Imperial Council)*. [honsi.org]

[208] In Czech, only friends, family members and intimates are addressed in the second-person singular. All others are addressed in the second-person plural. These two forms of address are used in most European languages. Modern English uses the word "you" in all instances.

[209] Podmoklí almost certainly refers to Podmokly, the name of four places in Czech Republic. Here the place in question has a railway station, so it is by near certainty Podmokly by Děčín. It was the last station before the German border and is indeed in the opposite direction of Budějovice.

The town was until 1945 largely populated by German-speakers. Podmokly is now part of Děčín and the station has been renamed Děčín hlavní nádraží *(the main railroad station)*. It is the last stop before the German border and all trains from Prague to Berlin stop here. [honsi.org]

[210] Gorgonzola her refers to the famous blue cheese from Gorgonzola by Milan. The cheese has a history that goes back more than one thousand years and was obviously very well known also in Austria-Hungary. It was among other places produced at the dairy in Hall in Tirol (who also produced Emmentaler *(Swiss)* and many other well known cheeses). [honsi.org]

[211] *The card gambling game also called "eye takes", "oner", or "eyelet", is similar to the Black Jack card game. It is usually played with a deck of 32 cards of the German type, so-called "mariášky". The banker deals one card to each player, including himself. The first player on his side (whether left or right) places his bet in front of him - the obligation of the first minimum bet can be agreed - and asks for another card. The banker adds the same amount from the pot to the bet. It is possible to bet up to the amount of the pot, while the player can "hop", i.e. add to the bet, at any time before taking the next card. The object of the game is to reach or come as close as possible to the sum of twenty-one, or the "eye". A player can claim any number of cards*

until he is satisfied with his total. When a player surpasses 21, he immediately loses his bet, which goes to the pot. [svejkmuseum.cz]

[212] A small four-wheeled carriage drawn by two horses.

[213] Krejcar, from German Kreuzer (*crosser*), because of the double cross, ("Kreuz" in German) on the face of the coin, [en.wikipedia.org] *was a small coin, valid in the monarchy. It was introduced in the Czech lands already during the reign of Ferdinand I in 1561. It was also valid during the First World War, when a parallel, crown currency had already been introduced.* [svejkmuseum.cz]

[214] Dr. Alexandr Sommer Batěk was a Czech doctor of chemistry and very prominent in the fight against the twin demons of alcohol and tobacco. He was also a vegetarian, sci-fi writer, scout-activist, YMCA-activist and pacifist. For a long period in 1919 he held (almost) daily lectures at Staroměstské náměstí so it is probably these the novel refers to.

More than 100 of the lectures featured in a collection of installments printed by publisher Kočí in 1919. His Sto jisker ethických (*One hundred sparks of ethics*) is included in the collection but the timing indicates that Otto Katz could hardly have known about them at the time so here the author has mixed in contemporary elements and moved them back into history by six years. Batěk also published the mentioned lecture as a separate 16-page pamphlet. He was very productive; the catalog of the Czech national library lists more than 500 items under his name. The other pamphlet mentioned, "*Let's declare a life and death struggle against the demon of alcohol...*", is not listed in the catalog.

He also lectured for the Czechoslovak abstinent's association, together with Pavla Moudrá and others. [honsi.org]

[215] A translator can use the original word in the translated text for various reasons. One of them is that the given word represents a unique phenomenon or concept. 'Juniper booze', i.e. 'jalovcová kořalka' does not have in the Anglo-Saxon world such a strong reputation and position, which 'borovička' enjoys among the Czech, Moravian and Slovak people. Therefore it is worth calling the Czech variety by its genuine name in an English text. However, a reader with no knowledge of Czech is denied not only the experience of drinking 'borovička' during his first, virtual encounter with it, but he is also denied its association with 'pine'. In Czech, that is the language of Švejk, 'borovička' is a diminutive of 'borovice', i.e. a tree known in English as 'pine'. Thus the first sense of the word is 'young pine' or 'pine sapling'. Unless a Czech is a drinker or has read Švejk, or in some other roundabout

way accidentally found out the connection between 'borovička', i.e. 'juniper booze', and 'jalovec', i.e. 'juniper', in his reader's imagination he is induced to attempt capturing on his virtual tongue the taste of pine, be it its wood or needles. Whence our insertion of the words "that liquor that tastes like pine wood" in the original edition of this volume. Both the readers of the original and the readers of the English translations find out the connection between 'borovička', i.e. 'juniper booze' and 'jalovec', i.e. 'juniper', three sentences later: "If it had been at least the genuine article, for instance, a distillate from juniper, like the one I drank in Moravia." In Bohemia, in Moravia, and in Slovakia 'jalovcová' is commonly called 'borovička'. It is worth noting that the Slovak word for 'jalovec', i.e. 'juniper', is 'borievka', and 'borovčie' denotes the Czech 'jalovčí', i.e. 'juniper bushes'. It is then altogether legitimate to guess that the Czech word 'borovička', popular inebriating distillate, is derived from the Slovak term for juniper. [Translator's note]

[216] Moravia is a historic region in Central Europe which is no longer an administrative unit. Together with Bohemia and a small part of Silesia it makes up Czech Republic. The capital is Brno and the region is named after the river Morava (Ger. March).

Other important cities were Moravská Ostrava (industry) and Olomouc that was (and is) an archbishop's seat and a prominent center of education. Olomouc was also the reserve capital of the Habsburgs in periods when Vienna was under threat. During the times of Austria-Hungary Moravia had the status as Kronland (*Crownland*). In 1910 Czechs made up over 70 per cent of the population, but Germans (including Jews) formed a substantial minority. In cities like Brno, Olomouc, Vyškov and Jihlava they were in majority. [honsi.org]

[217] Bruské kasárny (*Bruska barracks*) refers to the now demolished barracks that were located in Klárov area of Malá Strana (*Lesser Town*), next to Klárův ústav slepců (*Klar's Institute of the Blind*). They were named after the small (mostly underground) stream Bruska (Brusnice) that flows past the site.

These barracks were for most of the pre-war period the home of the staff of Infantry Regiment No. 28, one or more battalions, the replacement district command, and *I&R Artillery Regiment No. 8*. Units were frequently moved around so who occupied the barracks could change as often as each year. In 1914 only the 2nd battalion of IR28 was garrisoned here. [honsi.org]

[218] The garrison in Vršovice probably refers to the barracks in Vršovice that were home of the IR73 at the time. In 1914 it housed the Regiment's Staff and three battalions. Unlike the other Bohemian regiments, they were allowed

to stay in their home garrison during the whole war.

Most of the military personnel left the barracks hastily after the revolution of October 28th 1918 and set off to their home region of the city Eger (now Cheb). The barracks were immediately taken over by local militiamen (Sokol) and a few days later the newly formed Czechoslovak artillery moved in. The site was used by the military until the 1950s and now houses the court of four districts. [honsi.org]

[219] Zbraslav is an area of Prague, 10 km south of the center, where the river Berounka flows into the Vltava. Zbraslav became part of Prague as late as 1974.

Zbraslav was in 1913 a community of 1,772 inhabitants in the okres of the same name, hejtmanství Smíchov. Zbraslav had both a parish and a post office. The district was however much larger with its 28,094 inhabitants. It contained several places that are mentioned in the novel: Záběhlice, Všenory, Mníšek and Chuchle. [honsi.org]

[220] Steinhof is referred to by the author as a concentration camp, but it is unclear which place he has in mind. Steinhof by Vienna is an unlikely candidate although the name fits. From 1907 it was the location of the largest psychiatric institution in the Dual Monarchy, but there was no concentration camp here during World War I. None of the [researchers'] suggestions fit the official overview of internment camps in Austria-Hungary. In 1916 there were three of them, located in Thalerhof by Graz, Nézsider (Neusiedl) and Arad (Oradea). [honsi.org]

[221] Smíchov is a district of Prague, located west of the Vltava, in the southern part of the city. Smíchov has a major railway station, is an industrial area, and is the home of the Staropramen brewery. Smíchov became part of Prague in 1922.

In 1914 Smíchov was the center of hejtmanství (*administrative district*) and okres (*judicial district*) of the same name. The district was very populous with 167,830 inhabitants (1910) - in effect larger than any district in Bohemia apart from Prague. The *judicial district* Smíchov alone counted 139,736 inhabitants of which around 95 per cent were Czechs. The area of the *administrative district* also contained the *judicial district* Zbraslav. Within the *judicial district* Smíchov itself, several places we know from *The Good Soldier Švejk* were located. Among those are Břevnov, Dejvice, Klamovka, Kobylisy, Košíře, Motol, Roztoky and Horní Stodůlky. [honsi.org]

[222] New Guinea was by 1914 split between the Netherlands, the British Empire and Germany but Australian forces occupied the German part already in

1914.

New Guinea is the second largest island in the world and is located just north of Australia. Today the island is divided between Papua New Guinea and Indonesia. [honsi.org]

[223] Polynesia is a subregion of Oceania, made up of over 1,000 islands scattered over the central and southern Pacific Ocean. The term "Polynesia" was originally applied to all the islands of the Pacific Ocean. The only major political and geographical entity is New Zealand. The American state of Hawaii is also in Polynesia. The islands are partly independent, partly belonging to other states (USA, Chile, France and Australia). Until 1914 Germany was also present (Samoa). [honsi.org]

[224] Joseph-Ignace Guillotin was a French doctor and politician who on 10 October 1789 in the National Assembly proposed a reform of capital punishment; applying the same method regardless of class, that the purpose was to end life quickly rather than torture etc. The result of the proposal was that development of a falling axe apparatus was started. From 1792 it was in regular use and led to a much quicker and less painful execution process, a great progress from the previously barbarous methods.

The guillotine is best known from the French Revolution where many prominent heads rolled. The apparatus was also used in Switzerland, and notoriously in Nazi Germany and occupied territories. In Austria-Hungary the official method of execution was hanging at the gallows.[honsi.org]

[225] Spain was in 1914 a kingdom and preserved its neutrality throughout the world war. Conflicts with Germany occurred because some Spanish ships were sunk, but there was never any armed action taken from the Spanish side. [honsi.org]

[226] The early legionnaires of the Česká Družina (*Czech Battalion*), which became integrated into the Russian army, were mainly Czech immigrants to the Russian Empire. In 1916 the Czech colony in Russia started large-scale recruiting among Czech prisoners of war to fight with them against Austria. However, after the Bolshevik revolution, Czech Legionnaires were trapped deep in the interior of the new Soviet Union. In a series of heroic battles, the Legions were forced to fight their way out of Russia and into the pages of history. After the war, these men became lionized in the First Czechoslovak Republic. [Translator's note]

České legie is Hašek's term for Československé Legie (*Czechoslovak Legions*) that he mentions indirectly when discussing field chaplains and their role at executions. He lists several examples to illustrate his point, among them execution of Czech legionnaires.

The Legions are barely mentioned in *The Good Soldier Švejk* so the reader may wonder why a page about the novel dedicates so much space to an organization the author touches upon only once.

The answer is that there can be no doubt that the Legions would have been a main focus in the three volumes of the novel that the author had planned but never finalized. Jaroslav Hašek dedicated two years of his life to the Czech independence movement, and there is every reason to believe that he would have continued to spice his novel with autobiographical details, add people from his own milieu and episodes from his time there, just as he drew inspiration from his far shorter time of service in k.u.k. Heer (*I&R Army*).

České legie (*Czech Legions*), more commonly called Česko-slovenské or Československé legie, is a collective term describing different groups of mainly Czech volunteers who fought for the Entente against the Central Powers during World War I and from May 1918 against the Bolsheviks (communists) in the Russian Civil War. Politically they reported to Československá národní rada (t*he Czechoslovak National Council*) in Paris (from February 1916), militarily they were part of the armies of the Entente powers that hosted them.

From 1916 the Legions were an important instrument in the National Council's campaign to convince the allies to allow an independent Slavic state in Bohemia, Moravia and Slovakia. As Professor Masaryk, the leader of the Czecho-Slovak independence movement and the first President of Czechoslovakia, later summarized: "a state without an army can hardly make a claim to independence".

Already shortly after the outbreak of war, units of Czech volunteers were formed in France and Russia (and later also in Italy). In the novel the author obviously refers to the legions in Russia because it was those he knew and had experience from. [honsi.org]

[227] Born in 956 and named Vojtěch, Saint Adalbert was the first bishop of Prague to be of Czech origin. Descended from the Slavník princes of Bohemia, he trained in theology at Magdeburg, Germany for nine years. At his confirmation he received his name from St. Adalbert, first archbishop of Magdeburg. Saint Adalbert spread Christianity in several countries. He became a Czech martyr and saint, who suffered death as a martyr in his attempt to convert the Balts, and later became a patron saint of Bohemia, Poland, Hungary and Prussia. [britannica.com] [honsi.org]

[228] Bremen is a city and port in northwest Germany, 60 km south of the mouth

of the river Weser. During the times of Švejk it had status as a Freie Hansestadt (*Free Hanseatic city*).

Although Švejk says he has been to Bremen, there is no evidence that the author himself ever went there, so it is not clear what might have inspired this story. A possible source is Zdeněk Matěj Kuděj who traveled to New York from Cuxhaven on March 17th 1906 and may well have visited nearby Bremen on the way.

What Jaroslav Hašek no doubt was well informed about was the Bremer Räterepublik (*Bremen Council Republic*) from early 1919, one of the two best known Soviet Republics on German territory. The revolutionary republic lasted for only one month. [honsi.org]

[229] The English Channel is a strip of sea that separates England and France. It is part of the Atlantic Ocean, and connects this to the North Sea. The channel is at its narrowest between Dover and Calais where it is 34 km wide. [honsi.org]

[230] Břevnovský klášter is a Benedictine monastery in the Břevnov district of Prague. It was founded by Saint Adalbert in 993 and was the first of its kind in Bohemia. The architectural style is baroque and hails from the 18th century.

The Abbot during World War I was Lev Mojžíš, a cleric who has been subjected to claims by Jan Berwid-Buquoy that he was a notorious alcoholic and also the model for Feldkurat Katz.

In 1951, the monastery was dissolved and the premises handed over to the *Archive of the Ministry of Interior* (Archiv ministerstva vnitra). In 1990, it was handed back to the Benedictine order. Today both the Hotel Adalbert and restaurant Klášterní šenk are located on the premises, in addition to the monastery. [honsi.org]

[231] Sport-Favorit was a German sports club in Prague, officially named Fussballclub Sport-Favorit. Despite the name and the main focus on football they also did athletics and cycling, at least during the early years. [honsi.org]

[232] Mödling is a town in Niederösterreich (*Lower Austria*), with a population number (in 2007) of around 21,000. The town is situated 16 kilometers south of Vienna and is often called Perle des Wienerwaldes (*Pearl of the Vienna Woods*).

Oberleutnant Witinger allegedly ran 40 km in 1 hour 48 minutes which suggests that the author didn't care much about numbers. The marathon (41,185 meters) world record as of 2016 was 2:02:57 and was claimed by Dennis Kimetto in Berlin in 2014. This is the first example in *The Good*

Soldier Švejk of the author's disregard for factual accuracy. Obviously Jaroslav Hašek could also have got the distance wrong, the actual distance between the towns (16 km) would be possible to run in 1hr 48min. That said, it may be that the author was perfectly aware of the distances and times involved and that he was simply making fun of the boastful Oberleutnant Witinger. [honsi.org]

[233] k.u.k. Militärärar was a term for the military treasury of Austria-Hungary, i.e. the property that belonged to Kriegsministerium (*Ministry of War*) and its property administration. The word should not be confused with Ärar, the wider term for all state property.

The term derives from Latin Aerarium militare and was considered an "Austrianism". It is no longer used in the German language, not even in Austria. [honsi.org]

"Militärärar" corresponds to the Czech "erár", the common colloquial term for state or army property. Although obsolete in modern German, the term survived in Czech as a living Austrianism. [Translator's note]

[234] The Vršovice church is without doubt kostel svatého Mikuláše (*the Church of Saint Nicholas*), a Catholic church in Vršovice. It is in baroque style and was built in 1704. The vicarage is next door to the church. The address information shows that František Dusil was the vicar in 1907.

Jaroslav Hašek knew this church well because in the spring of 1912 he lived in nearby Palackého třída (*boulevard*) 363 (now Moskevská 363/33). This was also where his son Richard was born on May 2nd 1912. Soon after, the family father left his wife and the new-born child. [honsi.org]

[235] Zambezi is Africa's fourth longest river and flows from west to east in the southern part of Africa. [honsi.org]

[236] Buryatia is an autonomous republic in Siberia between Lake Baikal and Mongolia The Buryats are a people of Mongolian descent, now a minority in the republic. In 1923 Buryatia became an autonomous Soviet republic (ASSR). The capital is Ulan-Ude and the Trans-Siberian railway goes through the republic.

In 1920 Jaroslav Hašek ran propaganda activities among the Buryats and even taught himself some of the language. It is proven that he visited the region and at least got as far as Гусиное Озеро (*Goose Lake*), close to the Mongolian border. [honsi.org]

[237] Mongolia is a republic in Asia, between Russia and China, that broke away from China in 1911. During the Russian civil war Mongolia changed hands several times, but from 1921 the communists led by Damdin Sükhbaatar got

the upper hand, something that led to nearly 70 years of communist rule and strong links to the Soviet Union. A legacy from this period is the use of the Cyrillic alphabet.

In 1920 Jaroslav Hašek was involved on the periphery of the political struggle for Mongolia and he indeed knew Sükhbaatar in person. In the story Malé nedorozumění (*A small misunderstanding*) he writes that he traveled all the way to Urga (now Ulaanbaatar). This story has not been verified and is surely an example of "mystification". Such a journey during the short time he stayed in Irkutsk would in 1920 have been practically impossible. [honsi.org]

[238] Hašek used the word "daltonista", a now apparently obsolete term for "color-blind." John Dalton was a distinguished British scientist in physics and chemistry, also known for his research into color blindness, from which he himself suffered. Daltonism has even become a byword for it in some languages, notably French and Spanish. It also appears as a synonym in many more, among them Czech and English. Dalton spent almost his entire life in Manchester. [honsi.org]

[239] Wyandotte is the name of several places in the US, but the name of this chicken breed is taken from the Huron tribe who also call themselves Wyandotte. The tribal headquarters are located in Wyandotte, Oklahoma.

The breed of chicken was officially recognized in 1883 and borrowed the name from the above-mentioned Indian tribe. In Europe a midget-variation was bred later.

Jaroslav Hašek obviously knew about this animal breed (and many others) from his time as editor of Svět zvířat in 1909 and 1910. During his time as an editor the magazine printed some stories about "wyandottky" and photos also appeared. [honsi.org]

[240] The region around the Sázava River

[241] Heine (born Harry, later christened Christian Johann Heinrich), was one of the most important German poets and journalists in the 19th century. He is often referred to as the last romantic poet and one who also survived the era. As a critical and politically engaged journalist and satirist, he was as much admired as feared. His Jewish background also underlined his role as an Aussenseiter (outsider) with many enemies.

His most famous poem was Die Lore-Ley (1824). In [4.1] the first lines of which is quoted by the drunk sergeant who interrogates Švejk in Dobromil.

Ich weiß nicht was soll es bedeuten,
Dass ich so traurig bin;
Ein Märchen aus alten Zeiten,
Das kommt mir nicht aus dem Sinn.

On September 15th 2015 Heine posthumously shared an unlikely stage with Jaroslav Hašek. Both were on this day inducted in the memory plaque gallery of Sterne der Satire (*Stars of Satire*) in Mainz, as stars no. 78 and 79. respectively. Present on the occasion was Richard Hašek (grandson of the author) and several notabilities from German political and cultural life. The 80th and final star in the series was awarded to the comedian Dieter Hallervorden. [honsi.org]

[242] It is their job to dig saps, long, narrow trenches that are dug to approach and undermine enemy positions. The sappers are formally known as the Corps of Engineers. [Translator's note]

[243] "U zlatého věnce" (*At the Golden Wreath*) refers to a tavern in Královská třída (*boulevard*) 59 named after the house Zlatý věnec (*The Golden Wreath*) in Pobřežní třída 30 that was attached to it from the back. In 1907, the owner of both buildings was Marie Holubová.

Newspaper adverts and minor notices from around the turn of the century show that there was a guest house here. The adverts announced meetings of a trade union and theater performances so it was probably a spacious establishment. At the end of 1894 the *Metal worker's* trade union was founded here.

The landlord in 1892 and 1896 was Antonín Beran who already in 1884 is listed as the owner of the house. In 1907, Marie Holubová is entered as the owner of both house 161 and 362 but no hostelry is listed on the premises. In 1910, Josef Tichý is the landlord but in 1912 no pub is found at this address anymore. [honsi.org]

[244] Nová Paka is a town in north Bohemia in the district of Jičín. It is located 22 km north of the district capital. As of 2016 the population was 9,208. The town hosts a museum and a historic town square. In 1913 Nová Paka counted 6,057 inhabitants, and all apart from 12 reported Czech as their everyday language. The town was the center of okres and hejtmanství of the same name. [honsi.org]

[245] Susanna in the bath was a biblical character from the Book of Daniel. This part of the book is apocryphal (of doubtful authenticity, although widely circulated as being true) and not included in Protestant bibles. Susanna has been painted by many artists - Rembrandt, Rubens and van Dyck being among them. She is also the theme of a composition by Händel. Several theater plays based on the theme have been performed over the years, some of them considered quite daring at the time.

The story revolves around Susanna, the beautiful wife of Joachim. Two elders (judges) get infatuated with her and try to blackmail her to have sex with them. One day when she is taking a bath they carry out the threat but she rejects their advances. They subsequently accuse her of infidelity and report her. She is given a death sentence but after prayers by Susanna, God intervenes, informs the prophet Daniel about the real situation, and the case is reopened. The two elders are now interrogated separately and their explanations turn out to differ. The result is that Susanna is cleared and her two tormentors executed. [honsi.org]

[246] Moselle is a wine region in Germany, named after the river Moselle that flows through France, Luxembourg and Germany and ebbs into the Rhine by Koblenz.[honsi.org]

[247] Papin was a French physicist, mathematician and inventor who is best known for having invented the pressure-boiler (machine à vapeur). It is this device that is mentioned in *The Good Soldier Švejk* and it was invented in 1679 in London (Papin had left France in 1675). [honsi.org]

[248] a short for the term Eau de Cologne (water from Cologne), the world famous perfume. It was invented in 1709 by Giovanni Maria Farina and soon trickled down through the various underlying layers of society. The original outlet in Cologne still exists and before World War I the company had a sales office in Vienna.

The brand Eau de Cologne was one of the early victims of the renaming frenzy during World War I. This happened in France in November 1914 as after a vote it was decided to rename the fragrance "Eau de Lovain" after the Belgian city of Lovain (Leuven) that was destroyed and looted by the Germans in late August that year. Other candidates were also considered but didn't get as many votes. Among them was Eau de Pologne (Polish Water).

The best known example of de-Germanization is surely Sankt Peterburg which as early as 1914 was renamed Petrograd, but it was not alone. In USA the mildly amusing name "liberty cabbage" was proposed as a substitute for sauerkraut, but it is unclear if it was ever introduced. [honsi.org]

[249] Johannes Brahms was a German composer, conductor and pianist. He was discovered in 1853 by Robert Schumann who wrote an ecstatic article about the young musical genius.

His big breakthrough happened in 1868 with Ein deutsches Requiem. Brahms spent 20 years on his first symphony but eventually more were produced. From 1872 until his death he lived in Vienna. [honsi.org]

[250] Vlašim is a town in central Bohemia, located in the Benešov district east of the Vltava.

Jaroslav Hašek visited the town in the summer of 1922. This was his last major excursion before his premature death six months later. He also visited the area together with Zdeněk Matěj Kuděj in 1914. The inspiration for the novel would surely have come from the first visit because this part of the novel was written already in 1921. [honsi.org]

[251] Saint Augustine was a Church father and philosopher from North Africa and one of the greatest of the ancient theologians. He was regarded a saint soon after his death. In "De civitate Dei" he reveals his skepticism about the Antipodes:

> "Quod vero et Antipodes esse fabulantur, id est, homines a contraria parte terrae, ubi sol oritur, quando occidit nobis, adversa perdibus nostris calcare vestigia, nulla ratione credendum est..." (*"But that there are Antipodes, that is, men on the opposite part of the earth where the sun rises when it sets for us and who tread with their feet opposite to ours, is in no way to be believed..."*) [honsi.org]

[252] Australia was in 1914 still a British dominion but with extensive self-government. The country contributed to the allied war effort; Australian forces were heavily involved in the campaign against Turkey in 1915 (Gallipoli) and in attacks on German colonies in Polynesia.

Australia is by area the sixth largest country in the world, and is also classified as a continent. The population was in 2016 just above 23 million. [honsi.org]

[253] Hašek's colloquial phrase "u uršulinek v klášteře" refers informally to the residence of the Ursuline nuns, which in English is best rendered as "the Ursulines' convent." Historically, this community occupied the institution known as Klášter Voršilek, a 17th-century Ursuline monastery with an adjoining church on Národní třída (formerly Ferdinandova třída). Founded between 1674 and 1676, the monastery provided boarding and education for girls and has been under heritage protection since 1958. [Translator's note]

[254] "sirotčinec u Benešova" (*orphanage near Benešov*) surely refers to the home for parentless children in Benešov, "Domov" (*Home*). It was built around the turn of the century, was owned by the town, and seems to have been located below Konopiště castle. [honsi.org]

[255] Benešov is a town in central Bohemia with around 16,000 inhabitants. It is located appx. 40 kilometers south east of Prague, and is a stop on the railway line to Budějovice. The well-known château Konopiště, that until 1914 belonged to Archduke Franz Ferdinand is located 2 km to the west. [honsi.org]

[256] Lourdes is one of the most popular Roman-Catholic pilgrimage destinations

in the whole world. It is located in south-western France, not far from the border with Spain. The number of inhabitants as of 2010 was around 15,000. [honsi.org]

[257] The story of John the Baptist comes to us from the New Testament, particularly the gospels (Matthew, Mark, Luke and John), and from Flavius Josephus' work The Antiquities of the Jews. After living an ascetic life in the desert, John emerged into the lower Jordan Valley preaching about the imminent arrival of God's judgment, and urging his followers to repent their sins and be baptized in preparation for the coming Messiah.

John the Baptist's preparatory message attracted hundreds, perhaps thousands, of followers from Jerusalem and Judea. He made it clear that he himself was not the Messiah, and foretold the coming of Jesus: "one who is more powerful than I, whose sandals I am not worthy to carry." (Matthew 3:11).

Many religious scholars agree that John's subsequent baptism of Jesus in the River Jordan, described in three of the gospels (Matthew, Mark and Luke) and by a number of other canonical and non-canonical sources, is almost certainly a historical event. The archaeological site at Al-Maghtas, Jordan (identified as the Biblical "Bethany beyond the Jordan") has been viewed as the baptism site since the late Roman-early Byzantine era. Most Christian denominations view Jesus' baptism as a major milestone and the basis for the Christian rite of baptism that has survived through the centuries.

According to Josephus, sometime after baptizing Jesus, John the Baptist was killed at the palace fortress of Machaerus, located near the Dead Sea in modern Jordan. Built by King Herod the Great, the palace was occupied at the time by his son and successor, known as Herod Antipas.

The Gospels of Matthew (Matthew 14:1–12) and Mark (Mark 6:14–29) recorded that Herod Antipas had John the Baptist arrested and imprisoned after the preacher condemned the king's marriage to his wife, Herodias, as illegal, because she had previously been married to his own brother, Philip. Herod Antipas initially resisted killing John, because of his status as a holy man. But after his stepdaughter danced for him at his birthday party, he offered to give her anything she desired. Prompted by her mother, who resented John's judgment of her marriage, Herodias' daughter requested the head of John the Baptist on a platter.

In The Antiquities of the Jews (Book 18:116-19), Josephus confirmed that Herod Antipas "slew" John the Baptist after imprisoning him at Machaerus, because he feared John's influence might enable him to start a rebellion.

Josephus also identified Herodias' daughter as Salome (the gospels don't mention her name) but didn't state that John was beheaded on her request. [history.com]

[258] "U Piaristů" is a colloquial term for Kostel svatého Kříže (*Church of the Holy Cross*), a monastery with church and a school located at the corner of Na Příkopě and Panská streets that until 1912 belonged to the Piarist order. It is a Catholic educational order founded in 1617 and is the oldest of its kind. Its main purpose is to provide free education for poor children.

The church, which is built in a classical style, was constructed between 1816 and 1824. Among those who studied at the school was Vrchlický.

After the introduction of a new school law in 1869, the state took over and one part became a Gymnasium (German) and the other a teacher's institute. In 1912 the Piarists finally sold the building. Today the church is run by the Catholic institute Society of St. Francis de Sales (Salesians of Don Bosco).

It was on the street corner by this church that Oberleutnant Lukáš was to meet a lady, when on a walk with the dog Fox, he unfortunately bumped into *Col onel* Kraus.[honsi.org]

[259] According to the canonical Gospels, Joseph was a 1st-century Jewish man of Nazareth who was married to Mary, the mother of Jesus, and was the legal father of Jesus. [en.wikipedia.org]

[260] Saint Serapion was a monk and soldier from the age of the Crusades who suffered martyrdom at the hands of the Moors and was later canonized. He was a member of the Mercedarian Order for Redemption of Captives whose goal was to release Christian prisoners in Moslem captivity. The background for this martyrdom was that he offered himself as a hostage in Alger in a prisoner exchange deal, but when the Moslem captives were not released in time he was mutilated and killed. Serapion was of British origin and probably born in London. [honsi.org]

[261] Saint Ludmila was, according to legend, a Czech princess and married to the first Christian ruler of Bohemia, Bořivoj I of the Přemysl dynasty. She was the grandmother and custodian of Saint Václav. Ludmila is said to have been murdered on orders from her daughter-in-law, and became the first Czech saint.

Ludmila is an important person in the borderland between Czech mythology and history. Antonín Dvořák composed an oratorio to her honor, lyrics provided by Vrchlický. A red wine from Mělník is also named after her.

Ludmila also had a church in Vinohrady named after her: Kostel sv. Ludmily at Purkyňově square (now Náměstí míru). It was here that Jaroslav Hašek married Jarmila Mayerová on 23 May 1910. [honsi.org]

[262] Saint Bernhard (Bernard of Aosta, Bernard of Menthon or Bernard of Mont-Joux) was a French missionary who operated in the Alpine region. He is the patron saint of Alpine dwellers and mountaineers. The chronological details of his life are unclear, including year of birth and death. [honsi.org]

[263] Gotthard Pass is a mountain pass in the Alps that is located slightly south of the border between the cantons Uri and Ticino. The pass has lost much of its importance since the tunnel beneath it was opened in 1980. There is also a railway tunnel under the pass.

The chaplain's somewhat nebulous monologue suggests that he rather has the St. Bernhard pass in mind, since Saint Bernhard built mountain huts there for travelers, among them many pilgrims. [honsi.org]

[264] Herod was a Roman vassal King of Judea, Galilee, Samara and the surrounding areas. Many historians regard him as an effective ruler who completed several large building projects, but he was also known as ruthless and tyrannical. He had several members of his family executed, among them one of his wives.

Herod is best known through the Bible and the role he played after the birth of Jesus Christ. According to Matthew's gospel he gave the order to murder all boys in Bethlehem of less than two years of age. This was after the newly born Jesus, his perceived rival as "king of the Jews", had been brought into safety by his father Saint Joseph. [honsi.org]

[265] Boccaccio was an Italian writer and poet. He is best known as author of the The Decameron, the book that is mentioned here. He is regarded as one of the all time greats of Italian literature.

This book was by some distance Boccaccio's most famous work. The plot is set during the times of the Black Death (1348) in the surroundings of Florence. It is a collection of 100 short stories, told by 10 people who have fled the city due to the plague. Each tell one story a day over 10 days, some of them very daring for their time. This was partly due to sexually explicit content, moreover satire directed at the church and its institutions.

The Decameron is considered a key work in European literature, inspiring, among others, Geoffrey Chaucer and later Miguel de Cervantes and Lope de Vega.

The book was banned and censored on several occasions during medieval times, but more surprisingly the US postal services were from 1873 required by law not to ship it. The ban was lifted as late as 1926.

There are some striking similarities between Jaroslav Hašek's novel and the Decameron. They are both satirical books, have been banned, and are fragmented in their composition. Another curious similarity is the large number of facts that are embedded: the Decameron mentions numerous places, people and institutions, just like Hašek's novel does.

Fifty years after Hašek's death three volumes of his short stories were published, exploiting the name of Boccaccio's famous book: Dekameron humoru a satiry (*Decameron of Humor and Satire*) (1968), Druhý Dekameron (*The Second Decameron*) (1979) and Třetí dekameron: Reelní podnik (*The Third Decameron: The Real Estate Enterprise*) (1977). [honsi.org]

[266] Militärgeistlichkeit (*Military Clergy*) was a collective term for the military clergy of Austria-Hungary. It included Catholic (the largest), Jewish, Greek-Orthodox, Muslim and Protestant clergy. The institution reported to Kriegsministerium (*Ministry of War*). To every division was assigned one divisional field chaplain and each regiment was assigned one regimental field chaplain. Serving in this role at Infantry Regiment No. 91 was Jan Eybl; he was at the Regiment from 1 January 1914 to 24 April 1918.

The head of the military clergy from 1911 to 1918 was Emmerich Bjelik. His title was the resounding Apostolischer Feldvikar (*Apostolic Field Vicar*). Bjelik knew one of the models for the figures in *The Good Soldier Švejk*, namely Ludvík Lacina. Another person who knew Bjelik was Zdeněk Matěj Kuděj who for a period served at the Feldvikariat (*Field Vicariate*) in Vienna. It may well be that Jaroslav Hašek drew inspiration for some of his field chaplains from what Kuděj told him. The two authors met several times during the period the novel was written.

The institution of military clergy plays a prominent role in *The Good Soldier Švejk* and it is probably the authority that is subjected to the most stinging satire of them all. Already in Chapter 1 the author dedicates a complete sub-chapter to an attack on military clergy as a world phenomenon. Later the object of scorn is solely the Catholic field clergy in Austria-Hungary. The field chaplains Katz, Martinec, Lacina and their pious colleague in Chapter 11 are either drunkards (and immoral), and those who are not soon slide into debauchery. Chief Field Chaplain Ibl, however, is only mentioned briefly, but as an idiotic preacher.

Lacina and, to a lesser degree, Chief Field Chaplain Ibl are both inspired by living persons - Ludvík Lacina and Jan Eybl respectively. Feldkurat Martinec and Feldkurat Katz have no obvious link to any existing persons and no field chaplains with these names are listed in Schematismus (*Military Register*) from 1914. The marginal Feldkurat Matyáš could, however, have been inspired by a real person. Jaroslav Hašek definitely knew Eybl from his time in IR. 91 in 1915, and it is very likely that he also knew Lacina in person. [honsi.org]

[267] "vojenská nemocnice na Karlově náměstí" (*military hospital at Charles' square*) refers to c.k. vojenská nemocnice č. 11/k.u.k. Militärspital Nr. 11 (I&R Military Hospital No. 11) in Prague, a military hospital located at the southern end of Karlovo náměstí. Today the building is used by the university hospital (Všeobecná fakultní nemocnice v Praze).

A significant number of the locations mentioned in the first part of *The Good Soldier Švejk* and in anecdotes throughout the novel are located within a 10-minute walk from the hospital, including U kalicha (*At the Chalice*). The author lived in this area for the first 20 years of his life, and frequently also later in life. He graduated both from the Gymnasium and the Commercial Academy only a few hundred meters from here.

The military hospital where Švejk spent time as a malingerer in was a part of it. [honsi.org]

[268] Militärintendantur (*Military Supply Administration*) was the administrative body of the k.u.k. Heer (*I&R Army*) the task of which was to supply the army and perform accounting. The main office was located in Vienna, but this no doubt refers to their branch of the 8th army corps in Prague. The offices were located on the second storey of the Lichtenstein Palace in Malá Strana (*Lesser Town*). See Korpskommando and k.u.k. Militärärar. [honsi.org]

[269] Božena Němcová was a prominent Czech writer, who wrote short stories, poems and fairytales. Her best known work is however a novel: Babička [*Grandmother*], regarded as one of the classics of Czech literature. The well-known film Three nuts for Cinderella (1973) is based on her fairytale from 1845 called O Popelce [*About Cinderella*]. [honsi.org]

[270] "Dlouhá třída" (*Long Boulevard*) is a street in Staré město (*Old Town*), Prague. It extends from Staroměstské náměstí (*Old Town square*) towards Poříčí (*Riverside* [street]) and is one of the oldest streets in the city. [honsi.org]

[271] Ústav šlechtičen (*Institute for Noblewomen*) was an institution for education of daughters of noblemen who were incapable of providing their daughters with an existence that was in line with their rank in society.

The foundation was created by Maria Theresa in 1755 and accommodated 30 ladies. It was located in Rožmberský palace at Hradčany. The abbess was always an unmarried lady of the house Habsburg-Lothringen, and from 1894 to 1918, Maria Annunziata, the sister of Archduke Franz Ferdinand, held the position.

On May 1st 1919, the nobility institute was dissolved and the palace transferred to the Ministry of Interior. The building is located on the castle premises and is today (2015) the property of the Czech State. It recently underwent extensive renovation and is used as a museum and exhibition area. [honsi.org]

[272] "z chrámu od Ignáce" refers to "kostel svatého Ignáce" (*Church of Saint Ignatius*), a church at the corner of Ječná street and Karlovo náměstí (*Charles' square*) which today serves as the main seat of the Jesuit order in Czech Republic. It is named after the founder of the order, Ignatius of Loyola. Construction started in 1665 and was completed in 1699.

Jaroslav Hašek knew the church very well. Not only did he grow up in this area but according to Václav Menger he was an altar boy there during the second last year at primary school (i.e. when he was around nine years old). His knowledge of Catholic liturgy is no doubt in part due to this experience. [honsi.org]

[273] Žižkov is an urban district and cadastral area east of the center of Prague. Administratively it is part of Prague 3 and partly Prague 8. The district is named after the Hussite leader Jan Žižka. From 1881 to 1922 it was a city in its own right.

The first and part of the second volume of *The Good Soldier Švejk* was written here. Jaroslav Hašek stayed with his friend Franta Sauer at Jeronýmova 324/3 from January to August 1921. Nearby at Prokop's square there is now a statue of the author. [honsi.org]

[274] Malešice is an urban district in eastern Prague, located in Prague 10 and Prague 9. It became part of the capital in 1922. [honsi.org]

[275] Saint John Chrysostom was a Greek Church Father who was proclaimed a saint with 13 September as his memorial day. He was famous for his rhetorical capabilities. The name of Chrysostom, which is Greek for 'golden mouth', refers to this ability. [honsi.org]

[276] Bordeaux is a city in southwestern France with approx. 250,000 inhabitants (the urban area approx. 1 million). It is the center of the wine growing region of the same name and it is this connection that makes its way into the novel.

This variety of punch may not be a well-known term today, but Bordeaux wine is its ingredient.

The drink was also on sale in bottles, as adverts bear witness to. The best known brand seems to have been E. Lichtwizt & Co from Opava (Troppau) who were also suppliers to the Imperial and Royal Court. Even more common were concentrated flavors in bottles and these are the ones that appear in the earliest adverts. The first mention of Bordeaux punch that can be traced in the Austrian press is from 1845 and refers to an event at Sofien-Insel in Prague (now Slovanský ostrov island). [honsi.org]

[277] U Exnerů (*At Exners'*) was a restaurant that existed at least until 1940. It was located on the corner of Primátorská and Královská boulevard in Libeň. In the address books from 1896, 1907 and 1910 it is listed under the name Na Palmovce (*At Palmovka*).

U Exnerů was also used for organized meetings and events; in 1915, it is mentioned in the newspaper in connection with charities, for instance for poor children. [honsi.org]

[278] The Drina is a river in the Balkans, and one the tributaries to Sava. Stretching 346 km, it is the border between Bosnia-Hercegovina and Serbia, in 1914 effectively the border between Austria-Hungary and Serbia. [honsi.org]

[279] No Wichterle is listed in the database of fallen from World War I (soldiers from the current Czech and Slovak republics). Nor is the name found in Verlustliste (*Casualty Lists*) or in Schematismus (*Military Register*) from 1914. The only item that appears on searches for Wichterle at the time is a tools manufacturer in Prostějov. In Czech Republic there live only 30 persons with this surname. Even rarer is the similar Wuchterle.

There lived a man of this name whom Hašek definitely had heard of and probably also knew in person. He was Josef Boris Wuchterle (1891-1923), a high ranking officer in the Legions and a national hero in Czechoslovakia. He was one of the very first who joined the Česká Družina (*Czech Battalion*) in 1914. He commanded one of the companies of the 1st Rifle Regiment (where Hašek also served) and was severely wounded during the battle of Zborów in 1917. After the battle he was promoted to captain. The small difference between Wichterle and Wuchterle is well within the margin of error in *The Good Soldier Švejk* and it could even be that Hašek deliberately changed the letter to avoid controversies. [honsi.org]

[280] Rawa Ruska is the Polish name of Рава-Руська (Rava-Ruska, i.e. *Russian Rava*), a town and railway junction in Galicia, near the current border between Ukraine and Poland. The town is administratively part of Lviv oblast. Until 1918 it was part of Austria-Hungary, in the inter-war period it

belonged to Poland, since 1945 the Soviet Union and from 1991 Ukraine. [honsi.org]

[281] In Schematismus (*Military Register*) of 1914 one Oberleutnant (*Senior Lieutenant*) Viktor Machek is actually listed. That year he served at 3. Tyroler Kaiserjägerregiment (*3rd Tyrolean Imperial Rifle Regiment*). On July 1st 1915 he was promoted to captain and was still enlisted with the same regiment.

From the list of wounded of January 21st 1915 it is evident that Machek was hospitalized in Vienna after having been shot in the lungs. It is also mentioned that he was born in Prague in 1886. In *Casualty List No. 116* from January 29th he is correspondingly listed as "Verwundet" (*Wounded*). The Czech newspaper versions are, however, confusing. In Čech and Národní listy the presentation may be interpreted as if he had been captured, because they printed only the names under a general heading such as "Casualty List", without specifying "wounded" or "killed". *National Politics* makes it clear that when nothing else is noted, the soldier mentioned in such a list is to be understood as wounded.

The rank fits, Machek was born in Prague and from Czech newspapers it's not entirely clear whether he was wounded or captured. His family lived in Vinohrady, a place Jaroslav Hašek knew very well. This indicates that the author may perhaps have linked his literary figure with the real Viktor Machek. [honsi.org]

[282] The Carpathians are the easternmost of the great mountain ranges of Europe. It extends 1,500 km on the territory of Romania, Czech Republic, Slovakia, Poland, Ukraine, Austria, Serbia and Hungary.

In September 1914 Russian forces pushed into the northern part of the mountain range and in early October they tried to break through the Uszok pass. In November they occupied Humenné for a short while and also entered Hungarian territory in Maramaros (now Maramureş in Romania). [honsi.org]

[283] "Mariánská kongregace" (lat. Congregatio Mariana) is a Roman-Catholic educational institution, established by the Jesuit father Jean Leunis in 1563 and always associated with the Jesuit order.

The Prague section of the society was founded on April 28th 1892. In 1896 the institution was located in Ječná street 505/2, with Father Jemelka as chairman. In 1907 and 1910 the address was Ve Smečkách 1354/32, not far from Vodičkova street (where Feldkurat Katz and Švejk drove past in their horse cab). The building has since been demolished. [honsi.org]

[284] Heavily armed cavalry. [Translator's note]

K.u.k. Dragoner (*I&R Dragoons*) was the term for some of the cavalry units in the Austrian part of the Dual Monarchy. In total, there were 15 Dragoon regiments in k.u.k. Heer (*I&R Army*), mostly from the German- and Czech-speaking areas of the empire. The structure of the cavalry in Austria-Hungary was quite complex - in addition to the Dragoons there were also Uhlans and Hussars.

In *The Good Soldier Švejk* the reference is surely to a local Dragoon regiment, and such a regiment actually existed: Dragonerregiment Nr. 14. From 1912 the 2nd and 5th Squadron were garrisoned in the barracks behind Invalidovna in Karlín (now U Sluncové 6). The staff was located at Brandýs nad Labem, and the rest of the regiment in Stará Boleslav and Dobřany. The recruitment area was No. 8. The recruitment command itself was located in Klatovy.

Several Dragoon regiments were recruited from the district of the VIII. Armeekorps and over the years other regiments were located in Karlín. In 1906 Dragonerregiment Nr. 13 occupied the same premises behind Invalidovna as Dragonerregiment Nr. 14 did from 1912. [honsi.org]

[285] Českomoravská vysočina (*Czech-Moravian Highlands*) is a historical term for the geographical area that is now called Českomoravská vrchovina (*Bohemian-Moravian Uplands*). The area roughly corresponds to the modern administrative region of Kraj Vysočina (*Highlands Region*) but is slightly larger. The administrative center in the modern Vysočina is Jihlava.

The highlands are strongly associated with Jaroslav Hašek, mainly because most of *The Good Soldier Švejk* was written here, more precisely at Lipnice. This is also where he died and where his grave still is. His descendants have since 2003 been running the inn U české koruny (*At the Czech Crown*), where the author lived from August 1921 to October 1922.

Hašek knew the region well, also from his trips before the war, and mentions several places from Vysočina in the novel. Apart from Lipnice itself he mentions Posázaví, Německý Brod, Chotěboř, Skuteč, Okrouhlice, Kejžlice, Jihlava, Pelhřimov, Jedouchov, Dolní Královice, Velké Meziříčí.

It should be added that when the author wrote this passage of the novel he had not yet moved to Lipnice. [honsi.org]

[286] Generalstab (*General Staff*) was an institution that in times of war or times of a threatening war was responsible for planning, execution and supervision of military operations. General Staff formally belonged to Kriegsministerium (*Ministry of War*) and was located in the same building.

The Royal and Imperial General Staff existed from 1867 to 1918 but the institution was already in place long before the Ausgleich (*The Compromise*) split the Habsburg Empire into two parts of equal standing.

Chief of staff from 1912 to 1917 was Field Marshall Conrad. He was demoted by the new emperor Karl I and replaced by infantry general Arthur Arz von Straußenburg who was to become the last ever Chief of Staff at k.u.k. Generalstab.

General Staff officers were permanently present at major military units; at district, divisional and brigade level. [honsi.org]

[287] Carthage was an ancient city state at the coast of North Africa, south of the Lake of Tunis in modern Tunisia. At its prime it is believed to have had up to 700,000 inhabitants. The Phoenician city was an important sea power.

The city was destroyed by the Romans after the Punic Wars in 146 BC and this is the event both conversations in the novel refers to. [honsi.org]

[288] Mount Pelée is a volcano at the north-western part of the French Caribbean island Martinique. It had an explosive eruption on May 8th 1902 that caused an estimated 30,000 casualties and was reported in Czech newspapers two days later. The island's main city, Saint-Pierre, was totally destroyed and few of its citizens survived. Švejk is however imprecise when he claims that the eruption destroyed the whole island of Martinique. It was mainly Saint-Pierre and the northern part of the island that were hit. [honsi.org]

[289] Martinique is and island in the Small Antilles in the Caribbean Sea and a French overseas département. The island is located about 450 north east of the South American coast and 700 km south east of the Dominican Republic. The island is as part of France, member of the European Union, and the currency is Euro. The population count in 2014 was around 384,000. [honsi.org]

[290] Zenger is by near certainty the professor that Švejk refers to in the conversation at the *Military Hospital at Charles' square*. It can however not be verified that Zenger wrote any article similar to the one Švejk mentions, but his studies of the connection between sunspots and seismic activity on earth makes him an obvious inspiration for the professor in the novel.

Zenger was a distinguished physicist and meteorologist and towards the end of his life he was even awarded the title "Hofrat" (*Court Councillor*). He published widely; in Czech, German and even French. He was particularly well known in French academic circles, but his name also appears in newspapers like Bergens Tidende (Norway).

He taught at the technical high school Česká technika (now ČVUT) in Prague and Jaroslav Hašek mixed a great deal with its students and has surely been aware of professor Zenger and his theories.

Zenger observed an approximate ten year cycle on volcanic eruptions, and linked this to a corresponding cycle of high solar activity. The first eruption that was included in the statistics happened in 1732, and with only two exceptions there were repeated eruptions in years that ended in two. The two remaining happened in years that ended in three, among these was Krakatoa in 1883.

Some months after the disaster at Martinique an article was printed in the very *National Politics* where Zenger's theories were linked to the mentioned eruption. The article quotes the newspaper L'Opinion from Martinique, but also other French newspapers wrote about Zenger and his theories.

Many years earlier Zenger had investigated the connection between solar activity and its effect on the earth. He coined the term "sun climate" and was an international authority within this research. For instance he provided some statistics that indicate a link between high sunspot activity and seismic events on earth, and it may well be that Švejk had noticed this. [honsi.org]

[291] *As the Field Chaplain Katz explained to Švejk, he always added a bet: "I hopped it all..." "Hop - blind" means the player announces that he will play the banker for the entire pot without looking at the first card he was dealt.* [svejkmuseum.cz]

[292] *"Na Zderaze" is a street in Nové město (New Town) between Karlovo náměstí (Charles' square) and the Vltava. It stretches parallel to the river from Myslíkova street to Resslova street. Next to the Stoletá kavárna (Centennial Coffeehouse) and Na Zbořenci the street splits in two. The street Na Zbořenci behind the Centennial Cofeehouse was the likely location of the tavern where the famous game of cards took place.* [honsi.org]

[293] *Mariáš is a lifting card game for two to four players. Mariáš is played with a pack of 32 German-type cards, so-called mariášky. These 32 cards are divided into four suits: Reds, Rounds, Greens, and Acorns. Each suit has eight cards: seven, eight, nine, ten, bottom, upper, king, ace. Upper is also called boy or filek. The Ace of Acorns is called kočičák (catface) or Beelzebub. The two basic variants are designation and bidding mariáš for three players. For two players there is the simplified licked mariáš and for four players there is the so-called pausing foursome. The unique method of increasing bets is the so-called flecking: the first increase is announced with the word "Flek", 2. "Re", 3. "Supre", 4. "Tuti", 5. "Shoes", 6. "Pants". The rules and art of the mariáš game are quite complex and without practical instruction, an explanation is impossible. Once upon a time, mariáš was played for penny coins. Today it is no longer possible to play, due to the physical absence of these coins in Czech currency. Nevertheless, in*

accounting, the crown is still divided into hundredths or pennies. So we have not only pennies, but also other small penny coins abstracts. Hašek would certainly not have overlooked this absurdity. [svejkmuseum.cz]

[294] "the pub behind the Centennial Coffeehouse" was most probably an inn that belonged to Josef Pavlíček. The pub was located at Na Zbořenci No. 7, two houses up the street from the *Centennial Coffeehouse*. The cook Pavlíček also owned the building; he bought it at a bankruptcy auction in 1904. [honsi.org]

Stoletá kavárna (*Centennial Coffeehouse*) was a café with address Na Zderaze in Nové město (*New Town*) that existed from some time before 1887, but it is not known with certainty when it started and when it ceased operation. Early adverts show a certain Slavík as the landlord. In 1908 these small adverts reveal that the landlord is Antonín Kolář and the address book from 1907 confirms him also as the owner of the building.

In 1909 the old building was demolished and a new one erected on the premises. Jaroslav Hašek surely knew both versions of the café, but the time of tinsmith Vejvoda was probably before the rebuild. In 1914 they advertised for a piano player, the place was also a dance and concert establishment. In 1915 the building changed hands after a bankruptcy and in 1916 it is referred to as the former café. In 1918 it had reopened and in 1920 the landlord was B. Michálek. On the present building the inscription "Stoletá kavárna" is still visible. [honsi.org]

[295] *Announcing "trop" means that I quit, I don't participate in the game, although I paid the deposit to the bank, I don't have a good card. Everyone "tropped out" - everyone was "trop", they didn't participate in the game. Vejvoda suggested they "cast a oner for a five," i.e. to play "one-and-twenty" with an agreed bet of five krejcary.* [svejkmuseum.cz]

[296] *A fee to the innkeeper for allowing cards to be played in the establishment - also "card fee". The reason for charging this fee is that card players engrossed in the game consume little of the drinks and food offered.* [svejkmuseum.cz]

[297] Myslíkova ulice is a street in Nové město (*New Town*) that stretches from Spálená street down towards the Vltava. One of the side streets is Na Zderaze.

Myslíkova ulice is a street Jaroslav Hašek would have known very well. Not only was it in the middle of his stomping ground in Praha II. - number 15 housed the editorial offices and print-works of Kopřivy (*Nettles*) and Právo lidu (*The People's Right*), publications of the Czechoslovak Social Democratic Labor Party. Hašek contributed frequently to both publications in 1913 and 1914. [honsi.org]

[298] Monte Carlo is the most prosperous district of the Principality of Monaco and is best known for its casino that indirectly is referred to in the novel.

The district's road to fame started in 1863 when the current casino was completed. The same year the well known financier François Blanc (1806-1877), until then director of the casino in Bad Homburg, was hired to manage the casino. It still took many years before Monte Carlo became a household name for gambling, but by the outbreak of World War I it was already famous world wide.

In the manuscript Jaroslav Hašek spelled the name Monte Karlo but during a "clean-up" of *The Good Soldier Švejk* in the early 1950's, this and some other "oddities" were corrected. The inter-war issues of the novel, published by Adolf Synek, kept Hašek's original spelling. [honsi.org]

[299] Chodov is the name of four places in Bohemia, one on the outskirts of Prague and the three others in the west of the country. The text in the quote is picked from five different folk songs. The first line is from a song from the Chodsko region near the border with Bavaria, so here it certainly refers to Chodov by Domažlice. [honsi.org]

[300] Bílá Hora (*The White Mountain*) is a hill on the western outskirts of Prague, between Smíchov, Břevnov and Ruzyně. Until 1922 it belonged to the village of Řepy in *administrative district* and *judicial district* Smíchov, and in the ninteen-sixties it became part of the capital.

It is primarily known for the battle on November 8th 1620 that effectively ended Czech independence. Habsburg rule was cemented and lasted until 1918. The battle is regarded as one of the most important events of the Thirty Year War (1618-1648).

The line featured here is from the well known folk song "Na Bílé Hoře" (*At White Mountain*). [honsi.org]

[301] Sancho Panza was the servant of Don Quixote in the classic novel by Miguel de Cervantes. Many literary scholars point to similarities between Panza and Švejk, but also add that Švejk, as opposed to Sancho Panza, is the main character in his novel. [honsi.org]

[302] Don Quixote is the main character in the classic novel Quixote de la Mancha by Miguel de Cervantes. The novel is one of the greatest in the Spanish language ever, a universal classic, and one of the most translated.

Don Quixote is a novel that *The Good Soldier Švejk* has often been compared to. On August 23rd 1926 Swedish literary critic Carl-August Brolander wrote a review of the German translation of Part One for the newspaper Dagens Nyheter. Here he declared Jaroslav Hašek a "Czech Cervantes" and also compared him to Rabelais. The French critic Jean-Richard Bloch wrote a similarly enthusiastic review in Les Nouvelles littéraires in 1932. [honsi.org]

[303] The duke of Almavira is supposed to have been part of the defending party during some siege of Toledo but it is uncertain to what historic event or literary work the author refers.

Later in the novel (Book 3, Ch.3) One-Year Volunteer Marek mentions an almost identical episode, but the cannibalistic deed is now located in Madrid during the Napoleonic wars (there is no mention of any Almavira or Fernando here). Even this is doubtful as the siege in question was very short. It has not been possible to locate any place in Spain with the name Almavira so it is surely a spelling mistake or the person in question is someone entirely different. Hašek may well have mixed together multiple stories or invented new ones. Eating a servant may be only a grotesque intermezzo in line with detective Bretschneider's death [Book 1 Ch. 6] or the story about a dog who devoured a baby [Book 1 Ch. 3]. [honsi.org]

[304] Toledo is a historic city in Spain, 70 km south of Madrid. In 1986 the city was entered as a UNESCO World Heritage site. The city prospered in medieval times, and was for a while capital of Castilla. Today the city is the capital of the Castilla-La Mancha region and a major tourist attraction.

The historical event in question could be from 930 to 932 when the city was encircled by the Moors during a Christian uprising. After a two year siege it surrendered due to hunger. A shorter siege took place in 1085 when the city was wrestled away from the Moors by Christians. [honsi.org]

[305] Swabia is a historical region in southern Germany that spans the borders of the current states Bavaria and Baden-Württemberg. The principal cities in the area are Stuttgart, Ulm and Augsburg. Jaroslav Hašek visited Swabia in 1904 and eventually wrote a few humorous stories from his travels here.

When writing "ve staré švábské knize" (*in an old Swabian book*) – Hašek refers to a book on the art of warfare, though the exact work is unknown. He wrote "Swabian book," but he might have meant a book written in švabach, (from German "Schwabacher Schrift"), an early blackletter typeface. Luther's earliest Bible editions were printed in Schwabacher. By Hašek's time, German printing had largely switched to Fraktur (Frakturschrift), yet Czechs commonly referred to German books printed in either Schwabacher or Fraktur scripts as "švabach". Therefore, Hašek's "Swabian book" does not necessarily indicate a book of Swabian origin; it could have been any old German book on military matters printed in one of these blackletter typefaces.

The English translator of *The Good Soldier Švejk*, Cecil Parrott, evidently assumes this when he translates the phrase as "an old German book." [honsi.org]

If Hašek meant "a book written in Swabian script", he was once again pressing against the confines of the language rules, because "švábské" is a feminine adjective, meaning "of Swabia" or "of cockroach". The "Swabschrift" originated in Nuremberg and its use spread in Swabia, but calling a book "of Swabia" or "of cockroach" when meaning "of Swabchrift" is a bit of a stretch, when "švabaške knize", "a book in Swabacher [Schrift]" could had been used. [Translator's note]

[306] Named for the long curved pipes most of them smoked. "Pipe" was also used to denote any older man: i.e., an "old goat," or an "old geezer."

[307] Graz is the second largest city on Austria and the capital of Styria. The city has appx. 250,000 inhabitants (2006). In 1910 the population counted almost 200,000.

It has not been possible to find a direct parallel to the case from 1912 about the captain who allegedly kicked his servant to death and was acquitted. Most probably the story is a product of the author's imagination and his tendency to grotesque exaggerations. That said, a newspaper that year wrote about several other incidents where officer's servants were involved. There are reports about servants who stole from their officers, servants who committed suicide, and one servant who failed in an attempt to kill his superior and thereafter failed in killing himself.

An article in the Graz newspaper Arbeiterwille from 1912 deals with a case where an officer's servant commits suicide after being harassed over time and finally unjustly accused of having stolen five tins of conserves. The article also puts the tragedy in a greater perspective. It deals in more general terms with the hopeless situation of the army servant. He was obliged to serve not only his superior officer but also the family. If the situation became unbearable he couldn't simply quit his post as his civilian colleague could. The article advocates scrapping the whole institution of officer's servants, and has certain parallels to the author's own description of the status of the officer's servant. [honsi.org]

[308] Dubno (Ukr. "Дубно", Rus. "Дубно") is a city in the Volhynia province of Ukraine, until 1917 part of the Russian Volhynia Governorate. The city is located 15 km south of Khorupan where Jaroslav Hašek was captured on 24 September 1915. The area by Dubno had at the time a considerable number of Czech immigrants.

Dubno was strategically important due to its fortress and the railway

connections to the north and south. Austro-Hungarian forces entered the city on September 8th 1915 after an unexpected Russian withdrawal. The latter reconquered Dubno on June 10th 1916 during the Brusilov offensive.
[honsi.org]

[309] Darnitsa (Ukr. "Дарниця") is today a district of Kyiv, east of the river Dnieper. Nowadays Darnitsa is a huge suburb, dominated by high-rise apartment blocks. There is a street named after Jaroslav Hašek here.

Darnytsa was a well-known transit camp that existed from 1915. In the beginning the camp was very primitive and lacked the most basic facilities. Diseases raged and mortality rates were scarily high. The camp was also pivotal in supplying the Czech anti-Austrian volunteer forces, who from 1916 were allowed to recruit in Russian prisoner of war camps.

According to Jaroslav Kejla, Jaroslav Hašek was interned in the transit camp here for three days in the autumn of 1915, in mid October. From here he was sent onwards to Totskoye in southern Ural. His prisoner card has him registered in Penza on October 6th 1915. Kejla reports that the prisoners walked the 300 km from the Dubno-region to Darnitsa on foot from September 24th, but this fits badly with Penza and October 6th. An explanation may be that the date is according the old Russian calendar, in which case the registration in Penza happened on October 19th.

There is also little doubt that Hašek revisited Darnitsa as a recruiter and agitator after he joined České legie (*Czech Legions*) in Kiev in July 1916.
[honsi.org]

[310] Kiev (Ukr. "Київ", Rus. "Киев") is the capital and largest city of Ukraine. It straddles both banks of the river Dnieper and has nearly 3 million inhabitants, making it the seventh largest city in Europe. The administrative center and historic districts are located on the hills of the west bank.

Kiev was, in 1914, the capital of the Russian Kiev military district and "gubernia" of the same name. It had been under Russian control from the 17th century, although with a noticeable Polish footprint. The city also had a large Jewish population.

The city and the province had a sizable Czech immigrant community and the Czech weekly Čechoslovan (*Czechoslav*) was published in Kiev until February 1918. During World War I the city was, together with Paris and Petrograd, one of the main centers of the Czechoslovak independence movement. Until the Russian October Revolution Kiev was relatively unaffected by the war apart from the general shortages and the fact that the city was the center of the military assembly area and an important military-administrative center. Kiev was also the headquarters of the Russian branch of the Czechoslovak National Council. The leader of the Czechoslovak independence movement, Professor Masaryk, stayed here for long periods between May 1917 and February 1918. It was in Kiev that on February 7th 1918 he signed the treaty of the transfer of the Legions from the Russian to the French Army. [honsi.org]

[311] Ukraine (Ukr. "Україна", Rus. "Украина") is a large and populous state in south-western Europe with Kyiv as capital. The main language is Ukrainian but Russian is widely used, mainly in the east and in the south. However, before World War I the name Ukraine had a rather different meaning. According to Ottův slovník naučný (*Otto's Educational Dictionary*) (1888) it was a term that refers to "the south-western part of Russia along the banks of the rivers Bug and Dnieper but whose extent is not precisely defined". According to the encyclopedia, the name originates from the 17th century and means "borderland".

Meyers Konversations-Lexikon uses approximately the same definition as Otto's Encyclopedia but does not mention the river Bug; instead, it states that Ukraine consists of the areas on both banks of the Dnieper. Nordic and English encyclopedias from before World War I use more or less the same definition as Meyers. [honsi.org]

[312] Tashkent (Rus. "Ташкент") was in 1915 capital of the Russian general governorate of Turkestan. It is now the capital of Uzbekistan after having been part of the Soviet Union until 1991. Today the city has more than 2 million inhabitants.

During the war there was a prisoner's camp in the city, and another one at Troytsky 30 kilometers from the center. In both camps the inmates were mainly prisoners from the Slav nations of Austria-Hungary. Because many Czech were interned here Jaroslav Hašek surely knew a few people who had stories to tell from Tashkent. [honsi.org]

[313] Sokal (Ukr. "Сокáль") is a regional capital in the Lviv oblast in western Ukraine. It is situated 80 km north of Lviv on the eastern bank of the Buh (Bug) and as of 2018 it had approximately 25,000 inhabitants.

From 1772 to 1918 the town belonged to Austria, in the inter-war period to Poland, after the Second World War to the Soviet Union and from 1991 to Ukraine. In 1881 the population was around 8,000 with a near equal distributions between Jews, Poles and Ukrainians. The town was situated approx. 10 km from the border with Russia. After the battle of Sokal Hašek was promoted to Gefreiter and on August 18th 1915 he was decorated with a silver medal (2nd class) for bravery demonstrated during the fighting around Poturzyca on July 25th. [honsi.org]

[314] Niš (Ser. "Ниш") is a city in Serbia by the river Nišava. Counting more than 250,000 inhabitants it is the biggest city in southern Serbia and the third in the country behind Belgrade and Novi Sad.

The city became the wartime capital of Serbia due to the exposed position of Belgrade at the border with Hungary. During the Central Powers' offensive in the autumn of 1915, Niš was conquered by Bulgarian troops on November 5th 1915 after the Serbs had abandoned the city. It remained under Bulgarian occupation until October 12th 1918, when Serbian forces liberated it.

That Austrian soldiers would have been participating in the storming of Niš (as the author suggests) is unlikely, as the Bulgarian army undertook the operations against the city in 1915. [honsi.org]

[315] Piave is a river in northern Italy. It flows from the Alps and after 220 km ends in the Adriatic Sea near Venice.

After the Central Powers broke through by Caporetto on October 24th 1917, Italian forces pulled back to the Piave where the front was stabilized in November after the enemy's attempt to cross the river failed. In June 1918 a second battle by the Piave took place. This was the last large-scale Austro-Hungarian operation in the war. The offensive failed and the *I&R Army* suffered nearly 120,000 casualties. On October 24th 1918 the Allies attacked across the river and the Austro-Hungarian front collapsed.

By Piave a division of Czech legionnaires was fighting on the Italian side. Those who were captured were publicly executed. On one single day, July 22nd 1918, no less than 160 legionnaires suffered this grim fate. [honsi.org]

[316] Prager Einjährig-Freiwilligenschule (*Prague One-Year Volunteer School*) refers to some reserve officer's school in Prague. These schools belonged to the individual regiments, but as it is never revealed at which regiment Oberleutnant Lukáš served, it is impossible to know where the school was located. The next step in the investigation is therefore to look at which infantry regiments still had staff functions located in the city in the winter of 1914-15. Those were Infantry Regiment No. 11, Infantry Regiment No. 73 and Infantry Regiment No. 102 and Lukáš surely served as an instructor with one of these. [honsi.org]

[317] In the novel, Hašek refers to the region as "českém jihu", literally "Czech south." This is simply the standard Czech way of naming the area. In English, it is rendered as "Czech south" to preserve the Czech perspective. By contrast, the term "Bohemia" is Latin-based and was historically used by

foreigners to designate the Czech lands. The more formal "South Bohemia" derives from this foreign usage, carrying a historical or administrative tone distinct from the native Czech designation. For reference, the corresponding modern administrative region is the *South Bohemian Region* (Jihočeský kraj), which encompasses much of the area Hašek evokes, but did not exist in his time. [Translator's note] The Capital is České Budějovice, by far the largest city in the region. Among other notable towns are Tábor, Písek, Strakonice, Krumlov, Třeboň, and Jindřichův Hradec. As an administrative entity it was created in 1949 as Budějovický kraj (*Budějovice Region*), and since 1960 it has the current name.

That South Bohemia has such a prominent place in the novel is closely related to the author's own background. Even though Hašek was from Prague, both of his parents were from the south, and already as a teenager he visited the region with his mother. An important impetus is also his grandfather Jareš, the pond warden from Krč, who told young Jaroslav many stories from the area.

In the end his father's birthplace strongly influenced what setting the author used for the novel from Book Two onwards. Because his father, Josef Hašek, was born in Mydlovary, his son also had the right of domicile here. As Mydlovary was located in the recruitment district of IR. 91, Jaroslav Hašek was in 1915 called up to serve with this Regiment, a fact that decidedly influenced the direction of the plot, at least in a geographical sense. [honsi.org]

[318] Harz is a mountain range in Germany. It is the northernmost range in the country and straddles the borders of Lower Saxony, Saxony-Anhalt and Thuringia.

The "Harzer Roller" is a breed of canary birds that was bred in the Harz mountains and was very popular in the 19th century. It is best known as a singing bird but is also used in mines to warn against poisonous gases. It is particularly sensitive to carbon monoxide. The center for breeding of this race is Sankt Andreasberg.

The breed regularly showed up in newspaper adverts from before World War I, for instance in Národní politika (*National Politics*). Jaroslav Hašek, who in 1909 and 1910 was editor of the animal magazine Svět zvířat, was very knowledgeable about animals, including birds. [honsi.org]

The canary bird is named after the Canary Islands where it lives in the wild. It is also present on the Azores and Madeira. It was imported to Europe as a domesticated animal, and in Central Europe it became particularly popular.

During the 19th century the Harz region became the main center of canary breeding. (The Canary Islands is a group of islands in the Atlantic Ocean off the coast of Africa that belong to Spain.) [honsi.org]

[319] Pohodnice Pankrác was a "knacker's yard", i.e. a station for disposal of animal carcasses. It was also called a "Thermochemical station". The animal remains were mostly boiled to make fertilizer, bone flour and other residual products. Those were often used as ingredients in soap and glue. The enterprise was also allowed to collect dogs, cats and other stray animals from the eastern bank of the Vltava (a similar enterprise in Břevnov catered for the western bank). Prague city at the time defined stray dogs as "an animal that walked on its own without a muzzle". The enterprises were licensed by the city, but privately owned and managed.

The dogs were kept in a quarantine station at Vyšehrad until their owner reported and paid the fine for allowing his dog onto the street "improperly equipped". Dog owners had to claim their pets within three days, otherwise the animal would be destroyed. The carcass processing factory was located on the open fields between Dvorce-Podolí and Pankrác. [honsi.org]

[320] Pelhřimov is a town in Vysočina with around 17,000 inhabitants as of 2010. It has a well preserved historic center, and also a certain industrial tradition, for instance in brewing. Contrary to what is claimed in *The Good Soldier Švejk* there was (and is) no railway connection to Třeboň. [honsi.org]

[321] rendition of the Czech "ze Židů" (*"from the Jews"*)

V Židech (*In the Jews*) - *that's what the Jewish city of Prague was called - the Jewish ghetto, the "hampejz"**, [pron. "hum-pays] *which extended approximately where nowadays there is the part of Prague called* **Josefov**. *With some exceptions (synagogues, the old Jewish cemetery, the town hall) the entire agglomeration was bordered by Platnéřská Street, rehabilitated and rebuilt on the right bank of the Vltava and Revoluční třída* (Revolution Boulevard) *at the turn of the 19th and 20th centuries. Until then, it was the site of narrow streets, many mysterious corners and houses stuck on top of each other. In this confusing environment crime flourished, especially prostitution, black market trading, profiteering.* [svejkmuseum.cz]

 * "hampejz", from German, stands for "den", "slum" or
 "brothel" [Translator's note]

Josefov is part of Prague, Staré město (*Old Town*). Until 1922 it was a separate urban district also known as Praha V. From the late 19th century onwards it went through a redevelopment that changed the character of the quarter drastically, and few of the old buildings survived.

Prague V. was the smallest of the districts in the city with only 76 houses. It also had the highest proportion of German-speakers of any district in the city. This was no doubt due to the high number of Jewish inhabitants. Josefov roughly consisted of the area west of Mikulášská třída (*boulevard*) towards the Vltava.

The Jewish community in Prague was next to extinguished by the Nazis during the occupation from 1939 to 1945. The most famous resident of the area was arguably Franz Kafka. Egon Erwin Kisch was also born here. [honsi.org]

[322] "U Štupartů" is a building in Staré město (*Old Town*) with a history dating back to the 14th century. The house is named after Peter Stupart von Löwenthal who bought it on October 20th 1664. His grandson sold it out of the family on September 10th 1732. In 1910 the house had two street addresses in Štupartská 14 and Jakubská 2 and had many tenants. Among them the pub named after the house, run by Rudolf Holeček. Its address was Štupartská 14.

The original building (surely this was the one mentioned in the novel) was demolished in the autumn of 1911 after much opposition. Klub za starou Prahu (*The Club for Old Prague*) and others wanted to preserve it due to its historical and architectural value but they were overruled by the city council. Already in December that year the new building was under construction, was ready the next year and still occupies the site. The builder was Josef Sochor from Prague VII.

Another author who wrote about U Štupartů was Alois Jirásek, Jaroslav Hašek's teacher at the Gymnasium in Žitná street. The novel "Temno" (*Darkness*) was first printed as a serial in Zlatá Praha and was published as a book in 1914. It mentions the pub U Štupartů opposite the church Sv. Jakub as čertova krčma (*a devil's inn*). This historical novel is set at the beginning of the 18th century. [honsi.org]

[323] Bavaria is the largest of the German federal states, with Munich as the capital and one of the country's major cities.

The Kingdom of Bavaria existed from 1805 to 1918 and in 1871 it became part of the new united Germany. The geographical extent was somewhat different to that of the modern state as the geographically separate Palatinate belonged to Bavaria.

The kingdom kept a degree of autonomy after the unification: the Wittelsbach dynasty continued its reign, and Bavaria provided its own army, postal and railway services. Bavaria had traditionally been an ally of Austria in conflicts with Prussia; it was at war with Prussia as late as in the German War of 1866. [honsi.org]

[324] "dog, the ugliest mongrel" is my rendition of "Balabán". [Translator's note]

This dog appears in several of Jaroslav Hašek's stories. It was so ugly that dogs, other animals and people avoided him. From one of the stories, Kolik kdo má kolem krku (*Who Has How Much Around His Neck*), it is apparent that the author actually owned a dog called Balabán. The name may also be a generic term for a decoy and is even a Czech surname.

Balabán also appears in Dobrý voják Švejk v zajetí (1917), the second version of the good soldier. Here it is the name of the dog that Švejk stole in Bruck for the benefit of Ensign Dauerling. In this story the dog is a Boxer and even Cadet Biegler gets involved with him. [honsi.org]

[325] Austrian cops wore hats with plumes on their hats. [Translator's note]

[326] Mehmet V. Reşat was the Sultan of the Ottoman Empire from 1909 to 1918. He ascended the throne after the coup by the Young Turks but had limited power. His only significant political act was to formally declare Jihad against the Allies on November 11th 1914. He was the empire's Sultan no. 35 and died only months before the empire collapsed.

His reign was marked by enormous territorial losses for "the sick man of Europe", a term first used to describe the Ottoman Empire in the 19th century due to its economic decline, political instability, and territorial losses. North-Africa except Egypt and almost all of the Balkans was lost from 1912 to 1913. During World War I the Arab territories and Cyprus followed.

Circumstances strongly suggest that the decoration that Švejk read about took place in March 1915 as a quote from Rozkvět's (*The Blossoming*) "*Brief Chronicle of the World War*" is to the letter reproduced in the novel. The content of the "*Chronicle*" also appeared is newspapers like *National Politics*, and many of these brief quotes appear throughout this chapter of the novel. The chronicle refers to the date of decoration as March 24th 1915.

Already on March 9th 1915 the Turkish news agency Agence Milli reported that the Sultan had telegraphed the Emperor and congratulated him on the great victories in the east. In the same telegram it is revealed that the Emperor will be offered the Imtiaz War Medal as an expression of the Sultans admiration.

On March 25th Agence Milli reported that Goltz Paşa had left Constantinople for Berlin in order to personally forward the award. It also added that the war medal was specially issued for the Emperor.

In April it was revealed that the Emperor had responded by awarding the Sultan the Iron Cross 1st Class. Again Goltz Paşa performed the formal decoration. He actually brought the medal back with him from the visit to B erlin, and the Sultan received the medal on April 11th. [honsi.org]

[327] Kronika světové války (*Chronicle of the World War*) was not a book like the context here indicates, but sub-titles in the booklet series Světová válka slovem i obrazem (*The World War in Words and Pictures*) issued by the publisher Emil Šolc in Karlín from October 1914 on. They were published every two weeks and were later assembled in six large volumes. Editor in chief was Adolf Srb who was assisted by a group of experts. The series is richly illustrated, is very detailed and is generally of high quality. In total it contains nearly 2000 pages.

It is obvious that Jaroslav Hašek used some of the installments/books from the series as a source when he wrote *The Good Soldier Švejk*. The quote from *Chronicle of the World War* regarding the photo of the heir to the throne Archduke Karl Franz Joseph is copied letter by letter from volume II, page 505. It should be added that these brief daily reports appear also in periodicals like *National Politics* and Rozkvět, but with a slightly different spelling. Therefore everything indicates that the author used *The World War in Words and Pictures*, and not any of the others. The picture also appeared in Český svět on June 4th 1915 with exactly the same wording.

In Chapter 14 fragments from the *Chronicle* appear repeatedly. The first example is the Sultan awarding the German Emperor the war medal, then general General Kusmanek who arrived in Kiev. The longest direct quote is however the sub-title of the picture of the heir to the throne. [honsi.org]

[328] Karl Franz Joseph (baptized Karl Franz Joseph Ludwig Hubert Georg Otto Marie von Habsburg-Lothringen) was in 1915 the heir to the Austrian and Hungarian thrones. He was the eldest son of Archduke Otto, brother of Archduke Franz Ferdinand. He became emperor and king when Emperor Franz Joseph I died on November 21st 1916.

His reign was less repressive than his predecessor's as he gave an extensive amnesty to political prisoners. He also tried to negotiate a separate peace with the Entente, albeit without notifying his allies. Karl was the last emperor of the Habsburg family. He was beatified in 2004.

Before he ascended the thrones he visited the front frequently, and he often featured in illustrated magazines like Wiener Illustrierte Zeitung. In the context of *The Good Soldier Švejk* the most important photo of him is one that was printed in *Chronicle of the World War* in 1915 and is reproduced verbatim in the novel.

The picture shows the heir to the throne together with two pilots who have downed a Russian plane. It was printed also in other newspapers, and then with additional explanatory details. The two airmen shown were the Germans Johann Offermann and Erwin von Sprungmann. The photo was taken by Czernowitz in Bukovina (now Чернівці in Ukraine) and hails from the first half of 1915. The heir to the throne visited Černovci on April 19th 1915 and the photo was probably taken during this visit. [honsi.org]

[329] Kusmanek was an Austrian infantry general and commander of the Przemyśl fortress during the two Russian sieges in 1914-1915. He was considered one of the more capable Austrian commanders and earned the nickname "The Lion of Przemyśl" in 1914. After the capitulation of the fortress on 22 March 1915 he and the nearly 120,000 strong garrison became prisoners of war in Russia. [honsi.org]

[330] Vojtěšská ulice is a street in Nové město (*New Town*), running parallel to the Vltava north of Myslíkova street. The street is named after St Adalbert (Cz. Sv. Vojtěch). The main attraction in the street is probably church Kostel sv. Vojtěcha většího (*Church of St. Adalbert the Greater*). There is also an identically named street in Břevnov but it is unlikely that Švejk had this street in mind.

It has not been possible to link the mentioned episode to any news items from the period in question. [honsi.org]

[331] Jindřich is the Czech equivalent of the German name Heinrich, used by the young lady in her German language missive (as indicated by the italics, used by the translator for a sign that the text was written or conversation conducted in a language other than Czech, which is almost always German. In the few cases of other than German language being used, the context is the clue).

[332] Třeboň is a town in South Bohemia with around 8,700 inhabitants as of 2010. It was one of the main centers of the Schwarzenberg estates, has a fine historic old town and is surrounded by fishponds, artificial lakes used for fish-breeding. It is also classified as a spa town.

In 1914 Třeboň had direct railway connection with Prague and Vienna, but contrary to what is claimed in *The Good Soldier Švejk* there was (and is) no connection to Pelhřimov. It is possible to travel by train between the two towns, but that means changing twice. [honsi.org]

[333] Memphis is here mentioned through the cigarette brand Memphis that was manufactured by the I*mperial & Royal Tobacco Monopoly*. The cigarettes were made in Hainburg and a number of other places. In 1882 there were 28

tobacco factories in Cisleithania, i.e. the Austrian half of the Dual Monarchy, but details on which factory made what brand are not available.

The brand was launched in 1897 and was in 1913 the third most sold brand in Cisleithania. The name refers to Memphis in ancient Egypt, not to the US metropolis. Many of the Austrian cigarette brand names had an Oriental association (Nil, Stambul, Sultan, Memphis etc.).

Memphis cigarettes continued to be produced in post-war Czechoslovakia and Austria, by the successor states' respective tobacco monopolies. In Austria the monopoly was abolished as late as 1996 and the Memphis cigarette existed as of 2019, although it was no longer made in the country. The last domestic tobacco factory (Hainburg) closed down in 2011. [honsi.org]

[334] The Dunajec is a river that flows through northern Slovakia and southern Poland. It is one of the tributaries of Vistula which it joins by Opatowiec, north of Tarnów.

From November 15th 1914 the 3rd Russian Army led by Radko Dimitrov crossed the river and advanced across Raba towards Kraków. On December 8th they were forced back (the battle of Limanowa) and by the end of the year the front had stabilized by the Dunajec.

Until May 1915 part of the front stretched along the Dunajec and fierce fighting took place through the winter. The situation changed to the advantage of the Central Powers after the breakthrough by Gorlice and Tarnów on May 2nd 1915 and the area was thereafter spared from further destruction. [honsi.org]

[335] Všenory is a village around 20 km southwest of Prague, by the river Berounka. In 2018 it had 1,640 inhabitants. [honsi.org]

[336] Paris is the capital and the largest city in France. The city core has a population of around 2.1 million, whereas the metropolitan area, which is the fourth largest Europe, has around 12 million.

The French capital was for a while in August and September 1914 seriously threatened by the initial German advance, but the enemy was halted in the battle of Marne. [honsi.org]

[337] Východní Beskydy (*Eastern Beskids*), called the Bieszczady in Polish, is a mountain region straddling the border between Poland, Slovakia and Ukraine. From the autumn of 1914 until May 1915 the front went along the mountains which saw heavy fighting during the winter battle of the Carpathians.

The novel apparently refers to battles that took place at the beginning of April

1915 east of Medzilaborce. Many of the official bulletins from this period mention the fighting in Ostbeskiden (*Eastern Beskids*). This assumption is supported by the fact that the author picked most of the information he used in the conversation between Senior Lieutenant Lukáš and hop trader Wendler from these very announcements.

The news entry in *Chronicle of the World War* from April 2nd 1915 mentions *Eastern Beskids* as well as Klosterhoek, Niederaspach and Mühlhausen. All these places feature in the conversation between hop trader Wendler and Senior Lieutenant Lukáš. [honsi.org]

[338] Moscow [Москва] was in 1914 the biggest city in Russia, whereas Petrograd was the capital. In 1922 Moscow became the capital of the Soviet Union and was also the center of the Bolshevik administration from March 12th 1918. It is the capital and biggest city of modern Russia, with more than 10 millions inhabitants. The city is situated on the river Moskva, 142 meters above the sea level.

In 1897 the city had 988,614 inhabitants and the vast majority were Russians. The largest minority were Germans and Jews but none of these groups counted for more than 3 per cent of the population. There were also a number of Czechs and several Czech firms had offices in the city. During the last decennials before World War I Moscow grew rapidly, had a diverse industrial base and was also the hub of the Russian railway network.

Jaroslav Hašek arrived in the city in mid March 1918 together Břetislav Hůla. It was here he joined the Czech section of the Communist Party and started to campaign for České legie (*The Czech Legions*) to remain in Russia. On March 27th 1918 he published an article in Průkopník titled "*To the Czech Army: why is one going to France?*". He argued against the Legions' transfer to the Western front and thought they should remain in Russia to defend the revolution.

His stay in the city was short-lived as he left for Samara in early April. In November 1920 he appeared in Moscow again, now on the way back to his homeland after working for two years as a Red Army commissar in the Ural region and Siberia. [honsi.org]

[339] Meclis-i Umûmî (*Turkish Parliament* or *General Assembly*) was opened in 1876 and functioned until 1920. It was the first attempt of a representative system of government in the Ottoman Empire. It was however dissolved by the Sultan already in 1878 and only revived in 1908 after the Young Turk Revolution.

The assembly consisted of two chambers, the Meclis-i Âyân (*Upper*

Chamber) and the Meclis-i Mebusân (*Lower Chamber*). The *Lower Chamber* was made up of elected representatives, the *Upper Chamber* had its members picked by the Sultan.

At the election in 1908 several parties were represented, with the *Committee for Unity and Progress* (Young Turks) as the largest group. Many nationalities had seats in the parliament: Turks, Arabs, Armenians, Albanians, Greeks, Slavs, Jews etc.

The 1912 election was however won by the *Committee for Unity and Progress* with an overwhelming majority, after an election campaign where democratic rules were pushed to the side. The ethnic composition of the house remained much the same. After this election Halil Bey, the chairman of the Committee, was elected president of the lower chamber.

In 1914 new elections were held, but after the losses in the Balkans Wars, the *Committee* had in 1913 taken power through a coup and in 1914 they were the only party participating. On 13 May 1914 Emir Ali Paşa and Hüseyin Cahit Bey were elected vice presidents of the lower chamber. Halil Bey was at the same time re-elected as speaker of the house with 180 of the 181 votes. The last ever election to the parliament took place in 1919. [honsi.org]

[340] Hali Bey (correct Halil Bey, later he took the name Halil Menteşe) was a Turkish politician and one of the leaders of the Young Turk Movement, and for a period chairman of the associated *Committee of Union and Progress*. Halil served as an MP from 1908 to 1918. He was educated as a lawyer, and completed part of his studies in France.

Some time before December 1909 he became chairman of the Committee, the de facto ruling party after the Young Turk Revolution (1908). In February 1911 he accepted the post of Minister of the Interior after some deliberation. It was a critical period with considerable unrest among the minorities of the empire. His first task was to deal with an Albanian rebellion, and he strove to alleviate the tension by allowing the Latin alphabet to be used in Albanian schools. On May 15th 1912 he became the speaker of the lower chamber of Turkish Parliament (re-elected May 13th 1914), on October 24th 1915 Foreign Minister and in 1917 Minister of Justice.

According to US ambassador Henry Morgenthau, Halil did not approve of the genocide of the Armenians, but still defended it officially. In an interview with Berliner Tageblatt in 1915, he stated that "the Armenians are traitors, we must finish with them". Halil was also politically active in the new Turkish Republic that was formed after the collapse of the Ottoman empire. [honsi.org]

[341] Ali Bey no doubt refers to Emir Ali Paşa. The author uses the term "bej", but this is a misquotation that appeared in some Czech newspapers, including *National Politics*, Rozkvět and *Chronicle of the World War*.

Emir Ali was the son of the Algerian national hero Abd El-Kader El Djezairi, who from 1855 lived in Damascus. Emir Ali Paşa was, from May 1914, a member of the Lower Chamber of Turkish Parliament and at the same time was First Vice-Chairman of the chamber.

In mid-March 1915 he traveled to Berlin to negotiate the transfer of British and French Muslim prisoners of war to the Ottoman Empire. The plan was to employ them in the war against Great Britain. On the way back he stopped in Vienna. The stay lasted from 28th to 30th of March 1915 and he stayed at Hotel Bristol. He traveled from Berlin to Vienna together with Halil Bey. From Vienna he returned directly to Constantinople.

The quote from *National Politics*, Rozkvět and *Chronicle of the World War* is nearly identical to the quote in the novel, and several other snippets from the same pages appear in the conversation with the hop trader Wendler. It is this brief news item about the visit in Vienna that, six years later, found its way into a world-famous novel. The incorrect news items in the Czech press that the author used complicated the effort to identify Emir Ali, but a comparison with similar quotes from the Viennese press puts all doubt to rest.

[honsi.org]

[342] Liman von Sanders was a German cavalry general and Turkish marshal, best known for his role as advisor and military commander in Turkey. He was instrumental in thwarting the British-French expedition force by the Dardanelles in 1915.

In 1913 he was given the task of re-organizing the Turkish Army after the disastrous setbacks in the Balkans Wars of 1912 and 1913. Initially he was Corps Commander of Constantinople but was on March 24th 1915 appointed Commander of the newly formed 5th Army and it is the news of this appointment that appears in *The Good Soldier Švejk* with the words of Senior Lieutenant Lukáš.

Towards the end of the war he was the Commander of the Asia-Corps, and after the war he was arrested by the British, accused of war crimes against Armenians and Greeks, but released due to lack of evidence. He returned to Germany in 1919 and settled in Munich where he lived for the rest of his life.

The timing of the appointment mentioned by Lukáš is at odds with historical facts. It seems that Hašek used printed material from 1915 to construct this part of the plot, but "moved" the event to December 1914. The phrase that

Lukáš uses is to the letter identical to that found in *National Politics* April 4th 1915 and also in *Chronicle of the World War*. Similar time-shifts occur elsewhere in the novel. [honsi.org]

[343] Dardanelles is a narrow strait in northwestern Turkey that connects the Aegean Sea and the Marmara Sea. In March 1915 allied forces attempted to force their way through the straits but were repelled. The defeat ultimately led to the forced resignation of the British minister of Naval Affairs, Winston Churchill. The first major battle was fought on 18 March 1915 and the allied invasion fleet was repelled. The defenders were led by Cevat Paşa, later known as the hero of March 18th.

Marshal Liman von Sanders was named commander-in-chief of the Dardanelles army on 24 March 1915, and the news about his new role was pasted directly in to the novel. It was cut from a summary of the latest events that was printed in Národní politika on Easter Sunday 1915 (4 April).

[344] Goltz Paşa was a German general, military historian and author. From 1883 he was responsible for reorganizing the Turkish Army, and after returning to Germany in 1895 he held several high positions; among them army corps commander and army inspector. In 1914 the now retired general was appointed Military Governor in occupied Belgium, and from December he became an adviser to Turkey.

The trip that Senior Lieutenant Lukáš refers to actually occurred: Goltz arrived in Berlin from Constantinople on March 29th 1915, not in December 1914 as the novel indicates. The phrase about Goltz is word by word identical to an item in *Chronicle of the World War* in 1915, and then in *National Politics* on April 4th 1915. This is one of many items from the conversation between the hop trader and the officer that are be borrowed from the same source.

He returned to Constantinople on April 4th 1915 and stopped in Vienna for a conversation with Emperor Franz Joseph I. [honsi.org]

[345] Constantinople was in 1914 the capital and the largest city of the Ottoman Empire, and was the capital of the new Republic of Turkey until 1923. From 1930 the city has been known as İstanbul. [honsi.org]

[346] Berlin is the capital of Germany and its largest city, counting around 3.6 million inhabitants as of 2017. It is located by the river Spree and is situated appx. 35 meters above sea level.

The city was from 1871 the capital of Germany and already before that the capital of the kingdom of Prussia and until 1881 the province of Brandenburg. Some of the political decisions that led to the outbreak of the war were taken here. In 1900 the population count was around 2 millions and was growing rapidly. The city had at the time a very different appearance than today, because it was largely left in rubble during the Second World War.

Berlin, in its own right, played a key role in bringing Švejk to international prominence. Erwin Piscator's theatrical adaptation, staged at the Piscator-Bühne on Nollendorfplatz, greatly contributed to the growing fame of the good soldier. The production was met with enthusiastic acclaim from both audiences and critics, and its success resonated beyond Germany's borders. Max Pallenberg featured as Švejk, while the script was penned by Hans Reimann and Max Brod. The play premiered on January 23rd 1928. Another Berliner who pushed Švejk into the limelight was Kurt Tucholsky who in 1926 wrote a raving review of the two first volumes of the novel (i.e. the translation). [honsi.org]

[347] Enver Paşa (İsmail Enver) was a Turkish politician and general. He was Minister of War during World War I, and was regarded by many as a de facto dictator. In retrospect, he is seen as a poor military leader; the campaign against Russia was unsuccessful. He is also largely held responsible for the mass killings of Armenians in 1915, whom he accused of being fifth columnists.

When the war ended, he fled to Germany and, later, Russia. After first cooperating with the Soviet government, he turned against them, and in Tajikistan, he was killed fighting the Red Army.

Enver was indeed decorated by Emperor Franz Joseph I together with Usedom Paşa and Cevat Paşa, exactly as Senior Lieutenant Lukáš told hop trader Wendler. The decoration was announced on March 30th 1915. He was awarded the medal Militärverdienstkreuz 1. Klasse (*Military Merit Cross, 1st Class*). There was also a fourth decorated officer mentioned in the official news. Admiral Merten was, however, left out by the author. [honsi.org]

[348] Usedom Paşa was a German naval officer and ultimately Vice-Admiral who, from August 1914, led the Sonderkommando Kaiserliche Marine Türkei (*Special Command of the German Navy in Turkey*). He also led the Turkish forces in the Battle of the Dardanelles and was given a large share of the credit for repealing the Allied invaders.

Like the other names that Senior Lieutenant Lukáš mentions to hop trader Wendler regarding the Turkish war effort, the quote is cut directly from *Chronicle of the World War*. The background is the fact that Usedom on 30 March 1915, was awarded the *Military Merit Cross, 1st Class* medal by Emperor Franz Joseph I, together with three other Turkish officers: Enver

Paşa, Cevat Paşa and Admiral Merten. [honsi.org]

[349] Cevat Paşa (pronounced "Dzevad pasha"), later known as Cevat Çobanlı, was a Turkish general and commander of the Gallipoli fortress who distinguished himself in the battle of the Dardanelles on March 18th 1915. He was also given the nick-name Hero of March 18th. Cevat was awarded the title Paşa after the battle, was congratulated by Emperor Wilhelm II, and from newspaper clips it is obvious that he was educated in Germany.

At the end of the month he was awarded *Military Merit Cross, 2nd Class* by Emperor Franz Joseph I and this is the event that Senior Lieutenant Lukáš refers to. The entire sequence about the decorations has been cut from *Chronicle of the World War*. [honsi.org]

[350] Vistula is with its 1,047 km the longest river in Poland. It flows through cities like Kraków, Warsaw, Torun and Gdańsk. The catchment area covers half of Poland.

Throughout the autumn of 1914 and until late summer 1915 the war zone engulfed parts of the river basin. In the context of *The Good Soldier Švejk* it is however the upper stretch that is the theme, as it was on Austrian territory. [honsi.org]

[351] Italy was in 1914 a kingdom that had been united since 1861. The capital was Rome and the population in 1914 was 37 million. On the eve of World War I the area was the same as today with the exception of Trentino, Alto Agide (South Tyrol) and Trieste. The latter territories belonged to Austria until 1918 and were handed over to Italy as part of the peace settlement. Italy was also a colonial power, possessing Libya (from 1912) and also parts of eastern Africa.

Austria-Hungary had a sizable Italian minority, predominantly on the Istria peninsula and in Trentino. Italian speakers made up 1.5 per cent of the empire's population, or about 750,000. Italian was one of 10 official languages and Italians were represented in the Austrian Reichsrat. Almost the entire Italian population lived in Cisleithania. The Italian minority of Austria was a source of permanent conflict, as Italy made claims to the areas in where they lived. These territorial demands were in the end the main reason for Italy entering the war on the side of the Entente. [honsi.org]

[352] San Giuliano was an Italian politician who held the post of foreign secretary when the war started. He advocated neutrality but was already dead when Italy entered the war on the side of the Entente, on May 23rd 1915. His real name was Antonino Paternò Castello. He came from a noble family on Sicily, and received a good education in Vienna, London and Catania. From 1882

he was a member of the national assembly, from 1889 minister of various ministries, and from December 1905 foreign secretary. Politically he was liberal and anti-clerical, in foreign affairs he tried to balance between the blocks to the benefit of Italy. Before he became minister of foreign affairs he had been ambassador to London and Paris.

His successor as foreign secretary was Sidney Sonnino who was one of the politicians who eventually led Italy to declare war on her former partners.

Many fragments from the conversation between the hop trader and the officer are picked from the *Chronicle of the World War*, and probably this also applies to details around San Giuliano. In this case it is from page 511 where the *Chronicle* mentions that he, as foreign minister, renewed the Triple Alliance treaty in 1912, exactly as hop trader Wendler says. [honsi.org]

[353] Meuse is a river that flows from France, through Belgium and the Netherlands before emptying into the North Sea. The total length is 925 km.

From 1914 to 1918 the battlefront was close to Meuse in the area around Verdun. The fighting mentioned by hop trader Wendler took place in early April 1915 and was reported in official announcements from Berlin on April 2nd. The author employs these quotes almost exactly as they were printed in Czech newspapers. [honsi.org]

[354] Combres (officially Combres-sous-les-Côtes) is a municipality in the Meuse-department in Lorraine in France. It is located east of Verdun and was on or near the front almost the entire war.

In late March and early April 1915 fierce battles took place here, and it looks very much as if the author used a news bulletin from March 28th in this sequence, repeated in the *National Politics* in a news summary on April 4th 1915 and not least the *Chronicle of the World War*. [honsi.org]

[355] Woëvre is a region in Lorraine in northeastern France. It is located near Metz and the famous battlefield by Verdun. The front passed through here for almost the full length of the war and the events hop trader Wendler somewhat imprecisely refers to seem to be taken from a news release issued by the German HQ on March 28th 1915. These news bulletins appeared on the front pages of newspapers in Austria-Hungary throughout the war.

In Národní politika (*National Politics*) Woëvre is mentioned again on April 4th in a summary of events from the previous week. Now it is in a wording very close to what appears in the novel, but in all the press reports there is talk of the Woëvre plain,, not a town near Marche, so hop trader Wendler is slightly imprecise. [honsi.org]

[356] Hartmannsweiler is the German name of Hartmannswiller, a small place in

Alsace on the eastern slopes of the Vosges, northwest of the regional capital Mulhouse. Like the rest of the region it was part of Germany from 1871 to 1918.

It was the scene of fierce fighting during World War I, particularly in 1915. The battles mainly concerned Hartmannsweilerkopf, a summit of 956 meters west of the village. Today there is a large war cemetery and a French national monument. The village itself was destroyed by artillery bombardments.

As with the other Belgian and French breweries mentioned by hop trader Wendler in the conversation with Senior Lieutenant Lukáš the brewery here is presumably an invention. It may of course have existed, but even if this was the case it is unlikely that the author had any knowledge of it. [honsi.org]

[357] Vosges is a mountain range in northeastern France that between 1871 and 1918 straddled the French-German border. During World War I the front stretched along the mountains and in late March and early April 1915 there was heavy fighting here, events that the author transforms into destruction of breweries. Whether these breweries were destroyed (or even existed) has yet to be confirmed. [honsi.org]

[358] Niederaspach is the German name of Aspach-le-Bas, a municipality in the Haut-Rhin department in Alsace, from 1871 to 1918 part of Germany. It is located west of the regional capital Mulhouse.

It has not been possible to verify the existence of any brewery here, and certainly not a gigantic one (as hop trader Wendler claims).

The front stretched through the area through most of the war. In November 1914 it was frequently mentioned in German Kriegsberichte (*war dispatches*) and it also appeared in April 1915. [honsi.org]

[359] Mühlhausen is the German name of Mulhouse, a city in the province of Alsace (Ger. "Elsass") near the border of Switzerland and Germany. As the rest of Alsace it was part of Germany from 1871 to 1918. [honsi.org]

[360] Klosterhoek (also Kloosterhoek) was a farm east of Pervijze in Flanders, by Stuivekenskerke slightly west of the river Ijzer (Yser). Heavy fighting took place here in October 1914 and in March/April 1915 and it is also mentioned in news items from 1916 and 1917.

German forces reached the river Ijzer (Yser) late in October 1914 when they crossed it and occupied Klosterhoek, etc. Some days later the Belgians opened the ditches causing the area to be flooded and the Germans withdrew. The next news came from German official bulletins that reported that on March 31st 1915 they had occupied the farm. On April 2nd the Belgians failed in an attempt to recapture it and the stalemate by Yser lasted until the end of the war. The area was bombarded to the ground, and towns like Pervijze, Diksmuide and Veurne were ravaged. Klosterhoek itself was never rebuilt and today the site of the previous farm is a field. [honsi.org]

361 Zagreb was in 1914 capital of the Hungarian-ruled autonomous Kingdom of Croatia-Slavonia. At the time it was also known by its German name Agram, a term that is rarely used anymore. Zagreb is now the capital of the Republic of Croatia.

The city presumably hosted several breweries, but it is not known whether any of them were owned by the city council. The largest of them was not doubt Aktienbrauerei und Malzfabrik (*Joint-Stock Brewery and Malt Factory*) in Agram, locally simply called Pivovara (*Brewery*), that in 1910 was the 6th largest brewery in the entire Austria-Hungary. Beer production that year totaled 26,226 hectoliters.

This large brewery was founded as a joint limited company in 1893 through a merger of several smaller breweries that were unable to expand on their original sites. It still existed as of 2019, known as Zagrebačka pivovara (*Zagreb Brewery*) and owned by Molson Coors Brewing Company. [honsi.org]

362 Warsaw has been capital of Poland since 1918 and is the biggest city in the country. It is located by the river Vistula.

In 1914 the city was the capital of the Kingdom of Poland, also called Congress Poland, until 1915 a Russian satellite state. During the autumn of 1914 the Germans made several failed attempts to conquer the city. Warsaw finally fell on August 4th 1915 and remained in German hands for the rest of the war.

It has not been possible to identify any Augustian brewery in the city. The largest brewery in Warsaw at the end of the 19th century was Haberbusch i Schiele, a position it held also in 1914. The company also operated its own bottling plant in Kiev. The company retained its leading position in the inter-war independent Poland, but was destroyed during the Warsaw Uprising in 1944. Other breweries in the city were Machlejd and Livonia. Warsaw was also an important center for hop trading in the Russian Empire, and in this context it was often mentioned in specialist publications in Austria. [honsi.org]

363 Sopron is a city in Hungary near the Austrian border, regarded as the country's oldest city. It is located 5 km southwest of the Neusiedler See (*Lake Neusiedl*).

In 1910 the population count was 33,932 and among these the Germans were just about the largest ethnic group. The city was (and is) connected by rail to, among others, Győr and Wiener Neustadt. Sopron was after the peace treaty of Trianon in 1920 to join Austria, but a referendum overturned the decision so it remained in Hungary. Today Sopron has more than 60,000 inhabitants.

The brewery was established as a limited company on March 30th 1895 by factory owner Julius Lenck and a beer consortium from Brno. At the start the capacity was 25,000 hectoliters per year. The official name was Első Soproni Serfőzde és Malátagyár Részvénytársaság, in German Erste Oedenburger Bierbrauerei- und Malzfabrik-Aktiengesellschaft. The brewery existed under this name until 1917 when it was bought by a larger Hungarian enterprise. The brewery was still operating in 2019, owned by Heineken.

Jaroslav Hašek visited Sopron in 1905 together with Jaroslav Kubín and František Wágner. This was part of a longer trip that was later described in some detail in Strana mírného pokroku v mezích zákona (*Party of Moderate Progress Within the Bounds of the Law*), and also well covered by Václav Menger. According to Václav Menger they stayed with the brewmaster in Sopron, a Czech. [honsi.org]

[364] Nagykanizsa is a city in the Zala county in Hungary, located appx. 40 km south-west of Lake Balaton and 15 km from the border with Croatia.

Jaroslav Hašek visited the city in 1905 and later wrote a couple of stories set there, and many more that mentions the city. In the *Party of Moderate Progress Within the Bounds of the Law* he recalls being welcomed by the Czech brew-master there, a certain Mr. Znojemský.

The brewery was established in 1892 and operated until 1999. It was in the years before World War I a medium-size brewery with an output of 47,000 hectoliters in 1912. In 1902 Jan Znojemský became brewmaster at the plant. This is without doubt the person Hašek refers to in his story as Znojemský was still there in 1905. In 1909 he assumed the same role at the brewery F.F. Bote in Jekaterinoslav in Russia (now Dnipro, Ukraine), but resigned shortly after the outbreak of the war. [honsi.org]

[365] Alexandria (Arab. الإسكندرية) is a city in Egypt, named after Alexander the Great, the city's founder. In ancient times it was known for its library and its lighthouse, both classified among the seven wonders of the world.

In 1914 Egypt was formally still part of Turkey but had been occupied by the British since 1882. At the outbreak of war in 1914 the country was made a British protectorate, which no doubt ended any beer import from Austria-Hungary that ever was.

Reports from 1903 reveal that beer products were exported to Alexandria and other harbors in the Mediterranean Sea via Trieste.

There are a number of places named Alexandria around the world so one can't be one hundred per cent certain that hop trader Wendler actually had the Egyptian city in mind. Beer was already exported overseas and the numerous Alexandrias in North America are possible candidates.

Closer to home there is a remote possibility that hop trader Wendler was talking about Nowa Alexandria in Russian Poland, sometimes referred to as simply Alexandria. The town is now called Puławy but was from 1846 to 1918 named after Tsarina Alexandra Feodorovna (1798-1860).

The Romanian town of Alexandria can likewise not be entirely ruled out, being situated close to the Hungarian border. [honsi.org]

[366] The Czech place-name "Zámecké schody" contains "zámek", which ordinarily means "chateau" (as opposed to hrad, "castle"). In Prague toponyms, however, "zámek" can also denote the residential and garden precincts belonging to the Castle complex rather than a separate manor house. Zámecké schody are the historic stairs linking Malá Strana (the *Lesser Town*) with these upper castle precincts of Hradčany (the *Castle District*), in continuous use since the Middle Ages and rebuilt in the seventeenth century.

For this reason, the established English rendering is Castle Steps. [Translator's note]

[367] "malý výčep piva" (*small beer tap-room*) surely refers to one of the pubs in Thunovská ulice, a street leading up to Zámecké schody (*the Chateau Stairway*). In 1907 the address book shows up three pubs in the street: at No. 14, 15 and 19. In 1910 the one at No. 14 was no longer listed.

No. 19 was located directly at the end of the steps so at first sight it appears to be the tap-room the author had in mind. No. 15 hosted the well known U krále brabantského (*At the King of Brabant's*) and according to Zdeněk Matěj Kuděj known as a gathering place for secret meetings. This fits the scene from the novel well, but it is odd that Hašek classified it as a small beer tap-room. [honsi.org]

[368] The Venetian Republic may refer to the city state of Venice that existed for around 1000 years until 1797.

An alternative is Repubblica di San Marco, a short-lived republic that in 1848-49 rose up against the Austrian rule. It was centered on Venice and consisted more or less of the current region of Veneto. [honsi.org]

[369] Havlíčkovo náměstí (*Havlíček's square*) is the former name of the square

Senovážné náměstí (*Haymarket Square*) in Nové město (*New Town*). The name that appears in the novel was in use from 1896 to 1940. The square has also been named after František Soukup and Maxim Gorky. The square is located north of the main railway station.

Jaroslav Hašek worked at Banka Slavia here for a short while in 1902 and 1903 until he was dismissed after two absences without leave. [honsi.org]

[370] "psinec nad Klamovkou" (*the kennel above Klamovka*) refers to a breeding kennel that was owned by publisher and dog breeder Václav Fuchs and located by the villa Svět zvířat (*The Animal World*) in Košíře above Klamovka. After Fuchs's death in 1911 the kennel was renamed Canisport and managed by his son-in-law František Pober.

The kennel advertised already in 1899, and from 1901 it used the term Hundepark Fuchs or similar in their German language adverts. In Czech newspapers the term Fuchsův psinec or similar is often found. The sales pitch was particularly noticeable in Prague newspapers like Prager Tagblatt, Národní listy and Bohemia, although adverts and news at times appeared in many other newspapers across Austria. The weekly Das interessante Blatt from Vienna also often carried the adverts and even some articles where the breeding kennel was mentioned.

Fuchs moved to Klamovka from Jičín in 1898 and seems to have started breeding dogs at the premises soon after. In 1906 the kennel advertised a dog exhibition that was open to the public and in 1909 and 1910 they claimed to have more than 100 animals on show. The assistant at the kennel was from 1908 some Ladislav Čížek.

One of the important customers of the kennel was Rittmeister Rotter from k.k. Gendarmerie who let his two German shepherd dogs be trained here. Rotter was featured in an article in Svět zvířat in 1909, and there was also a picture of him with his dogs. On February 1st 1910 the magazine also printed a letter of acknowledgment from him in an advert for the kennel.

In 1908 Ladislav Hájek, one of Jaroslav Hašek's closest friends, became the chief editor of Svět zvířat. It was he who in November that year brought Hašek to Klamovka and the latter now came in close contact with the kennel, an experience that later was reflected not only in *The Good Soldier Švejk*, but also in many of the short stories. Hájek soon fell out with his boss and resigned as editor. Hašek then succeeded him, this probably happened in February 1909. [honsi.org]

Klamovka is a park area in Košíře and Smíchov, named after the Bohemian noble family Clam-Gallas. The main attraction of the park was (and is) the restaurant with a terrace that at the time often put on concerts with military orchestras. Egon Erwin Kisch has vividly described the ambiance at Klamovka in his story Der Clamsche Garten (*The Clam Garden*) from the collection Aus Prager Gassen und Nächten (*From Prague Streets and Nights*) (1912). [honsi.org]

[371] Pasteur-Institut (Pasteur Institute) is a private non-profit organization whose main goal is to combat infectious diseases. They were founded by and are named after the world famous bacteriologist and chemist Louis Pasteur. Their headquarters are located in Paris but have research centers and clinics all over the world.

The first institute was opened in Paris November 14th 1888 and very soon others opened all over the world. Their main task until World War I was to battle rabies. Vienna was relatively late in providing a clinic for treatment of rabies and already in 1889 Wiener Allgemaine Zeitung noted that such an institution existed in Bucharest. Budapest soon followed.

The so-called "Pasteur Institute" in Vienna was created in July 1894 as a clinic at the Imperial–Royal Rudolfstiftung Hospital in the 3rd District — Landstraße. The founder was the renowned bacteriologist Richard Paltauf (1858-1924). The task of the institute was inoculation against rabies, both preventive and after the patient had been infected. Treatment was free but the patient had to pay for accommodation (for poor patients the bill was sent to his home municipality).

The clinic had no official name and the connection to the institute in Paris was probably merely that they used the methods of Pasteur in treating the patients. In address books they are listed as Schutzimpfungsanstalt gegen Wut (*Institute for Protective Vaccination against Rabies*). They mainly served Vienna but patients from other parts of Austria were also welcome. Newspaper clips reveal that patients from Bohemia were treated here regularly. [honsi.org]

[372] Sady Vrchlického or Vrchlického sady (*Vrchlický's Garden*) is a park in front of the Prague Nádraží císaře Františka Josefa (*Emperor Franz Joseph Railway Station*) (in 1914), originally named Městský sad (*City Garden*). The park was laid out in connection with the construction of the railway station after 1870 and was at the time much larger than today. It even contained a fish pond, and a waterfall.

Between 1972 and 1977 a major redevelopment of the area took place: the new entrance hall for the railway station, a new transit road, and parking spaces. This reduced the area of the park considerably.

On 10 March 1913 the Council of Aldermen in Prague decided to rename the park in honor of the recently deceased poet Vrchlický (1853-1912). The original proposal was aired in a meeting on November 26th 1912. Thus Sady Vrchlického was the official name of the park when Blahník and Švejk were sneaking around in the area. [honsi.org]

[373] Krč is a village in the Písek district in South Bohemia, 3 km east of the center of Protivín. In 1847 Kateřina Jarešová, the mother of Jaroslav Hašek, was born here. Her father, Antonín Jareš, was a pond warden nearby. These are circumstances that no doubt inspired Hašek to assign his grandfather's name to four different characters in the novel. [honsi.org]

[374] Vydra was surely — like most characters who appear to be fictional in Švejk — a real person. In this respect, a candidate would be František Vydra (1869-1921), a factory owner and inventor whom Hašek surely knew about.

Vydra was educated as a brewer and in 1893 he bought the brewery in Dobrovíz, but soon converted it to a foodstuff factory. In 1898 he moved production to a former sugar refinery at Na Rokosce in Libeň, which he converted and expanded. The official name was Vydrova továrna poživatin (*Vydra's factory of victuals*). It manufactured nutrition products, among them coffee substitutes, grog, fruit juice, baking powder, soup tins, etc. The factory advertised regularly and seems to have been well known at the time. In its most successful period before World War I, Vydra employed close to 300 people. Their best-known product was a coffee substitute made from rye malt. Whether or not Vydra ever owned a St Bernard dog, and if the animal was ever stolen, has not been confirmed. [honsi.org]

[375] Bredovská ulice is a street in Nové město (*New Town*). The current name Ulice Politických vězňů literally means "The Political Prisoners' street". [honsi.org]

[376] Jindřišská is a street in Nové město that is is perpendicular to Václavské náměstí. Many streetcar lines pass through it. [honsi.org]

[377] "Fuchs" no doubt refers to a real stationer, but it is difficult to say exactly which enterprise Blahník refers to. One must assume that it was a specialist shop, as pedigree forms for dogs were surely not available in common stationer's shops.

The surname Fuchs was very common in Prague, but there is only one stationer's shop Fuchs listed in the address book. Also listed is a paper factory in Česká Kamenice with head offices in Mikulášská třída in Praha. Both are places where Blahník may have bought the blank pedigree forms, but the former is the prime candidate.

Closer investigations reveal that both firms had the same roots. They were owned by two brothers and had existed as a single enterprise until 1908. The company can be traced back to 1793, but it was the father of the brothers, the Jewish businessman Ignaz (Cz. "Hynek") Fuchs (1824-1890), who led the company to become one of the leaders in this market segment.

In 1888, the sons Robert (1854-1925) and Artur (1862-1940) took over as owners of the company. In 1908, the Fuchs brothers decided to split and they divided the company into two parts. Robert now owned the factory in Česká Kamenice and an office in Prague, whereas the rest remained with Artur, who also retained the brand name Hynek Fuchs. Both enterprises remained official purveyors to the court.

The range of goods was extensive, as witnessed by a wholesale catalog of 670 pages. The company didn't only trade in paper products; they offered a whole range of office and school equipment. They also manufactured various forms, but the mentioned catalog did not include blank pedigrees. On the other hand, it refers to detailed price lists for retail goods, so one would assume that empty pedigree forms belonged in this category.

In inter-war Czechoslovakia, the firm still flourished and the branches in Vienna and Hamburg also continued to operate. After 1933, the Hamburg branch was "aryanized" by the Nazis and the entire company suffered the same fate after the Nazi occupation of the Czech lands in 1939. Artur Fuchs committed suicide in 1940 and several members of the Fuchs family fell victim to the Holocaust. What happened to the company Hynek Fuchs after World War II is not known. The paper factory of Robert Fuchs in Česká Kamenice is still operating, but it is not clear if production has gone on continuously. [honsi.org]

[378] Leipzig is the second largest city in the state of Saxony, and was in 1914 part of the German Empire. The city is known for it's trade fair, university and as an important transport hub. The name is of Slavic origin. [honsi.org]

[379] Nürnberg is the second largest city of Bavaria and the largest in Franconia, in 1914 part of Germany. To judge by some short stories he wrote, Hašek visited the Nürnberg region in 1904. [honsi.org]

[380] Nürnberger Verein zur Zucht edler Hunde (*Nuremberg society for the breeding of thoroughbred dogs*) cannot be identified explicitly from the address directory of 1904 (the only one available for the period), but two dog societies are listed: Dachshundklub Nürnberg and Fränkische Verein zur Förderung reiner Hunderassen.

The latter's name is so close that it could be assumed that this is indeed the society the dog thief refers to. It was located in Nuremberg and regularly arranged exhibitions and other dog-related events.

The association was founded around Christmas 1889 and in 1915 it was still operating although the war restricted their activities. In 1915 they had more than 100 members. [honsi.org]

[381] Herzogtum Salzburg (the *Duchy of Salzburg*) was one of the 15 Crown Lands of Cisleithania. It was included in Austria in 1816 as a result of the Napoleonic Wars, and thus became part of Austria-Hungary in 1867. From January 1st 1850 onwards the Duchy enjoyed the status as a Crown Land, with its own government, headed by the Landeshauptmann (*ProvincialGovernor*). [honsi.org]

[382] Mannlicher was an Austrian inventor and small armaments designer, best known for M1895, a series of automatically loading rifles that became the standard issue rifle in the k.u.k. Heer (*I&R Army*). The Czech term "manclicherovka" refers to this gun. The most common version was Infanterie Repetier-Gewehr (*Infantry Repeating Rifle*) M1895. The rifles were produced in Steyr and later also in Budapest. [honsi.org]

[383] Colonel Kraus was obsessed with this rifle and therefore got the German nickname Mannlichertrottel, i.e. *Mannlicher idiot*. [honsi.org]

[384] Schiller was a world-famous German playwright, poet, historian and philosopher. He belonged to the Romantic era and was strongly associated with Goethe and Weimar. His full name was Johann Christoph Friedrich von Schiller. [honsi.org]

[385] Vierordt was a poet from Karlsruhe who soon after the outbreak of World War I wrote an infamously bloodthirsty poem in ten verses: Deutschland, Hasse! (Germany, Hate!). From this poem, verse seven is no doubt the one that Hašek refers to in *The Good Soldier Švejk*. Vierordt otherwise wrote patriotic poetry and ballads, praising the virtues of his home area and his nation. After the Nazi take-over, he associated himself with the party and even wrote poems glorifying Hitler[1]. Vierordt was married and had one daughter. On his 50th birthday, he was awarded the title Hofrat (*Court Councillor*). [honsi.org]

[386] U mariánského obrazu (*At the Marian Picture*) was a restaurant in Hybernská street. It was located on the ground floor in number 1011, right opposite the departure hall of Státní nádraží/Staatsbahnhof (State Railway Station), present-day Masarykovo nádraží. The restaurant has a history at least back to 1877 in what was then house number 104. It was a large tavern, obviously popular with travelers. In the decade before World War I they served beer

from Smíchov and Plzeň and offered soup from five o'clock in the morning. [honsi.org]

[387] Kostel svatého Haštala (*Church of St. Haštal*) is a church in Prague's Old Town, built in Gothic style. It is named after Saint Castulus, one of the first Christian martyrs. The church is one of the oldest in Prague; the predecessor was erected in the 13th century. The current structure was consecrated in 1375 and was finished by 1399. Hašek may have picked the theme of the beggar and the church from the historical novel Mistr Kampanus by Zikmund Winter. It was published in 1906. [honsi.org]

[388] Na Příkopě is a well-known street in Prague, often simply called Příkopy, one of the more up-market shopping streets. During Austria this area was dominated by Germans and was one of the most exclusive streets in the city.

In German the street was known as Am Graben, a parallel to the similarly exclusive and like-named street in Vienna. The name is literally translated *On the Moat*.

The "German" Příkopy would not have been the street Hašek most frequently visited, but one incident is recorded. At 3 in the morning on January 1st 1905 Hašek caused a disorder on this street. Totally drunk he waved his arms around and also insulted German students. One of the witnesses to the incident was the "German philosopher" Paul Kisch, brother of the eventually famous Egon Erwin Kisch. The perpetrator admitted to being very drunk and said he couldn't remember much of it. A record of the incident is stored in the police archives, translated into Czech by Břetislav Hůla. [honsi.org]

[389] Panská ulice is a relatively short side street to Na Příkopě, extending south towards the main railway station. It reaches towards Jindřišská. Panská street (*Lords' Street*). Ger. "Herrengasse" was the home of, among others, Prager Tagblatt and the Piarists. [honsi.org]

[390] The dog stories, like most elements in *The Good Soldier Švejk*, have clear connections to the author's own life and experiences. For a short while in 1910-11, Jaroslav Hašek ran his own Cynological Institute below Klamovka. He allegedly falsified pedigrees, just like Švejk did (or more likely, his assistant did).

On March 31st 1915, Prager Tagblatt printed a small advert that asked for news about a stolen dog. The advert has some striking links to the dog story in the novel. It requested information about the dog to be delivered for a 30-crown reward at the Hotel Black Horse at Na Příkopě street. This is the very street where Colonel Kraus encountered his stolen pet. [honsi.org]

[391] Náchod is a town in eastern Bohemia, only a few kilometers from the

border with Poland. The distance to the front in the autumn of 1914 was about 300 km (Raba), so the claim about the sound of artillery was dubious and probably a popular saying.

Jaroslav Hašek visited the Náchod district in August 1914, a stay that finds its way into the novel via Josefov and Jasenná. [honsi.org]

392 "Heavens! Laudon!" - *purely military cursing from the time of the great general Laudon, probably when Austria was at war with Prussia during the 18th century. Laudon was an Austrian field marshal of German Baltic origin, and one of the most successful Austrian commanders of the 18th century. He fought in the Seven Years' War, the War of the Bavarian Succession and wars against Turkey. His troops captured Belgrade in 1789.* [svejkmuseum.cz]

Born into a noble family in present-day Latvia, Laudon first served in the Russian army before offering his services to Prussia, where he was rejected. He had more luck in Austria but, in the beginning, he was assigned to the irregular troops of the infamous Baron von Trenck, the so-called Panduren. When these were dissolved, he joined the regular army.

During the Seven Years' War (1756-1763), his exploits in the campaign against Prussia made him famous. Many of the battles took place on Czech territory and this is undoubtedly the main reason for his legendary status in the Czech lands. Here, the well-known folk song Generál Laudon jede skrz vesnici (*General Laudon is riding through the village*) bears his name and his fame lingers on in the expletive himmellaudon!, the very one that Oberleutnant Lukáš used in the novel. [honsi.org]

393 Košíře is a district in Prague and is located in the western part of the capital, between Smíchov and Motol. Košíře was a separate town from 1895 until it joined greater Prague in 1922.

Jaroslav Hašek officially lived in Košíře no. 908 from February 4th 1909. This was the address of the editorial offices of the bi-weekly animal journal Svět zvířat, the magazine where he worked for nearly two years as an editor. The villa was situated above the Klamovka garden but was demolished some time between 2011 and 2015.

From July 28th 1910 shows him registered further down in the town towards Smíchov, in Košíře no. 1125. Here he lived with his wife Jarmila who he had married May 23rd 1910. He stayed here (at least officially) until December 28th 1911 when he is recorded as residing in Vršovice. It was from no. 1125 that for a short period, at the end of 1910 and beginning of 1911, he ran his unsuccessful "Cynological Institute", buying and selling dogs and other animals.

It was probably during his time in Košíře that the author first thought up *The Good Soldier Švejk*, although in a very different format than the later world famous novel. The first story about Švejk was published on May 22nd 1911. [honsi.org]

[394] "Číňan Staněk" no doubt refers to the warehouse Maison Staněk. It was located at Ferdinandova boulevard 32, with stores and offices at the nearby Vladislavova street no. 13 (from 1896 no. 17). They imported and sold art and industrial goods from the Far East, tea, wine and rum. They also manufactured bamboo furniture. The firm was founded in 1876 by Vilém Staněk and adverts from after 1880 reveal that they focused on importing tea. The firm's name was Staňkův ruský obchod s čajem (*Staněk's Russian tea trade*).

Thus it was not a question of a "Chinese" in the true meaning of the word although the Chinese Li Gü was employed there and was well known in the city. One of the shop windows displayed a convex mirror.

The owner was born in 1853 and was only 23 when he established the enterprise. He had traveled a fair deal in British and French colonies, among them India, and had lived in Paris for a few years. The firm grew rapidly and full-page adverts in Prager Tagblatt etc. reveal details from their history. They were represented in several cities around the world, among them Yokohama and Hong Kong. In 1909 they opened a new outlet in Pilsen.

Every year Staněk attended auctions in Nishny Novgorod and London. He wrote expert articles on tea and also published the magazine Staňkův Světem (Staněk across the world). It appeared from 1889 to 1896, with content in Czech and German, edited by Hanuš Wahner. Staněk was regarded a master at marketing, helped by his younger brother Emanuel who provided illustrations.

Staněk died on November 22nd 1893 from lung tuberculosis, at a mere age of 40. His wife Kateřina (born 1866) took over the enterprise after her husband passed away. The company remained in business until 1938 when it went bankrupt. [honsi.org]

[395] Hašek managed to spell the name "Grenevil" in four different ways in four publications. The song is about Franz Folliot de Crenneville, an Austrian count, General of the Artillery, Privy Councilor, Imperial Adjutant General and Colonel Chamberlain.

He hailed from a renowned military family of French descent and entered the army as a boy. He became a lieutenant when he was only 16 and captain when he was 22. He distinguished himself in the wars against Italy and was repeatedly decorated. During the battle of Solferino June 24th 1859 he was severely wounded. In between his military duties he also held a post at the court of Emperor Ferdinand I. [honsi.org]

[396] Prašná brána (*Powder Gate*) is a Gothic tower and former city gate in Staré město (*Old Town*), erected at the end of the 15th century. Between 1878 and 1886 the tower was rebuilt in pseudo-Gothic style. The architect leading the reconstruction was the renowned Josef Mocker (1835-1899). The tower is located by Náměstí Republiky (The *Republic's square*) and is 65 meters tall. [honsi.org]

[397] This is the last of the 59 instances of the word "garrison" in this volume. The word "garrison" appears 35 times as part of "garrison prison", which in turn is a translation of "posádková věznice" (3x) or "**garnizóna**" (32x) [Translator's note].

Originally "garnison", a French term for a military garrison, was adopted into German - die Garnison, with the same meaning. In the Austro-Hungarian army this term was also commonly used as the **slang term for the garrison prison***, although the correct full name of the garrison prison in German is "der Garnisonsarrest" or "das Garnisonsgefängnis" - the garrison prison. So the Czech soldiers shortened it to: "garnizon", "garnizóna", or "garňák".* [svejkmuseum.cz]

The other 24 instances of garrison, including this last one, are a translation of "kasárna":

Kasárna, kasárny (from Ital. casa d'arme, *a house for arms, armory), Rus.* казáрма, *Fr.* caserne, *Ital.* caserma, *Eng.* barracks, *Germ.* Kaserne, *a building for permanent lodging of a larger or smaller formation of troops. - Otto's Educational Dictionary, Illustrated Encyclopedia of General Knowledge, Part Fourteen, In Prague: J. Otto, 1899*

Kasárna is a word borrowed from German; ... The word Kaserne *came into German from French. The origin of the French* caserne *is not clear enough. They interpret it from the Provençal word* cazerna *(lat.* quaterna*), i.e. a dwelling for four. It is said that it originally meant a shelter in the ramparts for four soldiers (later for six), who took turns on guard; later it was transferred under Louis XIV. to military lodging in general. The interpretation that the word caserne is composed of the words casa (house) and arma (weapon) is impossible.-* Naše řeč *(Our Language), Institute of the Czech Language of the Czech Academy of Sciences, 1923* [Translator's note]

casern: a military barracks in a garrison town (merriam-webster.com)

The Czech "kasárna" is used to refer to both the lodging facilities in the garrison as well as to the whole military installation of the garrison. Related to "kasárna" is "kasárník", translated in this volume as "confinement to the barracks" [Translator's note]:

It is a slang term for the military punishment of prohibition to leave the lodging quarters (German Quartier - Lager – Arrest), *barracks, camp.*
[svejkmuseum.cz]

In the 24 cases not referring to the military prison at a military post though, "garrison" as a translation of "kasárna" in this text is used to mean "a military post" [merriam-webster] itself, not the "barracks - a building or set of buildings used especially for lodging soldiers in garrison". Although the reviewer thought the instance of "garrison" in the first sentence of Chapter 13 should be rendered as "barracks", I decided against it: since Katz "lived off base", he wouldn't be referring to the barracks, the lodging portion of the "garrison" as the place where he picked up the circular, i.e. "an office paper". The Czech term "kasárna", just as the original French and German terms, is commonly used to denote the whole garrison, not just the lodging portion, referred to in American English as the barracks. And although the U.S. Army Installation Management Command lists its 56 garrisons in the United States, only three, Detroit, Hawai, West Point have "Garrison" in their name, 34 are Forts, one is Barracks. All 14 overseas installations, of which 8 are in Europe, are Garrisons. [Translator's note]

[398] Ohře is a river in northwestern Bohemia. The source is in the Fichtelbebirge in Bavaria. The river does actually flow into the Vltava, but by Litoměřice and not by Budějovice as the Colonel thinks. Its total length is 316 km and the catchment area is 5,588 sq. km. [honsi.org]

[399] Oberkommando (*Supreme Command*) in this context seemingly refers to k.u.k. Armeeoberkommando (*Supreme Army Command*), the highest military authority during the war. From the outbreak of war the formal head was Archduke Friedrich but the war effort was for most practical purposes directed by Generalstab (General Staff), headed by Field Marshal Conrad. At the time of the plot in *The Good Soldier Švejk* Armeeoberkommando was located in Teschen (now Cieszyn), in the palace that was incidentally owned by Friedrich himself.

In *The Good Soldier Švejk* the terms "Vrchní velitelství" (*Supreme command*) and "vojenské velitelství" (*military command*) both probably refer to *Supreme Army Command*, although commands at subordinated levels can't be ruled out. [honsi.org]

[400] Nekázanka is a short street in Prague II, connecting Na Příkopě and

Jindřišská streets. It has existed since the 14th century, under various names. The most important building was the Country Bank and the street had several restaurants. [honsi.org]

[401] Jaroslav Hašek did, indeed, publish two more parts of the Švejk saga. The next was called "At the Front," as promised. The third, however, was called "The Glorious Thrashing." Jaroslav Hašek passed away on January 3rd, 1923, while writing his fourth book, "The Glorious Thrashing Continued." It is but a fragment, 80 pages long. In this last fragment, Švejk is near the front lines, but yet to fight a battle, or be captured. [Translator's note]

[402] Jiří Guth was a significant educator and literary figure, also known as a member of the first Olympic Committee, and very active in the Olympic movement. He was also the master of ceremony at President Masaryk's office. From 1920 onwards he called himself Jiří Stanislav Guth-Jarkovský. He studied at universities in Prague and Geneva, and graduated in philosophy. He then became an educator in a noble family. Already from 1890 he was active as translator of French literature, and he also wrote short-stories using the pseudonym Stanislav Jarkovský. At the turn of the century he was teaching at a Gymnasium in Prague, was active in Klub Českých Turistů (*Czech Tourists Club*) where for almost forty years he published their monthly Časopis turistů (*Tourists' Magazine*). He promoted Czech participation in the Olympic Games and he was a member of the very first Olympic Committee from 1896. He also wrote travel literature - from the Mediterranean countries, France, Sweden, and others. [honsi.org]

[403] Saint Aloysius was an Italian Jesuit priest, later canonized. His real name was Luigi Gonzaga. He is the patron saint of the Catholic youth and chastity. He died when caring for plague victims, which made him a saint for protection against this disease. [honsi.org]

[404] Eustach is not identified with certainty. One possibility is the French painter, architect and abbot Eustache Restout (1655-1743). He does not seem to have been an author, though.

One of his namesakes was actually an author: Eustache de Refuge (1564-1617). However, there is no information indicating that he was ever a monk.

Milan Jankovič put forward a theory that the person in question was the Greek Eustathios. This assumption, however, seems improbable as Saint Aloysius lived some 500 years later, and the former could not possibly have got any whiff of that thunderous fart. [honsi.org]

[405] Laudová was a well-known Czech actress, and periodically active as a journalist. She performed at National Theater from 1899 to 1915 when she

had to quit after an accident. During her acting career she also performed abroad, notably in Serbia and Russia. After her forced retirement she became a teacher at the State Music Conservatory in Prague and resumed her writing. For the most part she wrote educational prose, including giving advice on how to behave at social gatherings. [honsi.org]

[406] Olga Fastrová (born Cikhartová) was a Czech writer, journalist and translator, considered the first female Czech journalist. In 1896 she completed her teacher's education, a rare feat for a woman in those days. In 1898 she married the dramatist and translator Otto Faster (1872-1907) with whom she had three daughters.

Her initial writing activities consisted in helping her husband is his various projects. This included translation, and from 1903 she is listed as a translator from French in her own right. In 1908 she published the novel Fata Morgana. From 1910 to 1936 she was permanent editor of Národní politika (*National Politics*), the first ever woman, who served in this capacity in any of the major Czech newspapers. Her focus was primarily fashion and other themes that were deemed of typically female interest (home decoration etc.). She often used the pseudonym Yvonna. Some of her articles were also published in North America, for instance in Cleveland.

Jaroslav Hašek knew Olga Fastrová personally; in the short story Za Olgou Fastrovou (*Let's go after/see Olga Fastrová*) he writes that they had met just after his return from Russia, and Fastrová had asked him if "the Bolsheviks really were eating human meat". The story was a reaction to a satire about the Bolsheviks that Fastrová wrote in *National Politics* on May 7th 1922. In the story Hašek arranges her death, claiming that she must have had very high fever when writing such nonsense. Fastrová never reacted in writing to the story and survived Hašek by 42 years. [honsi.org]

[407] "severní Čechy", the *Czech north* is a vaguely defined geographical area that refers to the area that today roughly makes up the regions Ústecký kraj and Liberecký kraj. Important towns in the area are Liberec, Děčín, Ústi nad Labem, Litoměřice, Teplice, Jablonec, Turnov, Most and Chomutov. The region is mountainous, industrialized and has extensive mining. Until 1945 the majority of the population reported German as their everyday language.

In *The Good Soldier Švejk* the Czech north hardly figures at all and Hašek spent very little time in the area. In 1904 he however had an intermezzo i Lom where he wrote for the anarchist newspaper Omladina (*Youth*) and took part in agitation among the miners. He also worked in a mine for a short period. The stay ended badly as Hašek and a friend went on a drinking binge, sold a bicycle that belonged to Omladina and consumed the profit from the sale. Editor Bedřich Kalina later added that Hašek's mother had to pay for the bike. To judge by the pieces he had published in Omladina his time in Lom lasted for only for a few weeks, starting in late June 1904. [honsi.org]

[408] Not only the name Švejk, but the verb 'to švejk', and words 'švejking' and 'švejkism' became an integral part of the Czech language, culture, academic discourse, and even politics. For example: Gustav Husák, the General Secretary of the Czechoslovak Communist Party, who replaced the Prague Spring reformer Alexandr Dubček in that post after the 1968 Warsaw Pact invasion and occupation of Czechoslovakia, and assumed the Presidency as well, exhorted the population in a speech during the 1970's period of "normalization" to STOP ŠVEJKING!!! The Czechs themselves speak of being a nation of Švejks. Švejk is for them a source of both great pride and shame. However, as you now know, there is some of Švejk in all of us. [Translator's note]

Note: The Endnotes entries sourced from websites were current as of summer 2025.

About the Author

Jaroslav Hašek (30 April 1883 - 3 January 1923) was an author and satirist from Prague, who he lived a short and extremely turbulent life.

He is best known as the author of the famous satirical novel *The Good Soldier Švejk* (literally *The Fates of the Good Soldier Švejk During the World War*) but also wrote more than 1,200 short stories/feuilletons/articles, numerous poems, and co-authored some cabaret plays. His literary output may have been even greater than these numbers indicate because he flooded newspapers and magazines with his stories and used at least 100 pseudonyms.

CHILDHOOD

Hašek's parents were from South Bohemia and had a background in the so-called educated peasant classes. His father was an assistant teacher and later an employee of Banka Slavia, but died in 1896. After the father's death, the family fell into economic difficulties and moved no fewer than fifteen times during Jaroslav's childhood and adolescence.

EDUCATION AND BUDDING WRITER

Despite the changing circumstances, Hašek obtained a higher education, but soon showed himself incapable of living an orderly life. He graduated from the Českoslovanská akademie obchodní (*Czechoslavic Academy of Business*) (1899 -1902) with good marks and, in the same autumn, was employed by Banka Slavia. He was dismissed within eight months after being absent from work twice without permission. Afterwards, he became a creative and prolific writer and journalist, despite his untidy lifestyle and high alcohol consumption. As early as 1901, while still a student at the commercial academy, he published his first stories in Národní listy, and one of his teachers recognized his literary talent, describing him a "Czech Mark Twain". In 1903 he published the poetry collection Májové výkřiky (*The Cries of May*), together with his friend Hájek.

WANDERINGS

During the summers from 1899 to 1905 Jaroslav Hašek undertook long journeys in Central Europe, and even into the Balkans. These provided rich material for his short stories and the later masterpiece *The Good Soldier Švejk*. During these travels, he was often penniless, slept outdoors, and traveled partly on foot. He saw the society from its lowest levels, which influenced his writing and political outlook. The region he visited most frequently was Slovakia, but he also traveleld to Bavaria, Switzerland, Italy, Galicia, Hungary, Austria, Slovenia, and Croatia. In addition, he visited the areas of modern Romania and may have set foot in present-day Ukraine and Serbia. It has also been claimed that he visited Bulgaria and Macedonia in 1903.

ANARCHIST AND POLICE ENCOUNTERS

Even before writing *The Good Soldier Švejk* (1921-22) Jaroslav Hašek had a reputation as a prominent satirist, but was also considered controversial due to a period as an active anarchist. Hašek had repeated conflicts with the police and was imprisoned several times, mostly due to drunkenness and public disorder. He was, however, also under surveillance because of his involvement in the anarchist movement. The most serious case was in 1907, when he was sentenced to a month in prison for inciting violence against the police during an anarchist demonstration.

PERMANENT EMPLOYMENT AND MARRIAGE

In early 1909, Hašek succeeded his friend Ladislav Hájek as editor of the popular fortnightly magazine Svět zvířat (*The Animal World*), where he enjoyed his longest ever period of permanent employment, keeping the job for almost two years.

Stable employment and income finally enabled him to marry Jarmila Mayerová, whom he had been courting since 1906. Her parents had been vehemently opposed to the relationship because of Hašek's anarchist connections and unconventional lifestyle. Nevertheless, they eventually consented after the prospective groom settled into a stable existence. The couple married on 23 May 1910.

The bliss proved short-lived, as Hašek was dismissed from The Animal World in the autumn of 1910. His appearances at the office had become increasingly rare, and, worse still, readers had begun to question the veracity of the information presented in the journal. These two factors were probably the main reasons why the magazine's owner decided to dismiss his editor.

The widespread claims that he wrote about imaginary animals such as werewolves are, however, unsubstantiated. His pranks seem to have been rather innocent, like allowing himself minor jokes at the expense of his friends Josef Lada and Vilém Kún (and perhaps others). That he assigned imaginary attributes to existing species is quite likely, but the extent is difficult to verify. In 1973, Radko Pytlík noted that he and other researchers found nothing in the magazine that, in itself, could justify termination (see Fun and Education).

After leaving Svět zvířat, Hašek and his wife set up their own dog-trading business called Cynological Institute, but the enterprise soon collapsed. Soon after, he was admitted to a psychiatric hospital, apparently after trying to commit suicide by jumping from Charles' Bridge in Prague.

THE EARLY ŠVEJK

In the spring of 1911, Hašek conceived *The Good Soldier Švejk*, and five stories about the soldier were published from May 22nd 1911 onwards. These are very different in style and content from the later novel. The stinging satire was absent, Švejk tells no anecdotes, and the stories lack the strong connection to military reality that the author's experiences in the army lend to the novel.

The name Švejk also appeared in a couple of cabaret plays around this time, again in roles unrelated to the famous novel character. In one of the plays, Švejk was the servant of the Holy Roman Emperor Charles IV!

In 1912, the five stories were published in a book called The Good Soldier Švejk and other Strange Stories. The book was illustrated by Karel Stroff.

A MOCK PARTY

At the same time as Švejk was created, Hašek, with some friends, founded a mock party called Strana mírného pokroku v mezích zákona (*Party of Moderate Progress Within the Bounds of the Law*). According to its manifesto, this occurred in April 1911. It was partly a forum for ridiculing the political elite and partly established to increase the turnover at the pub where the party meetings were held. Hašek wrote many stories about the party, in which he caricatured politicians and others. Presumably for fear of libel suits, these were not published until after the First World War, and only in part. The complete collection did not appear in print until 1963.

Family breakdown

On May 23rd 1910 Jaroslav Hašek finally married Jarmila Mayerová whom he had been courting since 1906. Her parents were vehemently opposed to the relationship because of Hašek's anarchist connection and his unorthodox lifestyle, but in the end consented after the groom for once became permanently employed. On May 2nd 1912 Jarmila gave birth to their son Richard, but soon afterwards, Hašek left the family, only to see them again in 1921. The constraints and rigours of family life did not suit him, and again, he took up his bohemian way of life. After leaving his family, his life spiralled downwards, and he virtually became homeless, sleeping at friends' houses. Again, he started to travel, but now within Bohemia, mostly together with his friend Zdeněk Matěj Kuděj. At the outbreak of war in 1914, he was staying with the painter Josef Lada.

In the Austro-Hungarian army

The war led to big changes in Hašek's life. Never having completed compulsory military service (probably for health reasons), he was deemed fit for duty in 1914. On February 17th 1915, he was enlisted with Infanterieregiment Nr. 91 in Budějovice, was sent to the front in Galicia in early July and was captured by the Russians on September 24th 1915.

His time in the army eventually provided rich material for *The Good Soldier Švejk*. In the novel, many geographical details and other circumstances reflect the author's experiences serving with IR. 91. Hašek's time with the Regiment is investigated in more detail in the entry Jaroslav Hašek in the *Who's who section*.

Captivity and the Legions

In Russian captivity in the Totskoye camp Hašek contracted typhus, a disease that killed thousands of his fellow prisoners. In the spring of 1916, he volunteered for the Czechoslovak Brigade (later a.k.a Legions), was released from the camp in early July; he was formally enlisted on June 29th 1916. In the Legions, he worked as a recruiter among prisoners of war. He was also a journalist at the tsar-loyalist weekly Čechoslovan (*Czechoslav*) in Kyiv. During this period Hašek voiced nationalist sentiments and even supported Tsar Nicholas II's regime, which he saw as the strongest supporter of a future Czech state. After several episodes that embarrassed the Czech volunteers, he was sent to the front as an ordinary soldier in May 1917. His satirical article *The Czech Pickwick Club* led to further disciplinary measures. On July 2nd 1917, Hašek took part in the battle of Zborów where the Czechoslovak volunteers, for the first time, faced their own compatriots as a unit.

Communist

The Russian October Revolution in 1917 and the ensuing peace treaty between the new Soviet state and the Central Powers made continuing the war from Russian soil impossible for the Legions. They were formally placed under French command, and it was decided to transfer them to the western front via Vladivostok. This was a decision that Jaroslav Hašek disagreed with. He preferred his countrymen remain in Russia, presumably hoping that the front against the Central Powers would be reopened.

From the beginning of 1918, he also became increasingly influenced by communist ideas. Witnessing the Bolshevik occupation of Kiev in February may have contributed to this shift. According to Josef Pospíšil, he judged the Bolshevik leaders as very capable. He may also have been influenced by the young communist Břetislav Hůla, his co-editor at Čechoslovan from November 1917 onwards. At this stage, many left-wing groups disapproved of Lenin's Brest-Litovsk peace treaty, and it would have been natural for Hašek to align with those.

In March 1918 Hašek and Hůla, fleeing from the advancing Germans, traveled to Moscow and reported to the Czech social democrats (communists). In April Hašek wrote in a letter that he left the Czech Army (i.e. Legions), stating that he disagreed with their transfer to France. During the spring of 1918, the relationship between the Czechs and the Bolsheviks deteriorated, and at the end of May, an armed rebellion broke out. This led Hašek into direct conflict with his former comrades. He and other Czech communists were branded as traitors, and arrest orders for the more prominent of them were issued, with a particular emphasis on Hašek (Omsk July 25th 1918). By now, all bridges had been burned, and from October he worked directly for the Bolsheviks' 5th Army.

In Russia Hašek's career made rapid progress. He worked for the political department of the 5th Army, and he journeyed all the way to Irkutsk. Hašek was mainly responsible for propaganda and recruitment among the many foreign prisoners of war who remained in Russia. He published in Czech, Russian, German, Bashkir,

Hungarian, and Buryat. In Siberia, he married Alexandra Lvova (Šura). This was despite him not being formally divorced from Jarmila. During his time in the Bolshevik 5th Army, he proved himself a capable organizer and also stopped drinking.

RETURNING HOME

In the summer of 1920 circumstances changed again. The Bolsheviks had in effect won the Russian Civil War, and the many foreigners in their service were no longer needed in Russia. They were deemed more useful as agitators in their home countries, and the Comintern issued directives that they were to be dispatched to help the national communist movements. On August 26th 1920, the Irkutsk section of the party received a telegram instructing Hašek to relinquish his duties and report to the Central Bureau of the Czech section of the Communist Party. On October 24th he left Irkutsk for Moscow, where he appeared on November 26th.

He arrived in Prague on December 19th after traveling via Narva, Tallinn, Stettin, and Berlin and having spent a week in quarantine in Pardubice. By then, the communist uprising that he was supposed to take part in had failed and the organizers had been arrested.

Back in Prague he soon reverted to his former habits and was of little use to the communist movement thereafter. However, he still contributed to their newspapers and never renounced his convictions. If Hašek was controversial in pre-war Prague, he was even more so now; there was the threat of legal proceedings because of bigamy, and he was widely unpopular due to his Bolshevik past.

Gustav Janouch also claims to have witnessed an attempt to lynch Hašek.

A SATIRICAL MASTERPIECE

Around February/March 1921 Hašek hit on the idea of rekindling his soldier Švejk, now in the form of a novel, and he started to write *The Good Soldier Švejk*, a book that was planned in six parts. The first part and at least the first chapter of the second was completed in Žižkov, and was initially sold in serial installments. Although *The Good Soldier Švejk* sold well, glowing reviews appeared in influential newspapers only after *Švejk* was performed on stage from November 1st 1921 onwards. Max Brod, Ivan Olbracht, and Alfred Fuchs were the first enthusiastic reviewers, having all written about The Good Soldier Švejk during November 1921.

Before the novel's breakthrough in November 1921, Hašek had

moved to Lipnice (on August 25th 1921), where he completed Part Two, wrote Part Three, and started on the fourth part of *The Good Soldier Švejk*. Unfortunately, his health took a downward turn; the hard life had taken its toll, and he had also become dangerously overweight. He never completed the fourth part of his epic novel and died on January 3rd 1923. The causes of death were stated as pneumonia and heart failure. The belief that he drank himself to death is widespread, and though alcohol was not the primary cause of death, it was undoubtedly a contributing factor.

BOOKS ABOUT JAROSLAV HAŠEK

Jaroslav Hašek is the subject of several biographies, although most are available exclusively in Czech. Autobiographical material is almost non-existent, apart from those elements of his own life that he frequently blended into his writing, both in *The Good Soldier Švejk* and his numerous short stories. This information must, however, be viewed with scepticism, as Hašek was an accomplished mystifier who convincingly mixed truth, half-truths and lies. Almost all that is known about him today is, therefore, based on the accounts from people who knew him and material from various archives and newspapers. The material that his friends and biographers wrote is often unreliable because the source was often Hašek himself. In addition, some of them tended to embellish the stories.

For the international reading public, the best source of factual information is no doubt The Bad Bohemian (1978) by Cecil Parrott, the author of the second English translation of *The Good Soldier Švejk*. Parrott's biography is, to a degree, based on Radko Pytlík's de facto standard Toulavé house (*Wandering Gosling*) (1971).

A rare but valuable book is Emanuel Frynta's *Hašek, the Creator of Schweik*. It comes with many illustrations and has been competently translated into English. It focuses on the artistic view of the author, rather than the biographical details that other biographies tend to emphasise.

There is also literature on Jaroslav Hašek in German, for instance, the well-documented but speculative *Der Vater des braven Soldaten Schweik* by Gustav Janouch (1966). Furthermore, Jan Berwid-Buquoy has written two books in German about Hašek. These are works that are entertaining but of dubious veracity.

The most reliable book about Hašek in German is no doubt Pavel Petr's Hašeks Schwejk in Deutschland (1963). Although only partly biographical, Petr's book is well-researched and it is impeccably documented. At the time it was published, it was arguably one of the most solid works on Hašek that existed, anywhere, in any language. [honsi.org]

Bibliography of Editorial Notes

Sources are listed in the order of their first appearance.

Literary Translation, Acantho I&C, Professional Translators and Translations https://www.acantho.eu/literary-translation

Několik editologických poznámek k románu Jaroslava Haška Osudy dobrého vojáka Švejka za světové války (*A few editological notes to Jaroslav Hašek's novel The Fates of the Good Soldier Švejk During The World War*), by Jiří Fiala,
https://www.academia.edu/831323/ACTA_UNIVERSITATIS_PALACKI ANAE_OLOMUCENSIS_FACULTAS_PHILOSOPHICA_PHILOLOG ICA_84_2004

Michelle Woods reviews The Good Soldier Švejk (Book One), Jacket 18 — August 2002 http://jacketmagazine.com/18/woods-r-svejk.html

A response to Michelle Woods' review of «The Good Soldier Švejk (Book One), Jacket 40 — Late 2010 –
http://jacketmagazine.com/40/sadlon-woods.shtml

The Report on the experimental project of the first edition of the "Chicago version" Book One
https://svejkcentral.com/The%20Report

Language Development across Childhood and Adolescence, Trends in Language Acquisition Research
https://api.pageplace.de/preview/DT0400.9789027295002_A24762029/preview-9789027295002_A24762029.pdf

Combining Lexical And Morphological Knowledge in Language Model For Inflectional (Czech) Language, by Jan Nouza, Jindra Drabkova
https://www.isca-archive.org/icslp_2002/nouza02_icslp.pdf

Die Krisis der europaischen Kultur (p.242), by Rudolf Pannwitz https://archive.org/details/diekrisisdereuro00pann/page/242/mode/2up

Mluvnice současné angličtiny na pozadí češtiny (*Grammar of Contemporary English against the background of Czech*), Electronic edition, Dušková, Libuše et al. https://mluvniceanglictiny.cz/uvod

Languages with stricter and less strict word order?, Linguistics Stack Exchange
https://linguistics.stackexchange.com/questions/557/languages-with-stricter-and-less-strict-word-order

Corto 's Reviews > The Fateful Adventures of the Good Soldier Svejk During the World War, Book(s) Three & Four
https://www.goodreads.com/review/show/2307476567?book_show_action=false&from_review_page=1

Literary translations, POLYGLOT https://www.polyglot.lv/en/industries/literary-translations#:~:text=Translation%20of%20literature%20is%20fundamentally,translation%20also%20has%20aesthetic%20functions

Aesthetic Elements in Prose Translation, by Jin Li https://francis-press.com/uploads/papers/qKMuBHjms6nw4t71RwBGzz132AA2AN8LAL2pSYQx.pdf

Amazon Customer Review, by Edmund Pickett https://www.amazon.com/gp/customer-reviews/R3DLHN058MZP9I/ref=cm_cr_othr_d_rvw_ttl?ie=UTF8&ASIN=1438916701

On the Rendition of Verbal Aspect in English and Spanish Translations of Zdeněk Jirotka's Saturnin, by Nikola Janotová https://theses.cz/id/vrg4q0/18025856

Grammatical aspect in Slavic languages, Wikipedia https://en.wikipedia.org/wiki/Grammatical_aspect_in_Slavic_languages

Grammatical aspect, Wikipedia https://en.wikipedia.org/wiki/Grammatical_aspect

Sloveso v překladu, (*Verb in Translation*), Slavica Pragensia, by Josef Václav Bečka [not available online]

Mr and Mrs, Ms, and Miss: Meanings, Abbreviations, and Correct Usage, Hannah Yang https://prowritingaid.com/mr-mrs-ms-and-miss#:~:text=Historically%2C%20we%20referred%20to%20men,contractions%20to%20distinguish%20marital%20status

missis, Collins online dictionary https://www.collinsdictionary.com/us/dictionary/english/missis

Mrs., Collins online dictionary https://www.collinsdictionary.com/us/dictionary/english/mrs

This map shows the US really has 11 separate 'nations' with entirely different cultures, by Mark Abadi in Business Insider https://www.businessinsider.com/regional-differences-united-states-2018-1

10 Popular Newspaper Fonts, Issuu digital publishing platform https://issuu.com/resources/topics-of-interest/design/10-popular-newspaper-fonts#:~:text=Times%20New%20Roman,-One%20of%20the&text=Its%20shape%20is%20narrower%20than,for%20many%20platforms%20and%20professions

Imprint

This edition was typeset and composed using LibreOffice Writer for a 6 × 9 inch page format. The text is set in Times New Roman, with mirrored margins and an expanded inner margin for perfect binding. Typography, page layout, and editorial apparatus were composed during the editorial process. The volume was printed and bound as a paperback by IngramSpark.

w.ingramcontent.com/pod-product-compliance
htning Source LLC
ergne TN
W091701070526
199LV00050B/2242